SILENCER

Campbell Armstrong

CORGI BOOKS

SILENCER
A CORGI BOOK : 0 552 14496 7

Originally published in Great Britain by Doubleday,
a division of Transworld Publishers Ltd

PRINTING HISTORY
Doubleday edition published 1997
Corgi edition published 1998

Set in Sabon 11/12 pt by Falcon Oast Graphic Art

Corgi Books are published by Transworld Publishers Ltd,
61–63 Uxbridge Road, London W5 5SA,
in Australia by Transworld Publishers (Australia) Pty Ltd,
15–25 Helles Avenue, Moorebank, NSW 2170
and in New Zealand by Transworld Publishers (NZ) Ltd,
3 William Pickering Drive, Albany, Auckland.

Reproduced, printed and bound in Great Britain by
Cox & Wyman Ltd, Reading, Berks.

This novel went through the careful
editorial hands of the following people:

Marianne Velmans, Alison Tulett,
Leda DeForge and my wife Rebecca. I'm
deeply grateful for their counsel and advice.

My thanks to Eugene Dorr, for his help.

Campbell Armstrong was born in Glasgow and educated at Sussex University. He and his family now live in Ireland. His bestselling novels, *Jig*, *Mazurka*, *Mambo*, *Agents of Darkness*, *Concert of Ghosts*, *Jigsaw* and *Heat* have placed him in the front rank of international thriller writers. His latest novel, *Blackout*, is now available as a Doubleday hardback.

Praise for *Heat*:

One hell of a fast-moving thriller'
Daily Telegraph

'Armstrong has discovered a way with words that raises him above the routine level of the marketplace.'
The Times

'Erotic seduction mixes with bareknuckle Chandleresque prose, in an intriguing psycho-drama that keeps you guessing right up to the last page . . . A book that has all the staples of the thriller genre plus a little extra class . . . crafted with surgical and seamless precision . . . Elmore Leonard, watch your back'
Cork Examiner

'A consummate psychological thriller . . . Without doubt, Armstrong is now in the front rank of thriller writers'
Books Magazine

Praise for *Jigsaw*:

'Armstrong creates electric tension'
Daily Telegraph

'Campbell Armstrong has outdone both Frederick Forsyth and Ken Follett with *Jigsaw*. *Jigsaw* features a villain to die for, plus the most unusual and haunting romance I've encountered in a thriller'
James Patterson, author of *Along Came a Spider*

'Armstrong has created a thriller where the sex is sexy, the horror horrific, and the plot is, as it should be, the skeleton for a well fleshed-out piece of storytelling'
The Times

Also by Campbell Armstrong

JIGSAW
HEAT

and published by Corgi Books

1

At an intersection in the middle of nowhere a stop sign appears in the headlights, and Reuben Galindez thinks, OK, this is heebie-jeebies time, I had enough, and he opens the passenger door and steps out onto the narrow blacktop.

'What the fuck?' the bearded guy at the wheel says.

'I changed my mind,' Galindez says.

'You *what*?'

'I been thinking. I ain't stacking groceries in some supermarket in Scranton or whatever you got in mind. I don't need that shit.'

The guy on the back seat, the guy with silver-yellow sideburns, leans forward and says, 'Let me remind you, Reuben. You signed on the dotted line. This ain't something where you got the option of changing your mind and strolling the hell away.'

'Watch me,' Galindez says and he slams the door and begins to walk down the blacktop, thinking he'll hitch a ride as soon as a vehicle comes along this lonely road, which may take some time out here, granted, but no way is he going back inside the van with the tinted windows. No way is he stacking shelves or installing cable TV in Queens or *anything* like that. Four weeks he's been locked up in the safe house in Phoenix, climbing walls. Closing his eyes nights and seeing the flowery pattern of wallpaper behind his lids. Trapping cockroaches in beer bottles and suffocating the fuckers just for the sport. Watching TV, spinning through the channels until you're brain-dead. Four draggy weeks waiting for 'arrangements' to be made, and that's enough. Imagine living the rest of your life restricted. It ain't for me, thanks all the same.

'Reuben!'

Galindez looks back. The guy with the beard is outside the van now. 'You made a deal, Reuben. You can't just *walk*.'

Galindez calls back. 'Whatcha gonna do? Sue me?' He laughs, eh-eh-eh, turns and keeps on walking, the darkness of trees pressing in on him from either side of the road. This is the sticks, he thinks, but he couldn't hack sitting in that van a second longer, had to get out. His patience was stretched to breaking point and a voice he associates with the willies was rising inside his head.

'Reuben! Get your fat ass back here!'

Galindez glances round again. 'Yeah, yeah, yeah.'

'This ain't smart, Reuben.'

Galindez pays no attention. It's a free country. You're at liberty to change your mind. OK, he signed some documents, so what? You scribble your john hancock on a few papers, that means chickenshit to him.

He's fifty yards from the van and the bearded guy

is still calling. 'Hey! Reuben! This is a real dumb fuck thing you're doing!'

Just keep walking, Galindez thinks. Keep cruising. Sooner or later they're gonna get tired shouting and they'll drive away, and then somebody's gonna come along and you'll hitch back to civilization. Happy days.

'*Reuben!*'

Galindez hears a faint breeze whisper in the trees. He doesn't look round. Screw them. Screw their documents and their promises, you got a life all your own to live.

The sound of gunfire freezes him. A single crack gouges the blacktop near his feet, and suddenly the night's filled with birds panicked out of trees and some scared furry four-legged thing dashes in front of him. He turns his face and there's a second shot that whizzes somewhere to his right and it's like the darkness is punctured and leaking air, and his heart is hot and thudding. This is some kinda joke, he thinks. But he's stunned and confused by the *fact* of gunfire because by rights – *by rights* – he ought to be able to stroll away, if that's what he wants to do, and fuck the agreement, which was only paper anyhow. And these guys – they shouldn't be *shooting* at him.

'*Just walk back, Reuben*,' the bearded guy shouts.

Galindez doesn't move. Walk back, he thinks. Yeah, right. Walk back to what exactly?

Another shot and the air around him fractures, and this time Galindez blinks at the flash of light and thinks, I've been hit. Dreamtime. Except it's no dream, it's no little carnival of the mind, because there's a pain in his arm and he feels blood against his skin. Jesus fucking Christ, he thinks. I'm shot. It ain't supposed to be this way. The world's all upside down and I'm bleeding.

'The next one goes in the brainbox, Reuben!'

They're going to *kill* you, Galindez thinks, and it's like a light going on inside the open refrigerator of his head. They're going to murder you just because you don't want to be a member of their goddam club. You did them a good turn, you paid your dues, but now you want out – only they won't let you. You're in, the door's bolted, and that's that.

Fuck them! Fuck Scranton, Queens, wherever!

Under a moon fogged by cloud, he suddenly runs down among the trees, crashing between trunks and overhanging branches, and there's blood streaming down his arm but this is no time to think Band Aid. This is a time for running and running and if you bleed, you bleed, and so what.

He's overweight and his flabby pecs bounce and his lungs don't know what to do with all this clean, up-country air. He's a city guy and a chain-smoker, but these are minor inconveniences, because the only goddam thing that matters is getting away. He hears a small voice inside his head urgently repeating the phrase, Chug, chug, keep going. Down through the trees and don't stop.

Branches whip at his body and exposed roots curl raggedly underfoot and a few more spooked birds flap blackly on huge wings out of nowhere. But chug chug, you keep going.

Thinking, It ain't supposed to be like this.

His head's like an overheated radiator. Gotta stop a moment. Gasping for air, sweating, he leans against a tree, face down. He's wheezing like a busted accordion. Gotta move. Gotta keep moving.

'*Hey, Galindez!*'

The voice is what, twenty, thirty yards away? Too close.

Then there's the second guy's voice. 'This is plain stupid, *asshole*!'

Thirty yards. You can't gauge distances in these woods, not after a lifetime spent measuring everything in terms of city blocks. Go three blocks west, two blocks north. But here it's different, no stars and the moon shrouded in the sky.

Galindez pushes himself away from the tree. Chug chug. Running. Arm going numb. For all he knows he could be chasing round in circles, clattering through fern and undergrowth and getting nowhere. And there's a funny taste in his mouth – which is fear. Bone-dry, metallic, like powdered rust in his throat.

And then next thing there's a flashlight scanning the trees and he ducks his head low, but his yellow silk shirt might as well be a beacon out here in the woods. He hears a gunshot and it echoes – *boomoomoom* – and he drops down on all fours and crawls through fern and fallen branches.

Another sound reaches him. Water. Fast-flowing. So, there's a river nearby and he thinks, If I can reach it I can float away. Downstream and outta sight.

The beam of the flashlight illuminates branches all around him. He hears the two guys clumping towards him, twigs snapping.

Galindez crawls towards the sound of the water. Sharp things snag his shirt and lacerate his body.

The flashlight is ten yards from where he's crawling. He tries to make himself smaller, hunches his body, hauls in the band of blubber and just concentrates on believing he's a whippet of a guy who's in a hurry to reach the water. He also tries to divert himself with pleasing thoughts: playing the slots at the casino on the Gila Reservation, screwing some plump, nut-brown Indian chick in a trailer smelling of joss-sticks and maybe a little reefer.

Who's he kidding? This is life and death. This is all about survival.

Gunfire again. It blasts through the trees with a noise like a nuclear weapon, and there's a sizzle of red-hot light on the edge of his vision. The water. Get to the goddam *water*. Submerge yourself and hold your breath and let the currents sweep you away from these armed maniacs behind you.

Suddenly *holy shit!* – no more trees.

Suddenly a smooth pebbled shore and a suggestion of white water frothing through the darkness.

Big Problem. He's exposed now and the yellow shirt's like a goddam distress rocket. He pads over the slick pebbles, grunting, scrambling. Get to the water, the goddam water.

He crawls to the edge of the river and eases himself into the chill current, but the water's only eighteen inches deep and he finds himself half in, half out of the river, and O Jesus the flashlight is right on his face like a malevolent eye, and he's blinded and electric pings of panic vibrate through him.

'I spy with my little eye', one of the guys says in a singsong voice, 'somebody beginning with R.'

Galindez takes a few jittery steps back, the bank dips abruptly about two feet, and just as he's about to draw himself under the surface a gun goes off again with the sound of a thunderclap.

And Reuben – who thinks he sees the cylinder of a slot-machine revolve in front of his eyes and all the jackpot cherries appear simultaneously in the magic window – cries out, falls and slips away, turning over and over in relentless currents, leaving a spiralling trail of blood in the white wake of the river.

2

Amanda had been fishing since daybreak with no luck, trying to keep in mind what Rhees had told her about patience. You learn how to wait, he'd said. Remember, you're under no pressure.

Rhees lay on the bank with his eyes shut, raising a lazy hand now and again to brush aside a fly. A man in repose. A man on first-name terms with patience. Amanda studied her line in the water, concentrating on the little red plastic float that shivered on the surface. She was coming to the conclusion that either there were no fish in this river or else they were cunning little jokers who knew a trick or two about survival.

She looked up at the cloudless blue sky. Heat was beginning to build, the sun climbing above the trees. On the opposite bank of the river sandstone already shimmered. She nudged Rhees, who opened his eyes.

'Maybe they've all migrated,' she said.

Rhees said, 'It's not the catching that counts, Amanda.'

'Tell me it's the waiting.'

'The waiting's part of it, sure. But there are other factors; how to contain a sense of expectation, an ability to be alone with your own thoughts.'

'It's a whole fishing philosophy,' she remarked. 'I bet it's called pisceology or something like that.'

Rhees smiled at her. 'This is more to do with self than landing a fish.'

'Do you charge by the hour?' she asked.

'Just watch the float.'

'I haven't taken my eyes off the float. My whole life is centred around the goddam float. I'll dream floats tonight.'

'Think about this as part of a simple healing process, if that helps.'

A healing process. A life lived away from all the old stresses. No pressure, Rhees had said. She returned her eyes to her line and watched how it rippled in the movement of water. She envied Rhees's ability to drift into contented torpor. He could switch off his engine any time he liked.

She lit a cigarette. A bad habit, one she wished she could abandon, but you didn't win all your victories at once. It was a sequence of steps, and being up here in the deep isolation of the forest was just one of them. Being here on this granulated riverbank, staring at the float, trying to think of nothing, seeking, as Rhees might have said, an inner zone of quiet, a place where you might find all the hairline cracks in your psyche fixed.

She felt him touch the back of her neck. Her hair, pinned back and held by a black clasp, was brown, flecked with touches of red. Wisps of it always strayed from her head. She had problems with hair management, and she knew Rhees found this disarray touching. He was in love with her flaws. There was a sweet easy flow to life with him. Six years along the road and she could barely remember past lovers except for the weird coincidence that at least three of them had been named Robert, and they all wanted to be called Bob. Plain old Bob.

Even their faces were spectral in recollection. If she considered them at all, she could recall only a sickly medley of deodorants and skin oils. Funny, her past love life reduced to a distillation of odours from bottles and spray-cans, and no memory of any one lover who transported her to a place where comets crashed through the skies and the earth reverberated underfoot. No interplanetary daredevil Bob.

She lay back, finished her cigarette and stared at the sky. Rhees kissed her cheek, laid a hand gently on her breast. She felt the sun hot against her face. The warmth had a certain tranquillity. She thought how easy it would be to slip into a light sleep, lulled by the fluting of the river. Four weeks up here and she was already becoming accustomed to the luxury of dozing off at odd moments.

Rhees stroked her breast again.

'Somebody might come along, John,' she said.

'Way out here? I seriously doubt it.' He slid his hand under her cotton shirt and she turned her face towards him. The kiss, Rhees's mouth, his breath, the intimate locking together of familiar parts. She imagined a day might come when familiarity novocained passion and everything became jaded and repetitive, but it hadn't happened that way with her and Rhees.

'Listen,' she said. She turned and looked through

the trees behind her. The gear-grinding sound of a vehicle was audible in the woods.

'I hear,' Rhees said. 'It's probably a gang of good old boys in a jeep. A keg of Bud and a cassette of Garth Brooks's greatest hits and it's party time. Whoop-de-doo.'

'If that's the case, we'll go back to the cabin,' she said.

'And finish what we were just getting into?'

She smiled at him. 'I thought you were a master of contained expectation.'

'Up to a point,' he said.

'You're such a fraud at times, John.'

She stood up, brushed specks of sandstone from her cut-offs, then turned once again towards the trees. She could see the vehicle between the trees now, a Bronco that kicked up fine coppery dust as it churned and laboured along a very narrow track. It emerged from the woods in a flurry of broken branches and scattered pine needles and came to a halt on the bank about twenty feet from Amanda and Rhees.

There was no gang of good old boys. The big man who stepped down from the cab had plump, benign features and his plaid linen jacket was crumpled. He wore sunglasses and moved with a limp – a familiar figure – but his unexpected appearance was baffling.

'Willie?' Amanda said.

'I know, I know. The last guy on earth you expected to see,' and he smiled, slipping off the shades.

Rhees was curt. 'Rephrase that, Lieutenant. The last guy we *wanted* to see.'

Willie Drumm glanced at Rhees, nodded, then

shook Amanda's hand two-fisted. He had big soft hands and they dwarfed hers. 'You're looking good,' he said.

'It's this simple life, Willie.'

'Agrees with you. Anything running? Rainbow? Catfish?'

'Not that I've noticed,' she said. 'They must be keeping a low profile.'

Willie Drumm gazed at the river. There was a moment of uncomfortable tension. Amanda knew what Rhees was thinking. Drumm belonged firmly in the past, and he wasn't welcome because the past had no place here. He wasn't a part of her life any more. Those days were dead and buried. Rhees regarded Drumm as a dangerous gate-crasher, a homicide cop from the grim abattoir of the city. Somebody who dragged that environment on his shoulders like a bag stuffed with soiled laundry.

Drumm said, 'Boy, this ain't the easiest place to get to.'

'That's the whole idea,' Rhees said.

'Yeah well. Sure. I finally found the cabin, saw your car parked there, figured you couldn't be far away.' Drumm fidgeted with his glasses. He was uneasy.

'You're a detective, after all,' Rhees remarked. 'A piece of cake for you.'

This sour note in John's voice. Amanda felt a shadow fall across her mind, provoked by Drumm's arrival.

'You haven't come all this way to pay a social call, have you, Willie?' she asked.

Drumm looked at Rhees before answering. 'I'd be lying if I told you that.'

Rhees said, 'She quit, Willie. Q–U–I–T. She's no longer involved. She's out of it.'

'Yeah, I know, John. I just figured she'd be interested in what I have to say, that's all.'

'Maybe you figured wrong,' Rhees said, and slung an arm around Amanda's shoulders, a protective gesture. He wants to keep the world away from me, she thought. Especially that part of it where Willie Drumm belonged, that greased slope into despair. He doesn't want me sliding back down into that abyss.

She said, 'Willie's come a long way. It would be bad manners, John.'

'Far be it from me to be uncivil,' Rhees said. He stared at Drumm, who was wiping his wide forehead with a handkerchief.

Drumm said, 'Lookit, I don't mean to cause a problem, John. This is awkward.'

Amanda said, 'It's OK, it's OK.'

'Oh sure, it's just fine. Amanda says so.' Rhees stepped away from her. With his hands in the pockets of his jeans, he slouched, staring at the ground.

'What's on your mind, Willie?' she asked.

Drumm said quietly, 'Something connected with our old friend Sanchez.'

'Sanchez?' She had an odd experience of darkness, as if the shadow she'd felt a few moments ago had lengthened in her head. A sensory malfunction. There was a kind of faltering inside her. *Sanchez.* The chill claustrophobic space of a courtroom entered her memory and she heard refrigerated air rush from a wall-duct and the sharp knock, knock of a judge's gavel and the quiet tapping of the court reporter; babble she didn't need, but it filled her head regardless.

She fumbled out a cigarette and lit it, aware of Rhees frowning and jingling coins loudly in his pockets.

Drumm said, 'I didn't want you seeing this on the eleven o'clock news before I had a chance to tell you in person.'

'Tell me what?'

'Something's turned up. Literally.'

'Explain, Willie.'

'I'm talking a fish,' he said. 'A very big fish.'

3

It was twenty-three miles to the morgue in Flagstaff. Willie Drumm drove slowly out of the pines. 'John was pretty steamed up back there,' he said.

'He worries about me. But he gets over things quickly,' she said. Where was the conviction in her voice? Rhees had stomped back to the cabin, having registered a couple of protests. *Butt out of this. This hasn't got a goddam thing to do with you any more.* She imagined him walking up and down the small rooms, burning off his funk. The wonder of Rhees was his inability to maintain a bad mood. He might go through the motions, but he didn't have the heart to keep a bad humour alive for long.

Drumm said, 'I still feel like the guy who turns up at the banquet too late to tell everybody the soup was laced with arsenic.'

'You were talking about a certain fish,' she said.

Drumm slowed at a yield sign. 'Right. Washes up in a shallow tributary of the Little Colorado River. No ID, nothing. Gunshot wound in the heart. So the body comes under the jurisdiction of the

Navaho cops, but Sergeant Charlie House isn't happy with non-native American bodies turning up on his reservation, so he ships the body to Flag, and a set of prints down to Phoenix. We run the prints, we get a match. Which is why I'm trucking up here to look at the body and talk with the coroner. Meantime, I'm thinking, it doesn't add up. Make any sense to you, Amanda?'

She searched the breast pocket of her shirt for cigarettes and matches. 'Reuben Galindez was supposed to be far, far away. He was supposed to be secure. That was the arrangement.'

'Right. So what's he doing in a river in northern Arizona? And who shot him?'

She lit a cigarette, shrugged the question aside. The morning had taken on a fuzzy dreamlike quality. One minute you're fishing and the day's sweet and rich with promise, the next you're cruising off to the morgue to look at the face of a dead guy, and the axis of reality tilts and you wonder if this is hallucination. Who shot Galindez?

'I couldn't begin to guess,' she said. She wasn't sure if she even wanted to try. This wasn't her business any longer – so why had she agreed to accompany Drumm to the morgue? Curiosity? A sense of disbelief that Galindez had turned up in a place where he didn't belong? That maybe the ID made from a set of fingerprints was a mistake and the corpse on the slab would turn out to be that of a stranger?

Drumm drove a mile or two in silence, a toothpick parked at the corner of his mouth. 'The only way I can figure this is that Sanchez is behind the slaying. Galindez turns State's evidence and Sanchez gets a room in the Death Row Hilton. He's going crazy in there, so he gets a message out and somebody does a number on Galindez. Revenge being sweet and all.'

'Yeah. Just try proving it,' she said.

They were in downtown Flagstaff now. The main drag was motels advertising waterbeds and cable TV, stacked alongside an abundance of fast-food franchises. Plastic flags hung motionless in the sunlit air outside car dealerships. Drumm rolled down his window and the smoke from Amanda's cigarette drifted away.

He parked the Bronco and turned to gaze at her. 'You don't really need to come inside.'

'I've seen dead men before, Willie.'

'It's up to you, Amanda.' Drumm got out of the vehicle. Always courteous, he stepped round and opened Amanda's door.

The room was chilly and windowless, lit by a grid of pale fluorescent lights. Charlie House was there, an enormous copper-faced Navaho whose tan uniform was immaculate. The deputy coroner, wearing a badge that identified him as T. Lavery, was also present. He was a lean man dressed in a starched, lime-green smock.

It was Lavery who slid open the drawer and said, 'Step right up, folks. See Moby Dick.' He had an irksome chuckle. He'd clearly developed a barricade of insensitivity against death.

Amanda hesitated a moment before she looked at the bloated corpse on the metal slab. There was a hole in the area of the heart. Ragged, cleansed over and over by the river, it suggested a large embittered mouth. The left eye was blood-red, the right gone entirely. The socket was filled with sediment from the river. The lips and cheeks and throat had been gnawed and slashed by predators – rats, vultures, whatever. The man's hair had the slimy texture of strands clogged in a shower-drain. On the middle finger of one plump, water-puckered hand was a ruby ring embellished with miniature gold leaves.

She looked away. She felt more tense than she'd expected. The smell of death became trapped in the back of her throat, a raw flavour of chemicals and decay.

Drumm said, 'Galindez.'

Amanda thought, Galindez, beyond doubt.

'Half his face is missing,' Drumm said.

'Sure, but you don't see a ring like that every day of the week,' she said. She remembered the item of jewellery, the habit Galindez had had of twisting it. Ruby and gold, flashy. He'd told her during one of their reviews of the testimony he planned to give that he'd won the ring in a game of poker with some fast company in Bullhead City. What the hell was he doing lying here in a morgue in Flagstaff?

Lavery said, 'The way it looks, he'd been in the water maybe two or three days, could be more, could be less. A single gunshot wound to the heart. Size of the wound, I'd say it was a forty-five. A secondary wound, left arm. Killed upriver, floated down. Speed of the current, he might have been shot thirty, forty miles away from where Charlie found him.'

Drumm asked, 'Anything else you can tell me?'

Lavery said, 'I'll give you a copy of my report. There's nothing out of the ordinary here. Clothes washed clean, no clues there. Shoes missing. No unusual detritus under the fingernails. Facial lacerations consistent with predatory animals: buzzards, coyotes for sure. They made a meal of him when he washed ashore. Speaking of food, if you're interested, this guy's last meal was spaghetti and meatballs with a side salad that included radishes.'

Drumm said, 'You don't happen to know anything really useful, do you? Like the name of the restaurant?'

Lavery smiled and gazed down at the corpse. 'Give me a few more days, Lieutenant, I might be able to tell you not only where he ate but also how much of a tip he left.'

'Droll,' Drumm said.

'In this job, droll's useful.'

Charlie House looked at Drumm and smiled. 'He's all yours, Lieutenant.'

Drumm said, 'A gift from the Navaho nation.'

'Render unto Caesar,' House said.

Lavery asked, 'Anybody mind if I stick Moby back in his box? These outings seem to fatigue him.'

Nobody objected. Lavery slid the drawer shut. Amanda heard the faint squeak of metal on metal. She thought of Galindez floating downstream, ferried by currents, spinning and spinning, and she wondered how far his body had really travelled.

Lavery said, 'Next time you figure on sending us something, Charlie, make sure it doesn't smell this bad.'

'I got enough on my hands without corpses that come floating into the reservation from outside,' House said.

Lavery looked at Willie Drumm. 'I need you to sign some papers, Lieutenant. Papers, always papers, a goddam ocean of papers.'

Drumm followed Lavery out of the room.

Alone with Amanda, Charlie House asked, 'You were the prosecutor in the Sanchez case, right?'

'Right,' she said. She was cold to the marrow. She moved towards the door that led out of the morgue and the big Navaho came up behind her.

'I read you'd quit,' he said.

She stepped into a corridor. It was air-conditioned space, but warmer than the morgue.

'Yeah, I quit,' she said.

'Weary?'

She turned and looked at Charlie House. He had sympathetic eyes the colour of roasted coffee. Death was jarring. She hadn't come all the way up here from the city to look at a corpse, especially that of Reuben Galindez. She'd abdicated her old life and was waiting, as if in a state of suspension, for a new one to present itself. She wanted to be weightless, unshackled by pressures, free of the past. When you don't like your life you change it, Rhees had said to her about a month ago. Which was what she'd been trying to do, a purifying process, a reincarnation, a new Amanda restored from the ashes of the old.

But a dead man had been washed out of a river, a man who should have been somewhere else and long gone, renamed and reinvented, hidden in the secret places of the Federal Witness Protection Program.

'Weary's close enough,' she answered House finally, and she heard a strange lifeless quality in her voice.

4

She thinks, I need wheels. she's never stolen anything in her life, she doesn't know how to begin. She's imagining unlocked doors, keys dangling inside, maybe somebody running an errand inside the shopping mall, a forgetful person. Theft's wrong, but maybe not when your life's at stake, maybe there's some kind of forgiveness under special circumstances and God makes allowances.

She walks up and down and she's dog-tired and scared because she doesn't know how long she's got before they find her. And she's sweating, she's melting away under the hot noon sun. It ain't pleasant, she needs a bath and a shampoo and perfume.

She stops, pretends she's fumbling inside her bag, a canvas thing that holds all her sorry belongings. O Jesus, she's come a long way down from the time she shared the big house in Carefree with Ángel, and the rooms all tiled blue and white, and fans that turned beneath the ceiling. And the greenhouse, the *conservatory* Ángel called it, where there were rows and rows of green foliage in pots, and the air was scented with herbs. But this is like a memory she stole from somebody else, a memory of mint and coriander.

She fumbles inside the bag, trying to look busy, because there's a security guy in a blue uniform standing at the entrance to the mall and gazing out across the parking lot and his gun shines in his holster. He's all glinting metal and his sunglasses are mirrors and she knows, she *knows,* he's watching her as she moves between the cars and glances in each one, looking for keys. She takes a Kleenex out of her bag and raises it to her forehead, and the security guy shifts his face a little. She wipes sweat from her brow and dumps the used tissue in a trash can.

People come out of the mall pushing carts. Kids and women, and she remembers Ángel once said, *We'll start a family*, but that was before it all went to hell, which happened real fast in the end. Now she listens to the clatter of cartwheels and a kid singing a commercial jingle for some pizza joint and a mother calling out to a stray child, 'Come back here, Terry. Don't go wandering away, you hear?'

She watches the mother catch the kid and lift him inside the shopping cart. The security guy is moving out of the doorway and coming across the lot, and this is exactly what she *don't* need. She rummages inside the bag again for something to do, and wonders if she looks like a bum because her hair's not combed and she don't have make-up on, or if she looks suspicious. What's she doing in Farmington, New Mexico anyway? She holds her breath. She hears the guard's boots on the tarmac; clack, clack, clack. She wonders what he wants. She wonders how long she's got before they catch her up. You wonder a whole lotta things when you're scared.

The guard says, 'You OK?'

She looks at him through her grease-smudged sunglasses. 'Yeah, yeah fine.'

'I been watching you,' he says. 'You look kinda distressed.'

'Distressed?' She says the word *deezteressed*. Her pronunciation, it's like giving something away. It's all fear and sunlight and sweat. Ángel used to say, *Learn how to talk right*. Big shot Ángel, learn how to talk right. I learned how to talk well enough, she thinks. Too well. The sky is coming down on her, blue and heavy, squeezing her dry like an orange in a drought.

The guard says, 'You sure you're OK?'

'Fine,' she says. Go away, she thinks. Quit watching me.

'It's a hot one,' the guard says.

She looks at him again. A hot one. Ah, yeah. He's talking about the weather now, the goddam weather. This is all she needs.

'It's heatstroke weather,' he says. 'Drink lotsa water.'

'Water, yeah.' She walks away, the guard watches her, then he turns and strides back to the mall entrance and she keeps going between the rows of parked cars. She's frantic, caught between the guard and the guys she imagines are maybe only a couple of blocks away. It's like a whirlwind of panic around her and she's dragged up inside it the way a leaf is sucked up in a cyclone.

Find a goddam car.

She crosses herself. Say a prayer. Ask for guidance. The saints are on your side. Except she has a sense they've abandoned her, because she wouldn't be in this shit situation if they were around.

Up ahead she sees an aged Datsun slide into a parking lot. An old guy gets out. He has a black-wood cane with a brass handle and his white shirt-tail hangs out over his black-green herring-bone pants and he moves slow, closing the door of his car, then turning and catching her eye and drawing one hand across the stubble on his chin. She looks away.

The old guy goes towards the mall. He uses the cane for support. He calls out to the guard. 'Hot nuff fer you, Jimmy?'

'Nah,' says the guard.

She hears the old guy laugh and say something that sounds like, 'Hot nuff to fry a damn ole egg on the sidewalk fer sure,' and she moves a few feet towards the car, seeing a set of keys lying on the passenger seat.

This is where it goes right or it goes all wrong.

She runs a hand through her hair and waits. The tarmac shimmers. She feels heat rise up through the soles of her shoes. She feels the air is filled with invisible devils. Fuck you, Ángel. You put me in this place, you did that. And I loved you once, I gave you my heart, and what did you do with it?

She touches the door handle of the Datsun. The metal burns right through her. Her skin's welded to metal. She stares in the direction of the guard. The old guy's reached the mall and the guard's laughing at something and she knows she's not gonna get a better moment than this.

She opens the door, gets in the car, picks up the keys, tries until she finds one that fits the ignition, then she turns it and the engine makes a noise like *karam-karam-karam*. If this car had lungs they'd be bronchial. The vehicle shudders, roars into life and belches smoke. She pulls the seat forward, presses a foot on the gas pedal, sticks the gears in reverse and backs out. She sees the guard come out of the entranceway shouting something, and the old guy poking the air with his cane and the blackwood shining, but she's gone, she's gone, she's moving, and although the guard is chasing after her she's out of the parking lot fast and onto the road. Then she's looking for a freeway sign, even as she knows the demons are congregating in clouds behind her, and her world is about as secure as a house on stilts in a country of earthquakes.

5

On the drive back to the cabin Drumm said, 'OK, Galindez goes in the Program. Then what? He decides he can't hack the confines of witness protection and wants to get back to his old haunts, only to be dusted by one of his old cronies. Or do we skip that and point the finger of blame directly at Victor Sanchez and consider the possibility that he managed to breach Program security and get Galindez?'

Amanda found herself remembering the sand and grit in the empty socket, the stench of dead flesh. 'I'm not getting clear pictures of how he'd pull that off.' *Breach Program security*. She didn't want it to be that. Something at the back of her mind was sending up pale smoke signals she didn't want to read. 'How would he get inside information? How did he make the arrangements?'

'First he'd need a paid informant with Program knowledge,' Drumm said. 'After that, a hired gun.'

Amanda gazed at the pine forest on either side of the highway. A paid informant, a hired gun. She felt the sun strike her face through the windshield. 'I don't want to go in this direction, Willie. It makes me queasy.'

Drumm looked regretful. 'I'm sorry I dragged you into this. I don't know why I didn't go straight to Flagstaff, and why the hell I took a detour to find you. I guess I wasn't thinking straight.'

'You didn't exactly press-gang me.'

'That's not the point,' Drumm said. 'You don't need good old Uncle Willie dumping the recent past on your doorstep. It was piss-poor judgement on my part.'

Amanda dismissed Willie's remarks with a motion of her hand. She looked from the window, saw that the Bronco had left the highway. 'What's your next move?'

Drumm shrugged. 'About all I can do at the moment is make out a report and send the paperwork down the line and it'll eventually land on the desk of somebody in the Program. Trouble is, the Program works in deeply mysterious ways which makes it tough for your average joe homicide cop to get a foot in the door.'

Deeply mysterious ways, she thought. Secrets that should have been impenetrable – except they weren't.

The cabin came in sight, located among dense trees. It had been constructed in the Seventies by Amanda's father, Morgan Scholes, who'd bought 150 acres of pine forest and spent weekends building his sanctuary. He'd worked with the devout concentration he brought to all his activities, sunk a well and installed a generator. Two tiny bedrooms, a kitchen, toilet and shower. A phone line had been brought in five years ago, a convenience

Scholes had paid for handsomely. The number was unlisted. The cabin was a capsule that could be reached only by means of a narrow dirt track through the forest, an isolated retreat from the grind of the city and the red-hot freeways.

Drumm parked near the cabin, but didn't switch off the engine. 'I don't think I should come inside, Amanda. Two acts of trespass in one day, serious overkill.'

She opened the passenger door and stared at the windows, looking for a sign of Rhees.

'I miss seeing you around,' Drumm said.

'The same for me, Willie.'

'I hear they already gave your old job to Dominic Concannon.'

'He's OK,' she said. 'He's a decent lawyer, if that's not an oxymoron.'

'But he's not Amanda Scholes.' Drumm placed a hand on her shoulder. 'Words of wisdom for you: put all this shit out of your mind.'

She stepped out of the vehicle and stood staring up at Drumm. 'All of it?'

'Every bit. Forget I ever came here. Just get on with your life.'

She shut the door, rapped her knuckles against it and watched Drumm swing the Bronco round and head back down the track. When it had faded out of sight she turned and walked towards the cabin. She hesitated a moment before going inside.

Rhees sat at the table, which was covered with his papers and poetry books. Last night he'd been preparing his lecture material for the Fall semester. His notes were written in a minuscule hand she couldn't decipher.

She had an affection for Rhees's quiet world of

poetry. He wrote some himself on occasions, such as her birthday, when she'd find a short poem sealed inside an envelope and attached to a gift. Glasses halfway down his nose, he laboured over his verse like a man with a scalpel. Sometimes he hummed old Welsh tunes quietly. There was a bardic streak in Rhees.

Without raising his face from his books, Rhees said, 'You just had to look, didn't you?'

She needed coffee. She spooned three scoops into the basket then plugged the percolator into the wall. She noticed her hand trembled a little.

'Why?' he asked. 'You like morgues?'

'No, I don't like morgues. I wanted to be sure.'

The coffee began to perc. Amanda played with a wayward strand of hair. She noticed a grey streak.

'Galindez was scum, Amanda,' Rhees said.

'Yeah, I know what he was,' she said. 'I became very familiar with his rap-sheet. A nasty murder in Tucson, reduced through the usual legal legerdemain to a manslaughter rap. Early parole. A couple of rape charges, but he walked on those because nobody wanted to talk. Assisting Sanchez in gun-running to some very peculiar people in Mexico.'

'So a violent man comes to a violent end. Poetic justice.'

Amanda took a fresh pack of cigarettes from a drawer and tore off the Cellophane. She stood with her back to the sink, smoking, smelling the coffee.

Rhees said, 'Look, you were the one who decided you'd reached the end of the line. You wrote the letter of resignation. There was no gun to your head.'

Amanda poured two cups of coffee and carried

them to the table. 'And I'm happy with the decision,' she said.

'But something clings to you,' he said.

'I don't want to think so.'

He looked at her over the rim of his cup.

'It just bothers me, John.'

'You're carrying useless baggage.'

'I'm not going to get involved again,' she said.

'Then drop it. Because Galindez turns up dead, suddenly you're ticking over.' Rhees waved the fumes of her cigarette aside. 'I wish you'd quit smoking.'

'It's on my list to stop.'

'This list of yours. Two things you haven't crossed off; smoking's one.'

Amanda put the cigarette out in an old jamjar lid filled with stubs. 'Galindez happens to have been a major witness I used. Without him, Sanchez might be a free man. You think *Galindez* was scum? He was a minor demon compared to Sanchez. But Galindez makes a deal. I wasn't exactly over the moon with that—'

He interrupted her. 'A month ago you were a very unhappy human being. Insomnia, immune system precarious, prone to flu bugs, eating junk food, chewing down Dalmane every night like it was going out of style. You walked round like a ghost evicted from a house she was haunting. You were wandering the borderline of a nervous breakdown. Remember?'

'I don't really need reminding, thanks.' The sense of living on an edge. The feeling that panic was always somewhere nearby. Shallow sleep overflowing with bad dreams. A deep dread she couldn't define. She'd felt fractured, falling to pieces. Now she couldn't even remember the words she'd written in her letter of resignation, only how Luke Basha, the State Attorney-General, had counselled her to think again. *All you need is a vacation*, he'd said. *You've been working too hard*. It goes deeper than that, Luke, she'd said. It goes a long way down. She couldn't recall the press conference either, the way she'd answered questions about her resignation, what reasons she'd given. She only remembered the popping of cameras and sounds coming out of her mouth and a dark jagged pain in her head.

Rhees said, 'We talked it over, Amanda. Your state of mind. Your health. But the decision was yours in the end.' He tapped the back of her hand in an agitated manner. 'The law sucks. Your own words. Just look at the way you've been this last month. Colour's coming back to your face. Sex-drive restored. You sleep nights for the first time in an age. Life's worth living again. The question is, does the law suck enough for you to cross it off this list of yours?'

She walked round the tiny kitchen and paused at the window. Sunlight sloped through the pines. Why couldn't she just enjoy all this and forget everything else? She approached him, placed her hands on his shoulders.

'Look, it's not like I'm reversing a decision I already made. I want to stay up here. I want to make myself feel, what's the word . . . *clean* again. I just happen to think I ought to talk to Lew Bascombe myself.'

'Who's Bascombe?'

'He's the liaison guy with the Program. I'll tell him he should look into a possible breach of security.'

'I don't understand why you can't get Drumm to do that.'

'Because I'm better acquainted with Lew than Willie is. I'll just dump it on Bascombe's desk.'

'And leave it there?' Rhees looked doubtful.

'Yeah, I'll leave it there. I'll drive down to the city tomorrow. You want to keep me company?'

'On one condition. We get back here by bedtime.'

'I promise.'

She opened the kitchen door and stared out into the pines. Deep in the reaches of the forest, coyotes howled, then there was the babylike cry of something dying. A small deer, a stray cat, something.

Amanda shuddered. 'I hate that.'

'Serenity has its downside,' Rhees said.

The whimpering died and silence closed in again. She imagined coyotes feeding: a flurry of blood and fur. She remembered Galindez and she drew closer to Rhees.

'Let's go to bed and get into something passionate,' she said.

Rhees shut the door. 'I just remembered,' he said. 'I left my fishing rod on the bank.'

'It's not your fishing rod I have in mind, John.'

6

The woman reads the green sign through the bug-smeared window of her car. Tuba City.

Chooba City. Where the hell is that?

There's a coffeeshop up the street with a light blinking. I'll stop there, I gotta stop somewhere. She's exhausted, she feels the weariness in her bones, deeper than that, deeper than the marrow even – in her heart, what's left of it. She parks the car behind the coffeeshop so it can't be seen from the main drag. The night is dark and hot and dry and she feels like a landslide victim, smothered and blind and struggling for something to breathe.

She goes inside, takes a table away from the window and watches the waitress walk towards her with a pad in her hand. The waitress has this slinky sideways manner of walking, like an old beauty queen, maybe Miss Tuba City 1964, something. The light in this place is bad, low-wattage.

'Coffee.'

'Coffee. We got some nice Danish, you interested?'

'Just coffee. No cream. Please.'

Coffee – black and strong. She knows she needs to move again, get back in the car and drive, because no place is safe. She looks at her watch, but what's the point? Time don't matter, time don't have a significant meaning, only distance, distance is everything.

She opens her purse, sees the sealed envelope with the scribbled note inside. She wonders if her handwriting is readable, if she's spelled things the right way. She doesn't have a home address, only the office. If it goes to the office, they'll forward it. What if they don't?

The coffee comes. She sips it, taps her fingers on the table, watches the window, sees cars passing down the strip, cars heading out into the hot dark night, cars going everywhere and nowhere. She takes a napkin from the dispenser on her table and crumples it in her hand. Gotta go, keep moving, because you don't know what's behind you. Only one thing you know, the men are back there in the dark and they're coming. Only thing you can be sure of.

The men.

The napkin falls into the coffee and she pulls it out. It's sodden and brown and she makes a wad of it in her fist. There's no ashtray so she drops the wet thing on the floor, but now her hand is wet and she has to take another napkin from the dispenser to dry her palm. All this fuss, these napkins all joined together coming out the slot. She can hear the sound of herself falling apart.

She covers her eyes with her fingers. She needs sleep, she needs to put her head down and sleep. How long since she lay on that narrow iron bed in the mildewed motel room with the broken-down swamp-cooler? Her hand is shaky. She wonders if anyone notices, but nobody's looking at her. They don't care in a roadside place like this, nobody cares, nobody cares anywhere, no matter where you go it's the same thing.

She finishes the coffee, gets up, walks into the rest room and washes her face, avoiding the mirror. She doesn't want to see her reflection: a ruin. The rest room smells of heather or lilac, she can't tell which. It all comes out of an aerosol can anyway, it's all chemicals. She goes back into the coffee-shop.

'There a phone?' she asks.

The waitress points with a yellow pencil to the far side of the room.

'Thanks,' she says.

She goes between tables to the payphone, closes the door and digs coins out of her purse. This is another thing on top of everything else; running low on funds. She picks up the receiver, something happens inside her head, like an echo, like a ghost whispering in her skull. It's because she needs sleep, she can't keep going like this. You get hallucinations. You see stuff ain't there. You dream except you're not sleeping.

What she sees are flashes of light in the dark. She pushes the memory away, but it comes back immediately. How the night changed and the temperature tumbled to zero.

Coins in the slot. What's the number, remember the number; 6035 something, something, something. She punches the buttons and shuts her eyes. *Let her answer, let her answer.*

It rings and rings. She thinks of an empty house, the phone ringing and nobody to hear.

OK, she tries the other number. It's the same guy as before that answers.

'Are you the woman who called yesterday?' he asks.

'I'm calling from Chooba City,' she says, and wonders why she gives out this information. Off-guard, going round in a trance, fear makes you crazy.

'Listen, I'll give you the number where—'

She hangs up, a clattering sound. The man – she don't know who he is, could be anybody. Another trapdoor you fall through. She cries, salt liquid fills the back of her throat and sinuses. She weeps with her face pressed against the phone.

The letter. She opens her purse and she walks to the waitress, handing her the crumpled envelope. 'Please. Can you mail this for me?'

The waitress says, 'It ain't stamped, honey.'

She presses a couple of quarters into the waitress's hand and hurries out of the coffeeshop. She's still crying as she rushes to the parking lot and unlocks the car and gets behind the wheel. There's a stink of fried-food wrappers.

Drive, just drive, don't think. Make-believe you're maybe on vacation, a woman just touring here and there, some carefree divorcée. She turns the key in the ignition. How far away are the men? she wonders. How far?

7

The city in the distance was the colour of a dull penny in the afternoon sun. On either side of the freeway heat shimmered in dry brown hills. Amanda opened the sunroof of the VW and a warm breeze ruffled her hair. 'Bascombe said he'd see me at three – in and out. Also I'd like to stop a minute at the house before we head back. I need to pick up some books.'

'What books?'

'A biography of Lincoln I was reading before we rushed off to the mountains. Also a saga I'm half-way through. It's nice to read something that isn't a legal brief.'

Rhees studied the road and said, 'Maybe we should drop in on your father.'

'Why not? He's always liked you, John. He likes to think you're a good influence on me.'

'A man of impeccable judgement,' Rhees said.

Amanda had her arm across the back of the driver's seat. She watched Rhees's face for a time, the line of his lean jaw, the thoughtful grey eyes.

There was a reliability about that face. He'd never disappoint, never betray. She felt safe with Rhees.

The freeway sliced through the heart of the city. To the left were the spires of downtown, concrete and glass shining. On the right, in purple shadows, were shacks and shanties and laundry hanging motionless on lines. Beyond, suburbs stretched away into a muslin haze.

Rhees said, 'We could live year-round at the cabin. I could easily cram all my classes into two days a week, if I grovel in front of the department chairman.'

Amanda glanced at him. He was perfectly serious about this. A permanent move to the cabin. He'd mentioned it before. 'What would I do with my time?' she asked.

'Read, learn how to fish. We'll get a snowmobile and you can whizz across the landscape.'

'I'll think about it.'

In truth, she hadn't given her future much thought. She had space in her life for the first time in years. She woke mornings knowing she didn't have two hundred appointments and interviews with cops and the mind-numbing stress of courtroom appearances. Liberty exhilarated her, but it was a condition she suspected couldn't last. She'd worked too hard for as long as she could remember – law school, two years in a firm where she'd shuffled corporate papers, three years in a DA's office in southern California, another two in northern Arizona, then eight years in Phoenix, the last three of which she'd spent as Special Prosecutor in the State Attorney-General's crime task force. Her CV was overloaded.

'I'd probably feel guilty not doing something,'

she said. 'Anyway, I'm not sure I approve of the idea of you supporting me when my savings run out. I'd feel like a kept woman.'

'A kept woman. Has a sexy ring to it.' Rhees smiled and headed downtown. He found a parking space a couple of blocks from the Federal Building.

She suddenly remembered she'd dreamed last night of Galindez, his body rocking through black water, creatures feeding on his flesh. She wished he'd been washed down another river in a state a thousand miles away. She wished she and Rhees had been in Hawaii or Fiji when Willie Drumm had appeared. Wish, wish, wish.

And now she was back in the city where there were too many reminders of the job she'd walked away from, the work that had squeezed her dry.

The law sucks, she thought. She'd been wrong when she'd said that. It was the way law was manipulated that had depleted and disenchanted her, the sleaze of bargaining with defence attorneys in the fashion of dope merchants squabbling about the price of coke, the lack of any moral coherence underpinning the decrepit machinery of justice. A sense of morality was unfashionable, derisory even. To get a conviction, you had to sleep with the enemy. You had to make all kinds of deals and some churned your stomach, others dripped like acid on your heart – like the commitment she'd made to Reuben Galindez. Give me everything you know about Sanchez, Rube, and in return you'll get a new life. Manslaughter? Rape? Illicit traffic of weapons in contravention of federal laws? Hey, no problem. Testify against Sanchez and *presto* you get a new identity and a house in a distant state and enough money to kick-start you. Welcome to the Federal Witness Protection Program, Mr Galindez.

She opened the passenger door, but didn't get out at once. 'Sometimes it just blows me away to remember how naïve I was,' she said. There was a trace of sadness in her voice. 'I used to believe the law had a purity of sorts, but every shitty deal you cut clouds the picture and diminishes your faith. Finally you become a non-believer.'

Rhees was quiet for a time. 'You really sure you want to see this guy Bascombe?'

'It's no big deal. In and out toot sweet.'

'I'll find a bar and have a beer,' Rhees said.

'Let's meet back here in half an hour.'

He kissed her. She wolf-whistled him as he walked away and he turned back, smiling. He was dressed in a beige linen jacket and black jeans and his skin was lightly tanned. He looked luminously attractive. Six years and her heart still went into orbit.

'Take care,' she called to him.

She went in the direction of the Federal Building, where she walked through the metal detector, then stepped past the armed guards and headed for the elevators.

8

'I haven't seen a police report yet,' Lewis Bascombe said.

Amanda said, 'Drumm wouldn't submit it directly to you in any case. It would go to Chief Kelloway. You'll get it through whatever your regular channels are.'

Bascombe tapped his desk with a ballpoint pen which had on it the legend, '*Shop'n'Go 24 Hrs*'. Sunlight was thinly sliced by the drawn slats of a blind. The walls of the office were bare except for a photograph that depicted Bascombe and former President Bush handshaking.

Bascombe was an unimposing man with a toupee the colour of a mouse. 'The guidelines say I need a copy of a police report, Amanda. I need confirmation.'

'*Confirmation?* Of what? The body was definitely Galindez, and he'd definitely been shot. What is this, Lew?'

'I have to have a report from a law enforcement officer.'

'Lew,' Amanda said, 'why can't we skip your guidelines here? If there's even the *slightest* chance of a security screw-up, you can't fart around waiting for a report.'

'I'm not saying I doubt it was Galindez, and I'm not going to shed any tears over him, but put yourself in my place.'

'I spent the best part of my career bending the law to make it work. If it didn't fit, I had to twist it, and if that didn't work, I had to tweak it again. One thing I know about guidelines. They're malleable.' She was impatient. 'All I'm asking is that you notify the proper authorities immediately, Lew.'

'You don't have official status these days, Amanda.'

'So call me a concerned citizen, if that makes it easier for you.'

Bascombe appeared to consider this statement. Amanda couldn't tell anything from Bascombe's face about his inner world. Maybe he didn't have one. Maybe he was all surface, the bad wig and the sweat-rings in the armpits of his shirt. He liaised between the US Marshals Service and the Department of Justice in the operation of the Federal Witness Protection Program, which meant he worked in a secret hinterland, an altogether cloudy place. Maybe his lack of expression was a prerequisite for the demands of this shadowy territory.

She said, 'I placed Galindez in the Witness Program, Lew. He turns up dead in a place he should never have been, so naturally I'm concerned. If the Program's fucked we should know about it.'

Bascombe continued to tap his pen. 'Presumably you considered the possibility that Galindez left the Program of his own accord?'

'Of course I considered it, but I don't gamble when it comes to people's lives. Do you?'

'I work in the dark, Amanda. My job is to make sure witnesses are well protected before and during their testimony. After that, I don't know where they go, and I don't want to know. They're taken into custody by US marshals and then they vanish inside the Program in accordance with Title 18, *Crimes and Criminal Procedure*, Section 3521, *Witness Relocation and Protection*. The less I know the better for my own safety and for security in general.'

'Lew, don't go spouting title this and section that at me.'

Bascombe rolled his pen back and forth across his desk. He had stubby fingers. Amanda glanced a moment at the photograph on the wall. Former President Bush was smiling like a man trying to hang tough through a prolonged bout of constipation.

Amanda sighed. 'All I want is for you to make contact with the Program, tell them about Galindez. A favour to me, that's all. And if you won't do it, if you *can't* do it, give me the name of somebody I can contact personally.'

'A name?' Bascombe shook his head, as if Amanda's request were too preposterous to consider. 'The story going around is you'd lost your enthusiasm, Amanda. Turned your back on things.'

'I think of it as lawsick.'

'For a lady with no appetite, you sound pretty keen to me.'

'I don't like the idea of a leak, Lew.'

Bascombe nodded his head slowly. There was a bovine quality about the gesture. He studied the logo on his pen. 'OK. OK. I'll send along the message on Galindez today, but I think what we'll find is that he made the stupid decision to go walk-about and found his way back among his old cronies, and one of them administered the *coup de grâce*. Criminals have shit for brains, Amanda, as you well know.'

'I appreciate this,' Amanda said.

'And if anything comes up you need to know about, I'll be in touch,' Bascombe said.

Amanda gave him the telephone number at the cabin. Bascombe scribbled it down on a piece of paper and stuck it in the drawer. 'Something else on your mind?' he asked.

She hesitated, then shook her head. Nothing, she thought, just some vague unfocused disturbance way at the back of her mind, like wind blowing on a distant lake. The feeling faded as quickly as it had come.

She rose from her chair. 'When did you meet Bush?' she asked.

'About nine years ago.'

'Likeable?'

'A regular guy,' Bascombe said. 'But I didn't vote for him.'

'Why not?'

'I didn't vote period,' Bascombe said.

'Undemocratic of you, Lew.'

Bascombe said, 'You might not believe this, but I have a quiet rebellious streak deep inside, and sometimes it just bubbles up.'

'You're a dark horse. You take my breath away, Lew.'

9

Anthony Dansk was attending early evening mass when the cellular phone buzzed in his pocket. He shut it off at once, but not before it had drawn the attention of other worshippers, some of whom turned to stare. The priest heard it and frowned across the faces of his congregation.

Dansk slid out of the pew and walked up the aisle. In the vestibule, he pressed a button on the phone and said, 'I can't talk now, McTell. I'll get back to you.'

Dansk severed the connection and glanced at leaflets tacked to a bulletin board. Hot-line numbers for manic depressives, alcoholics, battered wives' support groups, a schedule for a kindergarten class. He also noticed dust on ledges and an old cobweb with a skeleton of an antique fly hanging under Christ's armpit.

He stuck the phone in his pocket, re-entered the church and slipped quietly into a pew at the rear. Churches impressed him: he liked the majesty and the mystery. His mother used to tell him he was a mote in Jesus's sunbeam. For years he'd thought of himself as a fleck floating in mid-air, with only Christ keeping him from falling. The things you believe.

He watched the priest, the rose-coloured scalp glowing under subdued light. Dansk pondered the concept of chastity, what it would be like not to get laid. Unreal. Pecker for-ever in your pocket, unless you had a taste for choirboys and indulged yourself with much fumbling of cassocks in the quiet of the sacristy.

When Mass was over Dansk walked outside and lingered on the sidewalk. The other worshippers drifted out. They were a well-scrubbed crew; wives with sculpted hair, men in suits. These people had homes to go to, kids to look after.

The priest appeared on the steps and looked at him.

'Visiting?' the priest asked.

'Yeah, more or less,' Dansk said.

'I thought your face was new.'

'New? It's thirty-five years old.'

'Pardon?'

Dansk said, 'A joke. You said new.'

'Oh, right. Yes. Forgive me.'

'Me forgive you? Shouldn't that be the other way round, Father?'

The priest laughed this time, but uneasily. Dansk often had an unsettling effect on others. He'd recognized this in himself long ago. People he met sometimes sensed a nebulous danger in him, a dark core. It was as if they were receiving vibrations that unhinged them a little. He considered it a kind of power he had. He fingered the Swiss Army knife in his pocket.

'Good Mass,' he said.

'We have a nice bunch of people here,' said the priest. 'My name's Father Hannon. Brian Hannon.'

'Anthony Dansk.'

'Are you staying long in our city?'

'It depends on business.'

'Ah. A man of commerce.'

'Commerce, right.'

'Well, if you decide to worship with us again, Anthony, you know where to find us. Just remember to switch your phone off next time.' The priest wandered off to chat with members of his congregation.

Dansk walked to the end of the block where he'd parked his rented car. He sat behind the wheel, took out his phone and punched the button that connected him with McTell.

'OK,' Dansk said. 'Talk.'

'We traced her.'

'You traced her before, I seem to remember,' Dansk said.

'This time's different.'

'It was different before,' Dansk said.

'I know, I know. But this time, I swear.'

'What are you swearing to, McTell?'

'She gassed her car on Thunderbird about forty-five minutes ago.'

'Thunderbird. What is that?'

'Name of a road. The guy filling her tank said she was unglued. Dropping coins, crying, the shakes, talking to herself. The guy figured a loony.'

'And?'

'Pasquale is on her.'

'Even as we speak?'

'Yeah,' McTell said.

Dansk considered this. 'I don't want you calling me later just to hum the same old tune, McTell. Don't get in touch unless you can sing me a lullaby.'

Dansk cut the connection. Through the windshield he watched Father Hannon shake hands with his departing flock. Dansk thought about white suburban houses and morning newspapers landing on porches and cookies baking in ovens and kids laughing in backyards. This life he led was one of hotels and endless highways and greasy spoons open all hours and lonely demented strangers.

He changed the angle of the rear-view mirror and looked at himself, the thick red hair, grass-green eyes, lips almost cherubic, pale skin. Thirty-five. He could pass for twenty. Baby face.

He twisted the mirror away, shoved the phone inside the glove compartment, then locked it. What he'd do was go back to his hotel downtown and wait for McTell to call again.

He glanced along the sidewalk at the priest. *Commerce my ass.* You don't know, Father, he thought. You probably think computers or life insurance or hotel supplies.

Wrong. My commerce is darkness without end.

10

Morgan Scholes shook Rhees's hand effusively, then embraced Amanda. He had thick white hair cut short. He smelled of Old Spice, a scent Amanda always found comforting.

Morgan Scholes said, 'I keep telling you, Mandy, marry this man. You don't, one day he'll just slip through the cracks.'

'I don't think I'm about to slip anywhere, Morgan,' Rhees said.

Amanda said, 'We've discussed matrimony, Dad. It's a subject we circle warily.'

'Nonsense,' the old man said. 'It's an ocean, and you plunge in head first and go with the tides. Is it cocktail hour yet?'

'There's a perfectly plausible theory that it's always cocktail hour somewhere on the planet,' Rhees said.

'See, Mandy. This is my kind of guy.' Morgan Scholes clapped Rhees on the shoulder. 'First time I ever liked any guy you brought home. Some of the cretins you used to hang out with, all those upwardly mobile types with one eye on their portable phone and the other on my money – I could sniff those guys a mile away.'

'Hey, they weren't all fortune-hunters,' Amanda said.

Morgan Scholes uttered a dismissive snort. 'They were wimps, girl. Transparent as all hell.'

She saw no point in pursuing the matter of old boyfriends, so she let the topic slide. Morgan's opinions tended to be cemented in his brain and therefore unshakeable anyway. Besides, she knew that the matter of her past lovers, even if they meant zip to her, wasn't high on Rhees's list of favourite conversation subjects. He had an endearing insecurity at times.

She followed Morgan inside the house, which clung in defiance of gravity to the side of a mountain, and consisted of three wings built around a central courtyard where a clay mermaid lay in a fountain. There were arched walkways, open spaces. In the sunken lounge, stained-glass windows handcrafted in the Baja filtered and changed the late afternoon sun. Traditional Western art hung on the walls; cowboys in glossy wax coats, a chuck wagon by campfire.

'Gin and tonic OK?'

The old man, dressed in grey slacks and sand-coloured shirt, made the drinks. He passed them out, then sat down next to Amanda and said, 'You look good in white. Like an angel.'

'Flattery, Dad. The old silver tongue.'

'Flattery doesn't enter into it. I never lied to a woman in my life. Made it a rule. Broke it only once and that was when your mother asked me outright if her disease was terminal. I told her no, said she'd get well. Three weeks later, dead.'

'An excusable lie,' Rhees said.

'You don't look the woman you love in the eye and tell her she's dying from cancer.'

Amanda tasted her drink. What she remembered of her mother was the voice, soft and Virginian. She'd died when Amanda was three. After that, there had been a series of 'companions' who came and went quickly because they couldn't compete with the dead. Morgan was more interested in the brutality of business than the delicate structures of relationships anyway. He'd made a fortune pioneering greetings cards with high-art reproductions on their covers. He'd parleyed this into even greater wealth in a series of speculative land deals in the days when property could be bought one morning and sold the next for fabulous profit.

'It was a damn good marriage,' the old man said.

'You were fortunate,' Rhees said.

'Sure I was fortunate. I used to wonder about remarrying, having more kids. Then I'd think, hold on, I've probably used up a whole lifetime's luck with Amanda's mother. You two staying for dinner?'

Amanda said, 'Not this time. We want to get back before it's too late.'

'That cabin grows on you,' Scholes remarked. 'I think you did an admirable thing when you quit, Mandy. You don't like what you're doing, dump it. Move on. You're young.'

'Relatively.'

Morgan Scholes waved this aside. 'Forty-two.'

'Three.'

'Three then. That's young. Right, John?'

'Absolutely,' Rhees said.

'And if you get bored at the cabin, enrol in some

college courses, study something different – economics, business. Something practical. It's not like you have money problems.'

'I have some savings,' Amanda said.

'Pah. Nickel and dime. I'm talking about your inheritance. I shuffle off, you're a very rich woman.'

'Let's not talk about shuffling off,' Amanda said.

'There's nothing wrong with inheriting money, Amanda. What do you want me to do with it? Leave it to some charity? I don't understand why you're always so damn narrow-minded and Bolshevist about it. It's not like it's tainted, for God's sake.'

The subject of her inheritance, which Morgan raised at every opportunity he could, made her uncomfortable. At some point on the graph of her life, she'd decided it was an injustice that one person should inherit another's wealth because of an accident of birth. During her years at law school in Los Angeles she'd worked nights and weekends as a cocktail waitress in a Brentwood hotel, instead of accepting her father's persistent offers of tuition and expenses. It came down to the fact that she wanted to be her own person, not the brat offspring of a rich man.

She didn't need her father's money, and she didn't like the way wealth influenced Morgan's life. He was always consorting with ossified people who just happened to be as rich as himself; industrialists, powerbrokers, men whose wives were face-lifted and ditzy and spent their days in listless shopping or fund-raising for Third World countries they couldn't find on a map if they tried. Wealth bred in some people a kind of blind ignorance, isolated them in a cocoon.

The old man, in a rare display of tact, changed the subject. 'You're better off out of law anyhow. It's a joke in this country, unless you've got money to burn. Lawyers like only one thing, and it's the folding green. Justice? What's that? John deserves better than a lawyer for a wife when you get right down to it.'

'How many times, Dad? We're not contemplating marriage.'

'She ought to have her head examined,' the old man said to Rhees.

Rhees smiled and said, 'I don't think there's much wrong with Amanda's head, Morgan.'

'You always take her side, John. Don't encourage her. I want to be there when you and she walk down that aisle, all sweetness and light.'

Amanda glanced at Rhees over her gin and tonic. 'He doesn't know when to quit, John.'

'Carve that on my stone,' the old man said. He finished his drink and looked at Amanda for a time, then he said to Rhees, 'She's stubborn and strong-willed. Don't know where in the world she gets it from.'

He winked at Rhees, then stood up and laughed. 'Bad habit telling other people what's good for them, huh? Can't break some habits at my time of life.'

'You mean well,' Amanda said.

'But the road to hell is paved, yadda yadda,' the old man said. 'Another drink?'

'I'm driving,' Rhees said.

'Not for me,' Amanda remarked.

Morgan Scholes said, 'I'm in the company of lightweights,' and fixed himself a second drink. Then he looked at his daughter. 'Say. I just remembered.

Some woman's been phoning here for you, Mandy.'

'Here? What woman?'

'She called first time two nights ago, then last night again. I must speak to Amanda, she says. I'm in Tuba City, she says.'

'Tuba City?'

'That's what she said. I tell her you're not here, and before I can give her the number at the cabin she hangs up.'

'She doesn't leave her name?'

Scholes shook his head. 'No, she doesn't.'

'Describe the voice,' Amanda said.

'It's low, whispered. Kind of Hispanic accent. She sounds frantic and then she hangs up like she thinks somebody's listening in, or she's in a big hurry. Who do you know in Tuba City?'

Amanda looked down into her drink. Bubbles of tonic popped on the surface. A woman calls and hangs up again quickly. What did that mean? Her mind blanked.

She gazed at Rhees, who was watching her thoughtfully. She saw dying sunlight come in a pale-blue haze through stained-glass. 'Why didn't you call and tell me this, Dad?' she asked.

'I've been pretty busy what with one thing and another,' Morgan Scholes said. 'Who is she anyway?'

She finished her drink. 'I don't know,' she said.

11

'I'm racking my brain,' Amanda said in the car. 'I don't know a soul up in that part of the state.' She lit a cigarette and inhaled smoke a little too quickly. *Frantic* was the word Morgan had used. *I must speak to Amanda*, Yours truly, Frantic, Tuba City. *Hispanic accent*. She didn't want to think.

A shadow rolled through her head, the same smoke signal she'd expelled from her mind when she'd been discussing Galindez with Willie Drumm, the same little shiver of concern she'd felt in Bascombe's office. She shut her eyes. Tuba City, the back-end of beyond. She thought of an endless arid landscape and a voice travelling through telephone wires and the way Galindez had been ferried downstream by the river.

'Why would somebody phone you at your father's number anyway?' Rhees asked.

'Maybe she tried our home number first, then when she got no response she looked up Morgan in the book. I don't know.'

Rhees was driving towards Scottsdale from

Phoenix. All that remained of the sun were a few spectacular streaks the colour of blood. Downtown Scottsdale was a sequence of traffic lights, all seemingly red. Rhees took a left turn off the main street. He drove until he reached the cul-de-sac where the house he shared with Amanda was located. He parked in the driveway and Amanda strolled ahead of him, unlocked the front door and turned on the lights.

Inside the air was stuffy. They'd been gone a little less than four weeks and yet she felt like an intruder. She went into the living room, Rhees followed her. More lights. She looked round the room. Their possessions – books, TV, furniture – had that alien quality you sometimes experience when you come back after a vacation. The geometry of the house was all wrong, ceilings too high, windows too large.

Rhees said, 'Weird.'

'You feel it?'

'Yeah, I feel it.'

'It's like somebody else's house,' Amanda said. 'I expect if we go into the backyard we'll find duplicates of ourselves emerging from giant pods.'

She walked to the answering machine, then remembered she'd disconnected it before they'd left for the cabin, an act of deliberate severance. Kill the machine. *I don't need and I don't want messages.*

'You think this mystery woman will call?' Rhees asked.

'It's a possibility.'

'I need a drink. Want one?'

'Please.'

Rhees went inside the kitchen. Amanda could hear him rummaging for ice. She sat on the sofa, glanced at the Adams prints on the walls, chilly black and white rock formations. Objects formerly charged with easy familiarity were shorn of meaning. Even the framed newspaper and magazine clippings that concerned some of her legal cases were related to a person other than herself. It was as if somebody had come here when the house was empty and stripped away the veneer of recognition.

Rhees returned with drinks. 'We forgot to empty the refrigerator. Something disgusting is growing in there.'

'Sit beside me.' She patted the sofa. He sat down and touched her wrist. She sipped her drink. She was conscious of the silent black telephone located on the table at her back. She was suddenly uptight, jangled. She wanted the gin to relax her, numb her head a little.

In the distance the shrill whine of a cop car was audible. Night in the city. Deaths and accidents. Casual, drive-by shootings. She yearned for the forest.

'We should be heading back soon,' Rhees said.

Amanda didn't move.

Rhees got up. 'Maybe I'll just defuzz the fridge to pass some time while you finish your drink and wait to see if the phone rings.'

He went back inside the kitchen. She listened to the sound of things being clattered around. Jars and bottles, glass knocked on glass impatiently. He didn't want to be here any more than she did. She heard him say, 'Sweet Jesus, was this sodden mass once a bag of carrots?'

Fifteen minutes dragged past before the telephone rang, and when it did Amanda reached for the receiver at once and spoke her name.

The woman said, 'Manda, I been trying to phone for days, I can't get you, Manda.'

For a second Amanda couldn't speak. Electricity spiked through her. She was only dimly aware of Rhees materializing in the kitchen doorway with what looked like green compost in his rubber-gloved hand. She leaned forward on the sofa and tried to keep alarm out of her voice. 'Where are you? Where the hell are you?'

'It's gone wrong, Manda, the whole goddam thing. This isn't the way you planned it. I'm inside this nightmare where I don't belong.' The woman was crying and her words ran into one another in breathless little utterances.

'Just tell me where you are,' Amanda said.

'God, where am I? Jesus, I don't know.'

'Calm down, calm down.'

'They're coming after me, Manda.'

'Who?'

'These two guys, they're coming after me.'

Amanda's fingers were rigid on the handset. 'I'll help, just tell me where you are.'

'OK, where I am, this is,' and her voice faded. Amanda heard the clank of a telephone being set down, then a creaking noise. 'Where I am. OK, this is a place called, wait a minute, I'm looking at the sign, the Canyon Motel, off the interstate. It's got a big blue light outside.'

'Which interstate?'

'What's the one? Seventeen. I-Seventeen.'

'*Seventeen?* You're here in *Arizona*?'

'Manda, help me. Come help me.'

'You're at a pay phone there.'

'A payphone, right. Say you'll come.'

'Stay where you are. Don't move.' Rhees was looking at her with curiosity.

'How long it gonna take you?'

'I don't know. Fast as I can get there.'

'Hurry, Jesus Christ hurry, please.'

'I'll be there.' Amanda hung up. Rhees was thumbing quickly through the Yellow Pages.

'The Canyon,' he said, reading from the directory. 'It's near Black Canyon City.'

Amanda could hear the motion of her blood. 'Even if I go like a bat out of hell, that's still twenty-five, thirty minutes. Do me a favour. Call Willie Drumm, tell him to meet me there.'

She rushed towards the door before Rhees – who looked puzzled and anxious – had time to say anything. She was all haste, her brain locked in that space where thoughts don't cohere and your head's filled with a strident choir of panic. She blew a quick kiss back at Rhees and said, 'Tell him it's Isabel Sanchez.'

12

She drove with concentrated urgency. The city thinned until there were no more orange lamps, only the unforgiving dark of the desert on either side. She tried to arrange her thoughts, piling them up like building blocks, but they wouldn't balance. Isabel calls from a place called the Canyon Motel on I-17. She's in trouble. Why is she there to begin with? And what had she been doing in Tuba City before that? Think *think* – but the bricks kept slipping and tumbling, and the letters of the alphabet made no sense. The night was cracked, and the pieces didn't fit, and Amanda couldn't make them.

Out into darkness, out into space. Freeway signs that read like gibberish, a cluster of orange lights, then more blackness for miles, and oncoming traffic rushing past her into a void. When she saw the blue light of the Canyon Motel she realized she'd lost all sense of time and distance. She swung off the freeway and raced up the ramp and braked hard inside the parking lot, opening the door and stepping out in one unbroken movement.

There was a payphone located outside the motel office. Nobody was using it, no sign of Isabel. She went inside the office. The clerk, a kid in a baseball cap, stood behind the desk. Willie Drumm was also there, beefy in his usual tight-fitting linen jacket.

'She's not here,' Drumm said. 'She's gone.'

'Gone?'

'I got here a minute ago—'

'You look around?' Amanda asked.

'I only just arrived, Amanda.'

Amanda looked at the clerk. 'Did you see her?'

The kid said, 'There was a woman out there making a phone call about ten minutes ago. Small woman, Mexican looking. She the one you mean?'

'Where did she go?'

'I wasn't paying close attention,' the kid said. He had a plump textbook open on the counter. *Gray's Anatomy.* Amanda glanced at an elongated sketch that might have been a cross-section of gland.

'Pre-med next month,' the kid said. 'I was studying actually.'

Amanda slammed the book shut. 'What the fuck did you see *actually*?'

The kid, who had a sharp little face, looked at Amanda with annoyance. 'Hey,' he said, 'you lost my place.'

'I'll ask again. What did you see?'

'This woman came in and wanted to use the pay phone, so I made change for her, then she went out again. I saw her go to the phone. She seemed sort of wigged.'

'Then what?'

'I wasn't really watching. I told you.'

'After she was finished using the phone, what did

she do? Did she drive away? Did she just walk up and down? What did you see?'

'I heard a car start up. I assume she drove away. Then this other vehicle came screaming through the lot.'

'What kind of vehicle?'

'Land Cruiser, something like that.'

'You heard this vehicle immediately after the first car?'

'Seconds, that was all.'

'You happen to see what direction these vehicles took?'

The kid pondered a moment. 'I don't think they headed to the freeway. I got the impression they were going in the other direction. Back there,' and he gestured with his thumb towards the desert.

Amanda looked at Drumm. 'We'll take your car, Willie.'

'Fine by me.' Drumm moved to the door and opened it. Amanda rushed past him. The cop, his right leg stiff from an old gunshot wound, stumped after her.

Amanda was buzzing, uneasy. She opened the door of the Bronco, sat in the passenger seat, watched Drumm lower himself behind the wheel.

'She can't be far away,' Amanda said.

Drumm backed up the Bronco, turned out of the lot, slid the vehicle into the road that ran at a right angle to the freeway, an unlit ribbon of blacktop. The blue neon of the motel faded quickly behind. The city became a remote yellow-orange constellation in the sky. Cacti loomed up in the headlights, some pock-marked by the gunfire of vandals at target practice.

'You want to tell me what's happening?' Drumm asked.

'She called me. She's in a bad way. She said some men were after her.'

'Did she say who these guys were?'

'She wasn't coherent.'

'You think this other car's chasing her?'

'Sounds that way. All I can tell you for sure is she's frightened and I want to find her.'

The Bronco dipped in and out of potholes and Drumm said, 'This road is the pits. You look your side, I'll look mine.'

'I'm doing that.'

'You can't see shit around here. What if she drove off the road? Headed out into the desert?'

'We'll stick to the road for the time being,' Amanda said.

'I don't see what choice we got. We go off the road, what direction do we take? People get lost in the desert all the time.'

Amanda beat a tattoo on the dash. She was trying to release tension, but it wasn't working. She thought of Isabel, tiny out there in the wilderness. Left, right, east, west. Drumm was correct. If they left the road, they'd be going nowhere.

'I thought she was long gone,' Drumm said.

'I thought the same thing,' Amanda leaned forward, scanning the night, the puny reaches of the lights. 'Stop the car.'

Drumm braked. Amanda rolled down her window and listened to a silence as big as a galaxy.

'You hear anything?' Drumm asked.

'Nothing. Drive on a bit farther.'

Drumm slid the Bronco forward. The blacktop

narrowed. The desert crowded in. After a mile or so, Amanda said, 'Stop again.'

Drumm cut the engine. Amanda focused on the night, still and enormous. What she longed for were distress flares, great plumes of white light to illuminate the landscape. She listened as she'd never listened before. She heard only absences and silences and the quickened rhythm of her own pulse. The desert was a vast infuriating secret.

She told Drumm to drive again.

Half a mile down the road, Amanda heard dogs barking far off. Drumm slowed.

'Coyotes,' Drumm said.

'They're dogs,' Amanda said.

'I'm a city boy,' Drumm remarked. 'Dogs, coyotes. What do I know?'

Amanda opened the door and got out of the car. She stood on the edge of the blacktop and listened. The dogs yapped and snivelled. Hounds, hunting dogs, excited. She couldn't tell where the sounds originated, how far away they might be. You could drive out there for miles and think you were heading directly to the source and you'd be wrong. Soundwaves zigzagged. There were acoustic distortions.

Drumm stood alongside her and surveyed the dark with a gloomy look. 'What do you think?'

'We may have to drive out there, Willie.'

'Like two blind people.'

'I don't like the sound of those dogs.'

'Maybe some good old boy's out chasing jackrabbits or something.'

'In the dark?'

Drumm shrugged. 'Anything's possible. You

want me to drive off the road, I'll do it. Christ only knows where we'll end up.'

Amanda got back inside the Bronco. A mile away, five miles, ten – the dogs could be anywhere. Drumm turned the key in the ignition.

Amanda hung one arm out the window and Drumm swung the vehicle off the blacktop and steered between cacti that resembled stick-figures petrified into stillness by the white slash of the headlights.

13

She's twisted her ankle and a heel has broken off her shoe and she's running, stumbling, trying all this time to keep quiet, but she makes gasping sounds because her lungs are bursting and her ankle's beginning to swell.

The dogs have the scent of her. They whine and yelp and she wishes she hadn't abandoned the car, even with the flat tyre, because she could have sat tight with the doors and windows locked, but even then, even then what good would it do? The men are following the dogs in a jeep. Always the men, the men.

There's no moon and the stars have gone out, and she finds herself scrambling up a slope. Dust rises into her nose and mouth and stings her eyes, and she wants to cry, but she's been crying too much lately, and she thinks, there's a time when you don't have no more tears.

She climbs up the slope on all fours now. Loose stones slither out from under her, and what she wants is to lie very still and pretend she isn't here and if she makes herself small maybe the dogs won't smell her. She loses her hold and slips a few yards and thinks, the landscape's against her, like everything else.

What she remembers is hitching rides from truckers who took her places she didn't want to go; Gallup then Farmington, New Mexico, the wrong direction, but she wasn't thinking straight for a while, and then she stole the car and drove back to Arizona.

The weariness, the car overheating, the air stuffy and stifling, this is what she remembers. Also how Manda's telephone rings on and on and even when she decided to try the other number all she ever got was a man. Maybe Manda's father. Maybe. You don't know who to trust; cops, strangers, you don't know. It's the world, the way of it.

She should have kept her mouth shut, but she spoke up about Ángel, yeah, *really* bright of her, very smart, Ángel who she used to love. Ángel who screwed her over real bad and treated her like shit and one time, with his razor, cut her in a private place. She doesn't want to think about him because love rots.

Running, driving long hours, panicky, drained, freeway lines painted inside her skull, one night in a small stuffy motel room and not knowing how long she can sleep because the men are always just behind her. She can't stay ahead of them no more and she knows it, and she's gonna die here and nobody gonna find her.

She wishes for moonlight, but then she thinks, maybe she don't want to see what's out there. Let it be this way, this dark. Better like this. She climbs again. Her fingernails are broken. One time she was proud of her nails and how long they were, she'd paint and buff and file them, when she wanted to look good for Ángel, when she loved him. When they had the big house and the *conservatory*, whatever it's called. The plants, she smells the plants, it's a dream of back then, that's all. A dream rotting inside her skull.

Her ankle feels like a crab is pinching. She's dragging the foot and it gets in the way of her movement, and the dogs are coming. She imagines them bounding through the dark towards her. She thinks of their hot breath, paws, sharp teeth. She thinks, the dogs gonna get me, no matter how hard I try to get away, the dogs are coming, and then the men behind them. They're coming at her in the night, and all she did was say what was in her mind, because all Ángel did was cause pain – he deserves what he got. But he don't roll over just because he's been put away, no, he don't do that: he sends out men and dogs to hunt her. Nobody else would send men and dogs after her. She can't think. She never hurt a soul. She was always kind, right from the time when she was a little girl and her grandmother dragged her from town to town selling those crazy herb potions for warts and insomnia and flatulence – dry towns and villages, Camargo and La Esmeralda and Ceballos. She remembers the cracked roads and her grandmother carving strips of yucca and muttering the secret holy words. She remembers the withered old bronze woman saying, *You're a good girl, Isabella. Always say your prayers and tell the truth and brush your teeth. And when a handsome young man talks to you, smile at him like you mean it.*

Manda you promised me. Manda you said everything gonna be OK. Just tell me this one thing, what good are your words now?

She slips again, clutching at nothing. She rolls over and over down the slope and dust chokes her and she's dizzy and the sky's off-centre and the dogs are louder all the time, and she feels the way a hunted rabbit would feel; all fear and wild impulses and thinking how to survive, how to get out of this place and just live.

Then suddenly the dogs are on her, out of the dark they come snarling, and she smells the meaty breath of the animals, and they whine and bark, snapping at skin and clothing, quick and savage. She sees their eyes gleam. She tries to cover her face and kicks at the beasts. The stench of their fur is strong and sickly, their bodies feel moist and hot against her skin. 'Mother of God,' she says. 'Mother of Christ.' Fangs, jaws, saliva, claws. She curls herself up into a ball. The dogs snap and bite and whine, how many: three, four, who can tell? Her leg is slashed, her hands are bleeding, the dogs are crazy for her blood. She tries to crawl out from under the pressure of their bodies, but they cling to her, they dig into her.

The sound of a vehicle. Slamming doors. A man's voice. 'Back, back. Get back.'

The animals retreat, sniffling, whimpering sullenly.

She looks up into the bright disc of a flashlight.

'Bitch,' the man says.

She knows this voice. Knows it.

Another man says, 'End of the road, sweetie.'

The first man says, 'I'll do it myself.'

The other man reaches down, grabs her hair and twists her face to the side. 'You don't look so good any more. You look tired and weary.'

He thrusts her face away. She's on fire where the dogs have lanced her skin. She says, 'You gonna do it, do it quick.'

'Think you're a brave little number,' the first man says. He kicks her straight in the heart and she moans. 'Huh? Huh? I'll show you brave, *conchita*.' He bends, pulls her skirt up, inserts his finger under her panties and thrusts it deep inside her and moves it up and down. Then he laughs and draws his hand away and she hears him sniff his own fingers. He laughs like the dogs bark.

'Get it the fuck over with,' the other man says.

She sees a gun, silver in flashlight. Jesus save me. She crosses herself with one bleeding hand.

'*Adiós*,' the first man says, and presses the barrel of the silver gun to the side of her head. And there's a click, a friction between her skin and metal, and then the flash.

14

Willie Drumm said, 'I'm tired, Amanda. it's gotta be at least two hours since we heard the gunshot, and I haven't heard the dogs either. The smart thing would be to quit, come back in the daylight with more help, give the area a thorough search.'

Amanda stared into the dark beyond the headlights. Her eyes ached. She knew Drumm's proposal was sound, and if she'd been looking for anyone other than Isabel she would have agreed to call it a night.

'Keep in mind Sanchez was my case too, Amanda, and I worked it long and hard. So don't take what I have to say the wrong way, but some might call this compulsive behaviour.'

'Maybe that's what it is.'

'I know we owe the woman big time. I understand your feelings.' Drumm indicated the wall of dark, moving his hand in a gesture of hopelessness. 'I heard of needles in haystacks, Amanda, but this . . .'

Amanda smoked a cigarette. She'd gone through

almost a pack in the two hours since the gunshot. Two hours of ruts and ravines and cacti, a hundred and twenty minutes or more in which she'd tried unsuccessfully to attribute the gunshot to another cause altogether – some jerk camper's kerosene stove exploding, a demented gold prospector's pick-up truck backfiring. There were all kinds of loonies drawn to the desert in the quest for gain, spiritual or material, God or gold.

But she was fooling herself. It had been a gunshot, unmistakable and dreadful. And just after the shot, she thought she'd heard a vehicle droning in the distance. She'd scanned the night but hadn't seen headlights. The landscape was pocked, hollows and canyons, a million hiding places.

'I'm getting sick of cacti,' Willie Drumm said. 'They're starting to develop personalities. Any time now, one of them's gonna say *you again?*'

Amanda was hunched forward in her seat. She'd been locked in this position a long time. 'Give it another twenty minutes, Willie. Then we'll go.'

'You think you remember the way back to the road?'

'We'll find it.'

Drumm edged the Bronco between stands of cacti. A jackrabbit ran mazily ahead of them. Once, a cactus wren darted in front of the vehicle, a feathered ball of light. Amanda barely noticed these disturbances. Her mind was elsewhere, probing her own private wasteland.

The Bronco bumped, thudded, bottomed out in a shallow arroyo Drumm had seen too late to avoid. 'Shit,' he said. He backed the vehicle up and the rear tyres span, and dust, thrown up by the wheels, clouded the air.

Amanda saw something then, metal and glinting. 'There,' she said. 'What's that?'

Drumm parked, removed a flashlight from the glove box. He left the headlights on, and they illuminated a late-1970s Datsun with a punctured front tyre. Drumm opened the passenger door and switched on the flash. Inside the car was a clutter of discarded fast-food wrappers and styrofoam coffee cups and empty Camel Light packs and crumpled Kleenex.

Amanda looked at the debris. 'Flash the back,' she said to Drumm.

Drumm moved the beam. In the back Amanda saw a heap of crushed clothing. Some of it was deadeningly familiar. A candy-striped blouse, a pair of jeans with a designer label, a blue T-shirt with a palm tree and the word Malibu.

'Hers?' Drumm asked.

Amanda nodded. She noticed a small pink thing among the clothing and she reached for it and held it in the palm of her hand.

'What's that?' Drumm asked.

'A barrette. A hair-clasp.' Amanda wrapped her fingers round the thin strip of plastic.

Drumm played the light on the ground around the Datsun. 'She had a flat and decided to hoof it,' he said.

Amanda studied the ground. There were footprints scuffed by paw-marks. Drumm was the first to see the shoe, which he picked up. 'You don't run too good in high heels,' he said.

Amanda took the shoe and noticed it was missing the heel. She tried to reconstruct the scene, but she didn't like the pictures she was coming up with. Isabel runs, her heel snaps, the dogs are after her.

'You want to keep going?' Drumm asked.

Amanda didn't. This was a trail she had no heart for. She felt empty and depressed. 'Sure,' she said.

Drumm trained the flashlight on the scuff of prints, Amanda followed. She didn't know how far she and Drumm walked; a quarter-mile, a half, more. The desert was beyond measurement.

'She comes this way.' Drumm stopped suddenly at the foot of an incline. There were indentations, disturbances, and blood.

Amanda squatted on her heels, picked up a handful of grainy dust and ran it through her fingers. She saw bloodstains in the grains, wet still.

'This is where it ends,' Drumm said quietly. He swung the flashlight around the general area. 'I see some tyre tracks over there.'

Amanda didn't look in the direction of the beam. She was thinking of dogs, wondering what it felt like to be hunted by them, trying to gauge hysteria, the sense of doom. This is where it ends. Drumm's sentence resonated in her head.

Drumm said, 'The dogs get her, they bring her down, then it happens. The gunman steps in and calls off the dogs. Boom.'

'And her body?' Amanda asked.

'He removes it.'

'Why not leave it here? You couldn't find a more isolated place for dumping a goddam corpse.'

'You got me,' Drumm said. 'What the hell. This whole goddam thing gets me. Two go in, two come out again.'

Two go in, two come out. Amanda listened to the desert, silent now, and eerie, where the dark land seamlessly met the dark sky.

15

During the trial of Victor Sanchez, Randolph Hanseimer, defence attorney, had tried to club Isabel Sanchez into submission. His tactics were crude, and once or twice Isabel had closed her eyes and swayed a little in the witness stand as if she were about to faint. *Aren't you just trying to get back at your ex-husband because he left you? Aren't you just mad at him for dumping you because you didn't live up to reasonable expectations as a wife? Isn't this just a seriously malicious case of sour grapes?*

Objection, objection, objection.

Amanda was replaying the trial in her head. She kept seeing Isabel in the stand, clenching her hands into small fists. Hanseimer tried to break her, but she always found the resolve to come back at him. The jury admired her. The jury saw an unassuming young woman abused beyond reason by a husband who was a cold-blooded killer.

Amanda stretched one arm across the bed. Her thoughts raced and her throat was raw from cigarettes and the desert still clung to her, the dread she'd felt, dread she was *still* feeling. Drumm's flashlight, the jackrabbit running, blood in the dust. The dogs, the goddam dogs: she kept hearing the way they yelped and whined. Isabel running from them, that fear, that solitude, just her and terror under an unyielding black sky.

She sat up. 'Two people I entrust to the Program. New names, identities, the whole Federal package. So what the hell were they doing back in Arizona?'

Rhees propped himself on an elbow. 'Maybe they were lured back somehow.'

'Lured?'

'Who would stand to get satisfaction from their deaths anyway?'

'Only Victor Sanchez. Lured though? I don't see how.'

'Sanchez wants revenge, but he wants it in a very special kind of way. What's the point of killing them in Idaho or wherever? That's remote. Better to draw them back here somehow and kill them where they're going to be discovered. Where *you're* going to know about it because it's your state, your own backyard so to speak. He's giving you the finger. He wants to show you he can cut through the Program like cream cheese, but he also wants you to be *aware* of it. He wants you to know that although you have him under lock and key on death row, he can still call the shots.'

She thought about this, then said, 'Explain why we couldn't find Isabel's body. If Sanchez was giving me the finger, why wasn't the body left right there?'

'Maybe you just didn't see it in the dark. Maybe she wasn't killed.'

'Drumm's going back in the morning with some help,' she said.

'Then he'll find her. If she's there to be found.'

Amanda didn't want to think about Drumm and his search-party. She remembered the many hours she'd spent with Isabel in a hotel room on the outskirts of Phoenix, where she'd been sequestered during the trial. Armed guards at the door, unmarked cop cars in the parking lot. She hadn't been taking any chances. She remembered how fragile Isabel had been. Her small face, dainty in its pale-brown perfection, had been taut most of the time. The atmosphere in the room had been a mix of tension and uneasy allegiance. It had been difficult for Isabel to testify against her husband, because even if the marriage had been a kind of crucifixion, even if Isabel had been hammered nail by nail into the splintered wood of matrimony, and Victor a bundle of unspeakable cruelties, there was still some stunted form of vestigial loyalty. At times Amanda had held Isabel, telling her she was doing the right thing, Victor belonged in jail and she could put him there for a very long time. *Don't think of it as betrayal, Isabel. I promise you'll be safe afterwards.*

Promise. Empty words, dry kindling.

She got out of bed, walked around the room, arms folded. She paused in front of a full-length mirror and caught her reflection in the faint moonlight. She looked frazzled, and she was four or five pounds too heavy, which was visible even under the oversized black T-shirt she wore. She turned away from the image and sighed.

Rhees was watching her. 'Sanchez has the key to all this. It's obvious.'

'There isn't supposed to *be* a key, John. The doors are meant to be locked tight. Nobody is supposed to be able to open them.'

'Sanchez found a way.'

'How?'

Rhees scratched his jaw. 'Come back to bed.'

'We're talking about something so secret even a guy like Bascombe doesn't know how the machinery really works. We're talking about sealed documents and secret codes. You don't just pick up a phone and ask for information about the new names and whereabouts of witnesses.'

Rhees flipped the bedsheet back and patted a pillow. 'Lie down,' he said.

'OK. I'll lie down.' She stretched alongside him, held his hand and brushed it with her lips. But she couldn't relax, couldn't *begin* to relax. 'I talked her into it, John. I persuaded her to go into court.'

Rhees stroked her forehead. 'You can't blame yourself.'

'I need to smoke. I know we have a rule about smoking in our bedroom but I'm about to break it.' She lit a cigarette. The sulphuric smell of the exploding match was awful. 'She wouldn't have testified if I hadn't forced her.'

'Forced? It was her decision in the end. Nobody shackled her and led her inside the court, she went of her own free will.'

Amanda shook her head. 'I bought her ticket. I put her on the justice train, which happened to be going nowhere.'

'Now you're choked up with remorse and you want to do something about it. But you'll be a damn sight better off going back to the cabin first thing in the morning and letting Drumm get on with it. Let Bascombe do what he has to do, you're out of it. It's not as if you have an official job these days anyway.'

'Bascombe said the same.'

'He's right. Now try to sleep.'

'How the fuck can I sleep, for God's sake?'

Rhees opened the drawer of the bedside table and removed a prescription bottle, took the lid off, slipped a red and yellow capsule into his palm. 'Take it.'

'I don't want it.'

'Do I have to stuff it down your throat?'

She opened her mouth reluctantly. He placed the capsule on her tongue and gently clapped a hand over her lips. She swallowed.

'Great bedside manner,' she said. Dalmane again. She hadn't used it for weeks and weeks. She'd been working hard to relegate the Sanchez trial to a basement room at the back of her head, and she'd almost managed to bury it.

Rhees said, 'I wonder what she ever saw in Sanchez.'

'That's easy. She was young, naïve and poor, John. Sanchez is a handsome guy, wads of money, knows how to blind her with flash. Flash loses its allure, so he comes up with other ways of getting her attention. He was careless with lit cigarettes when she was around. Once, just for the hell of it, he cut off one of her nipples with a razor blade. This is not a pleasant man.'

She'd seen Sanchez day in, day out for the best part of eight weeks in court, and what she remembered was the way he'd stared at her with a concentrated look of contempt. She remembered the trick he had of seeming not to blink. He emitted some very powerful waves of animosity, like a transmitter sending out a constant stream of malice. It had reached a point where she'd dreaded going into the courtroom and feeling the dangerous laser heat of his eyes.

'I don't mean this to sound callous, but you don't owe her,' Rhees said.

'I gave her my word, John.'

'Yeah, but it wasn't you that broke it.'

'That's not really the point,' she said. 'I came to like Isabel.'

'I know you did—'

'She survived a very damaging marriage, and she needed serious reassurance to go in that witness-stand. Thrown together in that kind of situation, you feel close to a person. We talked about a bunch of things; families, friends. We talked a lot about our fathers. I told her about the time Morgan gave me a brand-new car on my seventeenth birthday. The only birthday gift she could ever remember from her father was a cheap plastic barrette when she was twelve, which she kept. That made me feel kind of sad and kind of angry. I had this privileged upbringing I didn't ask for and she had nothing.'

Amanda felt the pill begin to kick in slowly. She could hear a slight echo around the edges of her words. There was a dryness in her throat. Rhees said something she didn't catch because she was drifting towards the peculiar numb darkness of drugged sleep.

She dreamed of Sanchez. She dreamed she was taking his temperature with a rectal thermometer. He was bent over, thighs splayed, and he was grinning, and the grin was terrifying.

She woke at dawn. The sky was the colour of a pale vein. She tossed the bedsheets aside. The inside of her head was like sludge at the bottom of a cafetière, but she knew where she was going.

16

Willie Drumm surveyed the desert. The sun was up, darkness banished. He said, 'Different place in daylight. Striking, if you like miles and miles of nothing.'

Amanda gazed at shadows in the distant foothills. A hawk crossed the sun with lazy ease. Four patrol cars, doors hanging open, were parked among cacti near the Datsun that contained Isabel's possessions. Uniformed officers stood round in groups and drank coffee from vacuum flasks. She counted a dozen men.

Among them she noticed Drumm's superior, Police Chief Dan Kelloway, long neck and lean, concave body and shaven head. A fitness freak, he was reputed to cycle twenty miles every morning before breakfast and survive on a diet of almonds and yoghurt. He was tanned and tall and wore an off-white suit, and his posture was invariably rigid. Between her and Kelloway was a chill zone, a permafrost which had its origins in a bitter disagreement a year earlier over a case Kelloway had been desperate to bring to trial. Amanda had considered the police evidence circumstantial, and the case – involving a young black man with the unfortunate name of Hood, who'd been caught in possession of a gun used in the fatal shooting of a pregnant white woman during a robbery – altogether unworthy of the court's time. Kelloway's frustration and anger with her opinion had been volcanic. He accused her of dereliction of duty, wilfulness, stupidity, hawking up a whole thesaurus of insults. It had seemed to her at the time that Kelloway's vibrating rage went some way deeper than the flawed Hood affair, as if he were driven by other more subterranean resentments she'd never quite figured out and didn't have the inclination to try.

She said, 'The brass is in evidence, I see.'

'Yeah. I guess he wanted to put in an appearance. The mood to get involved overtakes him. When he's not playing Mussolini at the office.'

Drumm ticked out a list on his fingers. 'OK, this is what we got: two shoes, one with a heel broken. One car, flat tyre. Assorted items of junk-food containers. One map of the United States in the glove box. Clothing and more footwear. Some blood in the vicinity, but significantly no corpse. We did find some dog hair, though.'

Amanda was barely listening. She stared at the car. 'New Mexico plates.'

'Yeah, we ran those already,' Drumm said. 'The car was stolen in Farmington.'

'Farmington?'

'What was she doing in Farmington, you wonder,' Drumm remarked. 'I couldn't even hazard a guess. Where she's been, what brought her back here. The only thing I can come up with is maybe she travelled all the way just to see you, Amanda. She was in some kind of trouble and you were the only one she could turn to.'

'She was supposed to be beyond trouble, Willie. That was the whole point.'

'She didn't trust anyone else but you. God knows, I spent hours trying to get through to her, but she never told me much. Must be the woman's touch.'

'Must be,' Amanda said. A tuft of dog hair, New Mexico plates, a carload of fast-food wrappers – it was like a list of ingredients you could never turn into a digestible concoction. She tried to picture Isabel driving long frantic distances to see her, ending up out here, panicked and forlorn and alone.

A patrol car appeared out on the flats. It kicked up a storm of orange dust as it approached. A uniformed cop, a sandy-haired, square-faced man with a moustache, stepped out of the car. Amanda recognized him as Sergeant Thomas Gannon.

He nodded at Amanda and said, 'Ms Scholes. Nice to see you again.'

'Sergeant,' she said.

Gannon said to Drumm, 'The tyre tracks you're interested in go way out there into that canyon where it's rough terrain, so we're looking at an off-the-road vehicle for sure. I couldn't take the car up there, no way.'

Amanda gazed off into the foothills again where shadows created sinister pools. The sun burned into her eyes and when she turned her face to the side her sight was streaked with zigzagging lines and flashes.

Drumm said, 'We'll send up a chopper.'

Sergeant Gannon said, 'No stone unturned, Ms Scholes.' He laid the palm of his hand on his pistol. 'I liked the woman.'

'Yeah, we were all fans,' said Drumm with a small forlorn note in his voice.

We were all fans. An epitaph, Amanda thought.

Drumm said, 'I know what you're thinking.'

'You know a lot more than me then.'

'We're gonna have US Marshals from the Program coming in droves. Probably guys from Justice. You can count on that,' Drumm said and touched her arm. 'Your best bet is to walk away. Walk the fuck away and keep walking and don't look back.'

'Or I'll be turned into a pillar of salt,' she said.

'Go live your life with John. Get your priorities straight.'

Amanda went back in the direction of the red VW. She was aware of Kelloway approaching.

'Miss Scholes,' he said.

She turned to him. Sun gleamed on his shaven head. He resembled a predatory bird, the nose a beak created for ripping flesh.

'Morbid curiosity bring you out here?' he asked.

He had a habit of attributing sleazy motives to people.

'I'm curious,' she said. 'Morbid doesn't come into it.'

'I don't need to remind you that this is strictly police business,' he said.

'No, you don't need to remind me.'

'I should hang a sign: "Civilians Keep Out."'

'I have a stake in Isabel,' she said.

'*Had* a stake. Had. Past tense. And I don't want you out here interfering with any of my guys.'

He made it sound like she had sexual molestation of uniformed officers in mind. He was more eclipse than human being, she thought. He enjoyed the dark little satisfactions he got from flexing authority.

'I'd love to chat more with you because it's always such a life-affirming experience, Kelloway, but I'm pushed for time.' She moved past him and sat behind the wheel of her car.

He stuck his face close to the window and smiled. He had a gold filling in an upper-left bicuspid. 'You're history, lady. Remember that. Any rights and privileges you enjoyed before, they're null and void. Your visa's withdrawn. Your credit's wiped.'

'Thanks for reminding me,' she said.

'My, do I hear testy,' Kelloway said, and brought his face a little nearer. 'Guess what?'

'Astonish me,' she said.

'Our old acquaintance Hood, the one you figured had a halo round his head?'

'What about him?'

'Busted him last night for illegal possession of firearms and conspiracy to distribute crack cocaine.'

She stared straight ahead. 'I hope it stands up,' she said.

'Oh, this one's watertight. This one's not falling apart because of some petty misgivings of the lady prosecutor.'

She turned the key in the ignition. 'They weren't petty, Kelloway.'

'They were piss-ant, and you know it.'

'Up yours,' she said.

She turned the car in a circle and headed for the

road. She waved at Drumm and then glanced once in the rear-view mirror and saw Kelloway smile, and then he was gone, leaving a reflection of the barren desert. She drove a few miles before she'd shaken Kelloway completely out of her system.

17

She found Bascombe in a coffee-shop near the Federal Building. He was halfway through a buttered bagel when she slid into the booth alongside him.

'I see our concerned citizen is also an early bird,' Bascombe said. 'How did you track me down?'

'I asked a secretary. You know why I'm here.'

Bascombe finished his bagel. 'I had a copy of a report from the Phoenix PD filed by Lieutenant Drumm. I know about your desert jaunt last night.'

'There was another jaunt this morning,' she said. 'I just got back from it. She's not out there. If she is, she's buried deep. Drumm had a dozen men looking. Including God, in the form of Kelloway.'

Bascombe sipped his coffee and looked impassive.

Amanda said, 'First Galindez, now Isabel. Face it, there's a serious breakdown here. There's a fatal flaw.'

'Yes, yes, there is,' Bascombe said. He rubbed his eyes, which were faintly bloodshot.

'You sent off your report on Galindez?'

'Immediately after you left my office yesterday afternoon, a fax went out.'

'You've heard nothing?'

'Amanda, they don't break open the brandy and the cigars because Lew Bascombe happens to send a message. A fax comes through, somebody picks it up, then it has to be directed to the person responsible.'

'What about Isabel? Have you reported that? Did you mention the fact that she phoned me last night in a state of distress?'

'Done. Half an hour ago. Another fax.'

Amanda crushed out her cigarette. 'Did you mark it urgent?'

'I drew attention to the fact that both Galindez and Mrs Sanchez were prosecution witnesses in the Victor Sanchez trial.'

'What does that mean? *Drew attention?*'

'It means I pointed out the background shared between Galindez and Mrs Sanchez. I cross-linked.'

'Is this Fed-speak I'm hearing, Lew?'

'You asked me what I'd done. I told you.'

'Drew their *attention*, for God's sake. *Cross-linked?* Why didn't you come right out and say the security's fucked? Why didn't you phone them? Why didn't you speak to a living human being? A fax. You don't even know if anybody ever receives a fax. They can go off into the ether sometimes. Mars.'

'These things are done by the book,' Bascombe said. 'The book says words on paper. The permanence of a written record.'

'Yesterday you were a rebel, Lew. What happened to you overnight?'

'What I did yesterday was a personal favour to you.'

'And I'm grateful.'

'But I can't ignore the guidelines all the time. I can't just disregard them because some former prosecutor with a bug up her ass breezes into my office.'

'A bug up my ass,' she said. 'That's a goddam funny way of describing my reaction to two dead people.'

'One dead anyway. The other isn't so clear-cut.'

'Because there's no corpse? Lew, I *want* to believe she's still alive, but even if by some remote chance she's wandering around the goddam desert barefoot and seeing visions of the Blessed Virgin on account of dehydration, the fact remains – security is shot. That's what this is all about.'

Amanda lapsed into silence. There was a fuse burning in her head. She could hear it hiss. She lit another cigarette. She smiled at Lewis Bascombe and changed the tone of her voice to something more reasonable. 'OK, I'm calmed down.'

'And better for it,' he remarked.

She kept the smile fixed on her face, but *Jesus* it was an effort. 'If security's on the fritz, Lew, you'd think they'd want to act at once. You'd think they'd go like greased lightning. You'd also think they'd be having a quiet word with Victor Sanchez, seeing as how he's the choice suspect here.'

'They'll talk to Sanchez, Amanda. Obviously he'll be top of their agenda. Just because I haven't heard, it doesn't mean they're not doing anything. Of course they'll act fast. They're not obliged to keep me informed of everything they do. In fact, they don't have to tell me a goddam thing.'

‘So you sit in the dark, knowing nothing.’

‘I’m just the guy who beats a drum. They hear it, they do something.’

‘And they don’t tell you what.’

‘They don’t have to.’

‘Secrets and more secrets.’

‘That’s how they designed it.’

‘They didn’t design it all that well, did they, Lew? Not if somebody can ferret out witnesses—’

‘The best-laid plans.’ Bascombe picked up the check, rummaged in his billfold, left a five-dollar bill on the table. ‘I have to get back.’

‘Tell me one thing, Lew. Is this the end of it? Do we never hear anything again? Do we never get to the root of it all? Why it happened. Why these two people weren’t properly protected. How security was breached. Is this where it finishes?’

‘I can’t even answer a simple question like that,’ Bascombe said, and moved towards the door.

Amanda sat for a time after Bascombe had gone, then she rose to leave. She had a moment of dizziness when she stepped outside. Too many cigarettes and no food, the way it had been before she’d quit, before she’d decided to make her break for freedom and good health.

Except she wasn’t free. She thought she’d dynamited her way out of the cave.

But she hadn’t.

18

In his hotel room Anthony Dansk flicked through a sex sheet, studying the ads for escort services. He liked hookers because they filled up a space inside. Fast-food sex, hygienic disposable wrapper. He liked how hookers didn't linger after, fishing for affection. They came and went with minimum fuss, just a basic lube job and thanks for the business.

When his phone rang he picked it up and heard McTell say, 'I'm in the bar.'

Dansk left his room, stepped along the corridor and decided to skip the elevator and walk down to the lobby. A little cardiac action did wonders. He believed in physical exercise. He was proud of his body.

The bar was shadowy. McTell, bearded and pale, occupied a table in the middle of the floor. Dansk sat and asked the miniskirted cocktail waitress for a club soda. He didn't like alcohol because it kicked the struts out under your judgement.

Eddie McTell said, 'Done. *Finito*.'

Dansk didn't speak. His drink arrived and the

waitress departed, leaving a pleasing mango fragrance in the air. He followed her skimpy little dress and long legs with his eyes, a reflex action.

'Pussy on stilts, hey,' McTell said.

Dansk ignored this.

McTell said, 'We got her. Out in the desert.'

'Spare me the details,' Dansk said.

'The dogs added a neat touch,' McTell said.

'That's a detail.'

McTell shrugged. 'So we can get out of this town now anyway. This fucking heat, you can keep it.'

Dansk sipped his soda. He looked at McTell's thin face. The beard was an attempt to give the face some hint of intelligence, but it didn't work. It looked glued-on, a spy's beard.

McTell picked up his lager. '*Vaya con dios*,' he said.

Dansk watched McTell slug his drink and asked, 'When you were a kid, how did you see your future?'

'My future? You mean, like ambitions?'

'You must have dreamed of something, McTell. Fireman. Engine driver. Superjock, last-minute touchdown, your pick of the cheerleaders. Making it big some way.'

'I used to be a wizard on ice-skates.'

'You thought hockey. A future in hockey.'

McTell shook his head. 'I tried out for a team in Boston one time, but I guess I lacked some quality they were looking for.'

'Maybe it was grace, McTell.'

'Grace. Yeah, maybe. Funny, my first wife was called Grace. Grace Spatsky. Polack broad with tits out to here.'

Dansk had no interest in McTell's matrimonial

history. He said, 'I had a notion of becoming a missionary. Doing good. Working in a leper colony maybe. I used to study maps. Places with names like Chad; the Ivory Coast.'

McTell grinned and stroked his beard. 'A missionary?'

'You think that's funny?'

'Just that kids think funny things. No offence.'

Dansk wondered why he'd bothered to mention this childhood fancy to McTell. Everything you said to McTell vanished inside a black hole. It was like sending a message into outer space because McTell was an inferior creature, barely a notch above the kind you saw all the time in K-Marts, pushing carts and surrounded by a squabble of snotty-nosed kids and waddling wives, or in late-night supermarkets stocking up on monster frozen pizzas and a gross of Danish. They lived in trailer parks with broken windows and crooked satellite dishes, or in subsidized housing with cockroaches and graffiti. They gorged themselves on Snickers bars and potato chips. They watched Oprah and thought they were checking the pulse of America. These people operated on weak batteries.

The sad thing, they didn't know they were empty and stupid. They had a certain animal cunning, but in reality they were on this earth to run the errands, to do the dark stuff somebody like Dansk wanted done.

Dansk pushed his glass away. He'd had enough of McTell's company. The beard depressed him, so did the light-blue jacket and the necktie the colour of a dead salmon.

Dansk stood up, reflecting on the fact that in this business you had to work with guys like McTell.

'Me and Pasquale, we'll just head out, I guess,' McTell said.

'Go to Vegas, stay at the usual place,' Dansk said. 'I'll be in touch. There's another piece of work coming up in Seattle.'

Dansk turned to leave.

McTell said, 'Oh yeah, Pasquale shot the dogs. Took them somewhere off the freeway and shot them. Smack between the eyes.'

Dansk knew McTell was telling him this because it might rile him a little. He pictured canine heads blown away and bloody fur. He kept going. In the lobby he passed the concierge's desk, stopped sharply and wheeled back round again. He approached the desk.

The concierge looked at Dansk with the general ass-clenched expression of concierges the world over. There had to be some kind of college where these characters learned how to patronize.

'Can I help you, sir?'

Dansk didn't answer. He picked up a newspaper from the stack on the guy's desk. The *Arizona Republic* with the word 'Complimentary' stamped on it.

'Help yourself,' said the concierge.

'Yeah,' Dansk said.

Halfway down the front page, a single column. There it was. A jolt. He walked back inside the bar.

He stood over McTell and said, 'Forget Vegas. Vegas is off the fucking menu.'

Dansk drew up the chair that was still warm from before and stared at McTell.

'Something wrong?' McTell asked.

Dansk tossed the newspaper down on the table. 'I take it you can read.'

McTell looked at the front page for a time without expression. Dansk snatched the paper back out of his hands and said, 'Let's take a stroll. Get some air.'

'I hate the air around here,' McTell said.

Dansk said, 'Move, Eddie. Don't give me any friction, I'm not in the mood.'

Outside in the heat Dansk sweated: the back of his neck and armpits. His perspiration displeased him. Liquid oozing through pores, impurities leaking from the system. He walked, followed by McTell, until he came to a small square on the edge of downtown where office workers, sprawled here and there on the sunny grass, ate health-conscious lunches. Men in white shirts, women in crisp blouses. They had the look of minor civil servants. They were clocking down their time until it was retirement day. Here's your pension. Enjoy.

A guy in wire-framed glasses laughed at something. The girl who knelt beside him, a half moon of pitta bread in her skinny hand, spluttered. There was a sense of things in their rightful place and lunches that lasted a regulation thirty minutes and amusing office gossip. Let's kill the supervisor. Let's poison his pastrami sandwich.

Dansk drew a hand across his wet forehead and sat under a shady tree. McTell hunkered down on his heels and let his arms dangle between his legs. Dansk had a feeling of anger so intense it seemed a thing apart from himself, a seething *doppelgänger*, another Anthony in another dimension.

He thrust the newspaper under McTell's nose with such vigour he might have intended to shove it up the man's nostrils. 'Quote unquote. "The body of Reuben Galindez, forty-seven, was found in the

Little Colorado River on the Navaho Indian reservation by Sergeant Charles House. Police reports blah, blah, blah, gunshot wound blah, blah, blah. Galindez turned State's evidence against Victor Sanchez et cetera et cetera. Homicide detective Lieutenant William Drumm of the Phoenix Police Department attended the forensic examination in Flagstaff rhubarb, rhubarb. With him was Amanda Scholes, the prosecutor in the sensational trial of Sanchez, now on death row. Neither Lieutenant Drumm nor Miss Scholes were available for comment." '

'Yeah, yeah, I read it, Anthony.'

Dansk said, 'I'm seeing Galindez float down a river like driftwood, and I don't like the image. I don't like it from any angle. I don't like any of this. You didn't tell me this was the way it happened.'

McTell said, 'Pasquale shot him, but the current was too fucking fast, and it wasn't like there was a full moon or nothing. We figured maybe he'd—'

'Maybe he'd what? Dissolve in the water like goddam Alka-Seltzer? Or were you under the illusion there were piranha in the river and they'd eat him?'

'Piranha?' McTell smiled his dull brute smile. 'More like decompose someplace, the river bottom, like that.'

'Dead people float, McTell. Unless you weigh them down, they have this unfortunate tendency to surface.'

Dansk sighed and looked up at the sky. How high and blue it was. Up, up and away. McTell acted on his thoughts the way a chunk of Kryptonite affected Superman.

'He drifts down the river, and *then* who enters

the picture? Look, *look*. Black and fucking white.'

'So what?'

'So *what*? He's only a homicide cop and she's only the goddam prosecutor whose last case was Victor Sanchez. I'm trying to run a discreet little disposal business here. Some business. Galindez floats out of sight down a fucking river and a woman the size of Minnie Mouse has you running your asses off.'

McTell shuffled his feet in the grass. 'Yeah, but we got her, Anthony.'

'Sure you got her. That's what you're paid for, McTell: getting people. Only now we have a goddam homicide cop *and* this former prosecutor bitch, and they're rolling around inside my head like very loud fucking marbles and I'm thinking, Maybe they're not just gonna drop this matter. Maybe they're gonna be intrigued, McTell.'

'Hey, they're a problem, no sweat, no big deal, we can fix them,' McTell said.

'A homicide cop and a former prosecutor and you can fix them, huh?'

'Listen. Anybody can be fixed.'

'All your solutions come down to the same thing: blow somebody away. Here's a problem, let's blast it into oblivion.'

'Saves time and trouble in the long haul.'

Dansk tried to imagine how Einstein felt in a bus station, say, surrounded by morons. How he felt standing in a cafeteria line for a hot dog and fries and listening to empty drones chatter about last night's soaps.

He looked across the grassy square. He admired how the freshly laundered office workers gathered up their trash before they left. House-trained.

Picky-picky. They worked in smoke-free zones and drank bottled water and belonged to health clubs and had mortgages and good credit ratings. They were respectable, central to the way the country worked. The machinery couldn't turn without them. Politicians drooled for their votes.

He found himself imagining what would happen if a passing gunman opened fire on this bunch just for the sport of it. He saw blood spilling across grass, white shirts red, people screaming and diving for cover, total chaos. He thought of snipers in towers and fertilizer bombs in vans parked outside government buildings and deranged sorts in the badlands who were at odds with revenue officials. This is America, bulletproof vest country, where you don't sit with your back to the door. The nation was bent out of shape.

He rose, brushed blades of grass from his slacks and looked at McTell. What was it about killers, why were they so well-endowed in the vicious department and so challenged when it came to brains? You took what you could find, he thought. It wasn't like you could go down to an employment bureau and ask for assassins. McTell and Pasquale came out of sewers. All they knew was death. It was a limited kind of understanding. They enjoyed killing, it thrilled them. It was their own crazed theatre.

He pondered this, what it would be like to buy a ticket and go inside. Snuff scenes at the Blood Bijou. People blown away. Carnage galore. And maybe when you slept you dreamed of human slaughter-houses and corpses hanging upside down from hooks, skinned and de-veined and raw.

He watched McTell yank a daisy out of the

ground and destroy it one petal at a time, and he wondered if flowers felt pain and anguish, if this daisy was screaming at some level beyond the range of human hearing. The thought intrigued him. Noises you couldn't hear, a place beyond the net of the senses.

He said, 'We'll wait, keep an eye on the situation, see what comes up. Then I'll decide. It's not like there's any bonus money in it for giving them the ultimate goodnight kiss, McTell.'

'No bonus money?' McTell asked.

'None. And if you don't like that, take it up with your union.'

19

The first thing Amanda heard when she returned to the house was a female voice. Rhees had a student with him in the living room, a willowy girl with straight, long blond hair. She looked as if she'd strolled out of a shampoo commercial. A yellow nimbus hung about her.

'Amanda,' Rhees said, 'this is Polly Svensen. Polly's doing post-grad work next semester.'

The student smiled. Amanda smiled back. Polly Svensen was, well, simply stunning. She had the kind of astonishing beauty that quickened men's hearts and sent thrilled whispers running through crowded rooms. Her neck's just a little too long, Amanda thought.

'I didn't expect Professor Rhees to be at home. I was just dropping off my paper,' Polly said. 'I heard he was out of town.'

'Lo and behold,' Amanda said, frost in her voice. 'Here he is. The man himself.'

Polly was all false modesty. She knew she was a knockout. Slender, five-eleven, faded skin-tight blue jeans and a white halter, and her cute little navel showing. She knew she changed the weather wherever she went.

Rhees frowned at Amanda and said, 'We were just discussing the role of nature in Dylan Thomas.'

'Mmm, interesting,' Amanda said. Rhees had access to a surfeit of girls. He met them one on one in his office, tutorial fashion. She wasn't normally threatened by these academic tête-à-têtes, but today things were just coming at her and she felt defenceless.

She said, 'The force that through the green fuse drives the flower, et cetera.'

Polly said, 'Right. You're familiar with Dylan.'

Dylan. Polly was just the type to be on first-name terms with dead poets.

Amanda said, 'A few lines, that's all.'

'He's worth getting into,' Polly said. 'There's this really marvellous deep underlying green thing. "About the lilting house and happy as the grass was green", you know?'

'And all this time I thought he wrote about jerking off. Goes to show.'

Polly had a distinctive giggle. Somebody had probably told her once it was real neat, so she reproduced it whenever she could.

Rhees got up from the table and cleared his throat. He indicated with a gesture of his head that he wanted a moment of privacy with Amanda. He went into the kitchen and Amanda followed. He shut the door and crossed his arms.

'You're being rude,' he said.

'Am I?'

'You know you are.' Rhees reached out and touched her shoulder. 'This isn't like you, Amanda.'

'Well,' she said, and shrugged.

'You sneaked off at dawn without saying where you were going. I can guess anyway.'

Amanda opened a closet door, rummaged around and said, 'I thought we had some Grahams here. Polly might want a cracker.'

'Unworthy scold,' Rhees said.

Amanda slammed the closet door shut. 'She's young and she's like some goddess. Her hair goes all the way down to her ass, for Christ's sake. What planet's she from?'

'Come here.' Rhees spread his arms and Amanda fell into them and shut her eyes. Rhees, her harbour. 'Polly's mostly bubbles, you're more my ideal.'

'How can I be anybody's ideal? Look at me.'

'You get better all the time, Amanda. I have you up on a pedestal.'

'I'm too heavy for your pedestal. I feel overweight and sluggish. And this.' She tugged at her brown hair, letting it slide through her fingers. 'They didn't find Isabel, John. They looked and they looked.'

'Maybe . . .' he said.

'Maybe what?'

'She's still out there somewhere.'

Amanda remembered the grains of dirt damp with blood. Rhees was trying to force open a little window of optimism in the face of evidence to the contrary. He was good at finding silver linings in the gloom. Please God let this be one of those silver linings. Let her be alive.

Rhees kissed her forehead. 'I'll give Polly the benefit of my wisdom, which should take all of seven or eight minutes, then we're out of here and heading north. How does that sound?' He moved towards the kitchen door. 'Before I forget, some reporter from the *Phoenix Gazette* phoned. Wanted to know if you had anything to add to the story of the Galindez discovery.'

'I hope you told him I was incommunicado.'

'My lips were sealed.'

Rhees left the kitchen.

Amanda's head hurt and she had an acid sensation in her stomach and a general sense of malaise, a weakening inside, as if her immune system was flagging. She looked out into the backyard. Neglected grass grew long in ragged brown stalks and butterflies flapped here and there, settling where the mood took them.

She watched for a time. She thought about Isabel. She couldn't cancel the thought out. She couldn't flutter away from it like one of those mercurial butterflies.

She walked into the bathroom, opened the cabinet, ransacked through a collection of bottles. Say hello to the old gang: ginseng, zinc capsules, iron, the whole spectrum of B-vitamins, garlic tabs, fortified C, some kind of painkiller. It was a regular health arsenal. She scooped out pills and downed them with water.

Then she put her hand in the hip pocket of her jeans and took out Isabel Sanchez's plastic hairclasp and studied it. It caught the sunlight streaming through the bathroom window. There were people in the world reputed to be able to locate buried corpses by caressing their possessions, but she wasn't one of them.

She had a mechanic's eye, not a mystic's.

She walked up and down the kitchen for a time before she dialled Directory Assistance, and wrote down the number she was given by the operator. Then she dialled it.

A man answered and introduced himself as Donald Scarfe.

She said, 'Don, this is Amanda Scholes.'

'We-ell, Amanda,' Scarfe said, 'it's been an age. What can I do you for?'

'I need to come see you.'

Scarfe said, 'You know the way.'

Amanda hung up. She left the kitchen by the back door, so that Rhees wouldn't see her. He wasn't going to be overjoyed about this stunt.

20

The window of Donald Scarfe's office in the Florence facility looked out over a hazy view of desert mountains in the distance. There was another vista directly below: the compound, watch-towers, barbed wire, high walls.

The compound was empty. Amanda glanced down, seeing shadows pressed against concrete. The watch-towers made her uneasy. Guards in shadows with guns. The penitentiary was a volatile place, heavy with violent potential.

'So you think he contracted out a killing,' Scarfe said.

'Everything points that way, Don.'

Donald Scarfe was tall and gaunt and his face had been hammered and dried by too much sun-light. He'd always reminded Amanda of a weathered fence post at the edge of a dry prairie. He wore a white short-sleeved shirt and a turquoise bola necktie, and looked more like somebody's idea of a middle-aged rodeo rider than an associate warden of a prison.

Amanda walked to the water-cooler in the corner of Scarfe's office and filled a dixie cup. She drank hastily. 'Mind if I smoke?'

Scarfe pointed to a no-smoking sign. 'Sorry.'

'It's OK. More and more I feel like a leper anyway.' She crushed the dixie cup and dropped it inside a wastebasket. She looked at Scarfe for a time. She'd met him at various seminars on penal policy and law-enforcement strategies several times during the last few years, and she'd liked his attitude, which was liberal, compared to the prevailing hard-assed positions concerning the treatment of prisoners. Stick them in goddam tents and let them sweat and feed them pig slop.

'I don't have any objection to this visit,' he said. 'I don't know what you expect to come of it, that's all.'

'I'm not anticipating a confession,' she said.

'So what are you expecting?'

'I don't know,' she said.

'You think you can tune into him, is that it?'

'I'm not sure, Don. Has anybody been to see him recently? Any visitors?'

'He doesn't get visitors, Amanda.'

Amanda looked at her watch. It was three-thirty in the afternoon. She remembered what Willie Drumm had said. *We're gonna have US marshals from the Program coming in droves. Probably guys from Justice.* So why hadn't anyone arrived yet? Bascombe's first message to Arlington, concerning Galindez, had gone out twenty-four hours ago. His second must have been received around noon today Eastern Time. And what had Bascombe himself said? *Of course they'd act fast.*

Bureaucrats. They doodled while cities caught

fire. They shuffled papers as volcanoes erupted. Perhaps they were still studying Bascombe's messages. Or perhaps somebody was in transit even now. She had no way of knowing.

'Are you up for this?' Scarfe asked. 'You look a little out of sorts.'

'It was a hot drive down here,' she said.

Scarfe shrugged and picked up one of the two telephones on his desk. He pressed a button and spoke to somebody. 'Chuck. Escort Prisoner eight eight sixty around to the interview room, would you? I'm bringing along a visitor. I want an armed guard in the room for the duration.'

Scarfe put down the telephone. He opened a drawer and took out a small laminated badge with the word 'Visitor' on it. She pinned it to her shirt.

'I'll walk with you,' Scarfe said. 'I ought to warn you though. He's been trouble from the start. He attacked another inmate with a screwdriver, which of course can't be proved because nobody saw anything. Punctured one of the guy's lungs.'

'He's a charmer,' she said.

'And last week he torched another guy's cell. He thought it was funny.'

'Offbeat sense of humour.'

'Black, anyway. I guess if you're living where he's living, nothing matters a damn in the end.'

They left the office and stepped into a long, chilled corridor. Halfway down, she stopped. She was approaching a transition here, a crossroads, choices. She had only to change her mind, turn round, walk back to the car, drive away and leave things be.

She moved forward.

The bridge was crossed and burning behind her and the fumes had a bitter-sweet smell, and she thought she detected in the smoke the strange scent of her apprehension at the idea of being in the company of Prisoner 8860.

21

The interview room, a table and a few chairs and a one-way observation window, smelled of floorwax. Overhead was a solitary fluorescent strip. Amanda, glad to see an ashtray on the table, lit a cigarette at once.

The door opened and Victor Sanchez, accompanied by an armed guard, a bullet-headed man with a long jaw, was led inside. The guard took up a position in the corner. Sanchez, with a slow motion imposed upon him by his ankle-shackles, shuffled to a chair and sat facing Amanda.

'The lady prosecutor,' he said. 'Life's all surprises.'

He was dressed in loose prison garb. He was sleek, muscular, handsome, more than six feet tall. He had long eyelashes that curled, and eyes the colour of a midnight with no moon. Girls would swoon and drown in those eyes. Isabel had.

'Smoke?' Amanda pushed the pack across the table. Her hand shook a little and she tried to still it.

'I conquered the habit,' he said. 'This a social visit or what?'

'No, not social.' Isabel had often referred to her former husband as Ángel, pronounced Anyel. It was a stretch to think of Sanchez as *anyelic*. He was spun out of darkness, a creature of vicious whim. If he had wings, they took him on flights into dismal regions of his own making. Celestial destinations weren't on Ángel's itinerary.

Amanda glanced at the guard, whose name tag identified him as Holland E. He was staring at a bare wall.

'How's prison life?' she asked.

'It's a ball. We got some real fuckwits there. Real clowns.' Sanchez gave her his withering look. She was determined to hold the gaze and not flinch, even though she was thinking about the border guards Sanchez had executed. He'd made them kneel and then shot them directly into their open mouths. Galindez, whose evasive manner in court had made him a less plausible witness than Isabel, had testified to this. Sanchez had ordered the guards to pray for mercy, then slaughtered them anyway. *Like a coupla lambs. Bleeding all over the place.*

'I guess it's not easy stuck in here,' she said. 'You appealing against the sentence?'

'I'm appealing any way you look at it.' He was amused. His smile was lethal. The sculpted body and the bronze skin were just extra tinsel on the Christmas tree. In another reality he might have been a male model of the Latin variety, white linen suit and two-tone shoes, strutting his stuff on the catwalk.

'What you here for anyway?' he asked. 'Talk about my sentence? Hey, maybe you got a pardon tucked in your pocket. You got a chit from the Governor or what?'

'No pardon, Victor. Just some loose ends.'
'I'm a loose end, huh?'
'Tell me how you got to them.'
'Got to who? You talk in puzzles, lady.'
'You don't have any idea what I'm driving at, I suppose.'
Sanchez laid a hand flat on his thigh. 'I like puzzles. I got this book with all these scrambled words in them and stuff, also join the dots and get a fucking donkey or eagle. I do crosswords. It gets pretty damn thrilling, I gotta say.'
'It's not crosswords I have in mind,' she said.
'You know what I think of you?'
Amanda shook her head. 'I don't read minds.'
Sanchez moved the hand on his thigh. 'Kinda proper, kinda aloof. But hot in the sack. Whooeee,' and he waved his hand loosely, as if his fingertips had been scalded.
'Games, Victor. I'm not playing.'
'What are you? Fortysomethin'? Late thirties? A lady in prime time, ripe and ready for plucking.'
'Is this the bit where you grab your crotch?' she asked.
'I watched you in court. You gave me these looks.'
'Chief among them was contempt.'
'Contempt my ass.'
'This may come as a surprise to you, but I don't see you as God's gift.'
'Know how many women I fucked in my life? Running close to fifteen hundred.'
'I bet you got testimonial letters from all of them.'
'I got no complaints. Most came back for more of the same, and some screamed with pleasure,' he said.

'Except when you were cutting off their nipples, I guess.'

Sanchez made a snorting sound. 'You believe that cunt's story? She walks into court like a Madonna, and she sits there and every time she opens her mouth out comes another lie.'

'She blackened your character, huh?'

'She fucking charbroiled me,' he said.

Amanda was silent a moment. Sanchez had led her on a detour and she'd followed. She was being drawn into areas of no relevance. She said, 'Let's backtrack, Victor.'

'You were talking puzzles, I remember.'

'You were the one talking puzzles. I was asking you how you did it.'

'I heard that tune already. Did what?'

'Galindez. Your ex-wife. You know what I'm talking about.'

'Pair of fucking vipers,' he said.

'How did you get to them, Victor?'

'Get to them how?'

'How did you have them killed?'

Sanchez pushed his chair back. 'Killed? You're saying they're dead?'

'Galindez for sure. He was shot through the heart. Isabel maybe. That's what I'm saying.'

Sanchez tilted his head back and stared at the ceiling. He moved his feet and the shackles rattled. He laughed, then he slumped back in his chair and his arms dangled at his sides and he looked serious. 'How do you mean Isabel maybe?'

'Just what I said. Isabel maybe.'

'Explain that to me.'

'Your people might have slipped up with her, I don't know yet.' A slim prospect, she thought, but sometimes you grabbed at such things because you wanted to hold on to a belief, no matter how marginal.

'My people? Meaning what?'

'The guys you hired. How did you arrange it? That's what I want to know.'

'Arrange it? That what you think?'

'That's my general inclination, Victor.'

'Look, lady, I sit in a cell and I do these puzzles in the book I got. It's a confined life.'

'Somehow you got a message to somebody,' she said.

'Oh sure, same way they allow me to send out for Domino's pizza and call-girls.'

He propped his elbows on the table and stared at her. Discomfited by the troubling black of his eyes, she was silent a moment. Sanchez lied instinctively. He probably considered truth a form of weakness.

She said, 'You wanted vengeance. You had the motive, Victor.'

'Sure I wanted vengeance. I sit in my cell and I dream up these real slow painful deaths for them, when I'm not joining fucking dots. If dreaming's a crime, I ain't been told. What you gonna do? Slap *another* death sentence on me?'

'They were in the Witness Protection Program, Victor,' she said. 'So how did you reach them?'

'Lady, you got a serious listening problem.'

What could you tell from Sanchez's expressions? What could you read into the body language? She shook a cigarette out of the pack and flicked her lighter. She was getting nothing here. She watched him tap his fingers on the table and had an impression of great energy held in check, but only just.

'For the sake of argument, let's take this big leap

and imagine you didn't do it,' she said. 'You got any idea who did?'

He shrugged. 'Nope.'

'Try a little harder, Victor.'

'What you want from me?'

'The truth.'

'The truth is what I been telling you.'

'I wonder why I'm not buying it.'

'Like I give a fuck.'

Sanchez smiled at her. She saw slyness in the expression, complicity even, or maybe he was a mirror in which you saw any reflection you wanted. 'You say I done it. OK, you figure it out, you're the brains. Me, I'm a common criminal. I'm lowlife.'

Sanchez gestured for her to lean a little closer to him, as if he wanted to say something in confidence. She inclined her head warily and drew her chair nearer to the table. She was conscious of his overwhelming physical presence, the way he projected himself. She imagined how women would go for this. You could look into Sanchez's eyes and see nothing there but romance and sea cruises and breezes blowing through chiffon and prolonged lovemaking, sometimes tender, sometimes brutal, in the penthouse cabin.

His hand rose and his fingertips touched her lips gently, and she didn't move, she held his eyes, smelled cheap prison soap on his fingers. This touch might arouse some kid, a naïve girl like Isabel or the fifteen hundred others he'd boasted about. She felt the hairs on the back of her neck go cold even as she knew it was important she didn't move away from him, that she meet him as far as she could on his own terms, whatever they were. Then he parted her lips and touched her teeth. He had long fingers.

Those same fingers had taken a razor-blade to Isabel's breast. Don't forget that. She hoped he suffered in his cell. She hoped he had times of dread. She wanted him to have bad dreams. Seeing himself strapped down in a gurney and wheeled inside the execution chamber, the IV drip attached to an open vein, the lethal concoction entering his bloodstream, and then goodbye, good riddance.

The maintenance of eye contact stressed her, and suddenly she was plunged back inside that foul courtroom, her head aching, nose stuffy, a drum pounding in her brain and the judge's gavel striking wood.

He whispered to her. 'Say, maybe you could kinda accidentally drop something on the floor, and when you bend down and pick it up you could find some way of entertaining me, then maybe I'll confess to anything you like . . .'

The guard said, 'Hey, Romeo. No contact. You know the rules.'

'Yes*sir*, Mr Holland.' Sanchez drew his hand back with exaggerated slowness. It was the motion of a man who didn't care about a goddam thing, who had nothing but disdain for authority, for the world.

Amanda stood up quickly, walked to the observation window and crossed her arms. She could still feel the lingering impression of his fingertips. *He can get to you even when you despise him.* She ran the back of her hand across her lips: an act of erasure, a small exorcism. But she felt vaguely askew, thrown off centre by Sanchez and that strange unwanted intimacy. The way he'd whispered. The way he'd imposed himself. Drop something, go down on your knees, entertain me while you're down there.

She strolled round the table.

He said, 'I don't have to answer your goddam questions. What's in it for me anyhow? Half an hour's exercise in the yard, maybe my own TV with multi-channels and a remote control? Big fucking deal. Suppose you gimme one good reason I should help you. You put me in this shithole.'

'You put yourself here, Victor. I was only doing my job.'

'Yeah, yeah, yeah, your job. Instrument of justice. Blindfold bitch. Fuck *you*.' Sanchez stared at her, challenging her.

She watched him a moment in silence, but now she couldn't hold his eyes because his look was hard and heartless and impossible to meet. She imagined that same expression on his face when he shot the border guards.

She turned away, feeling a tightness in her head. 'Let's see if we can put together a scenario, Victor. Let's say you managed to acquire some information. You got to somebody inside the Witness Program. Say you dangled the kind of money this somebody couldn't turn down. In return, you get Galindez's location, and Isabel's.'

'And I manage to do all this business from my fucking cell with no phone,' he said.

'You arranged it before the trial. You put it all together before the verdict.'

'Wow. And how did I manage all this?'

'I don't know how, but I'm close, Victor. I'm on track. Right?'

Sanchez laughed suddenly, then he stopped and his face was icy. He could go from tropical to arctic in a flash. She looked at him again, but it was still difficult to hold his gaze because it was as if he had some kind of electric force field around him, and if you listened hard enough you could hear a tiny little sizzle of danger.

He stood up and gestured to the guard. 'Holland, I'm through here. Take me home, country roads.'

'Wait,' she said.

'Wait for what? I don't have a whole lotta time, lady.'

She wondered how he could look that good and be so monstrous. Skin deep. Go down through the epidermal layers and keep going and you encounter a black heart, an unlit chamber.

She said, 'Nobody else had the motive, Victor.'

'Motive ain't proof, something you ought to know.'

'You're the only one,' she said.

He looked up at the ceiling a moment, then he moved. She hadn't expected it, nor had the guard. Despite the inhibition of the shackles, Sanchez acted with surprising agility. He lunged, bringing his forehead down hard on Holland's face. Amanda heard bone break and saw Holland drop to his knees, blood pouring from his nostrils. Sanchez turned quickly and with sheer brute strength forced her back against the wall, his solid forearm pressed like an iron bar to her throat. An alarm bell was ringing somewhere in the building. She heard it distantly because the pressure of Sanchez's arm was squeezing the air out of her and there was a roaring inside her head. She beat against the sides of his face with her fists but he wasn't troubled by her efforts, he just kept smiling, his expression one of – what? Some dark joy? A kind of twisted glee? He brought his face down close, his mouth almost touching hers. His breath smelled of toothpaste.

She was conscious of how her knees touched his and the way he had his body pressed against her. Weird little lights fizzed in her vision.

He whispered, 'Bad things come in threes, lady. You ever hear that saying? Two down, you can guess the rest. Keep it in mind.'

Holland had recovered his balance and taken his gun from the holster. His face was covered with blood. He said, 'Motherfucker,' and struck Sanchez on the back of the skull, but the blow didn't alter Sanchez's expression. The smile was fixed and immutable and dreadful. More guards were clattering into the room, three or four heavyweight types. One of them applied a stranglehold around Sanchez's neck and dragged him away from Amanda, another battered his ribs with a night-stick. Sanchez, covering his head with his hands, fell to the floor and lay in a foetal position. The guards circled him, kicked him a few times, then hauled him to his feet. His body limp, he looked at Amanda, who was trying to catch her breath and fight against the sensation of blackness that raged in her head.

'Remember,' he said.

She watched him being led out of the room. She heard the rattle and clank of the shackles and the sound of his laughter, then the swift crack of a night-stick, and after that there was silence from the corridor.

Donald Scarfe had appeared. 'Jesus. Are you OK?'

'Shocked, I guess,' she said. She coughed a few times into her hand.

'You need a medic? I'll call for one.'

She shook her head. Her legs felt like they were made of air. 'Nothing's broken. I'll be OK.'

'I was in the observation room,' Scarfe said. 'Then it all happened so fast. I should never have given permission for this—'

'Don, it's OK, I'm *fine.*' But it wasn't OK. She leaned against the table, shaken, light-headed, breathing a little too quickly. She lit a cigarette anyhow, imagined smoke swirling round her lungs as if she were seeing a live-action X-ray of herself.

'You heard the last thing he said?' she asked.

'He says things just to make your head spin.'

'Bad things come in threes. You heard that.'

'I'd take it with a pinch of salt, Amanda.'

Two down, she thought. *Bad things come in threes. You know the rest. Two down, one to go.* She had images of Galindez's white hand and his ruby ring and Isabel's blood and her cheap pink barrette, and she thought of herself lying on a coroner's slab and Rhees having to identify her. Bad things.

In the corridor fluorescent tubes hummed. She felt they were buzzing inside her.

'What now?' Scarfe asked.

What now. She wasn't sure. She felt hot and rundown and something else, something new, *scared,* and she'd have to drive home through relentless sunlight in a world that had abruptly shifted and cracked under her feet. She looked at Scarfe, but she said nothing. She was thinking of the smell of Victor Sanchez's breath and feeling the leaden weight of his arm and how the air had been crushed out of her. And she was hearing his words, over and over.

22

Dansk sat in his car in the cul-de-sac and watched the house. A dead-end street was a bad environment for surveillance. Traffic entering the street, eight houses on either side and one at the end, was usually local. A stranger who sat too long in his car would draw attention. Somebody would jot down his licence number, maybe even make a phone call to the local cops.

All the windows had little yellow or blue security stickers attached. Some were barred, others had steel shutters. This was profitable territory for the merchants of fear that sold home-safety systems.

The house Dansk watched was the last one on the left. He was parked diagonally across from it. It was the only house with an unruly garden out front. Some care was needed here, a little pride. There were neighbours to think about, the general appearance of the street, property values.

He looked at his watch. He didn't want to spend more than twenty minutes max in this place, any longer was folly, even twenty was stretching it.

He had a clipboard to which was attached a number of invoice sheets with the name of a dummy pharmaceutical company, and he started ticking items off with his pen and trying to seem occupied, like a salesman or a delivery guy catching up on a backlog of paperwork.

It was a strange thing about people. If they saw you with a clipboard they tended to glaze you out, thinking you were on some kind of legitimate business and unthreatening.

His cellular phone rang and he picked it up.

Pasquale had a voice like somebody coming down from a helium infusion: high-pitched, a little husky. 'On the way, Anthony. Maybe two minutes.'

'Right.' Dansk hung up and waited. He saw the car turn into the cul-de-sac, then it passed him and he watched it enter the driveway of the house with the overgrown garden.

He saw her get out.

She wore a navy-blue shirt and jeans. She swept a hand through her short brown hair. There was a slightly distracted frown on her face. Halfway up the path she stopped and plucked a leaf off a eucalyptus tree and sniffed it as if it were a rare perfume. Faces intrigued Dansk. This woman, for example. She wasn't what Dansk would call conventionally attractive. Good-looking in an idiosyncratic way, determined jaw, cheeks a little fleshy. She wasn't the type he went for. For one thing she had tits, and Dansk liked his women scrawny. He liked bones and angled structures and skinny hips. Another thing, she was outside his age limit. He preferred eighteen, seventeen. This one was what – forty?

But you never know. He wouldn't kick her out

of bed. An upholstered lady might be a change.

Smile more, he thought. Add a little make-up, change the hairdo, a touch of colour – sienna, say, or something outrageous and bright. Blond with a small pink streak. Turn a few heads.

She needed to pay attention to her posture. Too many years hunched over law books, hunting down precedents. Pick yourself up, inject a little elegance, ditch the blue jeans, and navy isn't your colour anyway. Get the best out of yourself. Nice ass, all the same. Usually at her age asses drooped, but hers looked firm.

He thought, I don't want to bring anything bad into your life, so don't make me. You're probably intelligent, concerned, dedicated. Don't be dedicated to the wrong things.

He leaned forward against the wheel, watching. She'd stopped again, like she was reluctant to go inside the house. What was it? Indecision? A forgotten door key?

A guy came out of the house.

Dansk was surprised because he'd somehow thought the place empty. The man was tall and on the lean side. Black jeans, a white shirt, thick dark hair going grey at the sides. He said something to the woman and she shook her head and Dansk sensed friction. The guy took a few steps towards her. The woman didn't move.

Who was the guy? Her lover?

On the one hand that might be problematic, on the other it might be nothing. It depended on the woman. Everything depended on her.

They were embracing now, repairing whatever was damaged between them. Dansk watched the guy's hand drop to the woman's ass. An easy intimacy. Dansk wondered how her laugh would sound. He imagined smoky and sincere, something you might hear at a crowded party and it would take your attention for a moment because of its hearty, good-natured quality.

Dansk never went to parties, never received invitations.

He watched the man slip an arm round the woman's shoulders and then they kissed, which involved an awkward craning movement downwards for the guy. They went inside the house – heading for the bedroom, he imagined. He zoomed in on an image of clothes cast aside, a clasp of bodies, the hot damp flesh of love, and the smells.

He drove out of the cul-de-sac. He went through downtown Scottsdale, took a turn off the main drag and found himself in a street of art galleries. Overpriced canvasses in windows, Native American Indian influence everywhere, Navaho and Hopi art, beads and goodies plundered from the reservations.

He kept driving. The early evening sky was leaking light.

Eventually he found the place he was looking for. It was a bar called Floozies that advertised topless girls. Inside, he found a big gloomy room doing nothing in the way of business – it was too early for the topless crew. The place smelled of spilled beer and the floor wasn't clean. Typical.

McTell and Pasquale occupied a table close to the stage, which was concealed behind a silver curtain decorated with naked women. Dansk sat down near a set of spangled red drums and a Yamaha keyboard.

McTell stroked his beard and said, 'She was at Florence for three quarters of an hour, I timed it.

She drove down there on her own. I didn't see any sign of this Drumm character. She went straight inside the slammer unaccompanied.'

Dansk looked round for the bartender and couldn't find him. There was no decent service in this country any more, everything was bad manners and have-a-nice-day insincerity. He said, 'She saw Sanchez.'

'That a question?' McTell asked.

'She goes down to Florence. Who else is she going to see?' He thought of the woman visiting Sanchez. So she was working up an interest. She was pursuing something she should leave alone. Too much persistence. Probably ingrained in her. Her world hung by a thread and she didn't even know it. Drumm hadn't gone with her, so maybe she was just poking around on her own.

Pasquale fiddled with a paper napkin. He folded it once, then a second time, and suddenly he had a little paper animal which he set on the table. It might have been a horse or a tiger, you couldn't tell. Whatever, it was sturdy, well-made. Dansk observed Pasquale's dark suit and white open-necked shirt. He had a thick lower lip and was overweight by about fifteen pounds. He had long elegant fingers and his hair was grey-yellow, with sideburns. He wore a gold pendant round his neck.

Dansk watched a guy come in and sit down behind the drums. He tapped the cymbals then cracked his knuckles one at a time. Dansk closed his eyes. Here he was in this tit and ass joint in the company of killers and a guy was cracking his knuckles, which was a sound that affected him like chalk squealing on a blackboard. Here he was sitting in a goddam drain with a sleazy curtain tattooed with nudes. He thought, This is what I do. This is how I make my nut.

McTell said, 'Why don't we blow the whole thing off and split? Why are we hanging here anyhow? You said we had other work.'

Dansk's patience was approaching meltdown. 'We need to know what she does, who she sees. How her behaviour might affect us. Information, Eddie. Know who you're dealing with. The more you know, the less likely an error of judgement. Suppose we split right now. Suppose we just get the fuck out. We don't have a clue what she and the cop might get up to behind our backs, do we? You see the problem?'

McTell nodded. He had a flat, almost concave forehead. He said, 'So she saw Sanchez. What's he gonna tell her? He's gonna laugh right in her fucking face.'

Dansk, hugely irritated by the world in a general way, turned to the guy at the drums and said, 'You intend to sit there tugging on your bones all night, fella?'

The knuckle-cracker had a weak lopsided smile. 'What's that?'

'That knuckle business,' Dansk said. 'It's frankly irritating.'

'Yeah? You got a problem with it?'

'I won't, soon as you get out of my sight.'

The knuckle-cracker looked at Dansk. If he was contemplating a verbal come-back, whatever he saw in Dansk's eyes made him change tack. 'OK, sorry, sorry, man. No sweat. I'll go sit on the other side of the room. Sorry.'

Dansk watched the guy slink away. The world was filled with nuisances, fringe disturbances, little whirlpools of agitation. All kinds of stuff he just didn't need.

He looked at Pasquale and McTell. They were watching him, waiting for instructions.

He said, 'I'll work the woman myself. Pasquale, you stay in your motel and watch cartoons until I need you.'

McTell asked, 'What about me?'

'There's a guy in her life, find out about him. Who he is, what he does. Just go gentle, if you know how.'

'Got it,' McTell said.

'OK.' Dansk rose. He wandered outside into the heat. A mandarin moon was suspended in the sky. He walked to his car, remembering the way Amanda had sniffed the eucalyptus leaf. He wondered if he could change the direction of his life through some perfumed avenue.

Dream on. Once you were in this line of work there was no way out. You made your living out of the dead.

23

The restaurant in north Scottsdale was French. Rhees had suggested the place. He liked his meat rare, bloody juices swimming on the plate.

Amanda saw a misty reflection of herself in the mahogany panel behind Rhees's head. They'd made love earlier and she'd detected in him a certain restraint. He'd been tense, and the absence of his usual verbal passion bothered her. Rhees never made love silently. Speech, even whispered in the incoherent language of lovers, was integral to the act where he was concerned.

'Are you still annoyed?' she asked.

'Yeah, I'm still annoyed. You sneaked off to see Sanchez without telling me.'

She looked down at the remains of her saffron rice, bright yellow on the plate. 'OK, I sneaked off. I knew you'd disapprove, so I didn't tell you I was going.'

'Share things with me, that's all I ask.'

She rubbed the back of his hand. 'I didn't ask for this situation, John.'

Rhees folded his napkin and placed it over the lamb bones and stared at her. 'So why bother with it?'

'Because it just fell in my lap and it's messy.'

'But not your mess. You gave your word to Isabel, fine, admirable, honourable. But she quit being your responsibility as soon as the trial was finished. What were you supposed to do? Hold her hand for the rest of her life? Maybe she should have moved in with us and you could have kept an eye on her twenty-four hours a day. Besides, I seem to remember all you were going to do was talk to Bascombe. In and out, you said. Toot sweet.' Blood seeped through Rhees's napkin. 'What did Sanchez tell you anyhow?'

'Nothing,' she said. She hadn't described the meeting to Rhees because she knew he'd react with horror. She played with a spoon, turning it over and over, remembering the way Sanchez had acted, bringing back the disturbing shock of the moment, focusing on the violence of the encounter: Sanchez forcing her against the wall, the blow of the gun on his head, the rap of a night-stick.

She thought about his threat, and suddenly there was an underlying strata of vulnerability. Faces in this restaurant, for instance. How could she know they were harmless? For all she could tell, at least one of them might be a Sanchez operative, watching, waiting.

She stopped herself. She let Donald Scarfe's words play through her head as if they were a kind of balm. *He says things just to make your head spin. A pinch of salt.* But Sanchez returned unprompted. *Bad things come in threes.* What credence could she give to Victor Sanchez's threat?

'He's into games,' was all she finally said.

'Did you expect anything else?'

'Not really.'

Rhees caught a waiter's eye and asked for the dessert menu and chose a meringue basket of pears baked in sherry. Amanda wanted only coffee. The waiter came back and Rhees plunged his spoon into the dessert. She enjoyed watching him eat. He did it with gusto.

'That's a mountain to get through, John.'

'I somehow worked up an appetite earlier.'

Amanda said, 'I don't understand why he hadn't been interviewed by anyone from the Program when I saw him.'

'You're dealing with a bureaucracy.'

'But this is a situation where you'd expect rapid response.'

'Maybe they're talking to him even as we sit here.'

'What I'd really like is to talk in person to somebody who works inside the Program,' she said. 'Get some straight answers, if there are such things.'

'You think that kind of access is possible?'

'Anything's possible if you go at it the right way,' she said. She picked up her napkin and dabbed Rhees's lower lip. 'You've got a stray morsel there.'

'Yes, Mother.'

'I can request a meeting,' she said. 'It's not like I just drifted in off the streets and I'm sticking my nose in. I'm an interested party.'

She dropped a cube of sugar into her coffee and stirred. Rhees said, 'Here, sample this.' He held his spoon to her lips. She tasted, found the meringue sickeningly sweet and the pears heavy on the sherry.

'Unadulterated cholesterol,' she said.

'Clogs the arteries. Slows the rush of blood to your head and makes you sluggish in your thinking.'

'Which is what you want, of course.'

'You know how I feel, Amanda.' He called for the check then went off to the men's room. He was gone a long time. When he came back they walked outside to the parking lot. The night was filled with hot dark enclosures beyond the beacons of lamplight that streamed up into the palm trees around the restaurant. There was the illusion of an electrified oasis. She didn't care for the shadows between the lights.

Rhees said, 'I think you're happy back in the swing again. The old pizazz. You never really wanted out of it in the first place, did you?'

'I wouldn't be too sure,' she said.

'You haven't forgotten that the razzmatazz comes at a price, sweetheart,' he said. 'Just keep that in mind before you start digging deeper into this whole wretched business.'

Digging: it was what she'd been trained to do in law school. Spade and shovel, examine the debris that came out of the earth, discard what was irrelevant and store what was useful. Legal archaeology. She hooked her arm through John's and, raising her face, kissed him. She found some very slight resistance in the kiss, almost as if he were trying to distance himself from her, but then he yielded, put his arms around her and drew her against him.

24

First thing in the morning, Amanda telephoned Donald Scarfe. 'Has Sanchez had any visitors yet?' she asked.

'You were the last,' he replied.

'No requests? No enquiries?'

'None so far.'

'That's all I wanted to know, Don. Thanks.'

'How are you today anyway?'

'I'm over the shock,' she said.

'I still blame myself, Amanda.'

'I absolve you totally, Don. I was the one that asked to go into the lion's den.'

Next, she punched in Bascombe's number.

'I haven't had my coffee,' Bascombe told her. 'I'm a goddam bear before that first cup.'

She was using the phone in the kitchen. The morning was rainy and humid and the long stalks of grass in the backyard buckled. A break in the weather. She liked rain.

'Explain this, Lew,' she said. 'Why hasn't anyone been down to see Sanchez? Has somebody at

Program control overlooked the connection between Sanchez and the two allegedly "safe" witnesses?'

Bascombe said, 'I sent the messages, Amanda. I don't have any say in the follow-up.'

'It's not acceptable, Lew.'

'You're speaking with your prosecutor's voice, Amanda.'

She watched Rhees, in a knee-length robe, put two slices of bread in the toaster. He poured a cup of coffee and sat at the table gazing out of the window.

'Lew, you might be quite comfortable working away in the dark, but it isn't a situation I find conducive to my peace of mind.'

'I'm not sure your peace of mind matters a damn to the people in Arlington,' he said.

'Did they acknowledge your messages?'

'We've been here before, Amanda.'

'I understand that. I'm just not very happy. In fact, I'm pissed. I don't like the way this thing works, if it works at all.'

'I hate it when I have to deal with shrill women first thing.'

'I am not being shrill, Lew.'

'Yes you are.'

'This is like trying to get through a brick wall,' she said.

'I can send off another message, see what happens.'

'Make it different this time. Add this rider: the former prosecutor wants a face to face with somebody in the Witness Program admin. And I'm not kidding, Lew.'

'You don't know what you're asking.'

'I know exactly what I'm asking.'

'They'll refuse.'

'Not if you mention that I intend to raise holy hell about the whole thing.'

'Meaning?'

She took a deep breath to ease the knot of pressure in her chest. 'It's really simple, Lew. Galindez has already made the papers, but the story didn't say anything about how he was supposed to be in the Program, nice and safe. And Isabel hasn't made the papers at all yet. All it takes is for me to phone some avid journalist and give an in-depth, behind-the-scenes account. Big problem with the Witness Protection Program, it leaks like a goddam sieve.'

'You wouldn't,' he said.

'Oh, try me.'

'You'd be jeopardizing criminal prosecutions all over the country, Amanda. A story like that—'

'A story like that is hair-raising, Lew,' she said.

'A story like that is going to make potential witnesses think long and hard about testifying. You're not giving this proper thought, Amanda.'

'*Au contraire*.'

'You're obsessing over Isabel Sanchez. This is a personal thing and it's also blackmail.'

'It takes what it takes, Lew. Get back to me before the end of the day. That's an ultimatum. I'll be waiting.'

Rhees looked up from his coffee. 'Hardball,' he said, with a sharp little note in his voice.

'What else works?' she asked.

She poured coffee. She felt a healthy vibrancy run through her like the struck strings of a zither. 'Goddam. I can't tell you how satisfying that was.'

'You think it's going to achieve anything?' Rhees asked.

'We'll see.' She clasped her hands round her cup and listened to the rain. It pattered on the roof, slinked over downpipes, stirred the grass. The doorbell rang. The sound made her jump. Rhees went to answer it. She heard him open the front door and after a couple of minutes he came back. 'Some guy selling magazine subscriptions,' he said. 'I felt sorry for him in this rain.'

'They count on your sympathy,' she said.

Rhees smiled. 'I told him I'd take *Sports Illustrated*.'

'You don't like sports.'

'The poor bastard was dripping. Besides, there's always the swimsuit issue. In any case, he didn't have the *New York Review of Books*. So what was I to do?'

'You'd give your last dime to any guy rattling a tin cup.'

'It's called charity,' Rhees said.

She paced the room. She wondered if Bascombe had telephoned Arlington, if she'd made him sweat enough to go that far.

The telephone rang. She reached for it at once. It was her father.

'I tried the cabin,' he said. 'Obviously you haven't gone back yet.'

'Not yet,' she said.

'I go out of town one night and I come back and there you are mentioned in the newspaper. You didn't say anything to me about this corpse.'

'Dad, I'm waiting for a call. I'm going to hang up and I'll get back to you.'

'You're back in business again, right? That's what I smell.'

'No, I'm not back in business. I'm only doing what I think I have to.'

'What is it with you? You got an aversion to peace and quiet? If I was Rhees, I'd stick you in the trunk of the car and drive you back to the cabin immediately and lock you there until you're thinking halfway straight. What's wrong with him anyway? You wrap him round your little finger like—'

'I'm hanging up, I'll call you back.'

'Don't you dare hang up on me, Amanda.'

She set the receiver down. She swept a lock of hair from her forehead. In a way, she liked the feeling of hanging up on Morgan, who longed to think she needed him *and* his money. The telephone rang again. This time it was Bascombe.

'Listen carefully,' he said, 'this is the deal.'

25

By early afternoon Dansk had almost finished going through the microfiche material in the newspaper morgue. He zoomed in on a photograph of Amanda taken outside a courtroom. Dressed in a dark suit with a double-breasted jacket, she was smiling into the camera. He gazed into her face. Was that fatigue he saw there? Or relief? He couldn't decipher the expression.

The caption read, SANCHEZ PROSECUTOR RESIGNS.

He skimmed over the story. 'Ms Scholes said she needed time for her personal life . . . looking forward to a vacation but gave no indication of where she plans to spend it . . . delighted the prolonged Sanchez case is finally over and that justice has been served.'

Justice served, and amen.

Behind Amanda in the photograph was a man identified as Lieutenant William Drumm. He had small slitted eyes and a benign smile. He was quoted as saying that the resignation of Special Prosecutor Scholes was a blow to the law-enforcement community. Amanda and the plump cop, a mutual admiration society.

The article also mentioned that Amanda's successor was a guy called Dominic Concannon, a graduate of Columbia. Concannon said that Amanda Scholes had set very high standards, she was a hard act to follow.

She'd had a fair amount of press in her time, Dansk thought. Magazine profiles, newspapers, mainly in-State publications, but also a couple of nationals. She had views on *big matters*. Capital punishment (against in some instances, for in others – cop-killers, child-murderers). Abortion (pro-choice). She was critical of the legal profession, the usual gripes: too many frivolous lawsuits, too many ambulance-chasers, too many deals cut in back rooms.

He left the building, stepped out into the rain, sat in his car, took out his little notebook and leafed through it. This Amanda was one determined woman. She sailed into battle with cannons blazing. In court she harried defence witnesses, squabbled with opposing attorneys, took flak from the bench. Gutsy, and brainy, give her that.

Then out of the blue she'd had enough. Abracadabra, gone. He wondered what lay behind this decision. Maybe she realized she'd chosen a career that didn't fulfil her, which wasn't a decision she'd make lightly. He had the feeling she didn't go into things in a superficial way, she'd figure the angles first, which was maybe too bad – superficial he could deal with.

He flicked the pages of his notebook to the biographical stuff. Father named Morgan Scholes, widower, rich business shark. Amanda had gone to law school in Los Angeles. She'd never married. Probably too busy being Ms Prosecutor, building the career, climbing the glory ladder. The fucking problem with microfiching your way into somebody's life was how you didn't get the full story, only the margins, and they were never satisfying.

For instance, did she have close friends? Old pals from college? People she'd confide in? People she'd turn to in an emergency? A support group? He wrote 'friends?' in his notebook.

He gazed out at the rain streaming across the parking lot. No sun, the city grim, passing cars making spray. Typical, you're in the desert and it rains. He drove back to his hotel, left his car in the underground parking. McTell was waiting in reception. They went inside the empty bar and Dansk ordered a 7-Up. McTell asked for a Coors.

He hunched across the table. 'The guy's called John Rhees,' he said. 'He's a professor. Teaches college here. Poetry or something.'

She'd want somebody smart, Dansk thought. 'Anything else?' he asked.

'According to this busybody neighbour I talked with, they've been living in a cabin up near Flagstaff past few weeks. Seems she was sick or something.'

Sick. Dansk wondered about that. Sick didn't tell you much. He settled back in his chair. 'You've been busy, Eddie.'

'Nice guy, Rhees,' McTell said.

'Don't tell me. You talked to him.'

'A few minutes.'

Dansk asked, 'What did you say, you were from the electric company and had to read his meter?'

'Trade secret, Anthony.'

'Did you see the woman?'

'Uh-huh.' McTell stared inside his drink. 'Whaddya think, Anthony? We gonna have to do surgery or what?'

Dansk said nothing. Surgery, he thought. Arteries ruptured, blood pumping.

'We can't like hang out here for ever,' McTell said.

'We like hang out until I say otherwise, McTell.'

McTell blew out his cheeks and looked sullen, resembling a puffer-fish in a bad humour.

Dansk pushed his chair back from the table. He thought about the French restaurant last night, the way Amanda and Rhees had held hands across the table. He was aware of a bleak little blue-yellow gas flame of loneliness inside his head. He recalled how she'd leaned across the table and dabbed Rhees's lips with her napkin, the concern that was maternal and sexy at the same time. Concealed behind a vase of carnations, Dansk had picked at his *salade niçoise* without any enjoyment.

He'd followed Rhees inside the men's room at one point and stood at the urinal next to him. In the strained manner of conversations conducted between strangers pissing side by side, Dansk had said, 'It's always a good sign when a restaurant has a spotless toilet.'

Rhees, zipping up, had agreed. Out of casual interest, Dansk had glanced very quickly at Rhees's flaccid penis – circumcised, mid-sized number, nothing to write home about – then he'd washed his hands and held them under the hot-air dryer.

Dansk said, 'Sanitary. Better than towels.'

Rhees said, 'Those gadgets don't dry as well as towels.'

'Towels carry germs,' Dansk had remarked.

Rhees had said, 'I guess it's down to personal preference,' and smiled affably, the smile of a man who knows his love is waiting for his return. Dansk had pictured this lean man with the easy smile fucking Amanda. He'd imagined Amanda's spread thighs and pubic shadows and moonlight on a window and Rhees saying he loved her, and he wondered what that was like, living your life as if you belonged inside it.

Dansk stood up now. Remembering Rhees depressed him. 'I think I'll rack out for a while.'

McTell said, 'Later.'

Dansk took the elevator up to his room. He hung the 'Do Not Disturb' sign on the handle and closed the door. He started to take off his jacket, then realized he wasn't alone. The man who sat on the bed wore a long black overcoat and a black cashmere beret. His breathing was shallow and laboured.

Dansk didn't move, didn't say anything. He was surprised by the guy's appearance, conscious of turbulence in his head. He had his jacket halfway off, an empty arm dangled at his side.

The man covered his mouth with a black-gloved hand and coughed a couple of times. His eyes were bloodshot and runny and, Dansk thought, disgusting.

The man opened his briefcase. He produced a thick wad of crisp banknotes, set it on the bedside table and said, 'Payroll time for your guys, Anthony.'

26

She entered the Biltmore at 10 p.m. *It's cloak and dagger*, Bascombe had said on the phone. *It's the only way they'll agree. Be punctual.*

The only way, she thought. What was wrong with a little openness now and again? They were infatuated with secrecy. They liked nocturnal meetings and whispered conversations in secure rooms.

She surveyed the reception area. This place, all the rage in the years after Frank Lloyd Wright had designed it, was past its shelf-date. Women with bad face-lifts dined here, balancing awkwardly on high heels and hanging on to the arms of silver-haired men who looked like traumatized bankers or golfers from the age of knickerbockers. There was the perfume of old money and the musty smell of quiet power. It was the kind of place where her father occasionally dined.

Amanda approached the desk. She asked a clerk for the key to room 247, as she'd been instructed. *Do it exactly the way you're told*, Bascombe had said. The clerk was supercilious. He pushed the key towards Amanda as if he thought she was here for the purpose of an illicit assignation. She wondered if her clothes were suspect. The knee-length black skirt and matching jacket didn't strike her as the garb of a working-girl. You couldn't tell, she supposed.

She took the key and walked towards the stairs. On her way up she encountered a party of old dowagers chattering among themselves like so many fluttery birds descending in a wave of chiffon and the choking smell of Chanel No.5. Amanda sidestepped, let them creak past her on their way down, then continued up.

She clutched the key in her warm hand. *Go into the room. Somebody will meet you there.* For an uneasy moment she suspected some kind of trick or trap. It was groundless, a case of nerves. She was going to have a quiet word with a grey-faced bureaucrat, that was all, somebody who'd allay her fears with a few appropriate phrases and maybe a lie or two thrown in for good measure. Somebody who'd tell her that the situation had been investigated and the repairs made, the holes sealed, it couldn't happen again. Sorry about Isabel Sanchez, by the way.

But still.

She walked down the corridor, searching for the room number. She reached it, paused, then kept walking. This affliction of nerves was downright stupid, so why didn't she just turn around, slip the key in the door and enter the goddam room? This is what you wanted, she thought. This is what you asked for.

She walked back. She looked at the key for a moment, then she opened the door. She stepped inside the room. It was empty. She checked the bathroom, also empty. She went to the window and gazed out, seeing falling rain caught in the lamplight on the lawn. Somewhere a band had begun to play, a tinny sound heavy on drums, music for people who wanted to shuffle through a geriatric foxtrot.

OK, so the Program representative was late, flight delayed, traffic jam, all kinds of reasons. She sat down in front of the dressing table and caught a glimpse of herself in the mirror. A little make-up, a touch around the eyes, the lashes, the lightest of lipstick, hair sensibly brushed and in place. She'd wanted to look down-to-business serious, the kind of person who wouldn't be swayed by platitudes and excuses.

She heard a key turn in the lock and the door opened. The man who entered the room came across the floor towards her. 'Amanda Scholes?' he asked.

She noticed tiny spots of rain in his hair. He reached inside his raincoat and said, 'Let me show you some ID.'

'Sure,' she said.

He handed her a laminated badge. She saw the words 'Department of Justice' and the guy's photograph and a thumbprint and a name typed just beneath it: 'Anthony Dansk'.

27

Her first impression was of a mauve birthmark, suggestive of a truncated map of Italy, situated between Dansk's jawline and ear. And then his eyes; greens were often restful, but not the green of Dansk's eyes, which had the sharp, just-too-bright quality of a traffic signal located on a lonesome road in the deep heart of nowhere. His hair was thick and red and healthy, brushed back and straight, and a faint gingery down fuzzed his cheeks. He wore a neat single-breasted grey suit and grey shirt and a black and grey necktie. His body was trim; clearly he worked out. He looked way too young, she thought, but so did a whole lot of people these days – physicians, cops, lawyers. They were like kids dressing up. You go over forty, and suddenly the world's filled with children running the show.

She lit a cigarette. She was still a little tense.

'I'm late,' he said. 'Flight schedules don't mean a thing these days. I wonder why they even announce them.' He sat, frowning at the smoke drifting from her cigarette.

'Yeah, I know. The health warning's on the pack,' she said.

Dansk said, 'What people inflict on their bodies is their own business. They want to take risks, it's up to them.' He leaned back in his chair. He smiled very briefly, which in that split second softened the starkness of his eyes and dimpled his cheeks unexpectedly. She could imagine him as a boy, apple-cheeked and freckled. He had perfect teeth. He puts a lot of effort into dental maintenance, she thought.

She looked for an ashtray. A length of ash dropped in her lap and she brushed it off, leaving a grey smudge on her skirt. Clumsy. Dansk watched her without expression.

'Do I call you Amanda or are we doing this on a formal basis?'

'Amanda's fine,' she said. 'So where do we begin?'

Dansk clasped his hands together. Well-manicured, except there was no nail on the pinky of his left hand, just puckered skin. 'Your concerns about the Program,' he said.

'That's a start,' she said.

He wandered over to the mini-bar, removed a can of Diet Dr Pepper and popped it. 'Under one name or another – Silencer, WITSEC – the Program's been around for thirty years, give or take. And you can't run something this sensitive for that length of time without the occasional mistake, a lapse here or there.'

'I don't call the fact that Galindez is dead a lapse,' she said, 'and I certainly don't call the likelihood that Isabel Sanchez is dead a lapse either. Euphemisms give me heartburn.'

He leaned forward in his chair. 'What I'm saying is, people are fallible, they get greedy. An official takes a bribe in return for somebody's address, then a witness you thought was well-protected turns up in the trunk of an abandoned car. I expect we'll find a bribe was involved in the situation with Galindez and Isabel Sanchez. We need some time to work on it.'

'How much time?'

'Impossible to estimate. These things have to be done very carefully. You don't want to alert the culpable party that he or she is under scrutiny.'

'How many people have access to the kind of information we're talking about?'

'I'm not allowed to divulge that.'

'What exactly are you allowed?'

'Try to understand, Amanda, the heart of this Program is secrecy.'

She said, 'Look. The glaringly obvious place to start is with Victor Sanchez. I already went down to Florence and gave it a shot; not that I achieved anything.'

'What impression did you get?'

'He's involved up to his neck. I just can't figure out how he penetrated your security. Also he threatened me.'

'Threatened you?'

'He said I was next on his hit list.' She made a slashing motion with her index finger across her throat. 'Which wasn't pleasant.'

'You think he was serious?'

'It's something I don't take lightly,' she said. 'He scared me.'

Dansk was quiet for a moment. 'We've arranged to interview him.'

My heart beats easier, she thought. 'You're finally getting around to that, are you?'

Dansk seemed impervious to her sarcasm. He said, 'My advice to you would be take a vacation and don't tell anyone where you're going. You'd be safer far away from here. Let me get on with my business, it's in good hands.'

'Funnily enough, I told Isabel Sanchez the very same thing,' she said. 'You're in good hands, sweetie. But I keep hearing the goddam dogs in my head.'

'The dogs, right,' he said. 'How close were you to them?'

'Hard to say. A mile, two, maybe more.'

Dansk looked pensive. 'You responded to a phone call from Mrs Sanchez, I understand.'

Amanda nodded. 'I was too late to help her.'

'What did she say exactly?'

'Didn't you see the report?'

'Sometimes the reports I get leave things to be desired.'

'She was scared. Men were coming after her.'

'Did she know these men?'

'She didn't say.'

'She mention how many men?'

'Two, she said.'

'Descriptions, anything like that?'

'No, no descriptions.'

Dansk shook his head. 'It's a bad business.'

A bad business was an understated way of putting it, she thought. 'I'm curious. She was in Farmington, New Mexico, then Tuba City. Finally she comes back here to Phoenix. Where did you relocate her?'

'I can't answer that, sorry.'

'What the hell *can* you answer? Galindez is dead, Isabel's missing and you come waltzing down from God knows what cubby hole in Arlington or Washington or wherever, and you're condescending. Oh, we're taking over, Amanda, why don't you go on vacation.' She checked herself, the way her voice was rising. She didn't want to alienate Dansk, because he had the power to close doors on her.

'Condescending?' he asked. 'I flew all the way down here to set your mind at rest.'

'And what if my mind isn't at rest? What if it's like a jumping bean?'

Dansk strolled across the room and sipped his drink. He switched the subject suddenly. 'You talked about going to the newspapers, I believe. I don't think that would be smart.'

'Is this some kind of warning?'

He sat down again and drew his chair close to her. Their knees were almost touching. 'All I'm telling you is this: if you decide to have a word in the ear of some inquisitive journalist – cases collapse because witnesses are too scared to talk.'

'But would you gag the journalist?'

'You think we have that kind of power?'

'I don't know exactly what powers you *do* have. I'm supposed to mosey off into the sunset while you people get on with your business.'

'You agree to stay out of this business entirely, and in return I'll let you know the outcome.'

'I stifle my curiosity while you get to work.'

'One other condition is you don't talk with journalists.'

'I see a problem,' she said. 'You could come back to me in a couple of days, a week, a month, and you could tell me anything you please, and I'd have to buy it.'

'That's not my style,' Dansk said.

Amanda stood up. She had pins and needles in her legs. 'You're asking me to trust you.'

'I'm asking you to be reasonable,' Dansk said. His voice was suddenly chill in a way she didn't like. 'I don't have to tell you anything.'

She turned and looked out of the window and saw Dansk's can of soda glint in the rainy pane. She watched his image move a little closer to hers.

'What if you don't get in touch with me? You're not going to give me a phone number where I can reach you any time I want, are you?'

'I don't want you to walk out of this hotel feeling you've just talked with somebody who's going to vanish inside some – what was the phrase you used – cubby hole in Washington?' Dansk took out a notebook from his pocket and scribbled something on a sheet. 'I'm going to be in town a couple of days at least. Here's a number where you can reach me.'

'You're not staying here?' she asked.

'This was just for the purpose of meeting you.'

A secure room, she thought. Cloak and dagger. They did it in style. She wondered if people whose profession revolved around secrecy became addicted to it, if a life of secrecy was like being immersed for a long time in a sensory-deprivation tank. If that numb, lonely suspension did something to the way you viewed reality.

'And when you leave town, where can I call you?'

'I'm adding another number. This one's highly confidential. I'm not always behind my desk, but you can leave a message and I'll get back to you as soon as I can.'

'I have your word on that?'

'Of course.'

She wondered about the value of Anthony Dansk's word. Then she thought, I'm judging him too harshly. He has his own code of rules and regulations, he has to play by the book the way it's written. And she ought to feel some gratitude towards him for flying two thousand miles just to talk to her – even if she'd had to apply pressure to get him here.

'Are we agreed?' he asked.

She thought a moment and then said, 'We're agreed.'

'Maybe a drink on the deal would be nice.'

He sounded like a kid asking for a date, she thought. He was watching her with a certain expectation she found vaguely embarrassing, and for a moment he reminded her of the high-school loner who could never get a girl, the one who stood on his own at the edge of a crowded prom, clip-on bow tie askew, eyes shyly scanning the dance floor.

She glanced at her watch. 'Why not. Gin, if there's any, and tonic.'

He walked to the mini-bar. 'There's no ice.'

'That's OK,' she said.

Dansk brought her the gin and tonic.

She sipped the drink and looked at him over the rim of her glass. She noticed he had a habit of turning his face to one side every now and then to hide the birthmark from sight. He had to go through life that way, she thought, his face for ever turned a little to one side. The birthmark obviously burdened him.

He said, 'Why did you quit law?'

'You've been researching my background, Anthony.'

'I'd hardly call it research. When I knew I was coming to meet you, I figured I ought to know who I was talking to, that's all. Your resignation's no big secret.'

'Why I quit law. Too many reasons. Mainly I was becoming polluted after years working with liars and flimflam artists and human eczema. I'd reached an unhealthy level of toxicity, and I wasn't prepared to go on paying the price.'

'Human eczema,' he said.

'Suppurations masquerading as people.'

'Harsh words.'

'You asked.' She listened to rain spray against the window. A wind was getting up and the trees shook outside, flickering the lamps.

She finished her drink. 'I have to be going.'

She shook his hand, then he opened the door for her in such a way that she had to duck under his outstretched arm. She stepped into the corridor.

She said, 'I was a little overheated before. I apologize for that.'

'Already forgotten, Amanda. I'll be in touch.'

'I look forward to it.'

'Meantime, you'd be wise to get away for a while. The rest is under control.'

She went down the stairs, crossed the lobby and walked outside. She sat in her parked car and looked out at the night and realized she didn't like the dark. Rain drummed on the roof. She'd done her duty, she'd dropped the whole mess in somebody else's lap. At least it would make Rhees a happy man. She turned the key in the ignition just as Dansk came out of the hotel and walked in a sprightly way across the parking lot. He passed within twenty yards of her car, but his range of vision was limited by his big black umbrella, and he didn't see her.

For some reason she had an urge to follow him, but she resisted it.

28

In his own hotel room, Dansk undid his necktie and hung it just so in the closet. There was a knock on his door. He went to answer it. The girl was about nineteen and waiflike. She had big brown eyes and a tiny oval face.

'You're expecting me,' she said. 'Chaka? From Romantic Liaisons?'

'Yeah, come in, come in.'

She asked him what he wanted and he said, 'Nothing exotic.'

'You got it,' she said. She undressed in front of him, stepped out of her white miniskirt, slid down her tights and her black panties. She wore no bra: she didn't need one. She lay on the bed and he placed his hand on her taut belly. Navels intrigued him. A navel was like a tiny eye of flesh.

She smelled of talcum powder. Her armpits had been shaved. Her pubic hair had been razored also. Vaginal topiary. He'd once seen a hooker in El Paso with her pubes cut heart-shaped, like a furry valentine between her legs.

He took off his pants and folded them over a chair. Chaka was watching him and waiting, checking her internal meter. Tick, tick, time is money. He removed his shirt. She put her hand inside his yellow and white polka-dot shorts and stroked him for a while.

'I don't feel anything stirring in here,' she remarked.

A breakdown of the machinery was the last thing he needed. He wanted release, his valve opened, pressure let out. The girl propped herself on an elbow and looked at him.

'You wanna watch me jerk off, get you going?' she asked.

'Sure.' His head wasn't sending signals down to the central furnace. Boiler-room failure. What's going on here, he wondered.

She spread her legs and rubbed a finger in the slit of herself. Her nails were red. Her little mouth was open. Dansk could see her fillings way back and the dark cavity of her throat. And then suddenly he was out in that goddam desert and he was wondering how close Amanda Scholes had been to McTell and Pasquale and their hounds. She'd said a mile, maybe two. Some margins were way too narrow.

Easy, easy, Anthony.

The girl had her hand inside his shorts again. 'I guess my charms ain't doing it for you. For extra, I could blow you.'

Dansk didn't like putting his cock in anybody's mouth. He'd tried it but he'd felt uncomfortably vulnerable, thinking what would happen if the woman had a brainstorm during the act, or some form of feminist-bitch revenge agenda, and decided to bite a chunk out of his dick.

Suddenly he caught her hand and squeezed it. Her bones were tiny. He imagined he had a small delicate bird trapped in his closed palm and how simple it would be to crush it. Squeezy-oh and snap.

'Ow,' she said.

For a moment Dansk found himself contemplating the notion of pulverizing the hooker's small hand. He thought of the noise the bones would make as they broke, a bag of brittle little sticks. As a kid, he'd once shot a pigeon with an air rifle, and he remembered how it dropped off a ledge and lay broken-winged and bloody on the sidewalk, a sickly substance oozing out of the beak. That bird had been a long time dying, spasming on the ground. His mother had told him, *You don't kill God's creatures, Anthony.*

It's only a pigeon, billions of them in the world, and God cares about one?

His eye is on the sparrow, sweetpea.

'Hey, *hey*, you!' the girl said, tugging to be free of him.

He released the girl's hand. He felt lopsided. The zip of the air rifle, the pigeon falling, what had he experienced at the time? A little surge of power or some kind of regret, he couldn't target it now. A kid blowing a bird away for the hell of it, just because the boy had a weapon and the bird happened to be where it was at that particular moment in time. Things converge, eddies of pure chance, like Galindez in that goddam river. Some things you can't foresee.

The girl rubbed her knuckles and said, 'I bruise easy, mister.'

Dansk gave the girl fifty bucks, two twenties and a ten. She was still rubbing the hand he'd squeezed and giving him a wary stare. He had an urge to grab her again and this time press his fingernails into her veins until he'd drawn blood.

She dressed. She had it down to a quick-getaway art as a safeguard against loony clients. He turned aside from her. He listened to all the sounds she made, the snap of panty elastic, tights rolling over flesh like a second skin, the meshing of a zipper.

'You're a real dipshit, buster,' she said.

Dipshit. He had an image of Amanda Scholes's face, and he wondered if there was some bizarre connection between his failure with the hooker and the encounter with the lady prosecutor, a distraction on a level he hadn't been aware of. He thought of the Sanchez woman phoning. OK, so her state of mind was one of dislocation, but that wasn't the point. She might have been lucid. It was no way to run a business like this. You couldn't depend on luck. You had to shape your destiny.

He walked quickly across the room. The girl had the door halfway open. He kicked it shut. 'Dipshit, huh?' He realized he was breathing a little too hard. He gripped her shoulder. He could feel bone and imagined he heard her heart beat. Anger foamed through him. He wasn't thinking, he was listening to this tide and the persistent voices it carried.

'I'm a dipshit? That what you called me? A dipshit?'

She said, 'Don't fucking touch me, I warn you.'

The girl tried to shrug his hand away but his grip was too tight. Just do it. *Do it, Anthony.* He punched her in the mouth, slammed her against the wall, punched her again and her head snapped back, but somehow she managed to get her teeth round his wrist, nipping his flesh with her teeth. It was like the pain of catching your skin in a zipper. He pulled his arm away and grabbed her by the hips and spun her round, striking the side of her face with an open palm. She crumpled into a crouching position. He stared down at her and the tide receded in his brain and then there was hollow silence.

The girl looked up at him. Already there was a discolouration around her mouth. He made a slight motion of his hand and she flinched, pulling her head to one side.

He turned away from her, didn't look as she got to her feet and opened the door. He heard a quick intake of her breath, as if she were struggling against tears. He studied his hand. He thought, You move certain muscles and a hand becomes a fist, a weapon. You give in to an impulse and discipline dies inside you. A moment of rage.

And here's the kicker: *weirdly pleasant.*

He heard the door close. She could go to the cops, he thought, but she wouldn't, not in her profession.

The problem with rage is you can't focus it; it overflows, goes in all directions, you strike out at whoever's within range. But you don't need rage. Everything's under *control*. You were Mr Smooth. You set out your wares and the former prosecutor, a discerning customer, listens to your pitch, and before she knows it she's buying. She's buying your plastic, your whole story, and then she's homeward bound, carrying her stack of purchases from Honest Anthony's Bazaar. She's home safe with her lover, her worries alleviated, her concerns eased.

But . . .

You never really know. Other people are

mysteries, planets unto themselves. *I'm at a loose end right now*, she'd said. This bothered him. A bright woman, formerly very busy, with too much time on her hands. A little bored. She wouldn't be the type to sit around crocheting or inclined over a cookbook studying a recipe for fucking bouillabaisse. And you couldn't see her serving soup in some tent-town for the homeless roaches of the nation. So what does she do with her time?

Dansk's Law: You can never sit back and get complacent. Another person's life was alien territory and you needed to map and monitor it until you were absolutely certain. And if it came right down to it, you needed to bring pressures to bear.

He was a master at pressures.

He walked up and down the room for a time, turning possibilities round and round. She'll drop it, she won't drop it. His fingers were beginning to ache from the impact of his punches. It wasn't a bad sensation.

He picked up the phone and dialled the number for the decrepit motel in south Phoenix where McTell and Pasquale were staying. It was called the Hideaway Knolls, situated on a busy intersection with nothing remotely resembling a knoll in miles.

McTell answered, first ring.

Dansk said, 'She was in the desert, McTell. The prosecutor was in the goddam desert at exactly the same time as you and your dufus associate. Have you any idea how close you came to having an eye-witness? She heard the *dogs*, McTell.'

'She see us?' McTell asked.

'You got lucky. But that's not the point, the point is carelessness. The point is keeping your eyes and ears open and making absolutely goddam sure there's nobody around when you work.'

'How were we meant to know somebody was out there? It's a big dark fucking place, the desert.'

'You don't pay close attention, Eddie. You smell blood and everything else flies out the window – like the possibility of an eyewitness. I'm trying to run this business in a professional way. *Professional*, McTell. You know that word? You heard it before?'

McTell said, 'I don't unnerstand your beef, Anthony. If she didn't see us where's the hassle? It's history. I still say surgery's the answer.'

Dansk ignored this. 'I want you and Pasquale to meet me. There's a Denny's joint off the interstate on Thomas. You'll find it. Forty-five minutes.'

He hung up and stepped inside the bathroom. He wanted to shower. He wanted the good feeling that came when pressurized water tingled against your body and all the grime and germs you'd accumulated during the day went swirling in grey-white foam down through pipes and into the rancid labyrinthine dark of the sewers.

29

Amanda drove until she came to a cocktail bar about a mile from her house. She parked outside, thinking about Rhees, who'd be in bed reading some heavy academic tome through the little half-moon glasses that made him look ecclesiastical. She went inside the bar, which was deep in shadow. A few lonesome drinkers, a mulatto girl playing the piano and singing 'I've Got You Under My Skin' in a feathery little voice.

She asked for a gin and tonic, fidgeted with a coaster, rolling it round between her fingers. She looked around the room. A sign in one corner read, 'Rest rooms. Telephone.' She didn't move at once. This behaviour came firmly under the category of sneaky activity, but the idea of further disapprobation from John didn't enchant her.

She scanned the bar again: shadowy faces, strangers, the girl at the piano. She was thinking of Dansk's advice. *Take a vacation. Go far away.* She tried to imagine his investigation, but she had no idea what it involved, and this niggled her. She was beset by an incomplete feeling, like a Scrabble tile she couldn't use, a solitaire card that wasn't playable.

Go ahead, *satisfy yourself*. Cut off that troubling little hangnail of doubt you have. She walked in the direction of the telephone. She took from her jacket the sheet of paper Dansk had given her. She fed a coin into the slot and dialled the number.

A woman's voice came on the line and said, 'The Carlton. How may I help you?'

'Anthony Dansk,' she said.

'One moment please.'

Amanda listened to the ringing tone. Dansk answered, a little breathless.

'This is Amanda Scholes,' she said. 'I hope I didn't wake you.'

'I was just getting out the shower.' He sounded cheerful.

'I realized I didn't give you our phone number,' she said.

'I figured you'd be in the book.'

'We're in the Phoenix directory, but you might need the out-of-town number, which is unlisted.'

'You've decided to go away?' he asked.

'We have a cabin upstate.'

'Sounds nice. OK. Pencil's at the ready.'

She gave him the number. He said, 'Got it.'

'Don't forget me,' she said.

'No chance of that, Amanda.' He said good-night.

She hung up the phone, lingered, tapped her fingers on the directory. *No chance of that, Amanda.*

She picked up the handset again and hesitated, then she pushed a handful of coins into the slot. She imagined a twenty-four-hour hotline, an operator who would pick up. Instead, she received a recorded message uttered by a man who sounded as if he had severe laryngitis.

'Department of Justice. You have reached the office of Anthony Dansk. Mr Dansk isn't available to take your call at present. Kindly leave a message. Your call will be returned as soon as possible. There is no need to leave the date and time of your message because this is automatically recorded. Thank you.' She put the phone back. An answering machine with a croak in its throat. The office of Anthony Dansk. The recorded message in a voice that wasn't his.

She wondered about this all the way back to her car.

30

She was aware of sunlight against her closed eyelids and the sound of the doorbell ringing. She heard John get out of bed and leave the room. She drew a bedsheet round her face and tried to get back to sleep, but Rhees returned and said, 'You've got a visitor.'

She opened one eye. The sun was a slit of revolting light. 'Who?'

'Dom Concannon,' he said.

'What ungodly time is it?'

'Eight-forty.'

'What the hell does he want at eight-forty?'

'Who knows? I'll brew some coffee,' Rhees said.

Amanda sat up. She dragged herself slowly inside the bathroom, brushed her teeth, ran a comb through her hair, then decided she didn't need to look her best. It was only Concannon, after all. She entered the living room in her robe and blinked at Dom, whom she liked well enough except for the fact that he was always bright and switched-on, irritating if you'd only just awakened.

He was sitting on the sofa, long legs stretched out. 'Got you out of bed, eh?'

She said, 'Just don't do your stage Irish bit, promise me.'

'And here I was practising bejaysus.'

She sat down facing Concannon. He had a big frank face and untidy fair hair. His family had emigrated seventy years ago from Cork. He was an expert on the subject of Celtic religious artefacts. Like Rhees with his sporadic Welshness, Concannon was another herb in the American stockpot.

'Just tink of me as yer postman,' he said.

'You promised, Dom,' she said.

'It comes over me and I can't for the life of me stop. What can I say?'

'As little as possible would be considered a start,' she suggested.

Rhees came in from the kitchen with a jug of coffee and three cups on a tray. He set it down on the table and poured. Amanda sipped and waited for the brew to kick in.

'What's this postman business?' she asked.

Concannon took an envelope from the inside pocket of his jacket. 'This came for you care of the office. It looks like it's been in the wars.'

She looked at the creased brown envelope. Her eyesight was out of focus. 'You didn't come just to bring me this, did you?'

'I've been missing you around and the letter gave me a good excuse, and anyway I happened to be in the vicinity. So, how are you doing?'

'OK for a person whose sleep has just been rudely interrupted by a fake Irishman. Don't you have cases to try or something?'

'Matter of fact, yeah. There's this interesting little

thing I've got in court in a couple of hours. Some guy selling humongous parcels of Northern Arizona that aren't his to sell. Complicated fraud, involving misuse of the US mails. The guy says he's been framed by an associate. Same old, same old. Your friend Randy Hanseimer is defending.'

'Kick ass, Dom.' She took another mouthful of coffee and turned the envelope over in her hand. She still wasn't focusing properly. She made out her name scribbled in caps with a ballpoint. The stamp was stuck on upside down.

'Funny business about Galindez,' Concannon said. 'I thought he was protected. The whisper going round is you're worried about witness security.'

She said nothing. She wondered about whispers, leaves stirring on the old grapevine. Gaggles of attorneys gossiping in stairwells, feeding on this snippet of truth or that crumb of misinformation.

'I understand they don't tell you shit, those Witness Program guys,' he said. 'I haven't had a whole lotta experience of them, but from what I gather they run their business like Fort Knox.'

'Allegedly.'

Concannon drew his long legs back and rearranged his sprawl. 'If I can help, let me know. Because if there's a leak in the Program, it's bad news.' He finished his coffee and then stood up. Six feet four and legs like stalks. 'Gotta run. Nail another shithead to the cross of justice. Oh, before I forget, you had a phone call day before yesterday. Bernadette Vialli.'

'Bernadette Vialli?'

'A blast from the past,' Concannon said. 'Said she wanted to talk to you about something. I said

I'd have you call her.' He touched his forelock in an exaggerated way. 'Good luck to ye, me dear.'

She picked up a cushion to toss at him, but he'd already slipped out the door and was gone. She wondered a moment about Bernadette Vialli, whom she recalled as a small bespectacled widow with permed hair. She remembered her son, Benny, and the shy way he'd answered questions in the witness-stand. A pale downtrodden kid, he'd directed his gaze somewhere into mid-air, never once meeting the eyes of the two defendants who stared at him with brooding hatred. Both were blood relations, Uncle Charlie Ravanelli and Uncle Giovanni 'Ironhead' Luccini, a couple of funereal mob types who'd seen too many Mafia films and had copied all the moves and the mumblings. Not the brightest kid on the block, Benny had drifted into the old family businesses: extortion, narcotics, prostitution. He was the invisible nephew and nobody paid him much attention. Run here, run there, fetch, fetch, fetch. The eager gofer. But Benny had a memory that was almost photographic, and when his time came in court he was an encyclopedia of names and places, dates and conversations he could remember verbatim. A prosecutor's wet dream.

Rhees said, 'I didn't hear you come in last night.'

'I didn't want to wake you.'

'How was your undercover meeting?'

She briefly told him about the talk with Dansk.

'You're suitably reassured,' he said, 'so now we can get back to the pines?'

'Sure.'

'I'm not hearing absolute certainty,' he said, and gave her a doubtful look.

She gazed again at her name on the front of the

envelope and noticed the postmark. She raised her face towards Rhees and felt blood rush through her head, and when she ripped the envelope open it seemed to her that her hands were numb and not her own and a strange wind, like a cyclone twisting through a canyon, stormed in her ears.

31

Pasquale was parked across from the entrance to the cul-de-sac. He had a map spread against the steering wheel and he was frowning like a tourist who'd lost his way in the complexity of a strange city.

He raised his face and looked towards the cul-de-sac. Nothing moved there. Iffy kind of morning. Bright sun, then clouds, then sun again.

His phone buzzed. He picked it up and heard McTell say, 'Lavatory cleaner. That would be the worst job I could think of.'

This was a game they'd been playing back and forth. McTell was parked a couple of blocks away. They changed locations every so often in accordance with Dansk's instructions.

'It don't beat morgue beautician,' Pasquale remarked. 'Lipstick on corpses, eye-shadow on stiffs, rouge on dead cheeks.'

McTell said, 'Naw, that's kindergarten stuff. Picture this. You come into work and it's the early a.m., you got your brush and your bucket and your disinfectant, you don't know what you're gonna find in the cubicles: vomit, unflushed shit, diarrhoea, piss all over the floor, used condoms leaking, junkie needles. Hey, I just thought of something worse even. A lavatory cleaner with a big momma of a hangover.'

'Pretty gross,' Pasquale said.

'You come up with anything better than a lavatory cleaner with a hangover like death, you call me. What's happening where you are?'

Pasquale said, 'Nothing.'

'I hate this waiting shit. You get all tensed up because you don't know if you're gonna do the job or if you ain't gonna do it. Waiting makes me pissed. Dansk makes me pissed. He wants us to create this . . . what's he call it? A diversion? Create your own fucking diversions, Anthony. Shove them up your ass.'

'He pays good money, plus some nice bonuses. You don't have to like the guy.' Pasquale tore out a square section of his map and began to fold it.

'Sometimes all I ask is some credit,' McTell remarked. 'He treats you like crap. He has you running here, running there, up and down this whole fucking state. He don't give respect where it's due.'

'He likes to think he's perfect,' Pasquale said.

'Perfect my ass.'

'He picks up the tab,' Pasquale said. 'He calls the shots.'

'Oh sure, he *calls* the shots, all right, but we're the ones do the actual *shooting*, Bruno. You don't see Tony Birthmark out there. He's like somebody just dropped in from another planet. You ever see this whole deal he goes through every morning before coffee?'

'No,' Pasquale said, working the segment of map between his fingers. Then he studied the paper dart he'd made, adjusted it and propelled it through the open window. It caught a pocket of air and drifted in smooth flight for some way before nosediving into shrubbery. Kamikaze.

McTell said, 'Check this, it's unreal. First, he flosses with mint-flavoured, wax-coated floss made in Holland or somewhere. Second, he has this Turkish or Indian wooden tongue-scraper that takes all the overnight shit off your tongue. Next, brushes his teeth with Sensodyne. Always Sensodyne. Then he rinses with this stuff, Per something, Peridex, I ain't sure. You'd think that would cover the oral hygiene, right? Uh-uh, there's more. He rounds things off with a salt-water gargle. Always bottled water, never straight outta the faucet, and always sea-salt. He carries round this little salt-shaker kinda thing. I wouldn't wanna be bacteria wandering loose inside Dansk's mouth. It'd be like a holocaust. And I haven't even started on the hair tonic and the whole shaving ritual and the stuff with the fingernails and the hundred quick press-ups.'

'It's what I said, Eddie. Perfectionist.'

'That's one way of putting it,' said McTell.

32

Amanda smoothed the pages and gazed out into the backyard without seeing anything in particular, the long grass, the swimming pool, the young grapefruit trees whose waxy leaves played tricks with the light. What she kept hearing was Isabel's voice, the way it issued from two pages of cheap notepaper.

She lit a cigarette and said to Rhees, 'I know it's too damned early but I need a drink.' She rose from the table, went to the liquor cabinet, poured a shot of brandy, sniffed the fumes and drank.

Rhees was bent over the letter, studying it the way he might study the long-lost first draft of a major poem. She wondered what he saw in it, if he was trying to read between the lines. She thought of the misspelled words, the lack of punctuation and the spidery, back-slanting letters and the curious alignments and how they reflected Isabel Sanchez's state of mind.

She finished the brandy. She'd read the letter again, for the forty-second time, it seemed. She wasn't counting. She walked back to the table. The brandy made a fiery lasso round her heart.

Manda, I hope this gets to you, they're behind me, two guys take me in this big kinda van
and Galindez is there also and this surprises me – I don't expect to be traveling noplace with him, he don't like me.
he sits up front with one guy and Im in the back with the other and this guy tells me how Im gonna like my new life
Galindez keeps saying he wishes hed kept his big mouth shut, so then it gets dark and we're drivin and then the bad shit happens – the van comes to a stop Galindez jumps out and the two guys go after him and
theres gunshots and Im scared and I think the best thing is for me to get the hell away before the two guys come back.
I get outta the van and I hear one of the guys say stoopid mother-fucker and the other says what we gonna do with conchita now.
I move real quiet into the trees.
I hear one of them calling out conchita where are you and I dont move, I dont know how long I lay still.
then here comes a truck and the driver gives me a ride so I end up in this place Gallup.

Amanda stopped reading and glanced at Rhees. He was standing framed in the window, watching her with his head inclined slightly to one side. She picked up the letter and stepped through the kitchen and out into the backyard. Rhees followed her. They walked together to the swimming pool. On the tiled bottom lay the corpse of a chlorinated frog, crouched and white. Clouds, stacked round the morning sun, were like smoke from a crematorium.

She spread the letter in her lap. She didn't want to read it again.

> then I get another ride to farmington – I phone the number you give me only nobody answers and I try the other number and there's a man answers
>
> and I think maybe I better head back to phoenix and get to you.
>
> I steel this car outside a store then I see the two guys again.
>
> I drive fast as I can but theyre behind me all the time except when I lose them near this park where Im writing
>
> and then I see the guys again and this time its outside Tuba city.

Amanda folded the pages. 'I can imagine her driving around in this stolen car, remembering all the promises I made . . .' She felt cold, like the edges of flu. The ice was in her bones and travelling. She gazed at the walls that bounded the yard and she thought, They wouldn't keep anyone out, anyone determined enough to come after her. She imagined shapes in the shrubbery.

She said, 'Galindez decides he doesn't want to participate, so he steps out of the van. The two escorts chase him and gun him down, and he's swept away in the river. Why didn't they just let him go? It's his decision. It's *his* choice. Why kill him?'

Rhees said, 'And because Isabel is a witness . . . what? She has to be killed too?'

'But why shoot Galindez in the *first* place? These guys are US Marshals, for Christ's sake. They're supposed to protect witnesses and whisk them off to a bright new life, not kill them.'

Rhees sat beside her and said, 'It's obvious they're not Marshals. They carry fake documents and ID good enough to convince anybody that they're charged with taking witnesses into protective custody, when in reality they're people Sanchez has hired.'

Cloud and sun, air heavy and lifeless. Amanda said, 'Why would Sanchez's people go through a charade like this? And why drive up into the boonies of Arizona? His hit men would do the job the first secluded place they came to.'

What we gonna do with conchita? The sun was sucked again behind clouds. The day was intermittent dark and light. She thought about Sanchez. She remembered the strength of his body and the touch of his fingers against her mouth and the smell of toothpaste and bad things coming in threes. How the hell did he get access to the Program? Who did he pay?

'You're trembling,' Rhees said.

'I know. Maybe a bug.'

'Let's go back indoors.'

Inside, she poured another shot of brandy. Booze on an empty stomach, like lighting a fuse. She needed a mega-infusion of vitamins and supplements, protein-shakes and immune-system boosters.

'Call Dansk,' Rhees said. 'Give him the letter, let him deal with it. Let's get the hell out of here and back to the cabin.'

The cabin, right. She was picturing Sanchez in his cell. People from Justice come to interrogate him, Dansk among them. They probe him long and hard. He doesn't have to tell them a goddam thing. He's a dead man, he can say whatever the hell he likes. Go fuck yourselves, he tells them. And maybe Dansk asks something like *Was your threat against Amanda Scholes serious*? And Sanchez just says *Eat shit* and smiles with contempt.

Rhees said, 'Call Dansk, give him the letter.' He picked up the telephone and held the receiver towards her.

She didn't take it from his hand.

'Call him, for God's sake. Arrange to deliver the letter. It's outside your domain. It belongs in the hands of the proper authority.'

Dansk. The proper authority. But Dansk was a stranger. He hadn't spent hours in Isabel's company the way she'd done, hadn't listened to the brutal story of her marriage to Sanchez, hadn't sat up at all hours comforting her, gently prompting her memory, sometimes embracing her while she cried tears of rage and fear.

She's still mine. She's still my business.

Rhees continued to hold the phone towards her.

She turned away. She walked inside the bathroom and shut the door. She pulled on jeans and a T-shirt and stuck Isabel's letter in her hip pocket, swallowed a handful of capsules and tablets, catching the acrid scent of brewer's yeast. Gimme strength. Help me think. She ran a brush through her hair. *What we gonna do with conchita now?* Kill her, what else?

Kill Conchita.

Rhees was waiting for her when she came out

of the bathroom. 'Where do you think you're going?'

'I need my sneakers,' and she edged past him. She found the sneakers, put them on and tied the laces. 'I have to go out for a while, there's something I want to check. I won't be long.'

'Let Dansk do the fucking checking. That's what he's here for. What is it with you? What is this need to fly solo?'

She headed for the front door. She was already stepping into the car when she saw Rhees appear in the driveway. She backed out. He had a hand raised in the air, a gesture that meant stop, but she didn't.

She thought, John, try and understand me. You don't belong in my world. She wasn't even sure she belonged in it herself any more. She wasn't sure if she still had the maps to it, if she understood the grids and interstices, or if she was rushing back in the direction of the same head-numbing sickness that had almost engulfed her before.

She drove out of the cul-de-sac, thinking about the last words of Isabel's letter.

you know sumtin?
this protection thing
it just dont work

33

Dansk, in baseball cap and dark shades, picked up his cellular phone on the first ring and heard Pasquale say, 'She just left.'

Dansk said, 'I'll be in touch.'

He was parked outside a Taco Bell. He waited until the red VW appeared, then slid out of the parking lot and cruised into traffic behind Amanda. The vehicle he drove was an anonymous Buick he'd picked up an hour ago from Budget. He believed in changing cars frequently as a matter of general strategy. He always went for mid-size cars in boring greys or dark blues with unmemorable wheels.

Headlines formed in his brain. FORMER PROSECUTOR KILLED IN FREAK ACCIDENT. You couldn't just bribe a crane operator to drop a six-ton slab of concrete on somebody's car. Here's a suggestion for you, lady: why don't you just drive across this construction site and under the crane with the big slab on the hook?

Then he thought, EX-PROSECUTOR DISAPPEARS LEAVING MYSTERIOUS NOTE. *I'm going away, I can't take it any more, forgive me*. But Amanda Scholes wasn't the kind who disappeared.

She was heading towards central Phoenix, high-rises in the distance, craggy brown peaks beyond. Please be doing something perfectly normal; going to the bank, the supermarket, picking up your dry-cleaning. Your everyday activities.

He was still pondering the fact that she'd called his hotel late last night, ostensibly to give him a phone number, but in reality *checking up* on him, which told you something about the way her mind worked. And he was still thinking about her trip to see Sanchez. She picked at fabrics just to see if they'd unravel. Pick, pick, pick.

Oh, lady. Let it be.

Downtown, clouds had lifted, traffic was snarled, drivers hung their shirtsleeved arms out of windows. Cigarettes were smoked, fingers tapped on side-panels. He could see her VW half a block away, stuck like he was. He took off the baseball cap. It was making his scalp itch.

Traffic moved again. The VW made a right turn. Dansk, six cars behind, followed. He wished he had a mask to filter out the fumes that hung in the air.

Amanda had found a parking space and was backing into it. Dansk drove past, reached a busy intersection, made an illegal U-turn and drove back past the VW.

Now Amanda was moving along the sidewalk. She ran a hand through her hair and Dansk thought, Rhees ought to give her a fine brush and comb for Christmas. Silver hair-clasps and a partridge in a pear tree.

He had to find a place to leave the Buick. He entered an alley clogged with cars, then he turned left and slipped the car into a metered space between a U-Haul truck and a busted-up old AMC Pacer with Nevada plates. He locked the Buick. Amanda was about fifty or sixty yards away. She wasn't looking his way. She wasn't looking at anything in particular. She was focused inward. She was dressed in jeans, white shirt and bleached-out sneakers.

In the French restaurant she'd looked smart and alive and attractive. She had the kind of sexiness that comes with maturity. A woman who knew all the points of the compass on her lover's body. Dansk wondered what she'd been like at seventeen and if he might have lusted after her. Probably.

No, *definitely*. Fucking the younger Amanda. Burying your face between her breasts and her hard darkened nipples in your mouth. Your cock inside her, and yeah, she's coming, she's coming in a noisy way, and you're beginning to feel your own derrick crank, and the geyser is rushing from deep inside you, and she's digging her fingernails into your spine and you can't get your tongue *deep enough* inside her mouth. You want it all, you want to consume her, your tongue all the way down inside her womb, and she's saying, oh oh oh, Anthony, oh, Anthony, and her whole body starts trembling and it's oh ah, God, oh, Anthony, Anthoneee, *do me, do me, do, don't stop, fuck my brains out*.

He could see all this. Smell it.

Slow down, Anthony. The key is detachment.

She paused on the sidewalk, reached inside her hip pocket and removed a couple of sheets of paper. Something in the way she held them struck him as interesting. Tight, possessive, as if they were important to her. From this distance, they looked like nothing more than some sheets ripped from a notebook. Maybe they were insignificant, a shopping list, say, reminders she'd written for herself. Things to do. But why clutch them like they were the secret key to a dead language?

Then one of the sheets slid suddenly from her fingers and a very faint breeze fluttered it along the sidewalk. She reached down quickly to pick it up, but the breeze tugged it beyond her and she went after it with a slight panicky movement, pushing her way forcefully past pedestrians, then trapping it beneath the sole of her foot. When she lifted the foot the paper blew away again, this time coming to rest under a parked car. She went on her knees, groped around, retrieved it, and in a crouching position smoothed the sheet against her thigh. She had an expression of relief on her face, a little half-smile.

She remained motionless for a few seconds, as if she were trying to reach a decision. Which she apparently did, because she folded the sheets and stuck them back in her hip pocket and then continued to walk.

The way she'd gone down on her knees to pick up the fallen sheet intrigued him. Whatever the papers were, you could dismiss the idea of shopping lists. Something else, something important to her.

She reached the Federal Building and went inside.

The Federal Building. Well, well. He loitered among pedestrians.

A mime approached, white-faced, a yellow helium balloon attached to a string in his gloved hand. He eyed Dansk a second, then changed direction abruptly and wandered away. Dansk had a serious contempt for these pests. Their plastic flowers that squirted water, the way they pretended they were walking against a storm. There ought to be a law against these assholes, and while you're at it another against former prosecutors who couldn't mind their own goddam business.

34

Lew Bascombe was crossing the lobby towards the elevators. Amanda called out his name and he turned.

'The bad penny again,' he said.

'Thanks for arranging the meeting,' she said.

'I trust it was fruitful,' Bascombe said.

'It was fine.'

'Does that mean I can look forward to some peace?'

She laid a hand on his arm. 'One last question, Lew.'

She looked across the lobby. Federal workers went back and forth carrying files and briefcases. An armed guard at the metal detector was quietly whistling 'Danny Boy'.

She said, 'You told me before that you'd passed Isabel Sanchez and Reuben Galindez along to agents from the Program. Right?'

Bascombe nodded his head in a tired way.

'US Marshals, right?'

'No,' Bascombe said. 'SS storm troopers.'

She wasn't in the mood. 'How many Marshals?'

'That's three questions, Amanda. I'm counting. You said you had one.'

'Please, Lew.'

Bascombe said, 'How many Marshals. I can't answer that.'

'But they showed you ID?'

'Amanda, what the hell is your problem? You blackmail me into fixing you up with a meeting with a Program official, which I do. Why didn't you ask him any questions you had?'

'I'm asking you, Lew.'

Bascombe drew her to one side, away from the elevator doors. 'This has got to stop, Amanda.'

'What did they show you, Lew?'

'They have a docket, stamped and authorized. I check the docket against a duplicate supplied to me by Arlington. If it matches, that's good enough.'

'They could be fake papers,' she said.

'I wish I had some kind of stuff in a canister I could spray on you. Send you into a temporary coma. As it is, I have half a mind to get the security people to toss you out on the street.' Bascombe pressed the call button.

Amanda said, 'The whole system sounds porous to me.'

Bascombe shook his head. 'The dockets have to match exactly. There's also a one-off code-number for each case, which is highly confidential. These are the safeguards.'

'OK. They show you papers. Do you accompany the Marshals when they pick up the witnesses, Lew? Make sure it all goes smoothly?'

'The logistics change from case to case, for security reasons. I'm not getting into that area, Amanda.'

She stared at Bascombe. The rug on his skull looked a little maladjusted today.

'Tell me one thing, Lew. Are you straight?'

'Straight?'

'Or are you crooked?'

'I don't think I follow,' Bascombe said.

You don't have the face and your hair's wrong too, she thought. You are what you are, a pencil-pusher with a house in the suburbs and two point something kids.

'Forget I ever asked, Lew,' she said.

Bascombe said, 'Now watch, Amanda. See me step inside this elevator. Imagine me rising to my tiny chamber upstairs where I like to be left alone. Got the picture?' He entered the elevator and the doors slid shut.

She turned and walked out of the building and back into the sunny street. She strolled through the crowds. She had a sense of being a cork afloat on an unpredictable tide. She felt the sun on her face and cold in her bones and indecision in her heart.

She moved across the street. She walked to the next intersection where she paused outside a drugstore. She patted her hip pocket, as if to reassure herself that Isabel's letter was still there.

Give it to Dansk. Take it to him now. You're wasting your time, burning up energy. She removed the two sheets, thinking how flimsy they were, feeling the cheapness of the paper, then she stuck them back inside the pocket and walked to a pay phone. She called the Phoenix PD and asked for Willie Drumm. She'd discuss the letter with Willie. He'd know what to do. He'd advise her.

She was informed that he was out of the office. Call back again in an hour or so. She hung up.

She stepped out of the phone booth and the glass door swung and trapped in reflection the face of a man several yards along the sidewalk, and for a moment she wasn't sure if she should turn and walk away. Then she thought, What the hell.

35

Dansk, stunned when he saw her step out of the phone booth and move towards him, squeezed out a smile.

'Amanda,' he said, 'this is a surprise.'

He was furious with the way he'd allowed himself to be bushwhacked. Your concentration slips a second and suddenly you're on the defensive, only you can't show it, you have to work to keep it out of your expression *and* your tone of voice, and this effort *grinds* inside your head.

'I had some business downtown,' he said. 'You too?'

'Nothing serious,' she answered. 'A chore, that's all.'

Nothing serious, he thought, just a trip to the Federal Building. 'You got time for a coffee?'

'Too busy with this and that. Sorry.'

'You were meant to be smelling the flowers, Amanda.'

'I'm getting round to it.'

Dansk took off his shades. 'You have to catch

them at the right time. Summer goes and before you know it, it's Fall.'

'Then it's dark old winter,' she said.

Dark old winter. You got it, lady. 'I had the impression you were going off to that cabin you mentioned.'

'Are you in some kind of hurry to see me leave by any chance, Anthony?' she asked.

'Hurry?' Don't push this, he thought. She's smart enough to sense any urgency in you. 'I just thought you were heading out of town, that's all.'

'I'll go tonight probably,' she said. 'Tomorrow morning at the latest. Have you been to see Sanchez yet?'

'I'm expecting a report any moment.'

'You're not interviewing him yourself?'

'Somebody else does that.'

'You don't do interviews,' she said. 'You don't have the knack for knowing when somebody's bull-shitting you.'

'No, I'm not saying I don't have the knack. It's just the way it works. Division of labour.'

She moved a few yards down the sidewalk and Dansk went along with her. 'How did you get into this line of work anyway, Anthony?' she asked.

'Through various channels,' he said.

'You're a load of information.'

'It's a habit.'

'Secrecy, you mean.'

'It's a lifestyle you get used to.'

'Some might say it's a strange lifestyle, Anthony.'

Dansk said, 'It's not what you'd call a sociable occupation. It's not the kind of thing where you have office Christmas parties and company barbecues.'

'Sounds quite lonely,' she said.

He hadn't meant to give an impression of loneliness. He hadn't meant to reveal anything of himself.

'The work has compensations,' he said. 'I'm doing some good.'

'Something for society.'

'We provide a service. We work in the shadows so people like yourself can put criminals where they belong. I believe in my work.'

'I don't doubt it, Anthony. You have a purposeful air about you.'

She looked directly at him. He understood he was being assessed somehow. He didn't like the frankness in her gaze. For a second he had the impression years had been stripped from her face and he was seeing her as she might have been in her early twenties, cheekbones less well-fleshed, an absence of those tiny lines around the corners of her grey-blue eyes, the eyes themselves bright with the future.

He glanced away, then looked back at her, but she'd shifted the angle of her head and the impression of youthfulness had left her and he experienced a certain relief. She flicked a lock of hair from her forehead and he realized he wanted to do this for her and clenched his hand and held it against his leg. Touching the lady prosecutor. Fixing her hair. Don't start *liking* the woman. Don't get drawn in. OK, you had one of those wayward sexual fantasies before, which meant zero, just random discharges of the imagination. Don't even think in terms of her being a woman, she's the subject of your scrutiny, that's it. She's what you're working on. This is your job. This is what you do with your fucking life, Anthony.

She slipped her hand inside her hip pocket. He thought about the papers she'd treated so preciously. He needed a pickpocket, a deft hand in Amanda's jeans. He needed to see these papers.

She asked, 'Do you ever lose people?'

'Lose people?' Dansk weighed the question. He had the feeling she was asking something completely different. 'You mean, do they ever stray?'

'Maybe,' she said.

'A few. They miss their old hang-outs. They wander off. Not often.'

'Are there stats available? How many people have walked away, for instance. What percentage stays with the Program. It would be interesting to look at the figures.'

Dansk said, 'Information like that would be confidential, Amanda.'

'Confidential. Of course.'

He looked at her. *Do you ever lose people?* It was more than simple fishing. Her question was a radar scan of deep waters, a probe for undersea life-forms. She was somehow different today than she'd been during the meeting at the Biltmore, only he couldn't quite figure it. She seemed more confident, self-assured. He wondered why. Maybe she'd stumbled on something by chance. *She knows something*. No way. What could she have found out anyway? There was nothing to find out. This whole thing was watertight, chained and padlocked.

Still.

His attention was drawn to a woman with a small rodent-like dog on a leash. The dog squatted, deposited excrement on the sidewalk, then shook its ass and strutted on.

Dansk stared at the little pile of shit and said,

'Goddam, I *detest* that. People let their dogs mess the sidewalks and just walk away. Morons throw beer cans from cars and pick-up trucks. The freeways are filthy. You find furniture just lying around outside houses. Mattresses, old refrigerators, beds, clothes, abandoned shopping carts. You have to wonder what kind of mentality is at work and why people can't keep the environment clean—'

Stop here, Anthony. Don't take this any further. Quit at this stage.

'This really gets to you,' she said. She looked at him with a little element of surprise.

'Goddam right it gets to me. Doesn't it bother you?'

'Yeah, but I can't honestly say I've given it as much thought as I should, Anthony.'

Dansk took a deep breath. Calm was the important factor here. He was supposed to be *detached*, not the kind of guy who'd get worked up over dog poop. Not that kind of guy at all.

In more measured speech, he said, 'That's just it; nobody thinks any more. They dispose of stuff but they don't do it properly, and somebody else has to come along and clean it up. The seas are filled with chemicals, rivers are poisoned. The air. Everywhere you look there's graffiti.' He ran the back of his hand across his lips.

'You're a tidy freak,' she said. 'You dispose of your own garbage in an orderly way, do you?'

'I try,' he said. 'I don't know about being a tidy freak.' Freak was a word he didn't like. Freak rubbed him all the wrong ways.

'Is this some kind of parable, Anthony?' she asked. 'You complain about litter and pollution, but really you're talking about something else.'

'I was talking strictly about trash.' He laughed. He heard a weird strain in the sound.

She glanced at him. 'Frankly, I'm more interested in other kinds of disposal: Galindez. Isabel.'

The way she said *disposal* – she gave it sly layers of meaning. She looked in a store window. A thousand kinds of old-fashioned candies in jars, stripes and swirls and a sense of rainbows trapped in bottles. She said, 'Fudge, look, butterscotch fudge.'

She entered the store and Dansk followed. The air was heavy with vanilla and cinnamon. Dansk studied an array of lollipops and liquorice laces and jaw-breakers. He was brutalized by scarlets and greens and screaming yellows. He'd never had a sweet tooth, and this kind of place made him feel as if silver foil had been placed directly against a metal filling.

Amanda bought a bag of butterscotch fudge. She popped a piece in her mouth before they were even back on the street.

'Want one?' she asked.

'No thanks.'

'Butterscotch fudge is my secret weakness,' she said. There was a bulge in her cheek. 'Do you have one, Anthony?'

'You mean a secret weakness? I don't think so.'

'Let me guess,' she said. 'Your secret weakness is so secret you don't even know what it is.'

Dansk smiled. She's playing with me. She's going too far. He thought, My finger's on the button.

'We were talking about your investigation,' she said.

'Right, we were.'

'This anticipated report concerning Sanchez may tell you nothing.'

'You never know.'

'And then what? Back to HQ?'

Dansk nodded. 'Right.'

'Back to your internal investigation. And when you learn something, I get to hear about it.'

'That's still the deal, Amanda. We shook hands on it.'

'Right, we did.'

'Call me old-fashioned, but a handshake means something to me,' he said.

'And to me, Anthony.' She rattled the paper bag containing the fudge. 'My secret weakness is really pretty tame when you think of what I could get up to.'

'What could you get up to, Amanda?' he asked.

'Oh, mischief, I guess.'

He looked at the slender little chain she wore round her neck and visualized twisting it until her eyes popped and her tongue hung out and that was the end of her. Then he imagined burying her alive. Soil falling on her face and darkness coming down on her, her hands upraised against the relentless rain of dirt. How she'd scream until her mouth filled up with earth and sand, and nothing to mark the grave, nothing to say, 'Here Lies The Lady Prosecutor'. Then he thought of her catching fire, burning. He imagined the air filled with cinders. *I have power over you, lady. I can fuck with your life like you wouldn't believe.*

They strolled until they came to an intersection. Dansk had a feeling of ropes tightly knotted inside his skull. *You're keeping me stuck in this burg when I have other places to go, other business elsewhere. I can't spread myself thin like this, lady.*

She said, 'My car's over there. This is where we part company.'

'I guess so.'

She shook the bag of fudge again. 'Sure you won't try one? Last offer.'

'You're persistent.'

'Oh very,' she said.

She opened the bag and he dipped a hand inside and came out with a crumbling brown cube, which he placed on his tongue as if it were nuclear waste. She smiled and walked to her car, and as soon as her back was turned he spat the candy from his mouth.

She drove past him and honked the horn twice and waved. He waved back. The sickly flavour of the fudge adhered to the back of his throat like sweetened chalk. He watched the VW disappear round a corner.

He went back to his car and sat behind the wheel. There were tracer bullets screaming in his head. His brain was a war zone. Trenches, casualties, men rushing with stretchers, the rumble of cannon, the dead littering the field of battle.

Mischief, he thought. I'll show you some genuine fucking mischief, toots. You have Anthony Dansk's personal guarantee. He had an image of his hand hovering over a control panel, lights blinking, his index finger poised, the pull of Amanda's gravity drawing his fingertip down and down to its destination.

One touch. Smithereens.

He phoned McTell.

36

She dialled Drumm's number from a pay phone at a filling-station. He was still unavailable. She left a message to say she'd called, then decided to phone Rhees. She watched traffic slide past and wondered if Anthony Dansk was nearby, if he'd really followed her downtown and seen her going inside the Federal Building, if he was following her still. Watching her moves. *You were meant to be smelling the flowers, Amanda.*

She'd surprised him when she'd popped out of the phone booth. He'd made a big effort to seem unflustered, but he'd reacted like a man caught in an act of voyeurism, an eavesdropper surprised behind a door, a whole flurry of give-aways: scratching his birthmark, nibbling the tip of his pinky. And then out of the blue the whammy, the bizarre diatribe against litter, white flecks at the corners of his lips.

A dog craps on a sidewalk and Dansk reacts badly. A neatness freak. Captain Hygiene. The thing that bothered her was the voltage in his eyes as he spoke. It was a zealot's intense stare, unblinking and focused on some remote place only he could see. The eyes had become hard bright emerald stones, and spooky. He meant what he said. He was a man who'd gone up the mountain and come down with a big-time revelation. Keep America clean.

No, it was more than that, more than litter and graffiti and shopping carts left all over the place. She had a low allegory threshold in general, but it seemed to her that he was saying, in his own roundabout way, something about the condition of the country. What? The heart of the nation was trashed? As a people, Americans had drifted too far towards a disregard of law and order, as evidenced by their tendency to litter the streets and let their pets shit anywhere they liked?

She wasn't sure, but his sudden outburst had made her uneasy, more than uneasy. There was clearly a very strange and worrisome compartment in Dansk's head, and for a moment she felt an odd sense of vulnerability, as if inside the phone booth she presented a clear target for a sniper nearby, her skull in somebody's scope, a nicotined finger on a delicate trigger. She looked across the street. The stucco building opposite was an office block, four storeys, blinds in windows, a solitary date palm outside. She gazed up at the roof, thinking, This is absurd. Dansk might be more than a little weird and scary, but he is an agent from the Justice Department, he is supposedly on your side . . .

And yet. She felt pressured by menace.

Rhees answered the phone.

She said, 'It's me.'

Rhees was quiet for a time. 'Where are you?'

'Glendale Avenue,' she answered.

'You're on your way back, I hope.' He sounded sullen.

'I didn't mean to rush out like that, John.'

Rhees said, 'You never *mean* to rush, Amanda.'

'I'm sorry,' she said.

'Now I'm hearing the contrite bit,' he said.

'OK, I'm contrite.'

'And furtive. I hate furtive.'

She felt a tense band across her forehead. 'Truce?'

'You can't just say that word and think it makes everything peachy. Have you contacted Dansk?'

'I saw him.'

'Tell me you gave him the goddam letter, Amanda. That's all I want to hear.'

'I think he's been following me, John.'

'*Following* you?'

'Watching me.'

'Why would he do that?'

'He wants to make sure I leave town. He doesn't want me hanging round. I also get the strong feeling he's a carrot short of a coleslaw.'

'So he's following you. He's watching you.'

'That's a gut instinct, I can't be sure—'

'But you're saying you don't trust him.'

She answered quickly. 'Yeah. I don't trust him.'

'You don't trust him to be honest with you? Or you don't trust him period?'

'Period,' she said.

'Why don't you just come home and we'll discuss all this face to face. Meantime, I'm still waiting to hear about the letter, which you managed to side-step quite neatly.'

She was quiet a moment. 'It's in my pocket,' she said. 'I'd like to discuss it with Willie before I do anything else.'

'Drumm, Dansk, I really don't give a shit who you give it to just as long as you get it out of our *lives*.'

He hung up. He'd never done that before. He'd never once just hung up on her in all six years of their relationship. She stuck the handset back. She felt slightly fragmented, as if some mild explosion had occurred inside the phone booth.

She stepped out and the hot sun zapped her and she suddenly remembered she was supposed to return Bernadette Vialli's call. She went back to the pay phone, searched through the tattered directory and called the number. There was no answer.

She walked to her car, drove a little way, checking her rear-view mirror, wondering how she could tell if she was being tracked through the stream of traffic. She steered into the parking lot of a shopping plaza, killed the engine and then she sat for a time, staring through the windshield and watching traffic come and go. So many cars, so many people, all movement eventually fusing together in one unbroken sunlit glow that after a time became surreal.

Her thoughts drifted to Sanchez, to the threat she could hear echo and roll inside her. She thought of shadows and stalkers, the possibility of harm lurking behind the glare of light.

Dansk.

Or somebody else, somebody hired by Sanchez.

How could you *possibly* know if anyone was following you through this crazy bright urban nightmare? And by the same token, how could you know the plastic Dansk had flashed at you was genuine issue? What evidence did you *really* have that he was who he claimed to be?

None.

37

Rhees was killing time fishing detritus from the pool – dead butterflies, limp insects, leaves – when the telephone rang inside the house. He laid the net on the ground and walked into the kitchen. He half-expected to hear Amanda again, but it was Morgan Scholes on the line.

'Is she around?'

'Not at the moment,' Rhees said. He looked across the backyard at the cedar fence. Water reflected by sunlight rippled against the wood, a dappled effect. A few yards down the alley beyond the fence a telephone lineman in a white hard hat was climbing down from a ladder propped against a pole. He vanished out of sight and Rhees heard doors slam and the sound of a van start up.

'You there, John?' Scholes asked.

'I'm here.'

'I call her, she says she'll get back to me, I don't hear a goddam thing.'

Rhees said, 'She's running an errand, Morgan.'

'Don't tell me. It's this stiff in the river business she's got herself into, right?'

'You know what she's like,' Rhees said.

'The back of my hand,' Morgan Scholes said. 'You're too soft on her, John. Who's in charge there anyway? You or her?'

Rhees said, 'We're equal partners,' and wondered how true that was. Sometimes he thought of Amanda in terms of a storm, a river suddenly flooding. His role was to stack sandbags along the banks and wait for the waters to recede.

'Equal, I don't think. She has you by the short and curlies.'

'That's not true, Morgan.'

'I blame myself. I gave her too much freedom when she was a kid and what good has that done? I should have laid down the law more.'

Rhees glanced at the kitchen clock. Half an hour had passed since he'd hung up on her. Maybe she was sulking somewhere, taking her time coming home, trying his patience.

'I don't think this has to do with you giving her too much freedom, Morgan,' he said.

'No?'

'One minute she wants the cabin and peace,' Rhees said, 'the next she's not sure it's inactivity she's really after. She's always had goals in the past. Now . . . I guess it's a question of redefining herself, which isn't easy for her.'

Morgan Scholes said, 'She's old enough to make up her mind, John, and you ought to tell her that.'

Rhees said, 'I'm trying.'

'Get her to phone me when she comes in.'

Rhees said he'd pass along the message.

He hung up, wandered through the house, room

to room, restless. In the bathroom he looked inside the medicine cabinet. He had an urge to gather together Amanda's vitamin supplements and immune-system boosters and just dump all that quackery in the trash. He studied the labels: dried seaweed, powder derived from a green-lipped mussel, whatever the hell that was. He imagined plants and creatures fished out of the deep sea, ground down and then stuffed into capsules.

There were a couple of prescription medications: Diazepam, Dalmane. Downers she'd used during the Sanchez trial when she'd needed to sleep, when she was fraught and wound too tight, and it was three a.m. and she was collating material or studying Isabel Sanchez's testimony, or poring over transcripts of her interviews with Galindez. When she was fraying at the edges.

And now, now she'd said Dansk was following her. Her gut feeling, she'd said. She usually had good instincts, but this time he had to wonder if she was interpreting the signals accurately, or if she was creating her own little melodrama because of Isabel.

A touch of paranoia? Possibly.

He shut the cabinet. He listened to the silences of the house. He wished she'd come through the front door and he could hold her and say something like, I'm sorry I hung up on you, let's talk. Let's clear the air about everything.

He walked into the kitchen. The door to the backyard was open. He thought he'd closed it. No, he *remembered* closing it to keep the cold air from the air-conditioning escaping—

He saw the tyre-iron but couldn't move out the way before it smashed into his ribs with an impact that forced all air out of his lungs, and he staggered, clutching the area of pain, aware of light being sucked out of the room, and he had the sensation of plummeting down a greased cylinder. The second blow struck the side of his head and the sense of slipping inside a darkening tube was even stronger now, and he gave up trying to keep his balance and went down on his hands and knees.

He raised his face. He made an effort to get up by clutching the edge of the table, and that was when the third blow was launched, sharp and dreadful, metal coming down so hard on his left hand that he could hear the sound of his finger-bones breaking. He slumped and the room was like one of those deranged rides at a carnival when you went spinning round and round in the air and the spectators far below you were just a sea of faces in white light. He rolled over on his back and dimly saw two guys wearing ski masks. He launched a foot, the best effort he could make, and struck one of the guys in the groin.

'You mother*fucker*,' the guy said.

The tyre-iron cracked against the back of his knee and he was dragged across the kitchen floor and out into the yard towards the swimming pool where his head was forced underwater and held there, and all he could see were pale red bubbles rising from his mouth. Drowned, he was being drowned. He wanted to scream, but then his head was yanked up from the water and the sunlight was blistering against his eyes and he was whacked again, this time across the shoulders. And then his face was forced underwater a second time, or maybe a third, he couldn't count, he was beyond making elementary measurements. Now the pain came roaring through him, gathering strength, but that was only the first stage, because after that he found himself entering a place of pain beyond pain, where a deep burgundy tide hurried into his brain.

38

Amanda drove into the cul-de-sac. She saw nothing out of the ordinary. There was no sight of Dansk or anyone else, no car behind her. She parked in the driveway.

OK. Time to get practical. Go inside the house and call the Justice Department in Washington, and ask through the central switchboard to be connected to Anthony Dansk. The private number he'd given her could be *anything*. If she found herself connected to his extension, then at least she'd know he worked for Justice. If the operator told her there was no listing for anyone called Dansk – but she wasn't ready to think this through to a conclusion.

She got out of the car. She turned and looked the length of the cul-de-sac. It was calm and somehow completely unsettling. It was as if a cortège had recently passed, leaving behind a sombre pall of silence. No kids, no pedestrians, no lawnmowers roaring, nothing. It was wrong, only she couldn't think why. Some form of charged static hung in the still air, like the atmosphere before a storm.

She opened the car door, glanced at the house, saw the sunstruck windows. Fiery glass blinded her. She walked to the house, unlocked the door and entered the hallway, where the shattered mirror on the wall reflected her face in a series of jagged slivers.

She didn't move. She understood at some level of memory activity that there was a procedure to follow in situations like this; you were supposed to back out of the house at once and call the police, you were advised not to run the risk of confronting the intruder if he was still on the premises, there were rules to follow if you wanted to survive. Rules didn't enter her head.

She took a step forward. Broken bits of mirror crunched under her sneakers. She glanced through the open doorway of the living room. A typewriter lay upturned on the floor. The drawers of Rhees's desk hung open. Papers were strewn all around.

Terror comes in variations on the ordinary. Papers where they shouldn't be, a typewriter lying upside down, a broken mirror. She edged closer to the door, conscious of the way a deep silence was clinging to the house, all noise vacuumed out of the place, dead space, just this void. She was numb, circuits down.

She entered the room.

'John,' she called.

His books were scattered. His files lay in utter disarray. A chair was overturned, a lampshade trampled and bent. No sign of Rhees.

'John!'

She moved to the kitchen doorway. No Rhees. On the kitchen table a jar of beets had been toppled and dark purple liquid dripped to the floor like a strange wine.

She was finding it hard to breathe. The space through which she moved was viscous. Go back, turn, get out of here. She walked to the half-open kitchen door and gripped the handle.

'JOHN!'

The yard was silent. Butterflies flapped over the long grass and her own voice returned to her as an echo she couldn't identify. Blue sky, frail bright wings, an echo dying. She went through the grass, drawn for some reason towards the pool, then stopped dead. The sun darkened.

He was seated motionless on the steps in the shallow end. His head was inclined forwards against his chest. His eyes were shut. The water, which rose as far as his waist, was ribboned with spirals of red.

This happens, this kind of thing, you read it every day in the papers – home invasions, suburban terrorists, dopers looking for quick cash, fix-money. This is the way it happens, only it's supposed to happen next door to somebody else, not to you.

No way. Never to you.

She rushed to where Rhees sat and, bending at the knees, gripped him under the shoulders, and then she pulled until she was breathless and her head was burning with a kind of fever and she'd hauled him out of the water and the air smelled of chemicals and damp clothing.

A mosquito landed on John's face, humming its blood song.

39

Dansk stepped inside the confessional. He noticed a scab of pink chewing gum pressed to the wall and a crayoned item of graffiti close to the floor: 'Jesus Saves at Citibank'. And here on the floor was a wrinkled condom dumped by some moron with a distasteful sense of humour. These signs of decline in the national fibre were everywhere – in churches even.

'I've sinned, Father. Fornication, hookers, call-girls.'

A thread of sunlight sneaking from somewhere illuminated the priest's skull on the other side of the grille, outlining a frizz of white hair, a halo effect. Dansk heard the priest yawn. Even priests suffered from the general malaise of things.

He thought of his mother and her unlimited piety. She lived in Patterson, New Jersey, occupying three brown twenty-watt rooms over the workshop of a blind violin repairman called Chomsky. To the accompaniment of plucking sounds coming up from below, she prayed a lot in front of a plaster statue of the Virgin that stood on top of the TV. Under the base of the statue were the words, *Souvenir from Knock, Ireland*. You grow up, Anthony, be an accountant, an optometrist, something people will respect.

Respect was her mantra. And always go to confession when you can.

Three or four times a year he phoned her, told her he was moving around from place to place, going where the oil company sent him in his capacity as a surveyor. He made up names for things that didn't exist. The *calsidron* broke down yesterday. There's one site near Amarillo that's probably the world's biggest deposit of *vobendum*.

His mother never asked questions, not even if he had a girlfriend and if she could look forward one day to being a grandmother. Whenever he thought about her he saw her stooped in front of that statue with her eyes shut, praying for her dead husband, Albert, who'd succumbed to a cardiac arrest on Dansk's fourth birthday. All Dansk could remember of his father was the smell of fried food that clung to his clothes from the fourteen-hour days he spent as a short-order cook in a truck stop on the edge of Patterson. Some memory. Some life.

'Do you believe in God?' the priest asked.

'I believe,' Dansk said. Confession boxes made him apprehensive. They were filled with the echoes of millions of sins, ghostly voices asking forgiveness.

'Ten Hail Marys,' the priest said.

Dansk said, 'Thank you, Father.'

'Bless you.'

Business done. Religion was a hurried affair like everything else in these days of acronyms and sound bites and nobody with the time to listen. Dismissed, Dansk stepped out of the box. I pay for sex, I consort with call-girls. I'm Chief Surveyor for Transamerica Explorations Inc. A man to be respected in spite of his sexual inclinations. I have nothing to do with death.

Ten Hail Marys, low-impact aerobics for the soul. You wouldn't even break sweat. He dropped some coins in a collection box for a Patagonian mission and went out to the street. He moved towards his car where a tall black man was leaning with folded arms against the hood. Dansk kept going, slowing his pace just a little, hearing the drone of imminent danger.

'You Dansk?' the man asked.

Dansk reached the car. He studied the man quickly. Black silk bomber jacket, black polo-neck, the face with the monstrous overhanging brow, huge hands, no rings. Dansk had the general impression of brutality.

'I wanna word,' the guy said.

Dansk said, 'I don't know you.'

'You're about to,' the guy said.

Dansk could feel it in the air around him, a kind of static, and somewhere in his head a sound that reminded him of Chomsky stretching a violin string to breaking point.

The black guy had his hands clasped in front of him. 'Let's you and me walk over there,' he said.

Dansk looked, saw an entrance to an alley, dumpsters, plastic sacks, one of which had broken and disgorged its contents. He saw chop-bones and a lettuce oozing brown slime. 'I don't walk into alleys with strangers,' he said. 'Rule of mine.'

The black man said, 'We can do this right here on the street.'

Dansk gazed the length of the street. He saw quiet houses, empty sidewalks, palm trees, and a few blocks beyond, the high-rises of downtown. Nobody moving. This was one of those upmarket streets, reclaimed from disrepair by lawyers, ad executives and local media types.

The black guy prodded Dansk's chest with a thick finger.

'This a mugging?' Dansk asked.

'You're gonna wish.'

Dansk looked into the man's eyes, which were the colour of smoked oak. What he saw there was a palpable dislike. 'So it's personal?' he asked.

The guy kept prodding, and Dansk backtracked.

'What you done to that girl's fucking shameful. Cretins like you need some serious discipline.'

The call-girl, Chaka, Dansk thought. She runs to her personal enforcer. She sets free the brute from her zoo. Dansk stepped a few paces back but the guy kept prodding. Keep this up, Dansk thought. I'm in the mood, and I'm one fit son of a bitch.

'The alley or right here. You choose,' the guy said.

'Touch me one more time.'

'And you're gonna what, Dansk? Slap me? Punch me a coupla times? I ain't some skinny little whore, if it ain't escaped your notice.'

The guy stuck his finger in Dansk's breastbone again. 'The joke's over,' Dansk said.

'Ain't no joke, asshole.'

'See if you find this funny.' Dansk had the Swiss Army knife out of his pocket in a flash, and before the big man could react he'd stuck the corkscrew attachment directly into the guy's right eye, hearing it puncture the gelatinous orb, a squelching sound. The guy said, 'Oh Jesus fucking Christ' and Dansk twisted the corkscrew round then pulled it free and the big man took a couple of unsteady steps to one side, his hand clamped over his eye and blood seeping between his fingers. Dansk kicked the guy's legs out from under him and he went down like an axed tree. He lay rolling around on the sidewalk and Dansk dragged him into the alley.

'What you need is a matching pair,' Dansk said.

The black man raised a hand to protect himself, but Dansk was way too fast for this cumbersome *asshole* and was already driving the corkscrew into the left eye, where he twisted it as if he were opening a bottle of cheap wine. The guy dropped his hands from his bloodied face and turned his head this way and that, his mouth open, no sound coming out, unless you counted the weird noise that suggested difficulty in breathing, some kind of shock reaction to his pain.

Dansk stood up, stepped back, feeling very calm, very detached. 'You fucking pimp,' he said. 'You piece of shit, worthless maggot.'

The guy started to groan. Bewildered, he stretched his hands out as if to grab something solid. Dansk crushed one hand with his foot, stomping it into the ground, then he walked to his car. Inside, he cleaned the knife with a tissue and stuck the tissue inside the ashtray.

He rolled down his window and called to the guy, 'You can always find work as a trainee violin repairman, Jack.' He drove away amused, pleased with himself. He looked at his reflection in the rearview mirror and laughed.

His phone rang, it was Pasquale. 'You oughta see her, Anthony. Pacing round outside the hospital and looking like her womb just fell out. It's a picture would break your heart.'

A picture.

'You know what to do next,' Dansk said.

'I'm moving.' Pasquale cut the connection.

Dansk laughed again and looked at himself laughing until all sense of self-recognition had left him and he was looking at somebody else, a roaring wet-eyed red-haired stranger, hugely satisfied with the day's work so far. A guy on a roll that didn't end here.

40

The physician was a stern young woman whose name-tag identified her as Dr Clara S. Lamont. She wore her hair in the tight bun of a pioneer's wife. She clearly didn't consider sympathy an implement in the practice of medicine. She spoke like someone reciting from a low-budget mail-order catalogue.

Two fractured ribs. Broken humerus. Three fingers of the left hand broken. Haematoma in the knee. A few blows to the head, but no internal damage. The patient would recover, given time and rest. He's not going to be mobile for a while. Clara S. Lamont had obviously seen every kind of human disaster and been numbed by calamity.

Amanda asked if Rhees was conscious and whether she could see him. Clara S. Lamont told her it might be hours yet and suggested Amanda make herself comfortable in the waiting room.

Make myself comfortable, Amanda thought. Tell me how, doc. Guide me a little before it's screaming time.

She watched Lamont turn and walk down the corridor.

The hospital was a maze of passageways and rooms painted in pastels designed to minimize the dread inherent in these institutions. The colour scheme didn't work for Amanda. This was no nursery. This was a place of pain and death, where screens were drawn round beds and people were rushed on rattling gurneys to operating rooms to be cut open and sewn up again. Two fractured ribs. Three fingers of the left hand broken. Haematoma. She thought about this, a subcutaneous swelling filled with blood, the pain of it.

She was aware of nurses and orderlies, but only in a dim far-away fashion. She slouched towards the waiting room where a strict no-smoking policy was in force. This was useless to her in her present state. She needed nicotine, vast quantities.

She went outside, and with a hand that trembled, lit a cigarette. She thought of the ambulance that had brought her here with Rhees. Rhees lying in silence, the orderly checking his pulse and blood pressure and flashing a light into his eyes, the slackness of Rhees's eyelids, the pupils that looked dead, the whites bloodshot.

I'm coming apart, she thought. Rhees is broken, and so am I, just in a different way.

The uniformed cops who'd come to the house had asked some questions in a manner that might have been desultory or delicate, she was too stunned to tell the difference. Had she seen anything? Did she know anything? Was anything missing?

Like I have time to search the fucking place looking for missing baubles, she'd said. Shock stripped you of basic manners, atomized your responses. You were raw all over.

The cops had talked to Clara Lamont, and then somewhere along the way they'd contrived to disappear. Reports to write. Narratives in triplicate. Get down the details while the blood is still fresh.

She walked up and down. She smoked and squinted into the sun. She sat on a wall, hands dangling between her knees. She couldn't stop herself shaking. What were you supposed to do in a situation like this anyway? How were you supposed to comport yourself? *Endure.* She closed her eyes. She didn't see Willie Drumm approach.

'Amanda.' Drumm's expression was sympathetic. He put his arms around her shoulders and she pressed her face into his plaid jacket. It smelled of dry-cleaning solvents.

'I came as soon as I heard. What's his condition?'

Amanda said nothing.

'The two uniforms say he took a bad beating,' Drumm said. 'You got any idea who'd do something like that to him?'

Amanda's mind was sand and silence, her own little Kalahari. She hadn't collected enough strands of herself to even think of apportioning blame. She shook her head and looked at Willie. She couldn't talk.

Drumm said, 'Hang in there, kid.'

That's what you're supposed to do. That's the phrase for every rotten situation. Hang in there. But what were you meant to hang from?

Drumm stepped back from her, a hand on her shoulder. 'You came home and found him, I understand.'

She nodded.

'Is he conscious?' Drumm asked.

'No, not yet.'

'When's he expected to be in a condition to talk?'

'I don't know. I'll wait. For as long as it takes I'll stay right here.'

'You got anything of value in the house, Amanda?'

'I had, only he's in this goddam hospital now.'

Drumm was quiet a moment. 'Things; jewels, money, that kind of stuff.'

She thought about the house and found she couldn't remember it exactly. How many rooms it had, what they contained. She knew it intimately but she couldn't force it into her head.

Drumm said, 'Maybe we should sit inside.'

'No. They don't let you smoke. I need to smoke.'

Drumm tapped a foot on the ground. 'People going round breaking into homes, beating the shit out of some poor bastard. It's an epidemic.'

Amanda looked up into the sun. It was strange to be part of the world and yet not, as if you were in a purgatory where you waited for Christ knows what. The sun in the sky, for instance, looked odd to her, shaped like a lozenge. And why did it make her feel this cold? She shivered and said, 'I can't get a handle on it, Willie.'

'Here.' He took a little pack of Kleenex out of his pocket and gave it to her.

She blew her nose and said, 'I can't get my head round it.'

Drumm was of the old school that believed in the mystical power of blowing your nose to feel better. He eased a fresh Kleenex into her hand. He was being kind and it touched her.

'John wanted to come with me when I left this

morning,' she said, 'but I drove away. I just drove away. I should have taken him along, Willie, then this wouldn't have happened.'

'You don't have a crystal ball, Amanda. You couldn't predict anything was gonna happen to him.'

Amanda walked in tight little circles. It was movement, something to keep the circulation going. 'I've been neglecting him lately. I haven't been paying attention to him. It's not like he demands much from me.'

Drumm took her hand. His palm was unexpectedly soft. 'Let's go inside, Amanda. Maybe we should think about talking to one of the doctors. Get something to settle you down.'

She allowed herself, without resistance, to be led back inside the hospital. Drumm told her to sit in the waiting room while he went off in search of a physician. She glared at the no-smoking posters and a diagram of a human skeleton that adorned one wall. She looked at the word humerus, known also as the funny bone. She imagined it was Rhees's skeleton. Poor John. He'd never hurt anyone in his life. He wasn't at war with anybody.

Fuck the warning sign. She lit a cigarette.

The only other occupant of the room, a man with an insurance-collar, said, 'I don't mind, you smoke all you want.'

Amanda said, 'I intend to.'

The man got up and set an empty Coke can on the table beside Amanda and said, 'Here, use this as an ashtray.'

'Thanks,' she said.

'I'm here on account of this neck.' He sat alongside her and leaned across her lap to adjust the position of the Coke can. His hair smelled faintly of crushed grapes. There was a brief contact of bodies she didn't like.

'Happened in a work-related incident,' he said.

'Really,' Amanda remarked. She didn't want to hear the guy's medical history. She looked elsewhere and edged slightly away from him.

'I'm suing because it wasn't my fault.'

'Good for you.'

'That's what the law's for,' he said.

The guy smiled at her and went out of the room. A moment later Drumm came back carrying a dixie cup of water. 'Here.' He gave her the cup and a small blue pill.

'What's the pill?' she asked.

Drumm said, 'The nurse said it would calm you.'

'Assuming I want to be calm, Willie.'

'Take the damn thing.'

Amanda stuck the pill in her mouth and washed it down with a sip of water. 'I want to see John,' she said.

'So do I,' Drumm said. 'Meantime, let's wait here.'

He patted her arm. She sat in silence for a long time, and when the pill kicked in she felt lethargic and light-headed. She must have dozed for a while because the next thing she knew Drumm was shaking her shoulder and saying, 'We can see him now.'

She was dry-mouthed and groggy, and when she stood up she was a little unsteady. She followed Drumm down a corridor to an elevator.

'You OK?' he asked.

OK in what way? she wondered. Physical mental spiritual. Delete what doesn't apply.

She stepped inside the elevator. Drumm said,

'He's in room three sixty. We've got five minutes, doctor's orders.'

She listened to the quiet whine of machinery and pulleys. She wondered about the kind of noises Rhees had made when he was being attacked. She didn't want to think. Some things were located just outside the scope of your imagination, like shadows beyond the reach of a campfire.

41

Rhees had a room to himself. He was propped up in bed with his eyes shut. The shades had been drawn against the sun and the only light came from a low-wattage lamp in a corner. Amanda went close to the bed and Willie Drumm lingered behind her.

'John,' she said.

His head turned slowly. 'I am *high*. Great drugs in here.'

She smiled at him even if it was the last thing she felt like doing. His left arm was in plaster. His left hand too. His face was bruised. His knee was an angry scarlet colour and bloated, and the ice-pack that had been wrapped around it had slipped out of position.

When he spoke, his words were lifeless, as if they'd travelled a very long and awkward distance to reach his mouth.

She wanted to touch him, she wasn't sure where. She decided on the back of his right hand, where she placed her palm gently.

Drumm asked, 'Can you answer a couple of questions, John?'

Rhees shut his eyes again. 'There were two guys, I think.'

Drumm waited. Amanda rubbed Rhees's hand. She wanted to tell Drumm that this wasn't the right time, Rhees needed to be left in peace.

Rhees said, '. . . in ski masks.'

'Ski masks, OK,' Drumm said.

Rhees started to add something but his voice dried up. Amanda held a container of water to his lips and adjusted the angular straw for him. She thought about ski masks. A terrorist nightmare in your own house, your backyard.

Drumm leaned closer to the bed. 'Did they say anything, John?'

Rhees opened his eyes. His pupils were black and enormous. 'Nothing. They had a . . . tyre-iron.'

This was the first time Amanda had thought about an assault instrument. It had been an abstraction before, but now Rhees had identified it, she could picture it rising and falling on his face and body. The brutality of it, the destruction of bones and tissue.

Rhees turned his face to the side and for a second it seemed he'd drifted off into sleep, but he hadn't. He looked into Amanda's eyes. She saw in his expression stress and puzzlement, only slightly obscured by the glaze of painkillers. She experienced a flutter of anger. Rhees had been reduced to this wrecked figure lying in a hospital bed. He'd been traumatized and diminished, and for what? Money probably. Credit cards. *Stuff*. Anything of value.

Rhees closed his eyes and this time didn't open them again.

'He's out,' Drumm said.

Amanda held his hand a moment longer before she stepped back from the bed. She leaned, kissed Rhees on his forehead, then walked into the corridor.

Drumm said, 'It sickens me to the gut. What do you do?' He shook his head in a slow side-to-side manner.

Amanda looked up at a fluorescent strip on the ceiling. A voice was issuing through the sound system: 'Dr Strapp to Emergency. Dr Strapp to Emergency.' More casualties. More damaged humans swept in from the streets. Smashed cars, bullet wounds, stabbing victims. What do you do? Drumm had said. You went up to the mountains, was the answer. You ran off up into the pines and you never came back, and if everything was going to hell in the city you didn't give a damn. You stayed where it was safe and the nights were as deep as all the oceans.

The elevator arrived. She and Drumm got in and rode down in silence. She slipped her hands into the back pockets of her jeans, thinking of Isabel's letter, expecting to encounter it with her fingers. She wished she'd never received the goddam thing. She wished it had been lost in the mail system, overlooked, shredded inside a franking machine, anything. She wished she'd never heard of Isabel Sanchez.

The letter wasn't in either hip pocket, and it wasn't in the front pockets.

She searched again, fumbling among keys and a bashed cigarette pack and a crumpled receipt chit from a Walmart and three washed-out dollar bills that must have gone through a laundry cycle.

No letter.

'Looking for something?' Drumm asked.

Without answering, she got out of the elevator and walked towards the waiting room, thinking she might have left the letter there, tugged it out of her jeans along with her cigarettes. She checked the room, saw the Coke can she'd used as an ashtray, but no sign of Isabel's two pages. Just an empty room painted lavender and grey.

Drumm, who'd limped behind her, asked, 'Lost something?'

She didn't reply.

42

Willie Drumm walked ahead of Amanda into the house. She was reluctant to enter. She was picking up on echoes, hearing the noise of Rhees's funny-bone snapping.

In the living room Drumm circled the fallen type-writer, the scattered papers and books with broken spines. 'They did a number here,' he said.

'I can't deal with this,' she said.

'A quick look round is all,' Drumm said. 'See if anything's missing. You keep jewels in the house, Amanda?'

'Any jewellery I had was in the bedroom, except for this silver chain I wear.' A gift from John, she remembered, with one of his poems attached.

'What about money?'

'John might have had a few dollars. We weren't planning to stay here.'

'Where's the bedroom?'

She showed Drumm the way. The closet had been ransacked. Her underwear had been rummaged through like lingerie at a frenetic post-Christmas sale. Panties in a heap, some of them flimsy and silken, sexy gossamer items. She thought of strangers crudely handling these intimacies and making off-colour jokes.

The drawers of the dressing table lay open. 'There should be a small black velvet box with a string of pearls inside,' she said.

'I don't see it, Amanda.'

'So they stole the pearls. I never wore them anyway.'

Drumm peered inside the bathroom. 'They didn't bother with this room,' he said.

She followed Drumm into the kitchen. He bent, picked up something and held it carefully, dangling it between thumb and index finger. It was John's brown leather wallet. He flipped it open. 'What did he keep in this?'

'An Amex card, a Visa, a couple of library cards. Probably some cash.'

'All they left were his library cards,' Drumm said. He wrapped the wallet in a sheet of waxy kitchen paper and stuck it in his pocket, then he stepped into the backyard and wandered off through the long grass, skirting the pool. She puzzled over what kind of inventory he was making. *One wallet, empty of cash and credit cards. One jar of beets, spilled. Frog in pool, deceased.* This wasn't his regular field of inquiry. He was here as a favour she hadn't asked for.

He came back indoors. 'They steal some jewels and a couple of credit cards and a negligible sum of money,' he said, 'but they don't take the PC or the TV and they don't rip off your expensive stereo system. That's a little strange. Usually it's the kind of stuff they make a beeline for.'

'They're not interested in carrying things,' she said. 'Maybe they're worn out by the physical exertion of beating up on John.'

Drumm laid a hand on her arm. 'I'll get some fingerprint guys in. And when John's feeling up to it, he might have more information we can use.'

She sat down at the table and looked through the kitchen door into the backyard. The setting sun was an otherworldly gold. A postcard. Wish you were here. Miss you.

She pressed her fingertips to her eyelids to ease the headache that was threatening. She glanced down at the puddle of beet juice. 'What makes them choose one house instead of another anyway? Why not the house next door, or the one next door to that? Is it like some kind of violent lottery, Willie? Spin the wheel, come up with an address?'

Drumm said, 'Sometimes.'

'Our house is the only scruffy one in the street. The yard's a mess. It doesn't exactly shout prosperity.'

'Exactly what makes it so attractive. Nobody comes to mow the lawn or clip the trees. Thieves watch a place. Who comes, who goes. They get the impression of vacancy and they think an easy score.'

'They watch,' she said.

'Sure they watch.'

They watch. They monitor. They drive past in the night, doing quiet U-turns in the cul-de-sac.

Anthony Dansk sailed into her mind.

She needed air. She walked out of the house and went to the bottom of the driveway and looked the length of the cul-de-sac. She glanced at parked cars. She moved until she came to the corner of the through street. Here, vehicles were tightly parked all the way along the sidewalks. Street lamps had come on, globes of orange-yellow light.

She stood on the corner, looking left and right, not at all certain what she expected to see. Maybe a guy behind a wheel, a woman staring idly into space, a man deep under the hood of his car, pretending he had engine trouble. Potential disguises were unlimited. Any innocent presence or movement was open to sinister interpretation.

She tried to imagine Dansk sitting in the vicinity, watching her coming and going, maybe even parked in the cul-de-sac itself now and again, brazenly observing the house. And if not Dansk, somebody who reported to him. And if not that, maybe Sanchez's people.

She went back, pausing in the driveway to look inside the VW, wondering if she'd dropped Isabel's letter on the floor. She checked under both front seats and found only a discarded Tab can. She flashed on the empty Coke can in the hospital waiting room, the guy in the insurance-collar, the way he'd sat down right next to her and how a certain amount of fumbling and body-contact had gone on while he'd adjusted the position of the can for her. *I don't mind, smoke all you want.* The memory was smudged. She hadn't been in a frame of mind to register details.

Drumm was standing in the doorway. 'What are you looking for, Amanda? You were looking for something at the hospital too.'

She leaned against the car and gazed up at the dusky sky.

Drumm was silent for a time. 'You still interested in the Sanchez matter?'

'I don't know what I'm interested in any more. I'm not thinking clearly, Willie.'

'A little bird told me you went down to Florence. You saw Sanchez. He became violent, made threats.'

'You've got good sources,' she said.

Drumm said, 'We sent up a chopper.'

She thought of the desert, Isabel's broken shoe, the shadow of a helicopter.

'The pilot found nothing,' Drumm said.

'Why didn't they steal the goddam TV and the stereo?' she asked. 'You said yourself it was unusual.'

'Back up. We were talking about the Sanchez thing.'

She looked at her watch. 'It's time I phoned the hospital.'

'Amanda. What do you know that I don't?'

'I just want to call the hospital.'

'You're being evasive. You don't trust me?'

'What kind of question is that?' she answered.

She went inside the house and Drumm followed. She called Directory Assistance, got the number of the hospital and dialled it. She asked to be connected to the nurses' station on the third floor. Immediately a woman answered.

Amanda said, 'I'm calling about a patient, John Rhees.'

'And you are?'

What was the appropriate word? Lover? Cohabitant? 'His fiancée, Amanda Scholes.'

There was the sound of a keyboard being tapped. 'He's stable, Miss Scholes.'

'When's the earliest I can see him?'

'Visiting hours are from ten a.m. until noon.'

Amanda thanked the woman and hung up. She

looked at Drumm and said, 'He's stable. That's hospital-speak.'

'*He's* stable. What about you?'

'I can't stay in this place. I'll check into a hotel for the night.'

'Smart idea.'

'Pack a few overnight things, I'm gone.'

Drumm caught her hand. 'Look. If there's something you're keeping back, this is as good a time as any to tell me. You left a message for me before. What did you want to tell me?'

It was an invitation to talk. Fine, why not? Break the goddam lid off the box and let the contents fly. She looked into Willie's eyes. There was never any guile in that face.

'This isn't for public consumption, Willie. This is strictly between you and me.' And she told him. About the letter, and the loss of it. The way she'd coerced the Program into sending Anthony Dansk to Phoenix. When she was finished, she felt vaguely relieved. She'd shifted a burden even if she hadn't removed it.

'Sweet Jesus,' he said. 'What I wonder is how in God's name Sanchez pulled it off. I mean, you're talking fake papers, funny badges, serious access to the inside track, knowledge of the MO of the Program, the location of witnesses, et cetera. You're talking more than a leak, this is the whole dam.'

'That's what it is,' she said.

'And this guy Dansk says he'll fix it.'

'That's what he says.'

'He never saw Isabel's letter?'

She shook her head.

'And you've no idea where you lost it?'

'None.'

'So Dansk says he'll investigate and let you know how it comes out. You got a problem with that?'

'Yeah, but my head's like a carousel going round and round and I can't get it to stop long enough to think clearly.'

'Talk to me some more, Amanda.' He put his hand under her chin and turned her face slowly towards his own. 'Unload. Dump the rest on me.'

Dump what? All she had was instinct, vague and fuzzy, like a photograph screwed up in the dark-room. All she had were reverberating doubts and the conviction that Dansk was seriously missing a hinge, and that made him dangerous.

'He has me under surveillance, Willie,' she said.

'You know this for a fact?'

'Not for a fact,' she said. It sounded, she thought, loopy. 'Next I'll be hearing voices.'

Drumm didn't smile. He'd always given her the courtesy of taking her seriously. 'OK. He wants to know what you're up to. What's he so lathered about, Amanda?'

'I made a threat about speaking to the newspapers, which went down like the Hindenburg. I guess he's uneasy because he can't be one hundred per cent certain I won't go through with it. He doesn't enjoy the possibility of me trespassing where I don't belong. Namely, Program security.'

'Program security seems a little thin on the ground at present,' Drumm said. 'Maybe he's covering his ass because he's got something to hide.'

'For example?'

Drumm took a toothpick out of his breast pocket and placed it between his lips, moving it from one corner of his mouth to the other. He tilted his head back. She knew this ruminative look so well she could practically hear wheels turning in his head. 'I'm just thinking out loud. Sanchez penetrates the Program, right. But he needed a whole lotta help. What if . . .' Drumm snapped the toothpick in two. 'What if he hired this character Dansk?'

'Sanchez hired Dansk?'

'Keep in mind I'm only saying what if, that's all. Dansk is running around doing some damage limitation on a situation he created himself. The monster he built for Sanchez is roaring out of control. He's got nothing to do with the Program. He's a freelance operator—'

She interrupted Drumm. 'And somebody else *inside* the Program is providing him with information?'

'Maybe. Just maybe.'

She pondered Drumm's speculation. Suppose Dansk's performance was all some elaborate masquerade. She remembered calling the number Dansk had given her, and the taped message in a voice that wasn't his. *You have reached the office of Anthony Dansk. Mr Dansk isn't available to take your call at present.* She wondered about this, tried to imagine the location of his office, and if Dansk really had any connection with the Justice Department. The office could be anything, rented space, an answering machine in an empty room. But whose voice was recorded on the machine? Then she remembered her earlier intention to telephone Justice, but when she'd entered the house and found chaos the notion had been swept out of her mind like debris in a flash-flood. And something else, another phone call she'd meant to make, but it evaded her. What the hell was it? She searched her shook-up memory.

Drumm said, 'What I can do is poke around, ask a few questions about this Dansk and see what comes up. A cop's badge still opens some doors, remember.'

'What doors do you have in mind?'

'For starters, Lewis Bascombe's,' he said.

'Bascombe? He's probably the most secretive man in this city,' she said. 'I don't know what you'll get out of him, even if he agrees to see you.'

'I'll kick my way in,' Drumm said, and smiled.

'And wave your thirty-eight in his face?'

She couldn't imagine Drumm getting anywhere with Lew Bascombe. She shut her eyes a moment. *Bernadette Vialli, of course.* That was the missing thought. Like so much else, it had drifted away from her.

'Do me a small favour,' she said. 'Remember the Vialli case?'

'Scorched into my memory,' Drumm said.

'Benny's mother tried to get in touch with me. I'm not in the mood for calling her back right now.'

'You any idea why she phoned?'

'No.' Amanda looked at John's typewriter on the floor and the scattered papers and books and all at once she heard a low-pitched humming reminiscent of wasps disturbed and zooming in crazy disarray. She recognized this anger, a delayed reaction to the fact that her world had been chopped like kindling, and somehow Dansk was the one with the hatchet, and a lit match in his fingers.

'You want me to contact the woman,' Drumm said.

'Would you?'

'No sweat,' Drumm said. 'Any favour you need,

come to me. Night, day, it doesn't matter. You got that?'

'Bless you,' she said. She kissed him on his plump warm cheek. Direct this animosity, she thought. Harness this rage.

'Meantime, I suggest you try and get a good night's rest,' Drumm said.

A good night's rest. It was the last thing on her mind.

43

At 7.30 p.m., Anthony Dansk and Eddie McTell stood in a park where a floodlit softball game was going on about two hundred yards away, a serious affair played with raw enthusiasm between one team in blue shirts and another in orange. The guy on strike had a massive roll of rubbery white flesh that leered between his shirt and waistband. A small crowd was gathered behind the wire fence at the catcher's back.

McTell asked, 'You uh like this game, Anthony?'

'I'm no big fan,' Dansk said. 'I just like to see people at their leisure, because I forget what leisure is.' He watched the fat guy swing and miss. Americans at play. An innocent contest under the lamps. Also shadows beyond the outfield where anything might lurk. A perv offering some seven-year-old a Snickers-bar bribe for a blow-job, or a sick dickhead junkie shooting up.

McTell stroked his beard. 'What's on your mind, Anthony?'

'A burden the size of a cathedral,' Dansk said. He

handed two sheets of paper to McTell, who held them angled towards the distant floodlights.

McTell read, then raised his face and gazed at the softball field. 'This is from . . .'

'You know who it's from. She sent it to the lady prosecutor and the lady prosecutor read it.'

'It don't name names,' McTell remarked and went into a defensive slouch, like a tired pugilist.

'And we're thankful for small mercies,' Dansk said.

'How did you get this letter?' McTell asked.

'Pasquale let his fingers do the walking.' Dansk took the letter back. 'I'd like to be happy, Eddie. Instead what I get are problems and headaches.'

'And you're blaming me and Pasquale, right? I gotta say this, Anthony, you never have a good word. You never say we did this right or we did that right.'

'What are you looking for, Eddie?' He raised both arms in the air and made a salaam motion. 'The mighty McTell, praise his name.'

McTell said, 'A kind word now and again is all. Instance. We did some terrific work on Rhees. You lay into a guy with metal, you run the risk of maybe puncturing a lung or breaking the skull and then it's serious. But we did it the way you wanted it; delicate, Anthony. Like fucking artists.'

Dansk stared at the softball field. Artists. McTell and Pasquale were up there with Van Gogh and Reubens. He pondered the letter. 'The lady's learned something she wasn't supposed to learn, McTell.'

'Ask me, I don't see where she's learned anything,' McTell said.

Dansk thought of pushing the corkscrew of his

Swiss Army knife into McTell's brain. 'Show me where the fuck it's written that you're paid to make judgements, McTell. You're reimbursed to kill, I'm the one paid to think and organize and forecast. And the problem here's not so much what she's learned as what she *thinks* she's learned, what she believes. Her brain's on overtime.'

'She don't even have the letter,' McTell said.

Dansk said, 'No, but I'll bet good money she showed it to Drumm.'

'So she tells this cop. What's he gonna do? Drag Sanchez outta his cell and interrogate him day and fucking night? Who did he bribe? Who did he buy? That kinda thing. And what's Sanchez gonna say? Jack shit.'

Dansk said, 'You're not taking into account the woman's persistence. She's like a termite. She's not happy unless she's nibbling away at timbers.'

'What you do with a termite is you drop poison.'

'Poison,' Dansk said. He felt entangled in a variety of possibilities suddenly. The softball game seemed very far away, miniature figures participating in a meaningless ritual under the lamps. His lips were dry. He took from his pocket a tube of salve and applied it. He tasted lemon.

McTell's voice was surly. 'So beating up on the guy was a waste. All that labour for what? Shit?'

'Without this goddam letter, she'd have withered on the vine, McTell. She'd have shrivelled to a puckered substandard little raisin. Without this hysterical fucking note from the runaway señorita, she'd have dropped out of sight and done her Nurse Nightingale bit and tended to her lover's wounds. But the letter arrives and she reads it and her head starts running and she can't stop it.'

McTell had a look that might have been exasperation. 'So what now?'

The phone in Dansk's pocket went off. He felt it vibrate against his hip. He flipped the device open and heard Pasquale say, 'I lost her, Anthony.'

'Lost her?'

'She was in the house with this cop Drumm for maybe an hour. He leaves and a coupla minutes later she comes outta the house and gets in her car. I follow her along Lincoln Boulevard, she pulls into a Circle-K, goes inside, ten minutes pass and she still hasn't reappeared. So I look in the store, only she's not there. I figure she's using the john, but when I take a look-see the john's empty and she's nowhere around. I walk back outside. Item, her car's still there. No sign of her.'

'So she slipped out the back?'

'Item, I go round the back. There's this alley. No sign of her. I check the front and her goddam car is still there. So I check the streets round the store; nothing. Then I haul ass back to the store again. Her car's *still* there. I can see it from where I'm sitting.'

'So this is like some magical illusion? She vanishes into nothing?'

'I don't know where she went.'

Dansk thought for a moment. 'Here's what I want you to do. Take her car, and don't tell me you don't have the keys and can't get it started. I'll call you back soon.'

Dansk snapped the phone shut and shoved it back in his pocket. She knew she was being followed, so she took steps to lose Pasquale. Nice. Did she ease through the back door of the store and into a maze of suburban streets? Stroll until she found a gas station where she could phone a cab? This lady has more than a degree of cunning.

'She skipped,' he said. *After talking with Drumm.*

'Anything you want me to do?'

Dansk was silent a moment. 'One thing,' he said.

'I'm listening,' said McTell, and inclined his body forward, his head tilted in what he considered his concentration mode.

44

From the window of the hotel Amanda could see the freeway, the lights of the suburbs stretching towards darkness. She drew the curtains briskly, dumped her overnight bag on the bed and opened it. *The motions, remember the motions. Focus.* She worked fast. She dressed in the suit she'd worn at the Biltmore. She went inside the bathroom and applied thick make-up. She painted her lips a high gloss red and drew exaggerated lines around her eyes with a fine brush, then sprayed gel into her hair and ran a comb through it. The glistening look. She walked back inside the bedroom and varnished her nails a dreadful nuclear pink that would glow in the dark.

A new Amanda. Overstated.

She opened the mini-bar and took out several miniatures of liquor, mainly brandy and gin. She loosened the caps a little and stuffed the tiny bottles in her purse, along with cigarettes and all the rest of the junk she'd need.

Then she thought of the car that had been

following her along Lincoln Boulevard. When she'd slowed down, so had the car. She pulled into the parking lot of a convenience store. The car had sailed past the store and then hung a U-turn at the next lights and come back. She'd stepped inside the store, walked towards the john and kept going, pushing the metal crossbar of the delivery door at the rear, and then she was running.

I can't go through with this. This loony plan. This trip to the moon. Drumm would disapprove and Rhees would have a cardiac arrest, but they don't know what I'm doing.

You're not even sure yourself.

Yes you are. This is called focusing your rage.

She felt an inner tremor, a doubt. Shove it aside, cast it off. No time for indecision. She let her hand hover above the telephone. Her fingernails looked like they belonged to somebody else's hand.

She picked up the telephone and called the operator. 'Connect me to Anthony Dansk,' she said.

'Hold.' Ringing, ringing, ringing.

'I'm sorry, the room isn't answering. Is there a message?'

'No message,' Amanda said.

She put the telephone down. How much time, she wondered. She couldn't begin to guess. She slipped her feet inside her black shoes, picked up the bulky purse and headed for the door. She rode the elevator downward to the reception area where a great chandelier spiked the air with light at all angles, like a wayward laser.

The concierge's desk was unattended. At reception there was only the young man who'd checked her in earlier. He had a smile designed to please.

'How can I help you?' he asked.

'I'm supposed to meet somebody here, but he hasn't shown up,' she said. 'He's a guest.'

'You know his room number?'

'I think its eight seven three four. I'm just hopeless with numbers.' The helpless shiny lipsticked smile.

'His name?'

'Dansk. Anthony.'

The clerk punched his computer. 'You certainly are hopeless with numbers,' he said, still smiling.

'Did I get the room wrong?'

'Miles out.'

'Typical. What is his number anyway?' she asked.

'Sorry, I can't say. Security reasons.'

'Makes sense these days,' she said.

'I'll call the room for you.' The clerk picked up a phone.

Amanda thought, Do it now. Do it before you lose whatever momentum you have.

She tipped her purse and it spilled open, tubes of lipstick, eyebrow pencils, a compact, a bottle of liquid hair gel, everything rolled across the surface of the desk in a variety of directions.

'Oh, Christ, clumsy me,' she said, and then the cigarettes followed, and six loose tampons, and the miniatures of liquor, which scattered across the desk leaking brandy and gin. 'Shit, shit, shit.'

The clerk said, 'It's no problem really.'

'My friends all call me Amanda Accident,' she said, in a bubbly airheaded fashion. 'I guess you can see why.'

'I'll just clean it up.' The clerk took a linen handkerchief from his pocket and began to swab the desk like a cabin boy. Booze was soaking through the tampon wrappers, making rainbow puddles around the eyebrow pencils and the tubes of lipstick.

'Jesus, it's a mess, it's a terrible mess. I'm sorry,' she said.

'It's nothing, really. I can clean it up in no time.'

'Let me help,' she said.

'I don't need help, really,' the clerk said.

'No, I insist.' She reached across the desk to retrieve some of the spilled items and she struck the computer screen with her elbow and it swivelled slightly towards her, even as a few of the cylindrical beauty enhancements dropped on the clerk's side of the desk and booze dripped onto his paper-work.

'Now it's all over your papers. I'm so damn sorry, really I am. I shouldn't be allowed out.'

7320.

'I'm fine, I'm absolutely fine,' he said.

Bless his heart, he was still smiling. Slapstick, she thought. I have a knack for it, a clown's gift.

The clerk had collected everything together in a wet mound on the centre of his desk. 'There, I think that's most of it. I guess you want me to dump this stuff.'

'Would you please,' she said.

'No problem.'

'You're very understanding,' she said. 'I come in here and before you know it, disaster.'

'I'm trained for emergencies, large and small,' he said.

She fished a wet five-dollar bill from her purse. 'Here,' she said.

'That's not necessary,' he said.

'Call it guilt money,' she said.

He took the bill tentatively out of her fingers.

She walked quickly out of the reception area. Act one over. She was conscious of time again.

She rode up in the elevator to her room. She looked at the room-service menu, picked up the phone and said, 'This is Mrs Anthony Dansk, seventy three twenty. Send up a Union Jack burger and fries. How long will that take?'

'Ten minutes, ma'am.'

She checked her watch. Ten minutes. Mrs Anthony Dansk, she thought. She wondered if Dansk had a wife. She couldn't imagine it.

She walked up and down the room. The slapstick was over. The next part was different. She sat on the bed, but her heart was like a racehorse and she had to get up again. She went inside the bathroom and looked at her face in the mirror. The surge of nervous energy that had transported her through the comedy of errors at reception was still flowing vigorously. All the time at the desk she'd wondered what would have happened if Dansk had chosen that moment to enter the hotel and he had seen her. A sliver of luck. You needed it now and again.

Let it hold.

She checked her watch again. She took off her shoes and left her room. She rode the elevator down and stepped out on the seventh floor. She found room 7320 and she waited outside the door. Ten minutes since she'd ordered from room service. Eleven. Twelve. This is no way to do things, the heart flat out. Dansk could appear. Dansk could materialize in the corridor. And then what? Hello, Anthony, I was just in the neighbourhood.

She heard the elevator in the shaft, the clank of cutlery. She saw the room-service waiter come into view with a tray balanced on one hand. He was a tall black kid in a striped vest. She smiled at him as he approached.

'I know, I know, you're gonna think I'm a total moron,' she said. 'I locked myself out. I'm not even wearing my shoes, for God's sake. I thought I heard somebody at the door, so I went to see, the door swung shut behind me. What do you put on the hinges here? Electromagnets? Now I'm standing here like an idiot.'

'Happens all the time,' the kid said.

'It does?'

'Oh sure.'

'So do I eat my dinner out here in the corridor or are you going to be like my knight in shining armour and let me back inside my room?'

'You're a damsel in distress,' the kid said.

'Distress is right. I think I'm beyond the age of damsel, though.'

The kid laughed. 'I never heard of an age limit to damsels.' He slipped a keycard from his shirt pocket.

'Will that work?' she asked, looking at the card and thinking, Hurry, hurry.

'This is a magic card. One size fits all.' He slid the card into the slot, turned the handle and said, 'See? Open sesame.'

She walked ahead of him into the room. He set down the tray and gave her a slip of paper to sign. She wrote *Mrs Anthony Dansk* and added five dollars in the gratuity column.

'Thanks a lot,' the kid said.

'You deserve it.'

The kid left the room, closing the door behind him.

She thought, *I'm in*.

45

Dansk, stepping out of his car in the parking garage, saw the man emerge from the shadows. Long black coat, beret, black gloves even. The man was seized by a fit of coughing and dug inside the pocket of his coat and came out with a small chocolate-brown bottle which he uncapped and held to his lips. He took a swig and stuck the bottle away again. His eyes watered. He looked as if he'd hawked up a chunk of diseased lung and was sickened by the taste in his mouth.

'What is that shit you're drinking, Loeb?' Dansk asked.

'Morphine in a syrup base.'

'Morphine?'

'Whatever it takes,' Loeb said. 'Anybody ever tells you there's dignity in pain is talking unadulterated crap. Let's get some air.'

They walked together through a door marked EXIT and entered an alley at the back of the hotel where Dansk saw dark-green plastic garbage sacks and cardboard boxes, all very orderly.

In his beret Loeb resembled a raddled, hollow-faced 1950s poet, a guy sitting outside a café on the Left Bank or in Greenwich Village, scribbling intense odes and drinking cheap red vino. 'I was wondering about our lady,' he said.

'This is territory I work my own way. This is mine,' Dansk said, keeping his voice in check.

'Yeah, it's your domain all right. But this work can contaminate a man. I've seen people get a taste for death. They develop a jones.'

'Oh spare me the fucking lecture,' Dansk said.

'Sometimes enthusiasm's great, Anthony. Other times it fogs a man's judgement.'

Dansk said, 'There's nothing wrong with my judgement, Loeb.'

Loeb said, 'You're so damn defensive these days, I wonder if you aren't just losing the place a little. I worry about your detachment.'

'I'm detached,' Dansk said.

'Maybe. But this work can get to you in such a way you wouldn't even notice it happening.'

'I'd notice,' Dansk said.

'So tell me about her. Share, Anthony.'

Dansk laughed. 'Share? What is this? Like a counselling session?'

'Carry too much inside, you get stressed, Anthony. I attend this group in Fairfax, it's people like myself living with a death sentence. And we talk things through, and it helps, because you realize you're not entirely alone in the universe.'

Dansk imagined a room filled with dying people. Incurables Anonymous. 'I don't need to share,' he said. 'I'm not the one sick.'

'Pardon me, I forgot, you're invincible. Captain Fucking Marvel. The occasional services of a hooker and a whistle-stop tour of a church or two, and suddenly you're walking on water.'

'Don't give me static, Loeb.' Dansk was irritated with Loeb prying, carping, carrying that dark bloom of death. He didn't want to be in Loeb's company. Hanging round terminal people was depressing. Even if you couldn't catch the other person's disease, you were vulnerable to the despair they hauled like leg-irons.

'She goes here, there, so I track her movements and I try to read her mind and see how much of a problem she is.'

'How much of a problem is she, Anthony?'

'I'm tired. This has been a long day and I feel like one of those plastic sacks there. There's grime attached to me, which I don't like. I need to shower.'

Dansk moved a few steps along the alley. Loeb followed, catching him by the arm. 'You think you can handle her, Anthony?'

Dansk shrugged the hand aside. 'I can handle her.' He thought about the letter in his pocket which he had no intention of showing to Loeb. Why give the nosy old fart something to criticize?

Dansk kept walking. He stopped only when he heard Amanda's voice:

'*Oh God, this is an emergency. I need an ambulance and police, and I need them five minutes ago.*'

'*Give me your address and the nature of your problem, please.*'

'*The address is three six one Kennedy. That's Scottsdale, near the Civic Center.*'

'*And the problem, miss?*'

'*My boyfriend . . . I think he may be dying . . .*

somebody came in the house and he's beaten up and I found him in the pool and—'

'Try to remain calm. I'll have somebody with you as fast as I can.'

'How fast is fast?'

'As fast as possible.'

'Hurry, for Christ's sake . . .'

Enraged, Dansk said, 'Jesus, you got a wire on her *fucking* phone.' He felt he'd been cuffed around the ears and the inside of his head was ringing, his skin stinging.

Loeb had a tiny cassette player in his hand. He said, 'Listen some more.'

Amanda's voice: *'I'm calling about a patient. John Rhees.'*

'And you are?'

'His fiancée, Amanda Scholes.'

'He's stable, Miss Scholes.'

'When's the earliest I can see him?'

'Visiting hours are from ten a.m. until noon.'

Loeb shut off the machine. 'And that's what you ordered, Anthony? You had the shit kicked out of her boyfriend?'

'It was a simple diversion,' Dansk said.

'Is that what you call it?'

'You had absolutely no goddam right, Loeb,' he said.

'No right to run an eye over your operation?'

Dansk said, 'The deal was you don't interfere, you don't question my decisions.'

'I question this one. Rhees is one half of a couple. You've trespassed into some very dicey emotional territory.'

Dansk said, 'Emotional territory? Where did you get your psychology degree? Some school in

Guatemala that advertises on the back of matchbooks?'

Loeb looked morose. 'You didn't take into account the obvious thing, Anthony. You've only tossed more kerosene on the woman's bonfire.'

Dansk said nothing. He was seething at the idea of Loeb criticizing him.

'You never used to put a foot wrong, Anthony, but what you didn't take into account is the fact that other people have strong feelings, and sometimes those feelings lead to unpredictable responses. Am I coming through to you on any known frequency?'

Dansk was silent. Let Loeb drone on.

'The question is, what's your next step, Anthony?'

'I go up to my room and I take a shower.'

'About the woman,' Loeb said.

Dansk said, 'I can take care of her.'

Loeb looked infinitely weary and sad. 'God knows why, but I'm your friend, Anthony. Maybe the only one you've got.'

'I don't need friends that go behind my back,' Dansk said. He listened to Loeb's ruined breathing. 'You know what I think? The drugs have addled you. You're stoned morning to night. You can't make judgements.'

'I don't believe I've ever seen the world more clearly in all my life,' Loeb said.

'Drugs'll make you believe anything,' Dansk said.

Loeb folded his arms and leaned against the wall. Under his eyes were dark sooty rings. 'This work we're doing, we're pushing boulders up mountains, and there's always more boulders. There's a job in Seattle should have been taken care of yesterday. Another in L.A.'

Open-mouthed, Loeb was sucking on shallow pockets of air. 'What I'm saying is we need to get the business done here because we're falling behind. I need to know you can finalize things in a straightforward way. I need to believe that this business you engineered with Rhees was just some brainstorm along the way.'

'I can cope,' Dansk said. Brainstorm, he thought. Loeb didn't appreciate intricacy. He didn't like filigree. Angles baffled him, curved surfaces bewildered him. His was the geometry of a wasted old pen-pusher. X belongs in this box, Y belongs in that. There's only one road from A to B, and that's the straight and narrow. Maybe for you, Loeb.

Loeb looked bleak. 'I don't want an extravaganza, Anthony. I don't want to hear about diversions. Give me quiet, and don't leave any mess. Bury your litter.' Loeb turned and moved in his slow-footed manner down the alley. He stopped and called back, 'I'm trusting you, Anthony. Just don't go off at tangents.'

Tangents. You brain-dead fuck. Dansk chewed on the small finger where no nail grew, a nervous mannerism he'd acquired in fifth grade. A brutally dumb kid called Skipper Klintz had smashed his pinky with a claw-hammer. It was all on account of Skipper's need to assert his tribal superiority over Dansk, whose birthmark rendered him odd and imperfect, and consequently a victim. The nail had never grown back again. Two weeks later, on a bleak sub-zero night, Dansk had waited in an alley for Skipper and battered his head with a baseball bat. He could still feel the whap of the bat in his hands and the crack of Skipper's skull. A home run and the crowd going crazy in the bleachers and the electronic scoreboard popping.

Now he watched Loeb go, a sick shambles of a guy shuffling away, dying with every step he took. *I'm trusting you.* Bugging phones behind my back, you call that trust?

Dansk walked to the end of the alley, reached the street where the hotel sign created a soft yellow glare and a uniformed doorman stood motionless on the steps, misted by the light falling all around him.

46

Amanda found stacked on Dansk's bedside table the following: a map of Arizona, a paperback entitled *Guide to Restaurants in the Valley of the Sun*, and an inky copy of something called *Phoenix After Dark*, which was a list of swingers and spouse-swappers, strip joints and gay bars and escort agencies. Dansk had circled some of these agencies in red ballpoint. Romantic Liaisons. Sweet Dreams. Phantasy Chix. Some had come-on lines, like 'Meet Miss Foxxy Foxx and get out of that rut.' 'See Petal, ripe for plucking.'

In the drawer of the table she found a packet of condoms, a set of old rosary beads and a plastic wallet-insert that contained a series of photographs.

She glanced at these snapshots. Dansk was unmistakable in each of them. Some depicted him as a kid, others as a teenager. A woman figured in every shot. In some of them she had an arm round Dansk's waist or a hand on his arm. Amanda guessed Dansk's mother because there was some slight resemblance. Touching, she thought. He carries pictures of Mom. And the beads. She tried to imagine him smoothing them with his fingertips but she couldn't.

She opened the drawers of the dressing table. The potent aroma of sandalwood emerged from a sachet that had been placed over a neat stack of boxer shorts. She dug around the polka dots and the paisleys, noticing how fastidiously they'd been ironed and arranged. The next drawer down contained a couple of shirts, still in their Cellophane packages, and a half dozen pairs of socks, coupled and folded. The third drawer was empty.

She walked to the closet and checked the clothes that hung meticulously on hangers: two suits, both designer labels, two sports coats, a couple of pairs of shorts. The pockets were all empty. They yielded nothing, not a coin, a scrap of paper, not even lint. What did he do? Vacuum them?

On the closet floor was a combination-locked aluminium case. She picked it up, shook it and heard what sounded like papers sliding around inside. She longed to open the case, but it was useless. She set the case back.

She entered the bathroom. Toilet items were lined up just so inside the cabinet. Aftershave, hair lotion, a mouthwash she'd never heard of and a toothbrush designed to reach the deepest recesses of the gums and God knows where else. A nail-file with a genuine ivory handle, a heavy-duty nail-clipper, a container of floss, a tortoiseshell hairbrush in whose bristles a matching comb had been inserted, and a wooden spatula-like device whose purpose she couldn't begin to guess. On the sink was a bottle of Italian mineral water and a razor and shaving cream in a tube.

And a salt-shaker. Did he gargle with brine?
This is what Dansk came down to. Expensive toiletries and empty pockets and a locked case and the fact that he used escort services.
Who the hell are you, Dansk?
She went back inside the bedroom. A printed card on top of the TV provided the information that guests could access a computer that would provide them with a detailed account of their bill. She aimed the remote at the screen, turned the TV on, selected Channel 22 as the card instructed. The name popped up: ANTHONY DANSK
Then:

ROOM RATE $175 TAX INC.	TOTAL $875.00
ROOM SERVICE	TOTAL $63.00
PHONE CALLS	TOTAL $4.25
LAUNDRY	TOTAL $48.50

She studied the room rate figure a moment, calculating. He'd been here five nights. He hadn't just come to Phoenix to meet her some twenty-four hours ago. *I flew all the way down here to set your mind at rest*, he'd told her. But you were already here, Anthony, already in place. Why the lie? Why go through that rigmarole?
You lie when you have something to gain.
Or something to hide.
She stared at the menu along the bottom of the screen and pressed sixty-seven on the remote, which gave her access to an itemized account of telephone calls.

PLEASE WAIT. TRY OUR YUCCA ROOM ON THE MEZZANINE FOR FINE WESTERN CUISINE!

Then:

DANSK, ANTHONY 7320

What followed was a list of calls he'd made. He'd placed four, all local, three to the same number. She wrote the numbers down on a scratch pad that lay on top of the dressing table, then she folded the sheet and stuck it in her pocket. She switched off the TV.

It was time to get out of here, and yet she had the feeling she was overlooking something, she hadn't explored deeply enough. But what was left to explore? Hotel rooms like this one didn't have a surplus of hiding-places. There was an air-conditioning duct, but she didn't have either the time or the tool to unscrew the grille. There was also the chance of something concealed under the carpet, but the task of searching would take too long. Down on her knees, hauling at the rug, popping tacks.

The mini-bar was the last place left. It was stuffed with miniatures, a half bottle of Californian Chardonnay, a jar of macadamia nuts and a tube of Toblerone. She rummaged, found nothing unusual and shut the door. Leave, she told herself. Leave now. You've already pressed your luck to its limits and then some.

She took a last quick look round the room and then stepped towards the door, and halfway there the mercurial bird of good fortune abandoned her, and she heard *click* as the coded key card was inserted into the lock and the door opened.

'Interesting,' Dansk said.

47

She raised one hand to her hair in a flustered manner, her nerve-ends jumping. The atmosphere around her had a tense zing to it, like the vibration left by a tuning fork. She moved, standing with her back to the window, crossing her arms in a defensive way. She was aware of the peripheral blackness of night behind her, and she imagined Dansk strolling towards her and casually pushing her through glass, and then she was falling, storey after storey, to the sidewalk.

She walked away from the window and thought, Nobody knows I'm here.

Dansk said, 'I guess there's a good explanation for this.' The letter from the señorita. That's what brings her here. She's shovelling and she doesn't know what lies underneath the soil. And if she knew, she wouldn't be here. 'You looking for anything in particular? Or was it just a general sniff around, see what you could find?'

She could still hear the air vibrate as if a huge menacing bird had just passed close to her face.

When she spoke her voice sounded cracked. 'You've been following me.'

'I didn't hear that. Louder.'

She cleared her throat and said it again.

Dansk looked annoyed. 'Following you? Is this because I bump into you by chance on the street and you construct a whole weird scenario around that encounter? Why would I follow you, Amanda?'

He undid his necktie and it dangled from his hand.

'You know why,' she said. She noticed how the silver tie caught the light and resembled a loose metal chain.

'You're speaking a foreign language. Translate for me.'

'You're running surveillance on me because you know I'm not buying into your deal.'

'Where is all this coming from, Amanda?'

'Rhees is in hospital with broken bones.'

'Rhees?' he asked. 'I don't know any Rhees. You can't just toss out a name at me, Amanda.'

She saw from the window the lights of radio masts perched on mountains in those black distances where the city faded. The anger and adrenalin that had driven her appeared to be slipping, and an edge of dread had replaced it. She felt very alone all at once. She looked at Dansk's reflection in the pane. He seemed to exist simultaneously in different dimensions, behind her in solid form, floating in front of her in a fuzzy spectral framework.

Why hadn't she told Willie she was coming here? Anything could happen to her and nobody would know. She turned, bringing Dansk back into focus. 'Rhees wasn't any part of this—'

'I'm hearing foreign still.'

'You didn't do it personally. You paid for it to be done.'

'Paid who to do what?'

'It was meant to look like robbery with serious violence thrown in. But it was badly stage-managed. Thieves *steal* things, Anthony. You should teach your thugs that.'

'I don't even know Rhees, so let me hear one good reason why I'd want him harmed.'

'As a warning to me.'

A warning, he thought. If she wanted to think it was something that crude, let her. People often misconstrued his intentions. Even the smart ones, like Amanda. They didn't set themselves demanding standards.

'You're off in the twilight zone, Amanda. I'm hearing that dooda-dooda tune. You just break in here and lay this shit on my doorstep and you don't have one solid thing to back it up. This is unlawyerly.'

'I'm not a lawyer these days,' she said. She stared at him. He gazed back, nonchalant, running the necktie through his fingers.

'You break in here and make a wild accusation. Is that normal behaviour?'

'You're familiar with normal, I suppose.'

He didn't like this remark. It rubbed him in all the wrong ways. He walked towards her and looked at her bright lipstick and polished nails. She wasn't cut out for these gaudy adornments, they cheapened her. 'What the hell is your *problem*? You break into my room, presumably you rummage through my belongings. What did you expect to find here? Spell it out for me. Tell me what's really on your mind.'

'Your Program. The way it leaks.'

'And that's all.'

'That's all.'

'I think it's more. You're unhinged on account of Isabel Sanchez and whatever it was happened to this guy Rhees,' he said. 'And now you're imagining funny things.'

There was an alteration in his mood. He leaned forward, placed his palms against the wall on either side of her face. She was imprisoned between his outstretched arms. She felt she was seeing him through a microscope. The fuzz on his cheeks, the ginger eyebrows, his pores, the birthmark, everything was blown-up in unnerving detail. She anticipated violence. She imagined Dansk striking her. She felt an inward flinch.

'Talk to me,' he said.

'I don't have anything else to say.'

He looked into her eyes and it occurred to him that he could strangle her with his necktie. The idea strobed through him in black and white flashes; the lethal laying on of hands, the deadly intimacy of it all, her eyes darkening as she died. Killing somebody, the way McTell did, or Pasquale. How it would feel. He imagined numbness, the heart anaesthetized, a plunge into a bewildering madness. He didn't want McTell or Pasquale involved when it came to this woman, he didn't want them getting within a mile of her. He wanted her for himself. But not here in this room, because even if she died without a sound there was still the daunting prospect of dragging a corpse into an elevator and out through reception, past clerks and porters and guests and security people. Unrealistic.

And then there was Rhees. Any final solution had

to involve him too, because he and Amanda had probably discussed the letter together. They were lovers, and lovers should die together.

He noticed the room-service food on the table. The hamburger smelled cold and the fries were limp.

'You haven't eaten your food,' he said. 'Lost your appetite?'

'I'm not that hungry.'

He gazed down at her feet. 'Lost your shoes as well?'

'I like not wearing shoes,' she said.

She looked at the sweat on his forehead and wondered where he'd been for the last twenty seconds or so, because he'd misted over like a window under a layer of condensation, and his jaw had set in a purposeful way and the muscles in his cheeks had been working as if he were chewing gum. He'd vanished in front of her eyes.

'Eat. You ordered the stuff.' He caught her wrist and tugged her towards the table. 'Sit down.'

'I don't want to sit,' she said.

He pulled back a chair and forced her into it. '*Now eat.*'

'I don't—'

'Eat,' he said.

He whipped the top off the bun and she found herself looking at a dollop of ketchup on the browned meat.

'Try the burger,' he said. His voice was chilly and brittle and angry.

She lifted the burger reluctantly. It fell apart between her fingers and she watched it drop on the plate, a soggy bun disintegrating and a crumbling disc of meat smeared with sauce. Dansk was hovering just behind her.

'Clumsy, clumsy. You need some help.'

He scooped up a handful of meat in his palm and held it to her mouth and she turned her head to one side and said, 'I'm not fucking hungry.'

'Kids are starving all over the world,' he said. 'And I hate waste, I hate the way people don't think about others less fortunate.' He pushed the meat forcefully into her mouth, and she shoved his hand aside.

'I don't *want* the goddam food,' she said.

'You *ordered* it,' he said.

Dansk could smell her perfume. He could smell fear on her too, and he had a sense of power flowing through him. He was wired to this woman in some fashion and he was draining energy out of her battery and it made him giddy. He reached down to the table and picked up a fork, speared an onion and raised it close to her face and let it dangle just in front of her.

She gazed at the hanging strand of onion and tried to shove her chair away from the table but Dansk obstructed her. He let the fork fall, placed his hands back on her shoulders and felt her shiver.

'I scare you,' he said.

'I'm not easily scared.'

He wanted to keep his hands on her. Suddenly he didn't want to release her, he wanted to open the buttons of her blouse and lay his head between her breasts. He kept the pressure on her shoulders. He thought, This is a step too far. So fucking what? He couldn't stop himself. He wanted to taste her breasts – a crazy idea, she meant nothing, she didn't even attract him that way, and in his head she was already a corpse. He reached over from behind and lowered his hands and fumbled with the buttons of her blouse and she didn't move, and he thought, She wants this. He slid a palm inside her blouse and felt the silky material of her brassière and slipped his fingers under it. Then he was touching her warm breast and it was a good feeling, the softness of her skin, her acquiescence, the power he had over her.

She moved abruptly. She swept the food and the plate from the table with a speedy motion of her hand and she picked up a knife, which she jabbed hard into his knuckles, and he stepped back. She rose, colliding with the table and toppling it over, then she spun round and held the knife towards Dansk, who held out his hands in a gesture that might have been one of appeasement, but it wasn't, because there was a vicious light in his green eyes. She was aware of the knife shaking in her fist and how breathless she'd become.

She could still feel the pressure of his fingers on her shoulders and the way he'd slipped his hand inside her blouse and how the ice-cold palm had covered her breast, the whole ugly violation of the moment.

Dansk casually examined the back of his hand where she'd jabbed it. 'What we have here is a slight misunderstanding,' he said. 'I guess I imagined . . . some carnal agenda.'

'*Carnal* agenda?'

'You turn up in my room. What am I supposed to think?'

'You don't think . . .' She wanted to laugh at his supposition, but she knew laughter would provoke him. Still holding the knife in front of herself, she moved towards the door and hurried out of the room. She ran along the corridor to the elevators, half expecting Dansk to follow her, but he didn't.

She entered the elevator and pressed the button for her floor and realized how tightly she was holding the knife in her tensed hand. Dansk had dragged her down to the place where he lived, his world of brutality. She entered her room, shut the door, slid the bolt in place and stood with her back against the wood, trying to catch her breath and steady her nerves.

Sweat stuck Dansk's shirt to his flesh.

He thought, She's past the point of no return. She's a long way past that.

He pictured her moving somewhere in the night. (Shoeless. Why shoeless?) He pictured her in bed, waiting for the hour to roll around when she'd visit Rhees in hospital. And then what? She'd sit beside him, feeling bad. She'd reproach herself. And what next?

He lay back and closed his eyes. He smelled the hamburger again, the stone-cold French fries. He looked at the overturned table, the scattered food, little globs of mustard and ketchup on the carpet. Messy, Amanda.

He lifted the phone and called McTell.

McTell said, 'I picked him up when he was leaving his office.'

'And?'

'OK. He drives to the suburbs, somewhere, north Phoenix, I dunno exactly. The streets look all the same to me round here.'

'Then what?'

'He parks outside a house surrounded by all these palm trees and yuck plants, yucca, whatever they're called—'

'Skip the garden tour.'

'He goes inside, stays a half-hour.'

'Whose house?'

'The name on the mailbox was Bascombe.'

Dansk was quiet for a time. 'Where is he now?'

'OK. He left Bascombe, stopped in a diner for some apple pie, cream, the works—'

'The point, McTell.'

'He's in another suburb, looks exactly like the last one. He's parked outside a house.'

'You got the name of the occupant?'

'I'm waiting to check the mailbox. You don't just walk up to it, Anthony: there's neighbours, a guy walking dogs—'

'Call me back when you know.'

Dansk hung up. He took Isabel Sanchez's letter from his pocket and stared at the scribbled words. He struck a match, applied it to the sheets and dropped them into an ashtray. He stirred the ashes with a fingertip, imagining they were the cremated remains of some tiny creature sacrificed, and then he opened his case and removed a bunch of faxes. He set these on fire too. Flame purified.

His phone rang. McTell said, 'Check this out. The name on the box is Vialli.'

Dansk said, 'Stay right where you are, McTell. Don't move an inch. I mean that.' He got up and started gathering his clothes together. He swept all his toiletries inside a leather bag and closed it. The sound of the zip closing reminded him of flesh tearing, of a sharp instrument slicing a vein.

He thought, This Is Your Life, Amanda Scholes.

The beginning of the end of it.

48

Drumm rang the doorbell, waited, shifted his weight a little. His leg ached from an old wound inflicted on him during the course of a liquor store hold-up when he'd been a rookie. He remembered the shock of the bullet ripping through his flesh and exiting along with tissue and blood and a chunk of bone. The ache was more pronounced at times of stress, such as now. He attributed the stabbing pain to his meeting with Bascombe. Talk about pulling teeth. Lew Bascombe was a dentist's nightmare.

A porch light came on and he blinked.

A woman's voice from inside: 'Who's there?'

'Police,' Drumm said. Even pleasant suburbs had become shotgun territory, he thought. People lived with guns in nightstands, guns in closets. Villains roamed the streets. Look at Rhees.

'Police?'

'I have ID,' Drumm said.

The door opened an inch. There was a chain between door and jamb. Drumm held out his ID card. The woman peered at it. 'This is kinda late to be calling,' she said.

'I apologize,' Drumm said.

'You better come inside,' she said. 'You know, I think I remember you. You were at the trial of Benny's uncles. Right?'

'Right.' Drumm stepped into the hallway. There was an overload of floral arrangements on various surfaces. The woman led him into a sitting room suggestive of a funeral parlour, more flowery arrays, mountains of lilacs and lilies, stacks of greenery in baskets.

'Sit, sit down, Lieutenant.'

Drumm lowered himself into a plump easy chair. The leg stabbed. Bernadette Vialli wore a blue robe. She had thick little fingers. The lenses of her glasses were grey-tinted, matching the colour of her short permed hair. She was a small woman and her feet barely touched the carpet when she sat in an armchair facing Drumm.

Family photographs hung on almost every available wall space, interrupted by a couple of paint-by-numbers watercolours. Drumm saw Benny Vialli in some of the photographs. Benny as a kid, Benny as a teenager. He had protruding ears and a cheerful smile.

'I'm here on Amanda Scholes's behalf,' Drumm said. 'You called her, I understand.'

'Yeah. A few days ago.'

'She asked me to follow up,' Drumm said.

'It's real nice of you to come in her place, except now I wish I hadn't called her. It's a waste of your time.'

'You must have had some reason when you phoned her.'

'I'm a mother. Worry about this, worry about that, then you're out of control before you know it and imagining all kinds of things.'

'I don't have any children, Mrs Vialli,' Drumm said. 'My wife died a few years back. We just never got round to kids.'

'I'm sorry,' she said. She took off her glasses. There were red ridges on either side of her nose.

Drumm thought about his little downtown apartment and the pantry loaded with Campbell's soup, individual servings in small cans. Jeanette, God rest her, had been some kind of cook. But that was past. He didn't dwell on her absence except when he had a can-opener in his hand and was wondering whether to choose the cream of asparagus or the cream of mushroom even though they tasted exactly the same: of corn-starch.

'Kids are a joy. Also a heartbreak.' Mrs Vialli rose and adjusted flowers, gathering bright clumps of petals between her hands. She did this for a while as if she had in mind some ideal arrangement she couldn't actualize. 'I got to thinking about Benny, that's what happened.'

'What about Benny?' he asked.

'It's just so . . . it's nothing.'

'I'd still like to hear.'

Mrs Vialli gave up on the flowers. 'Benny and me, we were real close, until his uncles hired him down to Tucson. With relatives like those guys you wish you could pick and choose your family. I hope they goddam rot in jail. They had Benny going like, yeah, a yo-yo. Drive this guy, drive that, deliver this package, deliver that. I don't believe he ever thought he was doing anything illegal. I'm his mother, and I love him more than anyone in the world, but he's always had this kinda lost thing about him. Day he was born, I took one look at his face and I thought, This world's gonna be a rocky ride for you, darling.'

Drumm heard the sadness in the woman's voice and it touched him. Mrs Vialli opened a cabinet and took out a small cassette deck. 'The battery's probably weak on this.'

She pressed PLAY. Initially there was hissing. The voice that eventually issued from the cassette sounded as if it had travelled from an abandoned space probe.

'Ma, it's Benny. I wish you was (*inaudible*) got (*inaudible*) two but (*inaudible*) I'm doing (*inaudible*) these guys are (*inaudible*) they say I can't call you (*Insert another seventy-five cents please*) Ma, I'm outta time, I'll call again real soon.'

The tape stopped dead.

Mrs Vialli said, 'That was two days after he went away. I've listened to it fifty times at least. I try to imagine where he was phoning from, what kind of place, what he was wearing, was he getting the right food, you know? He never did call back.'

Drumm thought the room felt like a box wrapped in Cellophane. One of the paintings on the wall depicted a harbour and a small anchored sailboat and gulls that were no more than a haphazard series of Vs.

I'll call again real soon. And he never had.

'My hobby,' Mrs Vialli said. 'Watercolours.'

'Very nice,' Drumm said. His thoughts drifted to Bascombe's hobby, the balsa-wood Messerschmitts and Spitfires he built in a workshop that smelled of glue and chemicals. He was some kind of World War Two airplane buff and he laboured in grim, patient silence. His tiny models hung from nylon strings tacked to the ceiling. *I don't like being interrupted in my own home*, Bascombe had said. *Make an appointment at my office.*

Mrs Vialli said, 'Benny's gone, and my husband passed away eight years ago. I miss the boy. It's a hole in my heart.'

'I'm sure it is,' Drumm said.

Mrs Vialli said, 'You got time to look at something?' She moved to a writing-bureau and opened it, and from a small drawer took out a white envelope. She handed it to Drumm.

'Go ahead, open it.'

Drumm took the message card from the envelope. It had a red heart on the front and the words 'HAPPY BIRTHDAY TO MY BELOVED MOTHER'.

Mrs Vialli said, 'The card was attached to a buncha roses. There's a message inside. Read it if you like.'

Drumm flipped open the card and read the message, written in featureless block capitals with a ballpoint pen. 'Dear Mom, I miss you very much, love, your son.'

'One quick phone message and flowers and that card in more than six months, nothing else,' Mrs Vialli said. She sat down and frowned. 'It's not much. I know, the Program protects him, I know the rules, but it's still not much. And there's something about the birthday card worries me.'

'What?'

'You have a kid, he's like this book you can always read, you just know how he behaves. And one big problem I have with this card is . . .' She paused and looked at Drumm. 'I know this is gonna seem very small to you and maybe you'll leave here thinking I'm a little crazy, but I'll tell you anyway. You heard the tape, he called me Ma. You read the card. How does it begin? Dear Mom, that's how. Dear Mom.'

'And?'

'When he was a very young kid, just starting to talk, he always called his grandmother Mom. Poor little guy couldn't get his mouth around the word grandma, I guess. Anyway, it was always Mom. I kept telling him life was gonna get confusing for everybody if he went round referring to his grandmother as Mom, so he called me Ma.'

'Always?'

'He'd come home from school and say what's that cooking in Ma Vialli's kitchen. What's that good smell, Ma. You change Ma to Mom, why it's like somebody who's called you Jack all your life suddenly deciding to call you John. Where's the sense of it?'

Mrs Vialli was right, it *was* a small thing, it was microscopic. But Drumm wasn't inclined to dismiss small things, because he understood from years of experience that they sometimes had significance way beyond their size. A fibre from a rug, a single pubic hair, a speck of dust, stuff like that had sent some people to jail, others to death row. You never overlooked small. He had a bad feeling, only it wasn't his leg this time, it was closer to indigestion, an eruption in his intestines, gassy heat round his heart. *I can't talk about the Program*, Bascombe had said.

This is serious, Lew. This is a homicide investigation and I'll be damned if you stand in my way.

'So if he calls me Ma every day of his life, how come all of a sudden it's Mom?'

'I don't know.'

'It crossed my mind . . .' Mrs Vialli let her sentence die.

'You can tell me.'

'OK. Maybe somebody else sent the flowers. Somebody made it up and sent it to me. And the question I keep coming back to is real simple: Why? If Benny didn't send them why not? Which is why I called Amanda Scholes.'

'Amanda resigned,' he said. Officially, he thought, but her heart had never quit.

'Resigned? Oh.'

Drumm nodded.

'Maybe *you* can help me then, Lieutenant. I'd like to see Benny, even for a couple of minutes, and if that's impractical, then maybe just to hear his voice on the phone, or a letter at the very least. I don't even need to know where he is, nothing like that.'

Drumm said, 'Have you written to the Program?'

'I've begun letters I don't know how many times. Then I thought of Amanda. She was the prosecutor in the case, she must have connections. It's depressing when you don't know about your own son. Probably I'm making a mountain outta nothing, but it would be a relief just to know that.'

Drumm rubbed his leg. Goddam switchblade of pain. He rose from his chair. *Tell me about this guy Dansk, Lew.*

He said, 'I'll look into it, Mrs Vialli. I promise.'

Her glasses reflected lamplight. 'Listen. You want some coffee? Maybe a slice of pie? I'm forgetting my manners.'

Drumm thanked her, but said no. He stepped into the hallway, and a weariness descended on him. Ma, Mom. What's in a name? Maybe a whole lot.

Maybe everything. Flip the coin, maybe nothing.

He turned to Mrs Vialli, who'd followed him along the hallway. 'Leave this with me. I'll be in touch.'

He stepped out of the house. Mrs Vialli called goodnight to him. He heard her shut the door and slip the chain back in place. He wandered down the path to the sidewalk. As he opened the door of his car, he sniffed the night air, which had the smell of week-old fish covered with fat blue flies.

49

McTell dislikes the creepy-crawly hush of the suburbs. He prefers downtown life and crowded streets and honkytonks and pussy joints. He'd rather be in New Orleans or Chicago than this place. Better still, give him Tijuana, where it's lawless and anything goes.

He sits in his car for a while, surrounded by the big silence of it all, and sees the cop drive away.

Minutes later, McTell gets out and strolls half a block through the warm dark. He pulls on a pair of leather gloves as he moves. They make his hands sweat.

He pauses. Looks around. Sidewalks empty. Keeps going. Busy night doing Dansk's work. Yessir, Anthony. Yessir, Mr Birthmark.

You got another disfigurement, Dansk. Inside your head is where.

He raises one hand and pats the perspiration from his brow. He checks his pockets. He's got everything he needs. He walks down a driveway and presses a doorbell. An outside light comes on.

'Who is it?'

McTell clears his throat and says, 'Drumm again.'

'You forgot something, Lieutenant?'

'Right.' Cough, cough.

He hears the chain slide back. The door's opened a slit. The woman is dressed in a big blue robe and has cold cream on her face. She looks like a wary raccoon.

She blinks and steps back, mouth turning into an o of disbelief. McTell sticks a hand across her face and spins her around. She kicks against him. He forces her to the floor and goes down on his knees and still holds one gloved hand clamped across her lips. He grunts and the woman's dumpy little legs kick in the air, and her hands thrash and cold cream adheres to McTell's glove, white and greasy. He keeps one hand across her face and from his pocket draws out a plastic bag, which he pulls over her head. Suck this air, lady, he thinks. She struggles, her little fingers turning into useless blunted claws, her legs still thrashing up and down and she's gasping inside the plastic bag.

She dies in a matter of minutes with her body angled in a position close to foetal. The plastic bag's been sucked a few inches inside her mouth and her eyes are open. She looks like somebody staring out of a rainy window at some horrible accident in the street below.

McTell wipes sweat from his face and gets to his feet. He's short of breath. He glances at the stairs and contemplates the next task. With some difficulty, he drags the woman upstairs, thump thump thump. Her head rolls from side to side.

He pauses halfway to get air into his lungs, then

keeps going. Inside the bathroom he sets her down on the tiled floor. He runs some cold water, splashes it across his face, then he checks the shower-curtain rail. He grabs it and pulls hard. It doesn't budge. It's been screwed deeply into the wall by somebody who knew his job. Unusual in this day and age.

He raises the woman into a sitting position and props her against the side of the stall. He removes the plastic bag and her head tilts towards her chest. He takes a length of rope from his pocket and prepares a noose that goes round her neck. The other end of the rope he tosses round the curtain rail.

Now pull.

He raises Mrs Vialli up from the floor inch by inch. Hard fucking work. The curtain rail trembles but doesn't pop loose from the wall.

He pulls until she's about twenty-four inches from the floor, then he makes a knot and watches the woman hang, her body turning very slightly. She brushes the edge of the shower curtain which makes a tiny creaking noise. Her big bunny-rabbit slippers are wet with piss which trickles down her legs. McTell has seen a lot of effluence in his time.

He finds a chair in a bedroom and carries it into the bathroom and places it on the floor under Mrs Vialli's feet. He wads sheets of toilet paper together and steps up on the chair, then he cleans the goo of cream from the woman's face.

He steps down, flushes the papers and makes sure they've been sucked away, then kicks over the chair.

Checklist.

Climbs up, *tick*, hangs herself, *tick*, knocks chair over as she chokes, *tick*.

Anything else?

He looks round the bathroom and goes down the stairs. He puts the chain back in place and turns off the hallway light, then walks with the aid of a pen-sized flashlight through the kitchen to the back door. He opens it, steps out, pulls it shut again behind him, hears the Yale snap at his back. No sign anywhere of forced entrance. No intrusion.

Just a very depressed woman hanging in her own bathroom.

50

Amanda, who'd slept badly, dreaming again of Galindez turning over and over in black waters, drank a quick coffee in her room at 7 a.m., then checked out of the hotel. She rented a Ford from the Avis office in the lobby. She drove past plazas and shopping centres not yet open. The world was uncontaminated in the early sunlight.

She entered a parking lot, idled outside a Walgreen's emporium, checked the street. The only vehicle that came along was a beat-up old van with the logo PEACE and a hippie floral design peeling from the body. Time-warp travel. Groovy.

She drove again. When she reached the Hideaway Knolls Motel she parked and sat looking at the jaded two-storey cinder-block construction. This was the motel Dansk had telephoned three times, according to the information from the hotel computer system. The other number he'd called turned out to be an escort service called Romantic Liaisons. A receptionist with a voice like smooth ice-cream had told Amanda, 'We can help you in ways the Red Cross never dreamed about, honey.'

Amanda lit a cigarette. The dashboard clock read seven-forty. Dansk had phoned the Hideaway Knolls three times. Who does he know here? She got out of the car. She'd sit in the coffeeshop and wait until it was time to visit Rhees. She put on a pair of sunglasses, walked inside and took a table in a far corner with a view of the door. She skipped quickly through the menu, ordered coffee and gazed round the room. This could be nothing, a waste of time.

The place was crowded. Some of the customers had the stunned dead-eyed glaze that comes when you're crossing the continent with your possessions in a U-Haul and wondering what your new lives will be like when you get where you're going.

New lives. Just what the Program offered.

She looked through the window at sun glaring off the pavement. She saw her image reflected in a knife on the table and she thought about Dansk and the sickening sensation of his fingers on her breast.

The waitress came with her coffee.

What was she expecting to discover in this place anyway? Dansk phones here, but you could hardly go from table to table asking people if they knew a man called Anthony Dansk, any more than you could trek from room to room knocking on doors. She went to the telephone and called the hospital. Rhees was fine and alert, the nurse said. He'd passed a comfortable night and eaten a good breakfast.

She walked back to her table, finished her coffee. She looked at her watch. Eight a.m. She wondered what Rhees might need, if there was anything she could take to him at the hospital. Reading material, maybe? Clean underwear for sure. Fresh clothes in the unlikely event they decided to discharge him in her care—

The door of the coffeeshop opened.

Startled, Amanda held the menu close to her face. *Don't panic.*

The man who came inside sat up on a stool at the counter and yawned. He checked the room with a casual movement of his head but he didn't see her. He wasn't wearing his neck brace, but this was the guy from the hospital waiting room. This was the one, she thought. This was who Dansk phoned here.

The thought raced through her mind that he might also be one of the pair who'd attacked Rhees. He resembled an athlete who'd let himself go; muscled, but slackly so. She watched him as he blew on the surface of his coffee. She looked at his yellow-grey hair and sideburns and his crumpled dark-blue suit. He turned to survey the room again and she laid the palm of one hand like a mask against her face, something to reinforce the dark glasses and the menu held in mid-air.

She couldn't play this hiding game indefinitely.

He was hunched on his stool, staring into his coffee. He yawned, stretched his arms, performed some business with his hands, applying the force of one against the other in a form of callisthenics, fingertip pushed upon fingertip. He tugged a tissue from the dispenser and in an absent-minded manner stroked it with his fingers.

It disappeared a second between his palms, and when he opened them the tissue had been transformed into a shape like the head of a white rose.

He pushed it across the counter towards the cashier, a teenage girl who smiled and said, 'Hey, neat little party trick you got there.'

There was an unusual grace and suppleness about those hands. They could play a cello, shuffle cards as if they were lubricated, conjure hankies or rabbits out of top hats, pick locks.

Amanda thought, Wait. Rewind all the way back to the moment when he'd leaned across her at the hospital, the soda can he'd suggested she use as an ashtray. The memory was like a scene filmed through cheesecloth, muted halos, soft edges.

Hands like those could pick more than locks. They could slide inside pockets, deft and weightless, they could remove two sheets of paper from the hip pocket of a highly distressed woman in the space of a breath. Two sheets of paper, gone in a whisper.

It was possible, more than possible.

He steals the letter. He slips a hand inside her back pocket and steals the goddam letter. She didn't want to think.

She dropped a couple of dollar bills on the table and hurried outside. Her dark glasses slid off her face and fell to the pavement and she stooped to pick them up. The left lens was cracked. She moved in the direction of her car. The world through cracked plastic. The tinted sun had a spidery fracture.

She reached her car and sat behind the wheel. OK, you didn't lose the letter after all. And all the time you were in Dansk's company, he knew you'd read it, you'd read Isabel Sanchez's hasty words that had dynamited the bunker of Program security.

She backed up the car into a green plastic dumpster that rocked to and fro, then she edged forward into the traffic flow. She avoided the clogged freeways. It took her twenty minutes driving along suburban back streets to get to her house. She parked and went indoors. She didn't look at the mess. She walked quickly inside the bedroom and found a freshly laundered shirt and a pair of jeans and clean socks and underwear, gathered them together hastily, then turned around to head back out again.

The telephone rang. She was tempted to let the answering machine pick up, but she reached for the handset before the recorded message kicked in.

It was Willie Drumm. 'Next time you go to a hotel, leave me the name of the place,' he said. 'That way I can reach you.'

'I wasn't thinking straight, Willie.'

'Whatever. Here's the run-down on my activity.'

'I'm listening.'

'First Mrs Vialli. She hasn't heard from Benny since he went inside the Program, except for some flowers on her birthday and a card she feels isn't kosher.'

'Not kosher how?' She clutched Rhees's clothing against her body as if she were holding the man himself.

Drumm told her. She listened carefully through an unexpected flutter of static on the line. She imagined Mrs Vialli reading and rereading a terse message she considered fake and replaying a taped phone message and thinking odd thoughts about a bunch of flowers long-since withered. She remembered Bernadette and the way she'd embraced her son outside the courthouse after he'd given his testimony, how she'd wept because she knew he was going away.

Amanda thought about this a moment. 'What are we saying here, Willie?'

'Maybe only that Benny's less loving and attentive than Ma Vialli wants to believe. She reads something into a message that isn't there. I don't know.'

Amanda thought Drumm's voice lacked conviction. 'When I spelled out for Benny what it would involve going into the Program, the only thing that bothered him was leaving his mother, nothing else. They're pretty close all right.'

'There's a note in your voice I don't like, Amanda. What are you thinking?'

'We know security's screwed-up. So . . . maybe there's some kind of connection between the apparent disappearance of Benny and the Sanchez-Galindez affair. Something we haven't thought about.'

'I don't see how there could be a connection,' Drumm said. 'Two different cases six months apart with nothing in common.'

'Except me, the prosecutor,' she said.

'So somebody's got it in for you personally? Dansk, say.'

'Until a few days ago I didn't even know he existed, Willie. I'd be inclined to dismiss anything personal.'

'If it's not personal, what is it?'

She didn't have an answer. Her brain was scurrying here and there, but coming up with nothing. 'I don't know what it is, Willie.'

Drumm was quiet a moment. He said, 'Speaking of Dansk. Let me just shift the scene to Bascombe a moment. This is a sensitive area, he tells me. Highly confidential. I tell him I don't give a rat's fuck how sensitive it is or who he works for, he's got no right to stand in the way of a homicide investigation. I mention Dansk's name has cropped up.'

'And what does he say?'

'Never heard of the guy. Total blank. So I press him just a little. He says he'll run a check on the name and get back to me this morning.'

Amanda let John's shirt slip to the floor and stooped to pick it up, balancing the handset between jaw and shoulder. 'That's the best he can do?'

'He says. I get the funny feeling he's gonna come up with nothing, even if he comes up with something. You know what I'm saying? He guards his territory like a killer Dobermann. He'd prefer to bite your face off than give you any information. I think it's time I had a word with Dansk in person.'

'You'll find him at the Carlton.'

'I'm also going to call Justice, check if they have anybody called Dansk.'

Something she'd meant to do. 'Contact me at the hospital as soon as you can.'

'Will do. Say hi to John for me.'

She hung up and left the house, stepped inside the car. She felt a shivery motion at the back of her mind, dark gauze shimmering in a draught.

Say hi to John for me.

It occurred to her then that if Dansk knew *she'd* read Isabel's letter, he'd assume Rhees had *also* read it. It was something she hadn't considered before, an oversight she attributed to the way events had whirled and jigged around her, but now she found herself worrying about hospital security and if Rhees might be in even more danger because he'd seen the letter, and in Dansk's distorted view of the world that made him a threat as much as herself.

She had a feeling of sinking through a sudden quicksand of panic. She thrust the key into the ignition and roared out of the cul-de-sac.

51

Dansk stared through the windshield of his car at the huge pink and aquamarine hospital, which bore some resemblance to a massive birthday cake. He turned to look at McTell in the seat. 'I want a gun, Eddie.'

'Say?'

'Something out of your private arsenal.'

'A gun,' McTell said and smiled in an uneasy fashion. Suddenly, outta the blue, Dansk wants a gun. Dansk's head was red flags, bad tides, No Swimming Beyond This Point.

'What kind of weapon can you give me?'

McTell said, 'I got a nice Heckler & Koch P7M8. Also a Ruger P89. You sure about this, Anthony?'

'I'm sure.'

'It's just when it comes to guns, me and Pasquale usually—'

'The Ruger,' Dansk said. He imagined the gun in his hand, the weight of it, the deadliness. He pinched the bridge of his nose. He was stuffed-up on account of this city air. His head ached, he was probably coming down with desert fever or whatever evil spore floated in from the hot canyons and clogged your nostrils and rooted itself like a fungus in your lungs.

McTell said, 'The Ruger's a joy. Square post front sight, square notch rear adjustable. It comes in blue steel, but I always had a soft spot for the stainless version.'

Dansk watched visitors getting out of cars and strolling towards the entrance with their flowers and candies. There was a certain type of person who thrived around sickbeds. They drew up their chairs and flashed their own epic scars. Here's where they did the bypass, a quadruple job, and down here's the appendectomy.

He looked for Amanda and saw no sign of her. Maybe she'd enter the building another way, a side door, a rear door, thinking she was being clever.

There's a note in your voice I don't like, Amanda. What are you thinking?

We know security's screwed-up. So . . . maybe there's some kind of connection between the apparent disappearance of Benny and the Sanchez-Galindez affair. Something we haven't thought about.

Dansk thought about the tape that had been delivered to his hotel at 9.15 a.m. just as he'd been finishing his press-ups. A brown padded envelope, no message. It hadn't needed any message. It was Loeb's way of telling him things had drifted too far. Well fuck you Loeb, I do this my way. Who needs a dying man's shit? He remembered sweat falling on the envelope. He'd called Pasquale immediately. His hand had left smudged prints on the phone.

'Is the gun handy?' he asked McTell.

'It's in the trunk of my car over there.'

'Get it for me.' Dansk watched McTell walk to his car, unlock the trunk and take out a brown-paper sack. McTell returned to the car and gave the sack to Dansk, who placed it in his lap, peered inside and saw the Ruger.

'Tell me about Mrs Vialli,' he said.

'What's to tell? It went off OK.'

Dansk said, 'You looked in her eyes, Eddie.'

'I don't think much about these things.'

'What did you see?'

'Like in her eyes?' This is Dansk. Dansk who never wants to hear details. All of a sudden he's interested. 'She just looked kinda surprised. She wet herself. She had on these furry slippers. Big fluffy things with like rabbit ears.'

Dansk thought of fuzzy dampened ears, the body discharging piss. He said, 'Here's what I want you to do, Eddie. Check the room Rhees is in.'

'Then what?'

'Just look inside, that's all.'

'That's it?' McTell opened the door and stopped halfway out. 'And if she's there with him? I just kinda look and walk away?'

Dansk said, 'Right. Buy a bunch of flowers, they'll make you appear legit. Go inside. Make it seem like you got the wrong room.'

'Rhees is gonna recognize me from that time we spoke.'

'Let me worry about that.'

McTell shrugged, stepped out of the car and walked across the lot.

Dansk regarded himself in the rear-view mirror and noticed a small brown wad of his morning toast stuck between his front teeth. He picked it out with his finger then wiped the finger on a Kleenex, a pop-up box of which he kept on the dash. Amanda Scholes had good teeth, he remembered. Strong and clean, healthy gums.

Good teeth. Everything decays though.

The hospital shimmered in front of him. All that sickness wrapped in a huge blue and pink cake. Terminal cases attached to machines, bony old women hunched behind screens.

On an impulse, he picked up his phone and called a number in New Jersey. He heard his mother's voice, faint and far away. Spectral.

'Anthony? That really you?'

'Yeah, really me. How are you?'

'It's been a while.'

'I've been busy, Ma.'

'Mr Chomsky was just asking after you,' she said. She had a quivery voice. It kept fading in and out.

'Where you calling from, Anthony?'

'Las Cruces, New Mexico.'

'You coming this way?'

'Soon, Ma.'

'I miss you.'

'Listen, I met a girl.'

'Yeah?'

'Nice girl, you'd like her. Maybe I'll bring her up there. Introduce you.'

'What's her name?'

'I can't hear you, Ma.'

'What's the girl's name I asked.'

'Amanda,' he said.

'Pretty name,' she said.

'Yeah, nice lady. Works for the same company as me.'

'I'll light a candle for you,' she said.

'You do that, Ma. I gotta go now. Talk to you soon.'

'I love you, Anthony.'

Dansk put down the phone on the passenger seat. The call would make the old woman's day, brighten her calendar. Sometimes you did what you could to spread a little cheer. He could see her hurry down the narrow gloomy stairs to the violin repairman's rooms where, surrounded by ancient amputated fiddles and a mountain of pegs and coiled strings, she'd tell Chomsky she'd just had a phone call from her son. He's got a girl called Amanda. She'd build it up into a big thing, a church wedding and decrepit Father McGlone conducting the service, and old Chom would tip his head in the manner of a blind person listening, and he'd smile in his gap-toothed way and say, 'Miracles happen when you least expect 'em. You gotta believe.'

Dansk leaned forward against the steering wheel. You tell a lie or two and they bring a little happiness. Where's the harm?

Amanda. It was the first name that had sprung to mind. He wondered about that, then decided it was on account of how much she occupied his thoughts, the way she eclipsed all other business. In one bizarre sense, he was more intimate with her than he'd ever been with any other woman in his entire life. He looked at the back of his hand, seeing the red mark left by the knife she'd used against him. Pathetic.

So somebody's got it in for you personally. Dansk, say.

Until a few days ago I didn't even know he existed, Willie. I'd be inclined to dismiss anything personal.

Personal, yeah. It hadn't started out that way, but somewhere along the line it had changed.

Dansk opened the paper sack, dipped a hand inside and gripped the Ruger. It had a lovely gravity. It seemed to emit a low humming sound, like a machine plugged into a power source. He took the gun out, passed it from one hand to the other, over and over. This killing device. This snuffer of human candles. He imagined saying, Open your mouth a little, part your lips just enough for me to slide the gun inside your mouth, Amanda. Let me bring an end to your troubles. The gun is foreplay. The rest is darkness.

He shut the sack. She was nearby and he knew it, he could sense it. He was tuned into her frequency. She was a clear image on his radar screen.

The wedge of pain had shifted to the front of his brain, and when he looked at the hospital it seemed to him that the edifice was disintegrating, like an ice-cream concoction melting in the heat.

A pigeon flew from the roof, flapping into the sun. Dansk watched it climb. He tightened his hold on the Ruger and imagined shooting the bird out of the sky. This was an unsettling junction where past and present intersected, and for a moment he seemed to hover outside himself, looking down and seeing a red-haired man sitting in a car with a gun in his lap and a freckled kid in the back seat clutching an air rifle. Both had murderous expressions.

52

She parked at the back of the hospital in one of the slots reserved for physicians and, wearing her cracked sunglasses, walked quickly between a fleet of ambulances. She went inside the building through double doors marked DELIVERIES, expecting to be challenged by hospital security guards. Nobody appeared.

She found herself in a wide corridor leading to the laundry. She passed a glass-panelled door, behind which she saw industrial washing-machines, enormous dryers rumbling, people in white smocks ironing and folding bed sheets. She took off the glasses when she reached the service elevator and punched the button for the third floor, where she emerged into a warren of corridors stretching into great pastel infinities. She took a left turn. Two security officers in chocolate-brown uniforms were talking together. They gazed at her, a moment of professional assessment, then turned away. She'd passed their scrutiny. A woman in a dark business suit, not worth challenging.

The door of room 360 was open.

He was propped up against pillows. His face was pale and swollen, his plastered arm in a white sling. His eyes were lacklustre. She drew up a chair to the side of the bed and Rhees managed a smile.

'How are we?' she asked.

'Prodigious amounts of Percodan in my bloodstream,' he said. 'I feel like a passenger on a slow-moving train crossing Kansas.'

She held his good hand between her own. Her and Rhees and nothing else. If only that small world could be restored. She watched him tilt his head back against the pillows. She wanted to protect him, make him safe. She wished she had the magic to turn back clocks.

He cleared his throat and said, 'Coughing's the real killer.'

The real killer, she thought. She looked at the window, seeing the frazzled morning gathering the kind of momentum that would lead to a hundred degrees and change, mercury exploding in glass tubes.

She said, 'I don't think they were burglars who came to the house, John. Dansk sent them.'

He looked at her for a time. 'He gets to you through me. Is that the idea?'

She looked round the room, the walls the colour of mango flesh, the wheelchair in the corner. 'I'm sorry for this, all this.'

'What's the point? I don't think you can help yourself. You're programmed to run in a certain direction, Amanda. It just happened that this time you ran into a bad place.'

'I might have disconnected the program,' she said. 'Ripped out the logic board. Anything.'

'You might have, but you didn't, and I didn't do enough to stop you.'

'I look at you and I feel like shit,' she said.

He closed his eyes and turned his face slightly away from her.

She said, 'Dansk got Isabel's letter from me.'

'How?'

'I was distracted. The point is he got it, he read it, and I think he knows you read it too. I don't know what conclusion he imagines I've reached.'

'Have you reached one?'

'I wish I could say yes. Willie's helping now.'

'You finally enlisted him? That's a step forward.'

'One I might have taken sooner,' she said.

Rhees flexed the fingers of his undamaged hand. 'How safe are we in this place?'

She looked through the door towards the corridor. People passed carrying flowers, bags of fruit, paperbacks, magazines. People visiting the sick. She wondered about them and their credentials, whether at least one of them had a hidden purpose. She walked to the window and gazed down at the parking lot. The roofs of cars were like tinted mirrors. Tension was rising inside her.

She was aware of Rhees watching her. 'Well?'

'I don't think we're safe, John.'

'Where is Drumm right now?'

'He said he'd call me here.' She looked at her watch. Ten-thirty. She had no idea when Willie would contact her. He'd talked about going to see Dansk, an idea that seemed to her suddenly loaded with menace.

Rhees said, 'You know what would be nice? A little protection. A cop posted outside the room. Somebody handy with a gun.'

A man appeared in the doorway. He was dressed in an open-neck shirt and held a plastic-wrapped bouquet of mixed flowers to his chest. He wore tinted glasses and his beard was neatly trimmed.

Jangled, Amanda rose immediately from her chair.

'This three zero six?' the man asked.

Amanda stared at the bouquet. Bright petals, green stems slick with water. They seemed fake, pressed out of synthetic materials. Anything could be hidden in those flowers. Plastic crackled against the guy's shirt and Amanda thought of explosives detonating miles away, like something you'd hear in the background of a TV broadcast from Bosnia or Sarajevo or wherever the world was at war.

'Three six zero,' Amanda said. This is what your condition comes right down to; a place where guns might be hidden in flowers and you hear bombs in the crackle of plastic.

'I guess I got the wrong room,' the guy said, and drifted back into the corridor.

Rhees was staring at the empty doorway. 'Last time I saw that guy he was selling magazine subscriptions on our doorstep. I signed up for *Sports Illustrated*.'

'That's the *same* guy? You're sure?'

'No question. We chatted a few minutes. It was raining and I felt sorry for him. It's no coincidence he's here, is it?'

'Dansk wants us to know how exposed we are,' she said.

'I guess that answers my question about safety. Call Drumm, Amanda. Do it now. Get him to come here.'

She lifted the handset from the bedside table. She

punched Drumm's number. A woman answered and introduced herself as Sergeant Betty Friedman.

Amanda asked, 'Is Willie available?'

'He's out of the office,' the sergeant said.

'If he calls in, get him to phone me at the Valley of the Sun Memorial Hospital immediately. My name's Amanda Scholes.'

'Amanda Scholes?'

'Scholes. You want me to spell it?'

Betty Friedman said, 'No, I'm pretty familiar with your name. It's funny though, because I saw Willie about twenty minutes ago and he was rushing out, and when I asked him where he was buzzing in such a heart-attack hurry, he said he'd received a message to meet you.'

'A message to meet *me*?'

'What he said.'

'I don't know anything about any meeting. Did he say where it's supposed to be?' Something caught and fluttered in her throat.

'He just boogied out the door. I guess maybe some wires got crossed along the way if he isn't with you.'

'Do you know where the message came from?'

'He never said. I'll see if I can find out. You want to hold?'

Amanda said, 'Sure.' A message, she thought. A message she'd never sent. She stared at the open door. People still passed back and forth along the corridor, a shuffling procession, funereal in its lack of energy.

Sergeant Friedman came back on the line. 'Nobody seems to know who received the message, Miss Scholes. Could be the officer has gone off-duty.'

'Can you contact Willie?'

'If he's not in his car, it's a problem. He carries a cellular, but he keeps it switched off when he feels like it. He says a man needs some private space, time to think.'

'The number here is nine four nine seventy seventy, extension three eight nine eight,' Amanda said. 'I need to talk with him – badly.'

'I'll get back to you.'

Amanda put down the receiver.

Rhees said, 'Problem?'

'Somebody left a message for Drumm to meet me.'

'We don't need three guesses, do we?' Rhees said. 'Dansk can predict your future. He knows you'll call on Drumm for help, so he lures Willie away with a story.'

She thought of Dansk trespassing in her head, forecasting her moves. He'd sent a message luring Willie away. Something about this bothered her. *Luring Willie away*. Before she could think it through any further, the telephone rang. She picked it up and heard Betty Friedman's voice.

'Sorry, I can't raise Willie,' she said.

'Please keep trying, it's important.'

Amanda hung up. This wasn't going to do it. Waiting here balanced on a piano-wire, waiting for Drumm. She couldn't just linger until some totalitarian head nurse told her visiting hours were over and ejected her, and she couldn't go, leaving John on his own. She'd left him once before and she wasn't abandoning him again. Ever.

'Who else can you call?' he asked. 'What about Drumm's boss. What's his name?'

'Kelloway's a hard-ass who doesn't like me.'

'The Irishman then. Maybe he could help in some way.'

'I don't see Concannon walking into a situation without knowing how the odds are stacked. What am I supposed to tell him? We need your help but it might be dangerous?'

'So we're in a box and it's just you and me,' Rhees said, 'and either we stay inside it or we try to get out.'

Amanda thought, This is no longer a hospital, but another kind of institution altogether, one of danger and high risk where a surgical mask might conceal a killer's face, a rubber glove a murderer's hand. She searched her mind for a small pocket of clarity. She thought of the parking lot at the back, getting John to the car, getting him away without being seen. She thought of waiting here in the hospital for Drumm to call. Inside outside, a bind.

'I'll get you out of here safely, John. I swear.'

'Then what? The house is out of the question. The drive to the cabin in my present state would be gruelling, and we can't go to your father's, because I don't see any reason to drag him into all this.'

Her father. She hadn't had time to think of him. She owed him a phone call, but this wasn't the moment. 'Then we drive downtown. The mountain goes to Muhammad.'

Rhees said, 'I hear the click of the little steel ball in the roulette wheel.'

'What you're really hearing is my heartbeat,' she answered.

53

She pushed the wheelchair close to the bed. 'We'll do this as quickly as we can. First the shirt.'

She slipped the hospital gown from Rhees's upper body and looked at his strapped ribcage. She draped the clean shirt she'd brought loosely around his shoulders. 'I need your legs next.'

Rhees groaned when he swung his legs in stilted fashion towards the edge of the bed. 'Jesus *Christ*,' he said.

She bent, drew the jeans over his bare feet and rolled them halfway up his legs. His bloated knee looked raw and awful. 'I've got to get you into the wheelchair, so I need you to stand up. I know it hurts. Grab my shoulder with your right hand.'

He reached out and moaned. His fingernails dug into the flesh around her shoulder. He was halfway up, his body bent forward awkwardly.

'I'm tottering, Amanda. The knee's fucked.'

'You can't afford to totter. Come on.'

He was upright now, all his weight on his good leg. She eased him into the wheelchair. She drew his jeans to his waist and buttoned them quickly and slipped his bare feet inside his canvas espadrilles.

She wheeled him to the door where she looked for the guy with the flowers, but didn't see him, which didn't mean he wasn't around somewhere, lingering, watching, waiting. Her whole life was a book lying open and somebody with the power of life and death was reading the pages.

Rhees had his upper body angled forward. His breathing was shallow. She tried to remember the way back to the service elevator. Her memory skipped a beat. Blank. She took a chance, turned right, then glanced back the way she'd come. An overweight woman in a baggy hospital gown stood propped up by a walking-stick, a kid with a bandaged head bounced a rubber ball on the floor, an old guy in a walker was being helped along by an elderly woman who had one leg in a metal brace. It was like the Lourdes Express had just disgorged its passengers.

She rolled Rhees through a door and faced another corridor. She recognized the colour scheme ahead; sky-blue and lemon. Quick, quick as you can. The service elevator was about twenty yards away. An orderly was waiting outside the door. The elevator arrived, the orderly held the door open for them and Amanda pushed the wheelchair inside.

The orderly looked at Rhees and said, 'He OK?'

'He's fine,' Amanda said.

The elevator started to descend with a cranking sound and a shudder. Rhees had his eyes shut. 'Looks like he needs rest,' the orderly said.

'I want to get him out of here.'

'Yeah, this hospital experience can really be a major bummer.' He was skinny and whitefaced and had the look of a guy who spent all his leisure time travelling the deepest arteries of the Internet until his eyes popped.

'Say, you taking this guy out without authority? This some kind of escape from the Gulag?'

'In a sense,' Amanda said.

'Cool. Anarchy.'

Amanda had the slight suspicion that this orderly had been dabbling inside the pharmacy, maybe a little speed to propel him through the day.

'I wonder if you'd do me a favour,' she said. 'My car's parked out back. Would you get it for me? Reverse it right up to the back doors, so I don't have to push this wheelchair all the way across the lot?'

'You're asking me to assist you in an unauthorized escape?'

'I guess I am.'

The orderly said, 'Sometimes I kinda imagine this whole place is a penal colony floating in outer space, you know? Like the patients are really prisoners of some oppressive regime that injects them with experimental drugs? And I'm on this secret mission to scope out the truth.'

'Outer space, huh,' Amanda said. Boy, you really know how to pick them. 'Maybe you can pretend my car's some kind of mini space shuttle.'

'Yeah, I could get into that.' The elevator stopped, the door opened. 'Just gimme the keys and point the way.'

'It's a yellow Ford parked near the ambulances.'

She pushed Rhees in the direction of the sign marked LAUNDRY. The laundry door was open and steam floated out and fogged the air. The exit was just ahead.

'Back the car as close as you can possibly get,' she said.

'Gotcha.'

She looked in the direction of the Ford, thirty yards away. She scanned the parking lot and saw a crew of guys washing ambulances. Pressurized water whizzed from black hoses, smacked against the panels and gathered in glittering oily puddles. BMWs and Jags were parked in the physicians' slots. No sign of the bearded guy with the flowers, and yet everything was charged and tense, as if somewhere near by, perhaps inside a trash can, perhaps stashed under the chassis of an ambulance, there was Semtex attached to a ticking clock muffled in old newspapers, or someone hidden in the shadows with a gun.

The orderly walked to the Ford, got in and backed up at speed, docking the shuttle.

He squeezed the car all the way inside between the open doors, a narrow margin. He got out and surveyed the distance separating car and door-frame, a matter of maybe a foot on either side.

'That close enough for you?' he asked.

'Terrific,' she said.

'Lemme help you get your friend in.' He opened the passenger door. There was just enough room for Rhees to slide in, but it was a difficult manoeuvre, even with the orderly's assistance. They raised Rhees out of the wheelchair, but when he had to bend to get into the passenger seat, he gasped.

'I think we'll rip off the wheelchair,' Amanda said.

'I'll fold it for you,' the orderly said. He collapsed the chair and placed it behind the front seats.

'What's your name?' Amanda asked.

'My earth name's Jonas.'

'Jonas, I owe you.'

'Consider me an agent of justice,' he said.

She got behind the wheel and slammed the car into the great bright vacuum of the day, tall date palms whipping past in a blue-green blur, groves of citrus trees flaring under the withering masonic eye of the sun.

'I don't recognize the car,' Rhees said.

'It's another story, John.'

He sat with his head against the back of his seat. 'It's going to get worse,' he said.

She wasn't sure if he was referring to the heat or his pain or something else altogether.

54

Willie Drumm waited outside the shopping mall. He drank coffee from a cardboard cup and checked his watch every so often. He was a patient man by nature, but this situation was beginning to test him. The message on his desk had read, 'Meet Amanda Scholes, Metrocenter, 11 a.m.' It had been received by a young cop called Lazarus, whom Drumm barely knew. Lazarus had gone off-duty, so Drumm hadn't been able to question him about the message. Had it come directly from Amanda? How had she sounded? Did she say anything else?

It was eleven-twenty now. He wondered how much longer he should give her. She'd always been a stickler for punctuality, at least when he'd worked with her. Her resignation had created a void in his life. He'd enjoyed the regular leisure hours they'd spent drinking, chatting, talking cases, crimes, the state of the nation.

He wandered up and down, scanning the parking-lot. It was packed with cars, people hurrying out of the sun and inside the mall as if this was the last shopping day in the history of the universe.

He realized he was hungry. Inside, you could get pizza, kebabs, stir-fry, anything you liked except it was all indigestible. He didn't want to go in and grab a sandwich because he didn't want to run the risk of missing Amanda when she showed up. He didn't like these consumer malls anyway. He preferred corner grocery stores and small family operations, when you could find them these days.

He strolled up and down. He'd give Amanda five more minutes then he'd call in and check his messages. She might have cancelled. He tapped the face of his watch.

This wasn't his day so far. He'd gone to the Carlton only to find that Anthony Dansk had checked out fifteen minutes before. No forwarding address, and now here he was waiting for Amanda.

She'd said she was on her way to visit Rhees, and that he should telephone her at the hospital after he'd seen Dansk. Maybe her plans had changed for some reason – hence the message, maybe she'd been delayed somewhere. He took the mobile phone from his pocket. He couldn't stand these things, they made him feel like a late-blooming yuppie. He didn't like electronic doodahs. Computers and modems and e-mail and all the rest of it were beyond him. Another world altogether.

Drumm punched the buttons and got himself connected to Betty Friedman.

'Finally,' she said.

'Why? You been looking for me?'

'Your friend Amanda called. Says it's urgent you get back to her.'

Drumm had an odd little feeling; somebody walking on his grave.

'She's at the Valley of the Sun Memorial. Got a pen, I hope?'

'I got a pen.' Drumm went through the pockets of his jacket and found a toothmarked stub of pencil attached to a frayed loop on his notebook.

Betty Friedman read him the number and the extension. He wrote it down.

'When did she phone?' he asked.

'About half an hour ago.'

'She sound OK?'

'Odd you should ask. She doesn't know anything about this meeting with you. It was news to her.'

'She didn't *know* about our appointment?'

'Nope.'

'That's weird.' More than weird, he thought. He had a prickling sensation in his bad leg.

'Call her. You're supposed to be in the business of clearing up mysteries, right?'

Drumm hung up. He dialled the number of the hospital. It was a while before anyone answered. You wouldn't want to be in the throes of cardiac arrest, gasping your last. Eventually an operator came on the line and Drumm asked for the extension number. It rang unanswered.

The operator broke in and said, 'That number doesn't reply.'

Drumm hung up and called Betty Friedman back. 'You sure you gave me the correct extension?'

'I told you what Amanda Scholes told me, Willie. Extension three eight nine eight. You probably wrote it down wrong.'

Drumm checked his notebook. No, he'd written 3898 exactly the way Friedman had given it to him. He dialled the hospital again – the switchboard took a long time to pick up this time too – and repeated the number. There was still no answer. Baffled and irritated, he called Betty Friedman yet again.

'I'm still getting no response from that number,' he said.

'Maybe the room's empty. She might have checked Rhees out.'

'He didn't look like a guy who was going anywhere when I saw him yesterday. I ought to get over to the hospital.'

'Willie, a moment's logical thought, huh?'

Drumm said, 'You're gonna tell me what to do. I can hear it coming, Betty.'

'A suggestion is all. She's bound to call here sooner or later, so it makes sense for you to come back to the office instead of wandering around a hospital she may have already left. At least you'll be here to take the call, right?'

'I hate sensible,' Drumm said.

'Men always do. See you.'

Drumm hung up the phone. Funny about that message. If Amanda didn't know about it, where the hell had it originated? But this whole business was funny, beginning with Dansk. Dead witnesses. A protection program that didn't protect. A mother worrying about her kid.

He tucked the phone away, scanned the parking lot and tried to remember where he'd left his car.

55

Dansk said into his phone, 'Give her bonus points for trying.'

McTell, driving behind, said, 'I guess.'

Dansk leaned forward against the wheel and watched the small yellow Ford ahead. He thought, She knows I'm behind her. She knows I'm in the vicinity. She might pull some utterly predictable stunt, like a sudden U-turn, but she'd have to dig deep inside her box of tricks to shake me off now. And it isn't going to be easy with the invalid on board. Rhees isn't exactly flexible.

When she'd roared from the rear of the hospital, McTell had picked up on her and Dansk had slipped in behind McTell. Sometimes he'd overtake Eddie, other times he'd let him lead. Alternating strategy.

'I'm enjoying this,' he said to McTell.

McTell's words floated on a ragged cushion of interference. 'This what?'

'This. This whole thing. Everything. The way you flushed her and Rhees out.' Dansk took the shooter out of the paper sack and laid it in his lap, fingering it with one hand. The day was vibrant all around him, a shade too bright, like a soap opera on Mexican TV, but he had a charge of exuberance going.

'This Ruger's sweet,' he said.

'You really sure how to handle it?' McTell asked.

'I didn't spend five years with the US Marshals making paper-clip chains,' Dansk said.

'Five years?' McTell said.

'Five years. I even represented DC Metro in a target-shooting competition in 1992, and came second.'

Inside his car, McTell thinks how little he knows about Dansk's history. Like he gives a shit anyhow. Dansk presses buzzers and you jump, end of story. He wants a gun, so he gets a gun. He always gets what he wants. McTell would have done it differently; straight inside the hospital, big fat silencer screwed on, perform the surgery fast and beat it outta this place where sunstroke was always two or three degrees away. But no, Dansk has to get intricate. Dansk has this game he's playing with this woman, he wants her to run and sweat and squirm through hoops. But sometimes you could cut somebody too much slack and then you had a major problem reining them back in.

What is it with Dansk? This business of flushing the man and woman out. He'd never mentioned that was his purpose. Just go in, McTell, check the room, carry flowers. But Dansk is devious. And why? *Because he wants to do the surgery himself!* He wants to pull the trigger, thinks he's got what it takes for the job. Doesn't want to do it inside the hospital, has some other place of execution in mind.

Let it go. This is the Anthony Dansk Show. He's the star and you're just Eddie McTell, warm-up comedian.

McTell said, 'If I was her, I'd head for the nearest precinct house and tell them I'm afraid for my life.'

'I'd do the same thing myself,' Dansk said.

'And this, like, don't worry you?'

'You don't see it, Eddie. You think if she wanders in off the street and pours out her yarn to some hard-assed cops, they'll sit around hanging on her every word? They'll listen, oh sure, because she used to be connected, but they'll be tapping their pencils slowly on their desks and thinking this lady's turned into a class-one conspiracy freak, this one's all the way from Woo-Woo Central. What a sad sight, emotionally unbalanced by recent events. Boyfriend battered and that poor Sanchez woman God knows where. She doesn't have a goddam thing to back up any suspicions she has. It's beayoo-tiful. So let her strut inside some precinct house and say what she likes. Here's a newsflash for you, McTell, sooner or later, she's gonna have to come out again.'

And I know where she'll go then, he thought, because I know what I'd do in her position. I'm scanning you, Amanda. It was like being twinned in some way, a bizarre kind of affinity, an intimacy. Like two lovers kept apart by fate and time.

'Drumm'll listen to her,' McTell said.

'Drumm, sure. Drumm'll listen. Right. He's Mr Empathy.' Dansk laughed, cut the connection and focussed on the Ford that glowed bright yellow in the sun. He imagined Amanda's hands sticky on the steering wheel. Your nerves are puppy dogs in a canvas bag on the way to the river to be drowned, sweetheart. You're running and running. You and your invalid lover running to see good old Willie Drumm for sympathy.

Sympathy. Right.

Ahead, the Ford was turning towards downtown.

56

Through the windshield of his car, Pasquale watched the cop cross the parking lot of the shopping mall. The guy had a slight limp. He was hurrying in an odd hip-hop fashion.

Pasquale drove slowly in the cop's general direction, then braked. The cop vanished between a line of parked cars for a moment and Pasquale, tapping his fingers on the wheel, waited for the guy to step back out into full view. He didn't like this situation, this waiting, all these shoppers going about their business. Waiting frayed his edges.

The cop re-emerged between a parked camper with a bumper-sticker saying DIVERS DO IT DEEPER, and a flashy new pick-up truck painted in blue and burgundy streaks. Pasquale remembered he'd had a bumper-sticker one time with Bruce Springsteen's face on it and an electric guitar. An old Camaro he'd owned when he was nineteen. Nice car. Babes liked it. Not like this one he was presently driving. This car was a total fuck-me embarrassment. It wasn't the kind of thing he'd want acquaintances to see him cruise around in.

He watched the cop pat the pockets of his jacket like he was looking for something. Shoppers walked in front of the car. One little kid stared at him and made a face, poking his ugly nose out of shape with a middle finger and pulling down the flesh under both eyes.

Pasquale rolled the window down. 'Your face'll stay that way, asshole.'

The kid flipped him a finger, then skipped away. Brat. Pasquale revved the engine. The cop was in open space, a bunch of keys in his hand, and Pasquale pressed his foot down on the gas pedal.

Go. This is your best chance.

The cop seemed oblivious to the car. He was elsewhere, wrapped up in his thoughts.

One hit, Pasquale thought.

He was a couple of hundred feet from the cop, who was still unaware of the car bearing down on him. It's gonna be one of those last second things, Pasquale thought, the cop raising his face just before impact, fear and surprise thundering through him when it was too late to take evasive action.

Pasquale floored the gas pedal.

The cop turned. His face had a stricken look, like this was all some kind of mistake or a sequence in a very bad dream.

You're not dreaming, buster.

The car struck the cop and tossed him in the air, and Pasquale felt the crack of impact and saw the guy tossed to one side, plaid jacket open and flapping in a draught of air, glittering coins falling from his pockets, a clutch of keys seeming to hang like a small silver kite.

In his rear-view mirror Pasquale saw the cop land

on his side and roll over and then – holy shit! – he was raising himself up on one knee. His jacket was covered in blood and he was shaking his head in a dazed, pained way, clutching his arm, which had to be broken because it was bent at a weird angle, and his mouth hung open and contorted.

A fuck-up, Pasquale thought. Big time. He stuck the car into reverse. No other way to do this, Bruno. He tightened his grip on the wheel and zoomed backwards fast, before the cop had a chance to react, and he heard the crunch of the rear wheels against the cop's body and the car rose a foot, suspension swaying, exhaust discolouring the air. He kept backing up, and then when he'd driven the front wheels over the cop he stuck the gear into first and rolled quickly over the guy again.

He looked in the rear-view mirror.

The cop wasn't moving now. He was lying there in sunlight and blood.

Pasquale hammered the car forwards and screeched across the lot and out into the street. It was two miles before he felt he'd covered enough distance from the shopping mall and it was safe to pull over. He parked in a street of tract homes and sat motionless, his breathing heavy.

He noticed a streak of blood on the lower right-hand corner of his windshield, a dark smear already drying in the hot air, and when his phone began to ring he let it go unanswered for a time, because it could only be Dansk checking how things had gone. Dansk, always Dansk.

He picked it up on the tenth ring.

It wasn't Dansk and it wasn't McTell.

It was a guy he'd never heard before, a guy with a deep cracked voice and a wild hack of a cough.

57

Stuffy inside the Ford, Rhees in pain, eyes shut, lids fluttering every now and again. Sometimes he'd lick his dry lips and try to dig out a small smile from a place far inside.

Amanda said, 'I'll stop someplace, pick up some aspirin. They might help ease the pain.'

'I'm more in a morphine mood,' Rhees said. 'Forget the aspirin. Don't stop, just keep going.'

She looked in rear-view and wing mirrors, but it was the old story; you needed to know what you were looking for before you spotted it, unless it was obvious, like the car that had tailed her a little too close along Lincoln Boulevard. But here traffic was glutted and cluttered and you couldn't single anything out.

A pick-up swerved directly in front of her and she wondered if the movement was designed to impede her. She changed lanes to avoid any possibility of impact, but the truck – booming hard-core Nashville, driver in a stetson with a long bright feather in the hatband – gathered speed and went past her and a Pabst beer can was tossed languidly from the cab. She imagined Dansk's disapproval; the world's a mess, the ozone layer's disappearing and the oceans are dying.

And so are people, she thought. Disappearing and dying, and not just because of harmful rays or seafood spiked with mercury.

She rolled down her window, lit a cigarette, then remembered what Dansk had said about smoking during their first meeting in the Biltmore. *What people inflict on their bodies is their own business. They want to take serious risks, let them.* She realized now he wasn't just passing a casual opinion on the perils of tobacco, he had in mind other kinds of risks more immediate than the long-term effects of cigarettes.

Rhees turned his face towards her. 'Doesn't it strike you that the guy with the flowers had the perfect opportunity in the hospital? You and me together in the room. All he had to do was shut the door, whip out a pistol. Why didn't he?'

She looked at Rhees. 'My guess is it's something Dansk wants to do himself.' And she wondered why she hadn't tried to plunge the knife into Dansk's goddam heart last night, why she hadn't at least attempted that last act. Because he was strong and would have disarmed her easily, because even with the knife in her hand she was afraid of him, just as she was afraid of him now.

She gave the car more gas, cutting in and out of the traffic flow. She headed south, neglecting the futile mirror checks now. Fear reduced everything to driving, just driving, concentrating on the distant towers, the heart of the city. The few clouds that drifted on the blue horizon were like smoke left by old cannon-fire.

Rhees asked, 'Are we close yet?'

'A few blocks.' Seventh Avenue and Washington, that was the place. Not far now, she'd see it any moment; the big beige building, patrol cars parked outside, cops coming and going. She'd park at the front and she'd ask a cop to help her get Rhees out of the car and into the wheelchair and she'd wheel him inside, and if Drumm wasn't there she'd ask for Betty Friedman. She had this much planned. Thinking your movements through brought an illusion of control.

She saw a clutter of cruisers, a few cops talking together and laughing, a hive of law-enforcement activity. Guns and protection, the safest place she could imagine. She parked the Ford as close to the building as she could, a no-parking zone, then she opened the door and stepped out. Her clothes stuck to her. She ran a hand through her damp hair.

She looked at the entrance to the building, saw the huge circular concrete flowerpots designed to prevent motorized assaults by madmen on the front doors, then lowered her face to check on Rhees, who was gazing at her listlessly. The line of her vision was drawn away from him and up, up over the roof of the Ford to the other side of the street, where she saw Dansk pass slowly in a car, wearing dark glasses and grinning at her, his hand hanging arrogantly from the open window, as if he were no more than a tourist driving idly through town, with nothing more than time to kill.

58

Betty Friedman had strong square hands and shrewd brown eyes that didn't miss much. 'Willie called,' she said. 'He oughta be walking through that door any moment. You want coffee, tea, anything while you wait?'

'Water, please,' Amanda said.

Rhees sat to one side of the sergeant's desk in the wheelchair. 'Water's fine,' he said.

She filled two dixie cups from the cooler and passed them out. Amanda gulped hers down. It had a faint chlorinated taste, but it was wet and welcome.

Rhees asked, 'Would you have a painkiller handy?'

'I got some codeine somewhere.' Betty Friedman, who wore her dark hair in a tight curled perm, rummaged in the drawer of her desk, opened a bottle and tipped out a couple of white pills. Rhees washed them down with his water.

'That message business is pretty weird,' Betty Friedman said.

'Yeah, it is,' Amanda said. She thought of Dansk

driving past and the way he'd grinned, and she wondered why he hadn't looked unhappy to see her outside the Police Department HQ, why he wasn't worried by the prospect of her walking inside the building. Because he's tricky, he's made a move I haven't taken into account, he's shuffled the deck and come up with a different hand. But what?

She felt she'd been manipulated, except she couldn't figure how. It was almost as if he wanted her to come to this place.

Because.

'Any idea who sent the message?' Betty Friedman asked.

Amanda said nothing. Dansk lures Willie away because – no, this was one of those roads she didn't want to travel. It went straight to a black destination.

'I guess it's something you'd prefer to share with Willie,' Betty Friedman said. 'Fine by me.'

Amanda looked at the clock on the wall. 'How long since he phoned?'

'Twenty-five minutes about, from Metrocenter.'

'He should be here by now.'

'Any moment. Relax.'

Amanda was thinking of Drumm out there in the city, maybe bogged in traffic, delayed by road-works, something. *Any moment.* He'd come through the door and he'd believe her story and he'd say *leave it to me* and she'd walk away from the whole thing, back to a private life. Mountain air, owls flying into the moon.

Any moment.

She looked at Betty Friedman and said, 'Try to reach him, please.'

The telephone on the desk rang then and Betty

Friedman picked it up, and Amanda watched her face go through various stages of change, from disbelief to shock, and then to some other expression, a kind of puzzled vagueness, an emptiness, spirit draining out of her.

Amanda couldn't sit, she had to move. She rose from her chair and paced the room and felt a disastrous darkness beat against her. *She knew.* She tried to distance herself from the external world, to silence extraneous sounds and sights, but she could hear Betty Friedman's voice anyway, scratchy and thin, like somebody on an ancient record. 'Did anybody get the goddam number? Sweet Christ, I can't take this in. I don't believe it, I talked to him maybe half an hour ago.'

Betty Friedman had put down her phone without hanging up, and the line beeped like the sound of an electrocardiograph emitting the bleak whistle of fatality. Surgeons took off their masks, sighed and washed blood from their hands. She pushed her chair against the wall and tilted her head back and appeared to be looking at the ceiling.

'It's Willie,' Amanda said. 'Something about Willie.'

Betty Friedman said, 'Run down by a car.'

Amanda flattened her hands on the surface of the desk and leaned forwards, and Betty Friedman said again, 'Run down by a car.' Her eyes had a faraway look. 'DOA.'

Rhees shifted his wheelchair a little. There was the sound of rubber tyres on the floor.

'Somebody . . .' Betty Friedman said, but her sentence gathered no momentum and she gave up on it and looked at Rhees as if his presence puzzled her. She picked up the handset but didn't hang it up.

'Some bastard,' she said. 'Some bastard hit Willie then backed up over him to make sure and then drove away and . . .'

Amanda felt like a long steel needle had entered her heart, an emotional biopsy. We need a small sample, Miss Scholes, to check your condition. Killed by a car. DOA. Betty Friedman got up and dropped the handset and it slithered from her desk and swung back and forth on its cord, a pendulum measuring nothing. Watching it, Amanda thought of Willie, and the image she received was of Drumm being struck and thrown, a killer's face in shadow behind a windshield, metal cracking bone, Drumm jolted, damaged by the impact, and then the car reversing over him. *Just to make sure*.

This is going to go away. Somebody will touch your shoulder and say it's time to get up.

She looked at Rhees. She went towards him and he caught her hand and held it against the side of his face. Betty Friedman had knocked over a waste-basket and papers spilled across the floor. She had all that unfocused energy of grief, the kind that burns without purpose. 'In the parking lot at Metrocenter, and all we got is a colour, and that colour's red, and a partial of the licence number, that's all. That's all we got. Just D–O–A.'

Betty Friedman drew the cuff of her shirt across her face. Amanda moved away from Rhees and reached out and touched the woman's arm. Whether she meant to comfort Friedman or comfort herself, it didn't matter which. A red car at Metrocenter and Willie's dead. Rushed to a hospital, the scream of an ambulance, Willie dying with an oxygen mask on his face and maybe blood spurting against the inside of the mask, and Willie's hands clawing air, life flying out of him.

And somewhere a man in a red car.

One of Dansk's people, she thought. One of Dansk's people sticking the hook into Willie's flesh and hauling him up out of the water.

Betty Friedman stared at Amanda in a hollow way and asked, 'Where the hell did that message come from?'

59

An elevator ride, Betty Friedman white and mute, Rhees hunched in the wheelchair, Amanda beset by a sense of sluggishly wading through water. A walk along a corridor to an office, a big room of panelled walls hung with various awards and civic honours.

Dan Kelloway stood behind his desk, sleeves rolled up to the elbows, arms burned brown, shaven head suntanned and gleaming. Another cop was present, a guy in a double-breasted suit and a lapel badge that identified him as Lt. Wom, S. He had Asiatic features, tiny hands and small feet in black patent-leather shoes. He lounged in the corner of the office, half in shadow, motionless.

Amanda thought, I don't know if these people will listen to me, and even if they listen whether they'll believe. But the telling of her story had become more important than how she gauged the mood of her audience, and even though she wanted Willie she couldn't have him, and that was something she couldn't change.

Kelloway told her to sit. Betty Friedman must have picked up on some sign from him, because she went out of the office, closing the door quietly.

Kelloway looked at Rhees. 'Who's this?'

Rhees introduced himself. Kelloway frowned and turned to Amanda. His voice was like an old-fashioned razor drawn across a leather strap. He sat down behind his desk, white shirt phosphorescent. 'OK, I'm listening.'

Amanda hesitated. She felt the solid wall of Kelloway's hostility. He had that hard-bitten scepticism common to career cops, and he had it in spades. You might have been a shit-hot prosecutor once, but you're history, and your history with me is a bad one.

She remembered Willie's kindness at the hospital, the depths of his concern for her, her face against his shoulder and the faint scent of dry-cleaning chemicals from his jacket, and the way he'd pressed Kleenex into her hands. She heard the room roar in her ears and saw Kelloway clasp his hands on the desk. 'We're waiting. You got something to say, Miss Scholes, say it.'

When she spoke she had no fluency, she fumbled over names and episodes. It didn't take long to tell the story – five minutes, ten, she wasn't sure. Neither Kelloway nor Wom moved. Kelloway watched her without expression, Wom studied his fingernails. She was dry-mouthed when she finished. She wanted to smoke, but it wouldn't have been allowed in Kelloway's sanctum.

Kelloway glanced at Wom. Wom shifted his head a little. Some kind of exchange passed between them. It was hard to tell what it meant. She didn't feel good about this little signal, whatever it was. She felt suspended, awaiting judgement.

Kelloway said, 'Pity about that purloined letter.'

Amanda didn't like the spin he gave the word *letter*. 'I wasn't the only one who read it,' she said. 'So did John.'

'I'm not denying it existed,' Kelloway said. 'All I'm saying is it would be useful to have.'

Wom spoke for the first time. His accent was East Coast clipped, maybe Boston. 'You say this guy Dansk is a resident at the Carlton downtown.'

'He is. At least last night he was.'

Wom picked up a phone on the desk and turned his back. He dialled a number and conducted a conversation in a low whisper. While Wom was on the phone, Kelloway said, 'What you're telling me is that Dansk is part of some corruption inside the Witness Program, and he's on the Sanchez payroll. And you also think this same Dansk is behind Willie's death because Willie was conducting an investigation Dansk didn't like.'

'Right,' she said. Her thoughts drifted to her last conversation with Willie, and she remembered Mrs Vialli's concern about her son. 'Willie talked to Lew Bascombe, also to Bernadette Vialli. My guess is he was followed to both places—'

'You told us that already.' Kelloway looked at Rhees. 'You were attacked by associates of Dansk, right?'

Rhees nodded.

'How do you know they were his associates?'

Rhees turned his face to Amanda for help. She read a certain helplessness in his expression.

Kelloway said, 'You're only going on what Miss Scholes said. Have you ever seen Dansk? Ever laid eyes on him?'

'No, never.'

'What are you getting at?' Amanda asked.

'I wasn't getting at anything, Miss Scholes. I just want to know if Rhees has ever encountered Dansk.'

Kelloway had a way of staring that made you want to turn your face aside, but Amanda held his eyes. She was damned if she was going to relinquish any of her territory to this hard-ass. 'I'm getting the strange impression you don't believe Dansk exists,' she said.

Kelloway said, 'You're over-reacting.'

Over-reacting. She liked that. Drumm had been killed and Dansk was out there scheming, and she was over-reacting.

'You just jumped to the conclusion that the people who attacked your boyfriend are associates of Dansk? Maybe the same people that shot Galindez and chased after Isabel Sanchez? Maybe even the same people that ran a car over one of my most experienced men? And one of these quote unquote killers is a resident at a place called the Hideaway Knolls, but you don't know his name.'

'I don't need your *scorn*, Kelloway. I come here, I tell you something is totally fucked inside the Protection Program, and you treat me like I'm some drooling idiot that just wandered in off the streets, instead of getting up off your ass and being practical.'

Kelloway was unaffected by her. He clasped his hands behind the back of his skull and cracked his finger-joints.

She said, 'Begin with something indisputable and work from there. Galindez and Isabel Sanchez – both protected witnesses, allegedly.'

Kelloway nodded. 'According to the elusive letter, Galindez was shot by the people protecting him and Isabel Sanchez ran away, et cetera. After that, what have you got? Some vague reference to Benny Vialli, which is a case I remember real well, but it doesn't seem to fit anything I can see.'

It doesn't seem to fit, she thought. Willie had said much the same thing. What was she doing? Looking for connections where none existed? Inventing structures that couldn't support any weight? And yet she was trying to forge something out of Bernadette Vialli's story, even if she wasn't sure what. I put Galindez and Isabel into the Program. I placed Benny Vialli in the same custody and nothing's been heard of him since. A kid out there somewhere – maybe he'd fallen in love, married, forgotten his mother. Maybe he'd found an altogether new life and the past was something he didn't want to resurrect.

No, she knew that wasn't true. It didn't square at all with the impression she'd had of Benny Vialli. But why did he send those flowers and the message that Bernadette thought was a fake? Answer: he didn't, somebody else did. Because Benny was in no position to send anything, because—

Wom hung up the phone and said, 'A man called Anthony Dansk checked out of the Carlton this morning.'

'Big surprise,' she said. Checked out and gone, she thought. Perfect timing. Dansk disappears into the sewers, planning to re-emerge when he's ready.

Kelloway said, 'Here's something puzzles me. If you know so much about Dansk, how come you're walking around to tell the tale? Why hasn't Dansk sent a car to run *you* down or get one of his killers to blow *you* away? Why didn't he stop you before you reached my office?'

Amanda looked into Kelloway's sharp blue eyes. 'Maybe because he's self-confident in a way neither you nor I understand. He lives in a demented world we can't quite fathom, Kelloway. And maybe he has other plans for me.'

'What kind of plans?'

'I can't read his mind, I doubt if anyone can do that. I only know his plans are lethal, whatever they are, and I'm feeling vulnerable because he's out there somewhere.'

Kelloway's phone rang. He picked it up, listened, then he rose. He said to Wom, 'Back in a second, Sonny,' and went out of the room.

Amanda heard the door close. She looked at Wom and said, 'I bet he stuffs dollar bills into collection boxes for religious missions in Patagonia. I bet he's active in the Big Brothers organization.'

Sonny Wom said, 'He's not a happy man today. None of us are.'

'Is he ever happy?' she asked.

Wom didn't answer. Kelloway came back into the room, carrying a piece of paper he spread on the desk. His skull shone like a hazelnut. 'What kind of car do you drive?'

'Car? A VW.'

He read something scrawled on the back of the paper. 'Registration number 4KL580?'

Rhees said, 'That's the number all right. Why?'

'Colour red?' Kelloway asked.

'Where is all this leading?' Amanda asked.

'It was your car that ran down Willie.'

'My car?'

'We found it abandoned a couple of miles from

Metrocenter. Front seriously dented, blood on the windshield, plus a strip torn from the sleeve of Willie's jacket stuck to a broken front light.'

Her own car. Willie's torn jacket. She couldn't think around this. 'I left that car last night outside a convenience market on Lincoln,' she said.

'By left, you mean you just walked away from it?'

'Somebody was tailing me. I decided to skip.'

'Who was tailing you?'

'One of Dansk's people,' she said.

'Naturally,' Kelloway said.

'So I dumped the car.'

Kelloway said, 'And somebody came along later and drove it away. And somebody sent Willie a message, using your name. And Willie walked into a trap.'

'Not somebody. Dansk.' How many ways could she tell Kelloway the same thing?

Kelloway tossed the sheet of paper aside. 'A suspicious person could look at all these things and interpret them in a dark way, Miss Scholes. A message you say you never sent. The fact your car was used in a hit and run. Somebody could add these things up and you'd come out looking murky.'

Rhees said, 'Crap, Kelloway. Are you accusing Amanda of something?'

Kelloway said, 'I'm just looking at the angles.'

'With some offensive results,' Rhees said. He sounded angry, even in his pain. Amanda rose and stood directly behind him, laying her hands on his shoulders. She felt heat rise from his body.

'I *saw* that goddam letter,' Rhees said.

'Did I say I disbelieved you?'

Amanda stepped in front of Kelloway's desk. Calm was the important thing. An air of reason.

'Don't you see what's going on, Kelloway? Dansk is stirring the pond, he's making the waters muddy. He leaves a message for Willie in my name, he uses my car, it's all diversionary stuff designed to confuse.'

'It's confusing all right. I grant you that.'

'He knows how to hide and he knows how to manipulate. Look, I don't have any motive for fabricating this story. I don't have anything to gain from making up fictions.'

Kelloway shrugged. 'I never accused you of making up fictions. Did I, Sonny? Did you hear me accuse Miss Scholes of that?'

Wom said, 'No, I missed out on that.'

Amanda smiled thinly. 'The pair of you are missing out on quite a few things, not least the fact that I was very close to Willie Drumm, and it hurts like fuck to think about what happened to him.'

'You're grieving,' Kelloway said.

'Goddam right I'm grieving.'

Kelloway tapped the surface of his desk. His tanned hand was bony. He looked at Sonny Wom and said, 'This lady won a few cases in her time. She came in for some courtroom glory. Sent some real bad guys away. She didn't do it all by herself, of course. No, we did all the shit work, built good solid cases for her. I don't think she ever once went into court on wobbly roller-skates. And the press she got. Jesus, you wouldn't believe it. Like a movie star. Cher or Michelle or somebody.'

Amanda asked, 'What am I hearing, Kelloway?'

Kelloway continued to address Wom. 'She had these profiles in the newspapers, Sonny. Magazines. How sharp she was. What a legal brain. Strange thing is, I never saw much mention of the back-room staff, the guys that lit the stage for her. The scriptwriters, the researchers, the little guys. She hogged it.'

Amanda stared at Kelloway. *The penny drops.* 'Oh Christ. How long have you been breast-feeding this grudge?'

'Grudge? What grudge?'

Exasperated, Amanda said, 'OK, I confess. You handed me cases on a shiny silver platter. Some of them were perfect, beyond perfect. Is that what you want me to say?'

Kelloway said, 'I'm not asking you to say anything, Miss Scholes.'

'Because you didn't get your share of the spotlight, you want to make life awkward for me,' she said.

'Awkward?' Kelloway feigned surprise. 'My department has always been the soul of co-operation, Miss Scholes. You'd agree with that?'

'Wholeheartedly,' she said.

'You'd also agree my people always walked the last few yards for you. Always.'

'More,' she said. She considered Kelloway's ego and what a delicate thing it had to be. Female prosecutor gets headlines and stories, macho Chief Kelloway gets none. So this was the source of his attitude; he was crying out for attention and he wasn't getting what he wanted and he was stamping his feet with a petulance that had been festering inside him for a long time, a resentment out of control. If you added to this the rancour he still hauled around because she'd refused to prosecute the Hood case, you got a guy who was a twisted bundle of bitterness.

'And now you need my help,' he said.

'Yeah, I need your help.'

Kelloway got up from his chair. 'Get one thing straight, Miss Scholes. The only important factor for me in all this is Willie Drumm. I'll have a man visit the Hideaway Knolls and check out the guy you claim pilfered the letter, so we'll need a description from you. I'll get in touch with Justice and see if we can arrange a meeting with somebody who knows about the Witness Protection Program, and we'll sit down together and look at this thing closely.'

Somebody who knows about the Witness Protection Program, she thought. The phrase created disturbances inside her. How could Kelloway know this somebody was trustworthy? And when it came to the question of trust, how did she know she could put any in Kelloway, riddled as he was with pettiness?

'As a bonus, we'll also talk to Mrs Vialli who's so worried about her kid. You see how co-operative we are.'

She said, 'I want you to understand one thing. I didn't write those goddam interviews. I didn't go out looking for publicity, and I still think the Hood case was too damn weak to take into court.'

'I don't actually give a shit who wrote them any more than I give a shit about Hood,' Kelloway said, and adjusted his belt buckle. 'I'm a mean-spirited bastard and I just got what I wanted.'

He smiled at her fiercely, an expression of satisfaction and voracious spite. She heard the whirr of feathers, wings ruffling then settling back in place. Lay an egg, Kelloway. Lay it so it chafes your ass.

60

Dansk checked into a hotel five miles from downtown. The place was a dump but he didn't plan on staying. It was a base, nothing more, a place to freshen up. The porter who touted for Dansk's case wore grubby black shoes and a tacky brocade vest with a grease-stained pocket.

Dansk chilled the bag-man with a stare, and got his room key. He went to the pay phones and opened a Phoenix directory. He found what he wanted and scribbled the information down inside his notebook.

He went up to his room. Stuffy. He opened the bedroom window just as his cellular phone rang.

Pasquale said, 'It went off OK.' He had a sullen distance in his voice.

'Go to a place called the Sidewinder on McDowell. You'll meet McTell. I'll be in touch.' Dansk cut the connection and looked out the window. Something was smouldering in the distance, a garbage dump, maybe garden trash. A stack of thin white smoke rose into the sun, like a pope had just been elected.

This would be a great room if you were thinking of suicide; long drop. Jumpers heaving themselves over the ledge, air whining in their ears as they fell, maybe even changing their minds halfway down, when it was too late to reverse the polarity of the situation.

Like it was too late for Amanda.

Amanda, Amanda. You got a guy that loves you. A guy you love. Life should've been more precious to you, but you took a wrong turning.

He picked up the telephone and dialled a number.

'Phoenix Police Department,' a man said.

'Put me through to Lieutenant Drumm,' Dansk said.

'He isn't in the office at the moment.'

I bet. 'When do you expect him?'

'It's hard to say.' This guy was following the official line; no death announcement at the moment. Keep a lid on it. 'Maybe somebody else could help you,' he said. 'I'll connect you.'

A woman came on the line and introduced herself as Sergeant Friedman. She sounded dispirited.

Dansk imposed a little authoritative weight into his voice. 'This is Morgan Scholes. Amanda Scholes is my daughter. She left a message on my answering machine, something about how she was going to see Lieutenant Drumm, something about Rhees being hurt and hospitalized. Is she around? Can I talk to her?'

'You just missed her, Mr Scholes.'

'Father and daughter, we're like ships in the night. You any idea where she went?'

Betty Friedman was quiet for a moment. 'She left

the building with Chief Kelloway and Lieutenant Wom.'

'She say where she was going?'

'All I know is they went to interview somebody.'

'What hospital is Rhees in?'

'He's here in the building at the moment. A physician gave him a pain-killing injection, knocked him out.'

'This world,' Dansk said. 'What the hell's it coming to when vandals can just go inside somebody's home?' He made a clucking noise of irritation and bewilderment. An older man's sound of bafflement at the condition of today's society.

'You wanna leave a message you called? If I see her I'll pass it along.'

'Don't bother. She'll be in touch with me soon, I'm sure.'

So, they were going through the motions, interviewing somebody. He guessed Mrs Vialli. Who else? Running a check on her. *Some flowers on her birthday and a card she feels isn't kosher*. Loeb's fuck-up, he thought. Correspondence was Loeb's department, but he'd failed to keep track of nuances and quirks and simple stuff like accurate birth dates. Ma. Mom.

And Rhees was drugged and dozing inside the police building. He'd wake soon enough and he'd have to come out, and Amanda would be pushing him in the wheelchair, very touching, lovers looking out for one another. Be my valentine.

He remembered he'd received a valentine once in his life. Aged twelve, a giant red rose and the words, 'You Are My Secret Love.' Unsigned. He'd wondered about the sender, hoping it was Louise Andersen who wore her yellow hair in Nordic braids and dressed in pretty frocks, who'd been the inspiration behind his first masturbation when he'd sat on the john with his underwear round his ankles and thought of what lay under her frock and her panties, and he'd jerked off and nothing was the same ever again. That feeling, that hot eruption, the discovery that you had fluids inside you never even knew about.

But when he'd looked at the handwriting on the envelope he'd recognized it as his mother's. A valentine from his own goddam mother.

He took the Ruger from his case and studied it. The exactitude of the architecture was impressive. You could lose yourself in the interior of the weapon, like you were something very tiny strolling a vast tubular passageway and the cartridges were the size of nuclear warheads.

He stuck the gun in his waistband at the base of his spine. His jacket concealed it neatly. He thought, Life can be good, Anthony. Life doesn't have to be pity valentines from your own mother.

He looked at himself in the full-length mirror.

Babyface Dansk.

He was ready now.

61

Bernadette Vialli wasn't answering her doorbell. Her maroon Toyota was parked in the garage and Kelloway was trying to open the door that led from garage to house, but it was locked.

Sonny Wom, who'd disappeared round the side of the house to peer through the windows, returned and said, 'I can't see anyone inside, and the back door's locked. Place feels empty.'

Amanda smelled the hot air of the garage, motor oil and a scent of paint-stripper. She moved outside and stood under a sumac tree and looked at the upper windows of the house, where curtains were drawn across what might have been Mrs Vialli's bedroom. One-thirty in the afternoon, curtains still shut. Maybe she popped sleeping-pills and slept through the sound of her phone ringing and straight into the early afternoon.

Kelloway emerged from the gloom. The temperature was well above a hundred. 'We'll give this one last try.' He laid a fingertip on the bell and left it there. You could hear the constant maddening chimes indoors.

Amanda gazed again at the curtains, thin and floral-patterned. She imagined light passing through the flimsy material and into the room. She moved out of the shade a moment but withdrew as soon as she felt the full force of the sun. The world was burning up. This climate lashed and punished you.

A scrawny woman dressed in Bermudas and a baggy silk blouse appeared on the edge of Mrs Vialli's lawn. Her mouth was set in a suspicious pucker. 'Is there a problem here?' she asked.

Kelloway showed her his identification, which relaxed her up to a point. She introduced herself as the next-door neighbour, Mrs Christian, spelled as in Jesus, she explained solemnly. 'Something wrong with Bernie?' she asked.

'She usually sleep this late?' Kelloway asked.

'She's normally up at the crack.'

'You happen to see her today?'

Mrs Christian shook her head.

Kelloway said, 'Her car's in the garage and she's not answering the doorbell.'

'Maybe she's sick,' said the woman. She fell silent a moment, making a worried sucking sound on her grey dentures. 'You need to go in and have a look, I got a key. Bernie likes me to keep an eye on the place if she goes away. I water her plants. Keep an eye out.'

'If it's no problem,' Kelloway said.

'Always help the police. Rule of mine.' The woman dug a cumbersome clutch of keys from her pocket. She separated one from the bunch and handed it to Kelloway. He turned the key in the lock and stepped inside the house. Amanda and Wom followed, but Mrs Christian, looking wary, lingered on the threshold.

The house had a moody silence. Amanda stood at the bottom of the stairs while Kelloway and Wom explored the ground-floor rooms. Her eye was drawn up to the shadows at the top of the stairs. Hot air was trapped in the house.

'Nothing,' Kelloway said.

Wom was already climbing the stairs, Kelloway followed. Amanda came behind, thinking of the room with the closed curtains.

Kelloway went inside the bedroom. The bedsheets were drawn back and the pillows indented, but Mrs Vialli wasn't there. He opened the curtains and the room burst into brightness. Amanda blinked and stepped back out into the hallway where Wom was already opening another door leading into a room that had obviously been Benny Vialli's once upon a time. Sports posters on the walls, Magic Johnson frozen in mid-flight above a hoop, a couple of dated rock posters, Madonna clutching her groin, a shot of The Rolling Stones before they became raddled capitalists.

Amanda wandered away from Benny's old room. Across the landing the door of the bathroom was open a couple of inches. Damson tiles, peach-coloured towels on a rack, a mirrored medicine cabinet that reflected a small area of the room's interior. Amanda moved towards this door and stopped. She saw something reflected in the mirror. A shower rail at a bad angle, a shower curtain twisted. Kelloway appeared at her back. He moved past her and stepped inside. Wom, directly behind him, blocked Amanda's view.

'Eureka,' Kelloway said.

Amanda shifted her position slightly, glanced over Wom's shoulder and saw how the shower rail had broken free from the wall at one end and the curtain was crumpled. A length of rope had been twisted round the rail and Bernadette Vialli lay in the centre of this tangle with a noose round her neck and an overturned chair a few feet away.

Amanda pushed past Wom into the bathroom. Kelloway, stretching out an arm, tried to hold her back, but she was already past him and kneeling over Bernadette Vialli, whose mouth was open, tongue swollen. Her robe was damp and her big silly slippers had slipped off her white feet to the floor.

Amanda looked at the nylon rope, the knot, the way it had cut into the dead woman's throat, the angry purple abrasions created by the tension of the noose. Kelloway, leaning forward, touched Amanda's shoulder and said something about how she shouldn't be looking at this. But Amanda ignored him, her attention fixed on the woman's open eyes, the whites bloodshot and a smear of cream that had adhered somehow to her eyelids and the darkness in the pupils. She found herself wondering if it was true that the eyes retained an image of the last thing a dead person had seen, or if that was just nonsense, a fantasy, and what did it matter anyway? Something about the cream bothered her.

'She got up on the chair and kicked it over,' Kelloway said. 'I guess the rail held out long enough for her to choke.'

'I don't buy that,' Amanda said.

'Let me guess. You think she was murdered and then strung up,' Kelloway said.

'That's exactly what I think.'

'By the mysterious Dansk.'

'Or one of his minions.'

'There's no sign of forced entry,' Wom said. 'No broken windows, smashed locks, anything like that.'

'So she opened the door to somebody she knew,' Amanda said, and finally looked away from Bernadette Vialli. She thought, A crushed plastic shower curtain with the tiny label 'Kaeskoo Products, Seoul' wasn't much of a shroud.

Kelloway asked, 'You're saying she knew her killer? How come?'

Amanda rose. 'I don't know how come.'

Kelloway was quiet for a moment.

She thought of Dansk, the way he'd tracked her. He must have watched Drumm come to this house, and the idea of a conversation between the cop and Mrs Vialli worried him to the point where he'd ordered the deaths of Willie and Bernadette. Let's just close this situation down, he might have thought. Let's nip this in the heart of the bud.

Amanda stepped out of the bathroom. She felt unwell, giddy. Kelloway followed her. Wom remained behind, notebook in one small hand, a scribe of death.

'No way was it suicide,' she said.

'Convince me,' Kelloway said.

'She's got some traces of moisturizing cream round her eyes. You think she slaps cream on her face before she hangs herself?'

'You're talking a trace, that's all. Maybe she started to apply the stuff then changed her mind. What the hell. I've seen suicides in tuxedos. You'll have to do better.'

She struggled against her dislike for this cop. But she had to accept the fact she needed him, she was dog-tired of going it alone, and he had behind him a large law-enforcement organization whose help she wanted. His scepticism, his abrasive manner, she'd tolerate these until it became impossible.

She stopped halfway down the stairs. A uniformed cop appeared in the hallway. It was Sergeant Thomas Gannon, whom she'd last seen during the fruitless search for Isabel in the desert. He touched his little moustache, nodded at her, then looked directly past her at Kelloway.

'I went to the Hideaway Knolls,' Gannon said. 'The only guy vaguely resembling the description Miss Scholes gave checked out this morning. He'd registered under the name of John J. Coleman.'

Kelloway looked at Amanda. 'Dansk checks out of his hotel, now this other character checks out. These people have quite a knack for timely disappearances, don't they?'

Amanda had a stifling sensation. She was caught up in filaments that, no matter how hard she tried to claw them from her skin, still clung to her. People check out, from hotels, from life.

Gannon said, 'I also have a message for you, Chief. Somebody from Justice will meet you at five in your office.'

'Quick response,' Kelloway said.

'Apparently this guy happened to be in L.A. and your enquiry was forwarded to him and he caught the first plane,' Gannon said.

'Lucked out,' Kelloway said.

Lucked out, Amanda thought. Mrs Vialli hadn't lucked out.

She reached the foot of the stairs and strolled past Gannon into the harrowing sunlight. She lit a cigarette and sucked smoke inside her lungs and wondered where Dansk was, what crevice of this city concealed him, what step he was planning next.

62

Eddie McTell and Bruno Pasquale sat in the big drab empty lounge of the Sidewinder Motel, a room that had the ambience of a charity clinic run by an indigent religious order excommunicated long ago.

McTell said, 'I've had it to the scrotum with crummy joints like this. Gimme Tijuana. Lead me to a bordello. Slamming tequila with some hot-blooded little chickadee sitting in my lap. Way to fucking go.'

'I never been in Mexico,' said Pasquale.

'I'll take you there one day, Bruno. Who needs shit places like this? The pits. Christ.'

Pasquale leaned back in his chair. He had a cinematic notion of Mexico, musicians with guitars strolling under fancy wrought-iron balconies. 'I hear they got cock-fights down there. I never seen one.'

'It's all blood and feathers and flying guts. You'd enjoy it.'

Pasquale was quiet for a time. 'I'm still thinking about this guy Loeb I met. He showed me some heavy ID, I mean, *impressive.* He's like up there. Way up. He knows everything going on, Eddie. You name it, all the work we done for Dansk, he knows about it. And it goes back a ways. I'm not just talking about recent stuff. And we're supposed to keep him posted on the moves Dansk orders, except Dansk ain't to know.'

'What I think it is, he's checking up on Tony Birthmark,' McTell said. 'Like a performance evaluation, something. How Dansk is handling the job. Maybe Loeb's got some doubts, which wouldn't blow me outta my chair with astonishment.'

'I don't like going behind anybody's back, Eddie.'

'If this Loeb's the big chief, you forget any doubts you might have.'

Pasquale said, 'He gave me his phone number, and we're supposed to call and keep him informed.'

'I don't have a problem with that,' McTell said. 'Dansk's head is wired all the wrong way.' He tapped the side of his skull with a fingertip. 'You ask me, the Birthmark Boy's got a fixation type thing about this broad. The way he talks about her, he gets this buzzing in his voice. Sometimes I think he's a death junkie and he wants to take a walk on the dark side, see how guys like you and me live. Only he hasn't admitted it to himself and now this woman comes along and stirs his juices and suddenly he's out of the closet and trigger-happy. It's like he's got a hard-on for her, swear to God.'

Pasquale played with a paper napkin, folding it, tearing it here and there, then spreading it open so it looked like a line of chorus girls. 'I didn't like the hit and run shtick,' he said.

'A cop into the bargain,' McTell said.

Pasquale said, 'A target's just a target. I don't

have any hang-ups who I work on. It was that dumb-fuck little German car in broad daylight.'

'You mentioned this hit to Loeb?'

'No. You think I oughta?'

'Loeb wants the skinny, you give it to him, man.'

'So I tell Loeb, you're saying.'

McTell sipped his lager and nodded. Pasquale placed a beer coaster on the edge of the table, smacked it with his hand and watched it rise in the air. He snatched it on the way down like a frisbee. 'I don't feel good about going behind Dansk's back.'

McTell shrugged. 'Me, I wouldn't think twice about talking to Loeb. Fact, you want to give me his number, I'll call him myself, because I got more than a few comments to make about Dansk.'

Pasquale plucked a slip of paper from his wallet and put it down on the table. 'Here.'

'You wanna go first?' McTell asked.

'After you, Eddie.'

'That's me,' said McTell. 'Always the guy that breaks the ice at parties.'

63

In the back of Kelloway's car Amanda thought about Willie Drumm and Bernadette Vialli. She pictured those little war monuments you saw sometimes in the leafy squares of backwater towns, the names of men and women who'd died in far-away wars for what was commonly referred to as democracy and liberty. No such rhetoric attached to the deaths of Willie and Bernadette Vialli. They'd been killed for reasons that had nothing to do with patriotism or honour or whatever pumped-up nonsense words were carved into granite to cover the fact of human sacrifice and bloodletting.

They'd been killed because of Dansk, because of Dansk's business, which clearly wasn't limited to Sanchez alone. Because if that were the case, Bernadette Vialli would still be alive in her split-level suburban home.

Something else, she thought.

Willie had speculated about a personal motive, but she wasn't buying this. It was more than that, but it was just beyond her reach, whatever it was, something she couldn't focus on. She wished she had Willie to talk it through with her. She wished for a resurrection.

She turned her face and looked from the window. Outside the car the city was a blend of glass and brick. Between the buildings were forlorn blue shadows. Wom was driving, Kelloway sat in the passenger seat, his body turned towards Amanda.

Kelloway said, 'You mentioned Mrs Vialli had a birthday card from her son, also a tape. We couldn't find either.'

Amanda said nothing. She looked at the windows of tall buildings. She imagined the sniper again, a telescopic lens attached to his high-powered rifle, a bullet slamming into her skull. Welcome back to happy hour for paranoids, when uneasy feelings were two for the price of one and the bartender had Dansk's face. She stared at the unusually deep cleft in the back of Kelloway's neck.

'Willie talked with Lew Bascombe about Dansk,' she said. 'That's an avenue you should be exploring.'

'You don't mind if we do this my way, do you?' Kelloway said.

'Bascombe was supposed to do some checking and get back to Willie—'

'My way,' Kelloway said. 'I mean that.'

Amanda lapsed into silence. Why not go direct to Bascombe now? Why not squeeze him hard? She wondered if there was any future in talking to Kelloway. He seemed to hear only what he wanted.

She looked at the digital dashboard clock. Four thirty-two. Somebody was coming from Justice at five, somebody who'd answer questions and allay the fears and suspicions. Yes indeed.

Wom parked the car in the lot of the Police building. Amanda stepped out into the volcanic afternoon. She didn't want to enter the monolithic beige-coloured building. She didn't want to see this somebody from Justice who'd have a plausible multi-layered story and a nice white shirt and the speech patterns of a real-estate salesman.

She followed Kelloway and Sonny Wom into the cool interior. 'I'll check on John,' she said.

'Sure.' Kelloway led her along a corridor to a tiny room. He opened the door. Rhees lay on a narrow cot. She entered the room alone and approached the bed. Rhees was drowsy from pain-killers.

'How are you?' she asked.

'I was having this dream we were in Fiji drinking coconut milk, only it wasn't milk, it was ink. You see any symbolism in that?'

'No, not really. How's the pain?'

'Numbed,' he said.

'I've got a meeting with some person from Justice shortly.'

'And then?'

She didn't know how to answer. She said, 'We'll see.' She ran a hand lightly across his face.

'Get brochures,' he said. 'Glossy ones from a travel agent . . .'

He closed his eyes, slipping into sleep. Ink and coconut milk, cave-writing on the walls of the unconscious. Rhees had hopes of blue distances and vacations, getting away from nightmares. She kissed his lips, then left the room.

Kelloway and Wom were waiting in the corridor.

'We'll go up to my office,' Kelloway said.

They rode an elevator in silence. When the doors opened Kelloway ushered her out. The corridor was quiet. A sense of bereavement hung in the air. A few cops sat at their desks and shuffled paperwork without interest. Here and there, in doorways and around a water fountain, they stood in small sombre groups. The fact of Drumm's death had permeated the building and alerted officers to the notion of their own mortality.

Amanda felt the heaviness in the atmosphere. The only thing missing was Willie's body inside a coffin on a plinth surrounded by floral tributes.

Kelloway entered his office with Sonny Wom. He went behind his desk and vigorously rubbed his arm with the palm of his hand. Amanda sat, struggling against her tension. Relax. Somebody from Justice is coming, the world is going to be set right, explanations will be forthcoming.

There was a knock on the door.

Kelloway said, 'Come.'

The door opened. Amanda didn't turn to look.

She heard a man say, 'I'm on time, I trust.'

Kelloway moved out from behind his desk to welcome the visitor and Amanda changed the angle of her head and saw a man dressed in a black suit and white shirt with a black tie. Over one arm he'd slung a coat. His hair was white and sparse and he moved across the floor in a shuffling way, no elasticity in his muscles.

I'm on time, I trust. Amanda had a sense of back-tracking, rolling in reverse on some kind of memory monorail through a tunnel filled with echoes.

'Chief of Police Kelloway?' the man asked.

'Right.'

'This heat,' the man said and smiled. 'How do you cope with it?'

'You get used to it,' Kelloway said. 'After twenty years, give or take.'

The man sat. He set a briefcase on the floor beside his chair. Amanda stared at him. His eyes were watery. She was still travelling backwards, still trying to compartmentalize something that had strayed out of place. But what?

The man opened a wallet and held out his ID. Kelloway looked at it, nodding his head.

The man turned to Amanda and asked, 'And you are?'

She spoke her name quietly. It had come back to her. It had come rolling all the way back to her.

She thought, This is wrong. This is out of tune.

64

Amanda asked, 'You just flew in from Los Angeles? Weather nice out there?'

The man said, 'Sunny like here, but less hot.'

Kelloway said, 'What's the weather got to do with anything?'

'Just curious.' Amanda noticed the darkness under the man's eyes, the lack of colour in his lips. 'What airline did you fly?'

'America West.' His voice was like grit inside a cat-litter box, cinders rolling back and forth, and he breathed with difficulty.

Kelloway said, 'Mr Loeb hasn't flown in to discuss weather or airlines.'

'Ralph,' Loeb said. 'Call me Ralph.'

'Last time I was in L.A., I stayed at the Marmont,' Amanda continued. 'Were you staying in a hotel?'

'No, with a friend in Westwood,' Loeb said.

Sonny Wom slipped out of the room quietly as if he'd received one of Kelloway's imperceptible signals. Kelloway was rising from behind his desk. His irritation was palpable. From the corner of her eye Amanda was aware of his bronze skin and white shirt.

'This chit-chat's entertaining, I'm sure,' he said. 'I'd like to see us get to the point, Scholes.'

Plain old *Scholes* now. Amanda ignored the cop and asked, 'How did you receive the message that brought you here?'

'Carrier pigeon,' Loeb said. He smiled thinly. 'By phone, of course.'

'In L.A. At your friend's house in Westwood.'

Loeb faced Kelloway and asked, 'Am I under oath?'

'What's the point of these questions, Scholes?' Kelloway asked.

Amanda stepped a little nearer to Loeb. 'Who was it that telephoned you in Westwood?'

'A colleague in Washington,' Loeb said with a certain patience. 'Let me take you through the steps, Miss Scholes. Chief Kelloway contacted the Justice Department with an urgent request to meet somebody connected to the Witness Protection Program, and his enquiry was passed along to me because, A, I'm associated with the Program, and B, I was less than an hour away by plane. That answer your questions?'

'Does this colleague have a name?'

Kelloway looked at Loeb and said, 'I'm sorry about this, Ralph. Scholes was a prosecuting attorney until recently, which she thinks gives her a licence to come off like the Grand Inquisitor.' He turned to Amanda, and his stare was unpleasant, and just for a moment Amanda had the tiny flash of a feeling that Kelloway and Loeb weren't entirely strangers to one another. But the sensation was smoke, and it dissipated as quickly as it had arisen, blown out of her head by the sharpness of Kelloway's angry voice. 'Ralph isn't here to play Trivial Pursuit, Scholes, and this isn't a court of law, in case that had slipped your mind.'

'I asked a simple question—'

'An irrelevant question,' Kelloway said.

Loeb smiled and said, 'You ought to have Miss Scholes fitted with an emergency brake, Chief.'

Kelloway said, 'I think it's a muzzle she needs more.'

Amanda said to Loeb, 'I can understand you might not want to tell us the name of your colleague at Justice. Confidentiality and so forth. What about your friend in L.A? What's his name?'

Kelloway had his hand firmly on her elbow now. 'Outside,' he said. 'I want a word.'

She allowed herself to be led into the corridor, where she yanked her arm free of Kelloway's flinty grip.

'What the fuck are you playing at?' he asked.

'He's not on the level, Kelloway.'

'How do you figure that?'

'Because I recognize his voice.'

'You're losing me.'

'Dansk gave me his private number to call in Washington. When I called it, I got an answering-machine, and the voice on the machine was Loeb's.'

'You phone Dansk and you get Loeb's voice on a machine. What's the big deal?'

'The big deal is they're in this together. Dansk and Loeb. They're *partners,* for Christ's sake. He's here to feed you bullshit. He'll tell you exactly what Dansk told me. He's going to talk about an in-house investigation of security leaks in the Program. He's going to tell you how they're in the process of being sealed. I've heard it before and it all sounds very plausible, but I'm not sitting through it again, thanks.'

Kelloway clenched a hand and tapped it like a mallet against the side of his leg. 'So you don't trust Loeb. Maybe you don't trust me either, huh?'

Amanda gazed along the corridor. A bubble rose inside a water-cooler and popped on the surface. She turned her face to Kelloway, whose sarcasm made her feel isolated. *Maybe you don't trust me either, huh?* Trust was fragile scaffolding and it swayed when you climbed it.

She said, 'All I'm telling you is that Loeb and Dansk are involved in this thing together, and Loeb's going to try and pass you off with pap. Christ, they've got it *sewn-up*, Kelloway. It's neat. They've got it nicely self-contained. Call Dansk and you get Loeb's voice. Messages for Dansk never go any further, they're always intercepted by Loeb.'

'So what have we got here? Guys that have entered into some sinister compact to bury a couple of witnesses on behalf of Victor Sanchez?'

'Exactly. Check Loeb's story. You can find out what flight he claims he caught from L.A. and the name of the friend he says he stayed with in California. My bet is he's covered his ass and you'll get nowhere. He can arrange well-rehearsed associates to back up anything he says. A flight attendant who seems to remember him, an old pal in L.A. who's going to tell you Loeb was his house guest.'

'Check Loeb's story. This is your best advice?'

'It's my only advice. This is a labyrinth. One wrong turn and you're lost.'

'Did you ever drop tainted acid back in the old

days and every now and again you have weird flashbacks?'

'Acid scared me, so I left it alone.'

Kelloway rolled up a sleeve that had begun to slide down his arm. 'You should have stuck to that principle, Scholes, leaving things alone.'

Sonny Wom came along the corridor and said, 'He checks out. He's with Justice all right.'

'Fine. Go back and keep him occupied, Sonny. I'll be with you in a minute.'

Amanda remembered Willie Drumm's speculation about Dansk. *He's got nothing to do with the Program. He's a freelance operator.* And somebody on the inside is feeding him information, somebody bought and paid for by Sanchez. Loeb.

It had to be. A sinister compact.

Kelloway said, 'So Loeb's the genuine article.'

'He works for Justice, which doesn't mean he's on the—'

'He's on the level until I find out otherwise, Scholes.'

'OK, OK, *OK*. Play it by your rules.'

'You still don't want to hear what he has to say? You're walking away?'

'First I have to think of someplace to walk,' she said. 'I don't like the idea of the streets. I don't know what's out there in all that sunlight.'

Kelloway said, 'Maybe that's all there is, sunlight and nothing else.'

'I seriously doubt it.'

He was quiet a moment. 'Why don't you ask me?'

'Ask you what?'

'Don't go coy. You need a favour.'

He reminded her increasingly of a hawk hovering

in the still air above hot canyons, scanning for soft prey. 'I don't expect favours from you,' she said. 'You don't like me. The chemistry between us is like frozen tundra.'

Kelloway shrugged. 'I have powers. You want to get out of here safely, don't you? And there's Rhees to think about.'

'There's Rhees, sure,' she said.

'But you don't like the idea of just walking away. Feisty lady prosecutor suddenly backed into corner, doesn't know who to trust. Injured man on her hands, serious limits to her freedom of movement.'

'You want me at your mercy,' she said.

'It's an appealing notion. The cops step in where the former angel of justice fears to tread.'

'You're an asshole, Kelloway.'

'Assholes can be powerful.'

'Power comes and goes.'

'Yeah, but right now I happen to have it, which is why you need me.'

'What are you offering?'

'You believe you're in danger. OK, you need protection. I'm thinking of offering you Thomas Gannon.'

Protection. Kelloway was right about one thing; Rhees restricted her activities. But if she walked away, it meant leaving everything to Kelloway. He inherited it all.

'Why the helping hand?' she asked.

'Willie Drumm thought the world of you. He talked about you like you were his favourite niece or something, and that counts where I'm concerned, because I liked Willie. Surprised?'

She tried to find a tiny kindness in his face at that moment, an underlying gentleness, but the face gave away nothing. It was all suntanned surfaces and hard angles. Whatever feelings he had were encased behind barbed wire, deep inside, where you couldn't get a glimpse of them.

'I'm wondering if you'll follow through,' she said. 'Or if you'll just buy Loeb's version and let everything slide away into obscurity.'

He drew a hand across his face. 'Let me explain something to you. When you say Willie was killed because this Dansk wanted him dead, I'd be remiss if I didn't look into your story, right? So that's what I'm doing: looking into your story. And meantime giving you protection. Doing my job.'

'I sit in the bleachers and you play the game,' she said. 'And Gannon is my guardian angel. Which is also pretty convenient for you, because he can report on me if I decide to step out of line.'

'That's what it comes down to. Pick a safe place.'

There was an echo here she didn't like; Dansk on their first meeting. *You agree to stay out of this business entirely, and in return I'll let you know the outcome*. Things had changed since then. Her world was haywire and she didn't have the resources to straighten it out on her own. A woman with a fractured lover; What could she do? Her boundaries had narrowed, her options diminished.

'Well?' Kelloway asked. 'Do I hear a thank you?'

She was thinking of the forest and the estuaries of darkness, the howl of coyotes and the sorry little pipsqueaks of their victims. She wasn't in the mood for expressing gratitude because she didn't feel any. It was another feeling she had, a kinship with those creatures of the pines that lived in fear of nocturnal predators with a craving for easy blood.

65

Dansk parked on the side of the mountain where a paved road had been laid close to the edge. Up here, people who'd accumulated great wealth built houses with amazing views of the city spread below. This was a place where you could stand on your balcony and sip your freshly squeezed orange juice on sunny mornings and say, Thank you, God, I've arrived. And maybe you'd spare a thought for the peasants toiling in the city far below, street-cleaners and janitors and maids, all the peons and wetbacks who laboured down there so you could live up here just a little nearer to heaven.

He got out of the car and walked through dusky light to a set of iron gates. He could see a house at the end of a driveway of rose-coloured gravel chips. The gates weren't locked. Up here, maybe people felt immune to the brigands in the city. Up here where private security cars patrolled back and forth, maybe they felt superbly secure.

Dansk pushed the gates open and heard his feet crunch on the gravel.

He heard an electronic beeping sound emerge from the house, faint but audible. He figured he'd set off an invisible alarm when he'd come through the gates. The sound stopped and a man appeared outside the house. He was dressed in neat brown slacks and a white cotton polo-neck. He had grey hair, well-trimmed. Dansk smiled and kept walking towards the man.

About six feet away, Dansk stopped. The guy had a stern look, slightly canine. Dansk tried to see some resemblance in the face to Amanda, but he couldn't find one. He remembered from his background research that Morgan Scholes was a widower and wondered how long ago his wife had died.

Dansk said, 'Sorry for the intrusion.'

Morgan Scholes had white hair on the backs of his hands. 'There's a sign at the gate,' he said. 'It says no trespassing, and that's precisely what it means.'

'I must have missed it,' Dansk said. Morgan Scholes's voice was authoritative. He gave an impression of crabbed impatience, belligerence held in check. A ruthless business type, Dansk thought, steamrolling the competition, amassing enormous amounts of cash and breaking bones along his merry acquisitive way.

Dansk kept smiling. 'My ID,' he said.

Morgan Scholes looked at the Justice Department credentials. This appeared to make him less aggressive. 'What can I do for you?'

'It's about your daughter,' Dansk said. 'I just want a quick word.'

Morgan Scholes said, 'Let's get out of this damn heat first.'

The house was all arches, Mexican tiles, ceramic pots and Western art. Dansk followed Scholes into a room filled with oil-paintings of cowboys.

'Sit,' Scholes said. 'Drink?'

'Maybe a soda,' Dansk said. He didn't sit. He never sat on command, that's what dogs did.

Scholes went into the kitchen. Dansk examined some framed photographs on a sideboard; Amanda on graduation day, gowned and mortarboarded and ready to shake plump fruits off the tree of the world. She looked fresh and innocent, hatched only minutes before. Her mouth had a slight enigmatic smile, but there was latent determination in the expression. He ran a fingertip across the glass, thinking he could almost feel the warmth of her flesh, the soft mouth. The next picture was that of a woman in a swimsuit. The resemblance to Amanda was obvious, so this had to be the dead mother. She had provocative lips and was staring evenly into the camera, like she was daring the photographer to disrobe.

Morgan Scholes came back carrying two ice-cold cans of root beer. He gave one to Dansk.

'So, what's this daughter of mine up to now? She's drawn into situations like a fly to horse-shit. Quits her job one minute, the next she's running around doing God knows what because of some stiff in a river. Too busy to speak to me on the phone, that's for sure.'

'The independent type,' Dansk said. He sipped the soda. Chemicals and carbonation.

'Independent wouldn't be my first choice, more like mulish. Gets her feet planted and won't budge. So what's happening?'

'I need to ask her a few questions,' Dansk said.

'Some clarification concerning the dead body, that's all.' This amazing calm he felt. It was like his heart-beat was down to five a minute and his nerves narcotized. 'But I'm having a problem trying to locate her. I tried her home in Scottsdale.'

'Welcome to the club.'

'You any idea where she is?'

Morgan Scholes shook his head. 'Not a clue.'

Dansk said, 'I understand there's a cabin some-place up near Flag.'

'I've been trying that number too. No luck.'

'Where is the cabin exactly?'

'Why? You think she's up there not answering the phone?'

'Maybe she's *en route*,' Dansk said. 'I don't know. I have to cover the possibilities.'

'I built that cabin, you know. With these,' and Morgan Scholes raised his hands in the air. 'The idea was a retreat away from everything.'

The self-made man, Dansk thought.

'Except I never spent much time at the goddam place. Too busy. Story of my life.'

Dansk wondered how long he could maintain the smile. He was beginning to feel lockjaw. 'I was thinking I'd take a run up there. If she shows up, fine.'

'If she's not there, you've driven a long way for nothing.'

'I'll take the chance,' Dansk said. 'What I'd like is the location of the cabin.'

Scholes looked hesitant. 'It's damned hard to get to.'

'I understand that, but it's important I contact her, otherwise I wouldn't be here bothering you.'

Scholes rose from the arm of the leather chair. He

stared at Dansk, a look of assessment. Just for a moment it seemed that the old guy was about to resist giving out information.

'You'll need a map,' he said finally. He went to a desk, took a sheet of paper and a pen from a drawer.

Dansk watched him draw neat lines on the paper.

'Leave Flagstaff on Route Forty heading west. Go about thirteen miles. You'll come to a track on the right that's poorly marked except for an ancient sign that says "No Hunting". The letters are faded. I'll mark that with an X. Go down this track about five miles. Two miles down the track you'll come to a bridge over a creek. I'll mark that B. Go slow there because that bridge is shaky. On the other side there's a path which isn't easy to find because it's overgrown. I wouldn't be taking any car of mine beyond that bridge unless it was four-wheel drive. It's rough.'

Dansk gazed at the map. X for turning. B for bridge.

'You follow the path for a mile, and you come to a fork. You keep going right. See this line I'm making? Follow that. It's the only access track to the cabin, and it's damn narrow, so stick to it. Go left and you're lost.'

'So I keep going right at the fork.'

'Exactly. You won't see much in the way of landmarks except a million trees that all look the same. I'm marking this C for the cabin. And if you run into my daughter, tell her I'm not too pleased with her right now.' Scholes handed the sheet of paper to Dansk.

'I'm obliged,' Dansk said.

'If Amanda happens to call in the meantime, I'll

tell her you're looking for her. You got a number where she can reach you?'

This tricky moment. Dansk had been waiting for it, expecting it. Say Amanda phones her father. Her father tells her somebody called Dansk has been asking for her. It couldn't be allowed to happen that way. His heart accelerated and the edge of his vision dimmed and he stared at Morgan Scholes who seemed surrounded by a sudden mist.

'Something wrong?' Scholes asked.

Dansk thought, Do this thing, do it now.

He whipped the Ruger out of his waistband and from a range of six or seven feet he shot Scholes in the head. He felt the kick of the pistol in his fist, and it reminded him of the sting of the baseball bat when he'd hit Skipper Klintz. He flashed back all those years, down through the fogged passages of time, and even as Scholes staggered back it was Skipper Klintz Dansk saw, a thick-skulled kid with a crew cut and snow falling lightly in the dark and blood in the snow and a scared cat screeching out of a trash can. Dansk lowered the gun to his side and stepped closer to Scholes, who'd fallen against his desk and knocked over a limestone paperweight decorated with some Navaho conceit. It had broken clean in two.

When you take your seat in the Blood Bijou you break some things, Dansk thought.

The map Scholes had sketched for him had half a dozen spots of blood on it. He picked it up, walked to the door, hesitated, then took Amanda's graduation photograph. He left the house and walked down the pathway, and this time he didn't hear the crunch of gravel under his feet. Goddam, goddam, he was thinking.

He reached his car. He sat without moving and stuck the gun back inside the paper bag. The picture of the young Amanda lay in his lap. He looked into her face. Amanda in my lap. Amanda lying near my groin. He nibbled on his pinky. I killed a guy. He stared down in the direction of the city, the layered pall of pollution. Suddenly street lamps came on. Scholes's light went out and the street lamps were switched on, like illuminations to mark the old guy's demise.

His phone rang. He picked it up in a hand that felt numb.

McTell said, 'She left the building. With Rhees.'

Dansk felt removed from himself. The building – the word seemed to have cast off meaning. He had to remind himself. The building. Police HQ.

McTell said, 'Minor problem, Anthony. She's in one of those four-wheel-drive Broncos with a cop driving. Looks like she got herself a little protection.'

Protection. Dansk closed his eyes. 'Any backup? Any other vehicles following?'

'None I can see.'

'Is Rhees with her?' I killed a guy and I don't feel a goddam thing.

'Yeah, he's with her. So how come she's got protection, Anthony? Cops believe her story after all? Something you didn't anticipate?'

Dansk heard a note in McTell's voice, an undercurrent of what – gloating? 'If they bought her story, they'd give her more than one cop inside the Bronco, McTell. Believe me. You'd also see a backup car you could spot a mile off. She's being patronized. The cop's like a condom she can wrap round her fears.'

'If you say so,' McTell remarked, that funny note still in his voice.

Dansk was jazzed a little, thinking about this unexpected cop. The lady had low-level protection, a fact of life you had to deal with. Things came up and you coped with them. Dansk's Law.

One cop wasn't a disaster. McTell and Pasquale could deal with the cop at the right time. The rest was his own business. Shapes formed and fell into place. Everything had its own little slot. The future was no mystery.

'Where are they exactly?'

McTell said, 'They're driving on I-Seventeen. Passing the Thunderbird exit.'

'Stay with them.'

He punched in Pasquale's number and asked, 'Where are you?'

'I'm on, lemme see, Indian School Road approaching the interstate.'

Dansk took a map from the glove compartment. He moved a fingertip directly north. It was just as he'd figured; she was see-through. I know you, babe. In another reality we might have been close and this affinity would have had a different outcome, but now I sit with a Ruger in a brown-paper sack and your face in my groin and think of unhappy endings.

'McTell says they're in a cop vehicle. I don't like that,' Pasquale said.

'Just keep going, Pasquale.'

Dansk drove for a while. The matter was settled in his mind, only the mechanics remained.

He called McTell back. 'Still no sign of backup?'

'Nothing I'd point a finger at.'

'Where are you now?'

'The sign I just passed said Flagstaff one hundred and eighteen miles.'

She was still on course. She'd feel safe now. She had a cop with a gun to comfort her. She'd be letting down her defences a little, saying soothing words to Rhees, holding his hand. Tra-la-la, everything in her garden was beginning to bloom again. She thinks.

He drove about ten miles. Much of the traffic was out of state, sun-seekers from the Dakotas and Nebraska who lumbered south in bulky motor homes, exchanging monotonous wheatfields for the furnace. The landscape reverted to desert. Cacti blazed gold out on the brown-red flats and the sun was dying in an extravagant palette of pinks and purples and yellows.

His phone buzzed and he picked it up, expecting Pasquale or McTell, but it was Loeb, sounding like a man trapped in a barrel of molasses.

'We need to talk,' Loeb said.

'What's on your mind?' He didn't like the idea of Loeb contacting him. Especially now, when he was preoccupied.

'Face to face, Anthony. I don't like talking into these gadgets. I know they're supposed to be secure, but I have a suspicious nature. Where are you?'

'The middle of nowhere,' Dansk said.

'Specifically,' Loeb said.

'There's some kind of road-house coming up,' Dansk said, spotting a ratty wooden tavern overlooking the interstate. An orange neon sign was lit. JACK'S DINER. STEAKS. RIBS.

'Is this important, Ralph?'

'Just tell me a place we can meet.'

Dansk pulled off the freeway and into the parking lot and explained where he was. 'Give me thirty minutes,' Loeb said.

66

Jack's diner was crammed with good old boys hee-hawing and playing eight-ball with cigarette packs tucked in the sleeves of their T-shirts. Country music came wailing from the place. Dansk walked up and down the parking area. The music annoyed him.

The sun had gone when a green Nissan entered the lot and parked. Loeb stepped out, his face dark and aggressive. 'What the fuck game are you playing, Anthony?'

'Meaning?'

Loeb expelled air in a choked manner. 'I just spent half an hour with the cops.'

'And?'

'The lady goes to the cops. The cops call Washington. I get an intercept. I meet the cops. The lady is present in the room for a time.' Loeb shivered although the night air was hot.

'They're not going to believe her,' Dansk said.

Loeb placed a hand on Dansk's sleeve. 'First off, she recognized me. Soon as she looks at me, I hear the whine of her brain hydraulics. She starts in with sharp little questions disguised as innocent enquiries. How do you suppose she knew me?'

Dansk said, 'Maybe she saw you talking to me somewhere. Maybe she did some spying.'

'What it comes down to is you were supposed to do the business with her, but there she is in the cop's office. No holograph, Anthony. The woman in the flesh, and not very happy.'

'I work my own way,' Dansk said. He was walking the boundaries of sheer displeasure now, staking little fence-posts of irritation on the perimeters of his property.

Loeb said, 'Work? What you're doing is building some Byzantine edifice. This isn't a fucking mosque under construction, Anthony. I told you before, no tangents. And suddenly there I am face to face with the woman.'

'The cops won't buy her story,' Dansk said.

'They shouldn't have been given the goddam opportunity to *hear* her story! You let her get to the cops. You allowed that. Fuck only knows what's going through your head. I can't keep track of you any more, Anthony.'

You'll never know what goes through my head, Loeb. 'So she talked to the cops, and you talked to the cops. What do they think of her story?'

'They think it's fluff. At least that's what they say.'

'I rest my case,' Dansk said. He looked at Loeb and out of nowhere he had the feeling the old guy wasn't being absolutely honest about something. He wasn't sure what.

'Premature, Anthony. Maybe in normal circumstances they'd cross the street to avoid her because she reeks of paranoia, except for a couple of important things. One of them is this dead cop. Cops don't like their colleagues dead. They become very tetchy. Small things get blown out of proportion. Fluff goes under the microscope, Anthony, and suddenly everything's complicated.'

Dansk looked at the night sky. You want to talk complicated, Loeb, lift up your eyes. Check out the firmament.

'A dead cop,' Loeb said, 'and a letter from Isabel Sanchez. A letter you didn't bother to mention to me.'

'There's no letter,' Dansk said, which was true, if you looked at it a certain way.

'Not according to what the prosecutor told the cops.'

'The prosecutor's full of shit,' Dansk said.

'Shit to one side, the cops think about their dead colleague and wonder about the contents of the alleged letter and suddenly they've got questions, and I'm the one who has to sit there and come up with answers, not *you*. You're too fucking busy playing your games. Life isn't a theme park somebody put you in charge of. I asked for simplicity. I asked for no funny sleight of hand.'

Dansk didn't say anything. He was wondering if stars emitted noise up there. If there was whistling and crackling in the galaxy or if it was just eerie silence to the end of the universe.

Loeb sighed. 'A dead cop, Anthony. For Christ's sake, why?'

Dansk felt a weary superiority. Grandmasters probably experienced the same feeling facing some patzer across a chessboard. 'I took him out of the picture because he was a sympathetic ear Scholes could rely on. Then when she comes in with her story, there's no Drumm to tell it to. It's called isolating your target.'

'Isolating your target.'

'Hanging it out exposed.'

'Exposed.'

'You don't see the strategy here, Loeb. You're on a whole different wavelength from me.'

'Everybody's on a whole different wavelength from you.' Loeb stared at Dansk in silence for a time. 'You got the tape I sent you. You heard the lady and Drumm discuss a possible connection between Galindez and Isabel and Benny Vialli.'

'Pure fucking speculation,' Dansk said. He was above all this petty shit.

'Yeah, but dangerous speculation, Anthony. The one plus is she obviously didn't mention this conversation to the cops, because they never raised it with me.'

'She's groping, Loeb. She's playing with mysteries. She's out of her league.'

Loeb said, 'Then your name came up. The cops asked if I'd heard of you.'

'My name was deleted,' Dansk said.

Loeb looked morose. 'Erasing your name from the computers is the easy part, Anthony, but you can't do the same with people's memories. The cops ask the lady prosecutor for a description of you and one of their artists comes up with a likeness. Then this picture goes out to such places as the FBI, Justice, the US Marshals Service, and somebody's going to say, "Hey, I know this guy, a US marshal. Wasn't he the one took compassionate leave from the Service a coupla years back on the grounds of depression caused by the death of his mother?"'

'My *mother*?' Dansk asked, jolted.

'Your mother. Slain by scumbag junkies for the few bucks in her purse. Remember?'

Scumbag junkies? What was this shit Loeb was talking? The old guy's marbles were broken and scattered. 'I talked to my mother on the phone this afternoon. She's absolutely fine. I never heard her better.'

'You *talked* to your mother? Is that what you're telling me? You actually talked to her. Talked? As in held a conversation?'

'Yeah, as in held a conversation.'

Loeb looked for a while into Dansk's eyes, then said quietly, 'Oh, Jesus.' He shook his head from side to side very slowly.

'What's your oh-Jesus problem, Loeb?'

'No problem, Anthony. Honestly. I'm glad she's in good shape. I mean that. I'm happy.'

He stroked his cheek with a fingertip. He looked past Dansk at the neon sign above the tavern. His expression was contemplative. His face had an unhealthy tangerine glow. 'It's over, Anthony.'

'What's over?'

'This. This work. I'm bringing down the curtain.'

'No way. No goddam way.'

'I can't let you . . .' Loeb smiled at Dansk in a soft sad manner. 'Look, Scholes has planted a seed and there's a chance it could grow up to be a plant, and the cops study this plant, and before you know it, it's got leaves and branches. Suddenly the cops are wondering how to classify it, because it's not in the usual books.'

Dansk said, 'Spare me the horticultural story, Loeb.'

'You kill the prosecutor, I'll tell you what happens.

The plant just bursts into an amazing flower, Anthony, and the gardeners are swarming all around it. They're analysing the roots, and that's the last thing we want, because the roots go places we don't want anyone finding. Kill the prosecutor and the cops are gonna take her story with a whole new level of seriousness.'

'Killing the prosecutor's the whole goddam *point*, because she's gonna keep prying and prying until she finds what she's looking for. You can't walk from that fact.'

Loeb gestured firmly, his hand slicing the air. 'Covering our tracks is the whole point now. The only point. We shut the book, we burn it and we try to make sure the goddam ashes don't blow all over the place.'

'The only thing we burn is the fucking woman,' Dansk said. His voice sounded thundery inside his head. He could hear his mother somewhere in all this ruckus, the mother Loeb said was dead, the mother he'd phoned that afternoon. Loeb was spaced on drugs. The prospect of death had unbalanced him. Sand was running out his egg-timer. A man looking down the tunnel of doom had to have profound difficulties concerning reality. You couldn't take him at face value, you couldn't trust anything he said. This story about his conversation with the cops, for instance. It didn't ring true. It had a counterfeit sound, like he was making some of it up.

'Let it sink in nice and slow,' Loeb said. 'We're shutting down, Anthony. Out of business. Trading conditions are adverse. We're looking at a whole dismantling operation because it's not secure any more, it's not like it used to be. I'm taking it apart brick by brick by brick. No more death. You following me, Anthony?'

'This is my work, Loeb. This is the way I live my life, and you want to close up my shop. You're out of your mind.'

'The work's devoured you, Anthony.' Loeb placed a hand on Dansk's shoulder, a gesture of comfort Dansk didn't need. He knocked Loeb's hand away.

Loeb said, 'Look, we accomplished a lot of what we set out to do back in the beginning. Remember that.'

'So it ends here,' Dansk said. 'Just like that. Just like that.'

'You'll be looked after,' Loeb said. 'I wouldn't leave you hanging, you know that.'

Dansk listened to the voice in his head. *Get people to respect you, Anthony. Don't get pushed around.*

'It ends here all right, Loeb, but not for me.' He reached quickly inside his car, stretched a hand across the framed photograph of Amanda, took the Ruger from the paper sack and turned and fired one shot into Loeb's forehead. Loeb collapsed slowly, his coat a tent about him. He lay like an old crow with spread wings. Dansk looked down at him. Blood, turned to orange by neon, flowed from Loeb's face. Dansk thought of juice squeezed out of oranges.

He got inside his car. Look on the bright side, Ralph, you don't need morphine now.

He picked up Amanda's photograph from the passenger seat and then, with a barely discernible notion of regret for things that might have been in an alternative dimension of dreams, he tossed it out of the window a few miles along the highway. He heard glass shatter and he thought, Goodbye, lady.

And goodnight.

67

Nightfall and darkness. Amanda sat in the back of the Bronco with Rhees. Rested, more alert, Rhees seemed to have negotiated a very fragile truce with his pain. Up front, Gannon drove with consideration, slowing when he came to bends.

'How you both doing back there?' he asked.

Amanda said, 'Fine,' but it was a lie, she didn't feel fine. It wasn't the fact that Kelloway had taken control of things, although it annoyed her to think of the way she'd been obliged to buckle and step aside. No, this was something else. *Pick a safe place*, Kelloway had said. Instinctively, she'd jumped at the idea of the pine forest as a secure destination, but now a dismaying sensation the colour of squid-ink was spiralling inside her head.

She said, 'Stop.'

Gannon pulled the vehicle over.

Rhees asked, 'Why are we stopping?'

Amanda looked at his face, then her vision drifted past him towards the empty blacktop. Clouds trailed across an insipid vanilla moon and the desert on either side of the highway was a landscape patched with tiny areas of spangle and shadow.

'The cabin,' she said.

'What about it?'

'I just have a bad feeling.'

Rhees said, 'You think Dansk knows about the place? Even if he does, it's not easy to find.'

'He *probes*, John. He's got the instincts of a psychotic proctologist, and somewhere along the way he finds out we've been living in a cabin near Flag.'

'You're saying he'll follow us,' Rhees said.

'He's driven. He has a relentless streak. He isn't going to drop this. He isn't about to let you and me off the hook.'

Gannon, who had a shotgun balanced against the passenger seat and a Colt .45 in a holster, said, 'Listen, I only know what Chief Kelloway told me. I drive you both to the cabin and play bodyguard until I hear otherwise. Now you're saying you don't want to go there because you're worried about this guy.'

Amanda pictured the small rooms of the cabin, but the intimacy of the place had dissolved, the idea of sanctuary had eroded. She was going passively back to the forest, and it was the wrong move. Unless she could somehow turn it to her advantage.

Traffic appeared on the highway, a cluster of four or five cars, bright lights. She wondered about their occupants. If Dansk was nearby, if he'd tracked her from Phoenix. A cop vehicle wouldn't deter him, she knew that. He'd consider it a minor nuisance.

Gannon asked, 'Is this guy working alone, or are we talking numbers?'

'Including Dansk, three at least,' she said. 'There might be more, I don't know.'

Gannon said, 'Nobody's told me the whole story here, but the buzz I hear is that this Dansk is connected some way to the death of Willie Drumm.'

'Connected some way is right,' she said.

'I don't like losing friends,' Gannon remarked.

'And I don't like running away from things,' she said.

Gannon said, 'Look, my brief is to guard you. Kelloway never mentioned anything else. Just keep an eye on the pair of you, he said.'

'The Colt .45 and the shotgun, what are they for? You need permission from the bald eagle to use them?' She listened to her own voice and how bellicose it had become. It was like the voice of a different person.

Gannon said, 'If there's a life-threatening situation, first thing I reach for is my friendly Colt, believe me. I don't stop to ask permission, Ms Scholes.'

Rhees shifted his body slightly and said to Amanda, 'I know what's running through your mind. You're wondering if Dansk can be trapped.'

'Maybe,' she said.

'No maybe, Amanda. I know you. You're wondering if he can be trapped and caught.'

'I don't like the direction of this,' Gannon said.

Amanda said, 'He killed Willie Drumm, Gannon. Your colleague. Your friend. My friend.'

'My instructions don't include capturing Dansk or anyone else.'

'I'm not asking you to disobey,' she said. 'You just do your job the way Kelloway wants it done. You protect us.'

'I have every intention,' Gannon said.

Rhees said, 'A trap needs bait. What bait are we talking about here?'

Amanda said, 'It's a risk.'

Rhees looked at her for a long time. He shook his head. 'No way. Absolutely no way. I don't want to hear the rest of this. Forget it.'

'Like I said, it's a risk.'

Rhees said, 'No. End of subject.'

'You can't just make Dansk disappear, John. If Kelloway's investigating, it could take days, weeks. Even then there's no guarantee he's ever going to get to the truth. He'll be shunted between Justice officials, US Marshals and God knows who else in the Federal machine. This guy Loeb who came from Justice, for instance, he and Dansk come out the same damn pod.'

Rhees said, 'We could go somewhere—'

'And hide? I can't live that way, John. Sorry.'

Rhees sighed. 'It's in the hands of the cops, Amanda. That's what really riles you. You've been decommissioned.'

'No, what riles me is the idea of doing nothing,' she said. 'And with respect to Sergeant Gannon, I don't feel very secure.'

Dansk's presence in the pines, his head filled with murderous notions, birds disturbed, wings suddenly fluttering through branches – no, she couldn't go through with that, waiting and waiting.

Gannon alone wasn't enough. She'd need more than Gannon's shotgun and the Colt in his holster before she could feel remotely secure. 'Pass me your mobile.'

Gannon handed her the unit with a little gesture of reluctance.

Rhees asked, 'Who do you intend to call?'

Amanda began to tap numbers. 'I want Dansk out of our lives, John. I want to hand him over to Kelloway and say, Here, here's the elusive Dansk for you, Chief. Why don't you grill him for answers? Why don't you shine a big bright fucking light in his eyes and make him talk? I just want things back the way they were before.'

Rhees said, 'Before? Remind me, Amanda. Refresh my memory.'

'It was a good life and I want it to be good again. It's that simple.'

'What is it really, Amanda? You feel you have some kind of appointment with Dansk you're desperate to keep?'

An appointment with Dansk, that was one way of putting it. But it had to be on her own terms and her own territory. 'I'm not running from this situation. Somebody else might, but not me.'

Rhees's voice was dry and flat and suffused with resignation. 'It's all or nothing with you, Amanda. It's always been that way.'

'You get to a point where you're sick of fear, and I've reached that point, John. I've reached it and I've outstripped it and I'm tired.'

She finished punching in the number that would connect her with Kelloway.

68

Dansk felt the darkness was fevered in some way. If the night was a human being, it would be running a temperature. He glanced at the Ruger on the passenger seat. The power of a gun. The stunning velocity of a bullet, the implosion of an eye, the demolition of brain tissue, flakes of bone spitting through the back of Loeb's head into the tangerine light, Morgan Scholes crumpling like an empty grocery bag. Death delivered in an instant. Life and death locked in an ammunition clip locked in a chamber locked in your fist. All that lethal energy. Death compacted and compressed in pointed cylinders.

You killed Loeb. You killed Morgan Scholes. No inner turmoil, no conflict with your conscience, no great upheaval of the heart. Just point the gun and pull the trigger. Real easy.

Somewhere far to his right a firework went off. A solitary burst of bright purple light, then a fine spray as the power ebbed out of the thing and it fell to earth. Some kid with a firework he'd probably smuggled back from Mexico. Dansk retained the impression behind his eyes for a few miles, a firefly flutter of powdered light.

He pulled into a gas station, got out of his car and approached the office. The old guy who appeared in the doorway had a discoloured glass eye. Dansk noticed the fake eye was blue-grey and the white around it viscous, milky.

''Bout to close up,' the old guy said. 'You got me just in time.' He shuffled out to the pumps and began to fill Dansk's car. 'See some eejit set off a firework. You get these drunk kids out in the woods. They don't think fire hazards. You just passing through?'

For ever, Dansk thought. He said, 'Yeah. Passing through.'

''Bout all Flag's good for these days, passing through. One time it was different. Air up here used to be sweeter than honey in my day.' He closed the gas cap.

Dansk followed the man inside the office, which was also a storeroom. It smelled of grease and rubber and stewed coffee. He spotted a Coke machine that issued soda in glass bottles. He asked for change and inserted enough coins for two bottles. He looked round the place, bought a flashlight, a box of Kleenex, thirty-six inches of clear plastic tubing, a bottle-opener, a disposable lighter and the largest wrench he could find.

The old guy rang the items up on his cash register. Dansk paid. Outside, a car idled near the darkened pumps, then drove away quickly in a squeal of rubber.

'I guess that's one fellow decided he don't need

gas,' the old guy said, 'or else he's in an almighty hurry, like everybody else these days.'

Dansk stepped outside, clutching his purchases, seeing tail-lights glow like cast-off cigarette butts down the highway.

69

Inside McTell's car Pasquale said, 'I gotta call Loeb, tell him it's done.'

'You attached it OK?' McTell asked.

'While Dansk was in the gas station. The thing's magnetic.' Pasquale removed his phone from his pocket and dialled Loeb's number. There wasn't an answer. He let it ring for a while. 'Funny, he said he'd wait to hear from me.'

'So he split. Back home probably. It's no big deal.'

'This whole thing's gone weird,' Pasquale remarked.

'You get new orders direct from Loeb, you go through with them. Nothing weird about that.'

Pasquale sighed. 'Loeb isn't a healthy guy, Eddie. I never seen a human look like that since my Uncle Bill on my mother's side croaked from pneumonia. He's like this zombie colour.'

'The only colour interests me is money,' McTell said.

Pasquale took a thick white envelope from the inside pocket of his jacket. 'Twenty thou in crisp hundreds. Severance pay, Loeb calls it. We get the second instalment afterwards.'

'Yo, May-eee-co,' said McTell. '*Arriba arriba!*'

'Yeah,' said Pasquale, 'it's gonna be a change.'

McTell said, 'I hate Dansk like a tumour in my chest, like a thing I gotta cut out at the root. It's got to where I can't hack the sound of his voice even, that little nasal thing he's got sometimes.'

'Tell you what I hate,' Pasquale said. 'This feeling of treachery.'

'You'll get over it, Bruno. Down in Tijuana the Birthmark Kid's gonna fade to black.'

Pasquale said, 'The thing is, I was inside the Protection Program, sitting in fucking Buffalo and bored outta my skull and just fucking *aching* for some action, and he rescues me from that meat-packing plant. He pulls me outta that situation and puts me back to my own kinda work. So I still feel I owe him, Eddie.'

'Listen, I was twice as bored in Pasadena managing a laundromat and sniffing all those fucking cancerous chemicals they got in them places,' McTell said, 'but I don't figure I owe Dansk a goddam thing. I'm sick of his shit attitude and the way he does things.'

McTell drove in silence for a time. 'Let's see the gadget.'

Pasquale removed a black plastic box from his right side pocket. It was about four inches by four, battery-operated. He flicked a switch and a panel lit.

'Who made that box?' McTell asked.

'Who what?'

'There a manufacturer's name?'

Pasquale turned on the map light and studied the

box. 'Cisco Electronics Inc., San Luis Obispo, Cal, it says here.'

'American. Call me a patriot.'

Pasquale peered at the red digital numbers on the box. 'The only condition Loeb laid down is we got to do the thing in an isolated place.'

'No problem,' McTell said. 'It's a big empty state, Arizona.'

70

Amanda kicked off her shoes, changed her clothes from the business suit to jeans and a long-sleeved shirt of John's. She lit a cigarette and drew smoke deeply into her lungs. The nicotine didn't relax her. The palms of her hands were damp and some kind of nerve worked like a pulse in her throat. The unlit rooms of the cabin cramped her. The night was all tension and expectation, the silence that of a very delicate cease-fire. The dark had a heavy stillness and the air smelled like a pine coffin and the moon was behind cloud and sailing.

She crushed her cigarette in the fireplace and thought of Gannon strolling quietly round the cabin. She'd called Kelloway and badgered him into contacting the Flagstaff PD to see if members of the local force might provide more backup, and he'd been grudgingly obliging. A mile down the path, two cops armed with rifles and night-scopes watched and waited for unusual sounds and sights in the dark, and another, a deputy called Clarence Griffin, was posted close to the old bridge.

And now she wondered if she'd done enough or if her idea was flawed, or if she should have listened to Rhees and changed tack and gone to another destination far away. But she'd made this decision and she couldn't back out even if she'd wanted to, and she didn't, despite the menacing quiet of the forest and the arrhythmic nature of her pulses.

She lit another cigarette. She tilted her head back and realized she was listening as she'd never listened before in her life. If a pine needle drifted from a branch she'd hear it. If a grass snake stirred, she'd register the whispered slither of its movements. She was fine-tuned to whatever happened outside the cabin.

She sat on the floor, her back propped against the wall. She studied the dim shape of Rhees in an armchair on the other side of the room. He'd defiantly refused the wheelchair. He'd turned down the suggestion of going to a motel room and waiting alone. He'd been adamant and unusually stubborn, as if he felt a need to match her determination with his own. If he couldn't make her change her mind, then he'd stay with her and to hell with his pain.

He sat in shadow and said nothing, and she wondered if there was reproach in his expression, or fear, but she couldn't see his face, just the pale outline of his plastered arm and the sling, and the white stripes in his shirt.

She flicked her cigarette into the fireplace. 'You OK?' she asked.

'You're whispering,' he said.

'Yeah, I guess I am. You think this is a bad move, don't you?'

'When it comes to you, Amanda, it's like being caught up in a whirlwind, and I don't see much point in criticizing a force of nature.'

'You didn't have to be here,' she said. 'You had choices.'

'The only feasible choice was to stay with you, at the eye of the storm.'

'You haven't answered my question,' she said.

'It's a bad move if it turns out wrong. It's a good move if it works.'

'Fence-sitting,' she said.

Rhees said, 'I'll tell you something I'm a touch more certain about: you don't *really* want Dansk captured, you want him gunned down by one of your posse out there. This notion you have about handing him over to Kelloway is one you'd *like* to believe in, but I get the sense you want blood. Tell me I'm wrong.'

Dansk's blood. Maybe there was a truth in Rhees's words she didn't want to acknowledge. Maybe a hardening had taken place inside her and she wanted him dead. But there were mysteries still, and they confounded her.

'I want him any way I can get him.'

'Dead or alive,' Rhees said.

'I'd prefer alive,' she said. 'The other way, he can't answer any questions, and I have a few I want answered.'

She lit another cigarette, masking the flame of the lighter in her hand.

'He kills Willie and Mrs Vialli. Willie, OK, I can understand. He's a cop poking around asking questions. But Bernadette? Your average suburban widow, for God's sake . . . except for one big difference. She happens to have a son in the Protection

Program and she's not happy because he's been silent too long. And when he does get in touch, it's in a form she finds iffy. Question: Where the hell is Benny?'

Rhees said, 'For God's sake, leave it to Kelloway, Amanda.'

She walked the room quietly, window to door and back again. She stopped behind Rhees and laid her hands on his shoulders and a dark thought formed in her brain.

'Benny's dead,' she said.

'You can't *know* he's dead, Amanda.'

'Benny's dead and Dansk's responsible, and the only goddam reason I can think he'd have for killing her was to keep her from discovering the fate of her son.'

'I don't know where you're going with this,' Rhees said.

The patterns in her head kept spinning and shifting. She heard herself say, 'Why wasn't Bascombe high on Kelloway's list of people to talk to? Lew was supposed to be digging up information for Willie, after all. So why did Kelloway call Justice first? And Loeb – what did the big Chief learn there? When I phoned him to beg for more bodies, he didn't mention his talk with Loeb. Why? Because it amounted to nothing? Because Loeb fobbed him off? Why?'

'Leave it,' Rhees said.

Leave it. Leave it all to Kelloway. Hail to the Chief. Her thoughts were greyhounds on a slippery track, and she couldn't follow them and the hare they chased was out of sight.

Rhees said, 'There's the more pressing matter of Dansk. If he's out there, he isn't going to walk blindly into a set-up, Amanda. He'd *know* you've got cops staking the place out. He may be outnumbered for all we know, but maybe he hasn't been out-thought. Which scares me more than a little.'

Amanda heard the sound of Gannon's quiet footsteps on the porch. She inclined her face, bringing the surface of her cheek against John's. 'I wish,' she said.

'Wish what?'

'Forget it. It doesn't matter—'

'Wish I wasn't here? Wish I'd stayed in some nice safe motel room so you didn't have to take any responsibility for me?'

'Yes. No. I'm not sure.'

He touched her hand. 'If there has to be bait, you'd rather it was just you dangling.'

'I want you to be safe, that's all. I don't want anybody to hurt you again.'

'Eye of the storm, Amanda. It's no place to be alone.'

'There's protection,' she said. 'I wouldn't be alone.'

'Four cops. An army would make me a little less uneasy.'

She kissed him. He rested his hand against the curve of her hip. She drew the flat of his hand across her stomach, and for a second she thought it was possible to believe nothing had altered. And then the telephone rang, harsh and unexpected. She picked it up on the first ring.

Dansk said, 'Nice quiet countryside, Amanda. Nothing moving except a few old raccoons, unless you count me.'

She didn't respond. Her hand on the receiver was stiff and suddenly she was cold.

Dansk said, 'The woods are lovely dark and deep, et cetera.'

She still didn't reply. She realized she was holding her breath.

Dansk laughed. 'You figured it all out yet, lady?'

71

Dansk left his car hidden under shrubbery a quarter of a mile from the old bridge, and moved through the trees, ducking now and again to avoid low-hanging branches. You had to be careful what was underfoot: roots, rotted trunks, gopher holes. He went cautiously, but with a certain ease. He'd back-packed in rough places, he'd put in hard time on survival courses courtesy of the US Marshals Service, spent weeks alone in remote Appalachian hill country where all you got was a knife and a box of matches and a length of twine and a safety pin, and fend for yourself, buddy. And I did it, he thought. With flying colours. This was a walk on the beach by comparison. Easy-peasy, watch where you step, *concentrate*. Listen to the language of the pines, what the landscape is saying. He stopped moving, crouched low, studied the darkness.

In the right-hand pocket of his dark-blue jacket he had a Coke bottle into which he'd siphoned gasoline from the tank of his car. He'd stuffed the neck with wadded Kleenex. He had a second bottle in his left pocket, also filled with gas and similarly fused. In his right hand he carried the hefty wrench he'd bought at the filling-station, the Ruger was in his left. He'd tucked the flashlight in his belt and the mobile phone was in his back pocket with the ringer switched off. The last thing he needed in the stillness of the night was a call from McTell or Pasquale, the sound of buzzing in the pines.

If they phoned.

Earlier, he'd tried to make contact with them from his car, but neither had answered. He'd assumed at first that they'd made a rendezvous, and maybe they'd left their cars to take a leak at the side of the road, but ten minutes later he was still getting no answer from either. One possibility was that they'd stopped for pizza or to grab a hamburger. They were always chowing down unhealthy fast-food fodder. Another was that they'd crapped out, decided to quit, go their own way. But they'd never run from a situation before, so why start now? Afraid of the cop presence?

Or something else.

Such as what? He wondered if maybe Loeb had contacted them, ordered them out of the picture, part of his dismantling operation. We're shutting down. We're hanging a sign in the window: Out of Business.

They'd both been off-centre recently, McTell more than normally sullen, Pasquale remote. Fuck them. Dansk was only half interested anyway, inclined to dismiss them. It was a shabby world. You can't trust people, they disappoint. What it comes down to over and over is that there's only one person to rely on in the end: Anthony Dansk. Your good self.

He didn't need McTell and Pasquale. He was weary of dumb killers and their idiot resentments. They were like boulder-filled baggage he had to haul, directing them to do this, go here, go there. They couldn't think for themselves, they didn't have enough brains to boil a fucking egg. He was better on his own because he'd always preferred his own company. Maybe he should have worked alone from the beginning, doing the surgery by himself. God knows he was capable of it, and he was comfortable with it.

He kept moving. It was surprising how little sound you made if you concentrated, if you were aware. The darkness was a warm embrace. Come on in, Anthony, there's nothing to fear.

The forest filled his head like sweet music. McTell and Pasquale would've been noisy, crushing twigs and cones underfoot, disturbing birds and alarming skunks. They wouldn't have heard the music.

Come in, keep coming, Amanda isn't far away.

He thought of her in the darkness ahead. Her and Rhees. He pictured her when she'd plucked the eucalyptus leaf outside her house. He saw Rhees's hand dropping to her ass. Oh that intimacy. He remembered the way he'd grabbed her wrist in the hotel room and forced food to her lips, and the feeling of power that spiked through him and the warmth of her breast.

He also remembered calling his mother to tell her about a girl named Amanda. His mother seemed very far away from him at this moment, a distance greater than two thousand and something miles. She seemed locked inside the prism of his memory like a butterfly pinned in a glass display case.

He stopped suddenly, alert to a slight alteration in the melody in his brain. A change of modality, major to minor. He stood very still under a tree that oozed a resinous odour. The sound was faint but he zoned in on it. He recognized it as the noise made by somebody's stomach, a churning of intestinal juices.

The source of the sound was somewhere to his right, five or six yards, maybe more. You had to make allowances for the way noise carried here. There was barely any light. The moon was shrouded by thick strands of cloud.

He stepped to his right. He had the sensation of floating just above the ground. He weighed the wrench in his hand, twelve inches of hard steel, something you could believe in. That's what you needed in life, something to believe in. Like this work Loeb had wanted to close down and walk away from. Close the book. Burn it. Leave the prosecutor alive and look after our own asses.

Right, rob me of my life, Loeb. No way.

The man in the trees was about six feet tall and wore a dark windcheater and black jeans. He had a holstered weapon on his hip and he was standing very still. Maybe he'd sensed something, aroused by a faint instinct to the fact that there was a change in the atmosphere, only he couldn't quite pinpoint it.

A guard, Dansk thought. He wondered if this was the cop who'd driven Amanda and Rhees up here from Phoenix, or if Amanda had managed to stock the woods with reinforcements. It was the kind of move she'd make. You see one cop in the Bronco, but what you don't see are the others in the pine forest. Just keep coming, Anthony. I have a few tricks left.

I'm ready for you, lady. Always have been.

He edged forwards. He felt a weird tingle in the tips of his fingers, as if the steel of the wrench had turned to ice and welded skin to metal, like the effect when you took something out of the deep-freeze.

The man turned his head a little, away from Dansk. Dansk stepped forward and swung the wrench with all his strength and felt it split the skin and sink into the base of the man's neck. The man went down at once and Dansk straddled him, noticing that one of the guy's eyelids quivered uncontrollably as if a circuit of nerve-links had been severed with the blow.

'How fucking many of you?' Dansk whispered.

The guy rolled his face to the side. Blood was flowing from the place where neck and shoulder had been punctured, and the eyelid kept flickering open and shut. Dansk brought the wrench down a second time into the side of the guy's neck.

Pine needles adhered to the guy's lips and teeth. 'Go fuck yourself,' he said.

Dansk was centred, he'd found a balance in himself. He hammered the wrench into the guy's head with controlled force. 'How many, fella?'

The guy moaned and said, 'Three . . .'

'Three where?'

'Two . . . a mile up the path.'

'And the third?'

'The cabin.'

'Thanks,' and Dansk smacked the wrench down again and again, three times, four, he lost count, it didn't matter. And then it was no longer what you'd call a face, it was bloody and broken and ugly; hard steel had splintered bone and demolished the skull and mouth and blinded the eyes.

Dansk stopped, listening for the sound of breathing. He heard none. This one was gone. Like that. Life battered out of him. Face, skull, blood pouring from shattered veins. Life is a skinny thread, snip.

He reached down and touched the guy's groin, wondering if there was a discharge of piss, but the guy was dry.

Dansk stood up and his eye followed the overgrown path as far as he could see in the diminished light. He was conscious of the scent of gasoline from one of his pockets, where a bottle had tilted a little and fuel soaked the wadded tissue.

Two other guards a mile along the path, and one at the cabin. Amanda and Rhees inside.

I'm coming, I'm on my way. There's no stopping me.

He went between the trees with the blood-wet wrench in his right hand, and he walked as close to the path as he could. It was choked with fern and stunted bushes and scrub. Here and there stray pine saplings had taken root but, overshadowed by the density of older trees, they grew stilted and starved. Survival depended on how much territory you could claim for yourself.

I claim this forest. This whole goddam thing and everything in it, especially the former prosecutor. This is my dominion. McTell and Pasquale could never have understood this.

The only thing they knew was thuggery. They didn't understand the true nature of killing, they thought of it as simple disposal. But you weren't just ending the life of somebody, no way, you were changing history. A man beaten to death was no simple brutal act, it had consequences you couldn't begin to foresee – bereaved wife, orphaned children, an empty chair at dinner, a coffin, lawyers checking last wills and testaments, insurance agents scanning policies. Killing was a form of rearranging the patterns of reality, breaking a sheet of stained glass into a sudden amazing kaleidoscope in which you could watch all the coloured flecks revolve in an infinity of configurations. Even on a simple level, the dead guy's clothes would need to be stacked inside boxes and donated to Goodwill, and somebody else would go round wearing them, unaware of the fact that they'd once belonged to a guy battered to death in a pine forest by a wrench.

You don't touch just one life in killing. It was a stone dropped in water; the rings spread and all kinds of people were changed, some in big ways, others in small. Some were heartbroken, others got used Levis from a charity store.

On your own you can change the world.

He kept going, his body hunched a little, shoulders down. He wasn't thinking now. He was all motion and hard focus and silence. He'd stepped up a gear. He was cruising through the trees, sensing treacherous dips in the earth before he reached them. His night vision was acute, vulpine.

He stopped.

There were two of them just ahead. There was also a vehicle of the jeep variety. One of the men was moving slowly round the vehicle, the other, smaller and younger, leaned against the door panel. They had rifles and wore uniforms.

Dansk calculated the distance to the vehicle; fifty yards, maybe less. He lowered himself to the ground and watched. To see without being seen. Invisibility was a kick. The cop leaning against the door sighed quietly. He didn't know somebody was out among the trees watching him.

Dansk moved closer.

The older guy stopped beside the younger and whispered something Dansk couldn't catch. The young cop shook his head.

Dansk got a little closer still.

The moment.

Showtime.

He removed the Coke bottle from his right pocket. The stench of gas was strong, but there was no breeze to carry it in the direction of the cops. The night was like a deflated lung. He hunkered down behind a bush and took out the cheap cigarette lighter he'd bought.

He adjusted the little lever to low before he applied his thumb to the lighter. He pressed down, got a tiny eye of flame from the plastic cylinder – and now this had to be quick. Lighter-flame to tissue, just a touch, then he stood up and tossed the bottle through the air and heard the musculature in his arm ripple. He watched the bottle rise and fall in a lit arc, spinning and turning as it fell, then exploding against the windshield of the vehicle, and instantly the air was luminous with flame and the younger cop, seared by an outburst of fire, screamed. The older guy had dropped to the ground, his flesh pierced with spears and shards of glass, and he was moaning about his eyes, how he couldn't see *a fucking thing*, and the young cop just kept screaming, rolling over and over in an attempt to douse the fire that melted his clothes to his skin.

Polyester shirt and pants, Dansk thought. Man-made fibre. Never trust it. He lit and threw the second bottle. It struck the jeep, which exploded.

The force of the blast made Dansk step back into the trees. The jeep combusted in blue and yellow flags of fire and the air was bitter with the smell of rubber and gasoline.

A thing of great beauty, this conflagration. Your own private war zone. Dry pines began to crackle, flame created sudden bridges through space, the forest was lit and the darkness dissolved. Birds shaken out of branches were turned gold and red by reflected fire, transmuted from ordinary bluejays and ravens into creatures with exotic plumage. The night burned and burned and burned.

And Dansk was already moving again, and thinking.

Of the cabin. Of Amanda.

72

Barefoot, she hurried out to the porch, where Gannon stood with his shotgun against his side, the barrel directed downwards. She'd heard somebody scream and then the explosions rocked the night and she'd seen unidentifiable debris rise and fall through the air. Now she stared at the fire half a mile away and watched it spread like an apocalyptic false dawn. Then Rhees was standing just behind her in the doorway, breathing hard and leaning against the frame for support. The heart of the fire was the place where the two cops had been parked.

Rhees said, 'The Bronco's parked out back. We could try to drive out of here.'

Gannon shook his head. 'Too damn risky. The path's blocked by fire, there's a good chance we'd fry, and there's no way to drive out except that path. You couldn't get a vehicle through the trees. Too dense.'

Amanda resisted panic. Be calm in the face of adversity. Dansk and his thugs had pierced the thin defences she'd arranged, which meant they'd got past the deputy Clarence Griffin at the bridge, then blown up the cop vehicle. They'd created this light show, all these special effects, and now they were moving somewhere in the shadows between the flames towards the cabin. As for Griffin and the two other cops – this was an area she didn't want to enter.

Gannon said, 'One stroke of luck is there's no wind. The way the fire's spreading I'd say we have maybe thirty minutes or more before it reaches this far.'

Amanda looked towards the pines that edged the path. They were burning, dry sticks in a bonfire. The scent of smoking wood drifted through the air, sweet, narcotic. But there was a secondary smell, a noxious undercurrent of plastic smouldering, oil on fire.

Amanda said, 'So either we sit here and barbecue or we get the hell out. Turning to hamburger doesn't attract me, and if we can't drive, we hoof it out of here and head away from the fire in the direction of the river.' She turned to Rhees. 'There's not a multitude of choices, John. You think you can make it?'

'Like you say, no choice.'

Gannon seemed suddenly decisive. 'OK, let's do it. Let's go for it.'

'Once we're about a mile clear of the cabin there's a dry creek surrounded by scrub, which might give us some cover for a time,' Amanda said.

'I know the place,' Rhees said.

In another lifetime they'd made love in that arroyo, she recalled, spontaneous and urgent in spite of the grit and the pestering flies.

She remembered she was barefoot. She stepped

into the cabin to fetch her shoes. The reach of fire-light hadn't penetrated the rooms, so she flipped a switch, saw the shoes near the fireplace and slipped her feet into them.

He was standing by the open window on the other side of the room. His face was smoke-stained, his jacket was smeared with soil and pine needles, and there was blood on the back of the hand that held the gun. He was about six feet away and reeked of gasoline.

'Say nothing, Amanda,' he whispered.

She registered the open window, the bits and pieces of forest that clung to Dansk, who resembled some creature long dormant, emerging from an underground cavern, half human, half some other kind of being. He stepped towards her, caught her and turned her around, and she felt the pressure of his body against her spine, the gun and his breath upon the back of her neck.

'The door,' he said.

He forced her outside to the porch.

Rhees leaned against the rail, and Gannon stared at the flames like a man trying to gauge the rate the fire was spreading. She thought of giving a cry of warning, an elbow smacked into Dansk's ribcage, into his heart, a sudden turn and a rake of his face with her fingernails, trying to grapple the gun away from him. Then she felt Dansk's mouth against her neck, his lips, teeth. A kiss.

Rhees turned his face and said, 'Jesus.'

Gannon looked round then, but it was too late for him, the shotgun he held was pointed down-wards and he didn't have time to bring it up into a firing position, and even if he'd had days to figure out a move he couldn't have fired because Amanda was a shield protecting Anthony Dansk. Dansk levelled the pistol, his hand an inch or so above Amanda's shoulder. She tried to lean into him, collide just enough to force him into an erratic shot, but he was too quick, he'd already fired the gun and the sound was like a landmine in her ears. She felt sick in her stomach and sour saliva came flooding into her mouth. She thought she heard Dansk say, 'Not very smart, Amanda,' and then she was conscious of how Gannon was thrown back against the rail and the shotgun fell out of his hands. The rail yielded and Gannon dropped out of sight through wood that had snapped with the impact of his body.

Rhees, dragging his useless leg, took one halting step forward, as if he were considering an act of bravery. She told him to stay where he was in a voice that was thick and half audible to herself.

Dansk laughed. 'Listen to the lady, Rhees.'

Rhees said, 'Let her go.'

Dansk laughed again. It was a quiet laugh, restrained. 'Let her go?'

Amanda stared at Rhees. His face was illuminated by flame, his expression was numbed. And all the time there was the deafening roar in her head of the gun firing and the pine trees crackling.

'You thought you'd be nice and safe here,' Dansk said. 'A flash for you. Nowhere's safe. It's that kind of world.' He surveyed the fire a moment. 'It's time we got out of here.'

'Where?' she asked.

'To a place where all your curiosity ends.' He looked at Rhees. 'It's a rough walk for you, I guess. Maybe you'd prefer to stay? Or maybe you're just as curious as your lady here.' He pointed the Ruger at Rhees.

Rhees said, 'I go where she goes.'

'Figures.' Dansk released Amanda and gestured with his head towards the forest. 'We'll go round the flames back to the bridge.'

'And then what?' she asked.

Dansk seemed not to hear her question. He said, 'Pity about the trees. You take something out of nature, it disturbs the balance of things. I don't like that.' There was a look of mild regret on his face. 'Now walk. Just walk. I'm right behind you.'

73

They moved between trees, along the edges of flame, past the burning jeep. She saw no sign of the cops and hoped they'd somehow managed to survive, but she knew this was a dim prospect.

The going was rough on Rhees. Amanda had to take his weight against her body, an effort that confined her thoughts to the immediacy of things around her; the sound of Rhees's breathing, the architecture of fire. She had no sense of a future. It was a matter of walking out of the forest, and wherever they went next was up to Dansk. This place he had in mind. *Where all your curiosity ends.*

Rhees said, 'I need a moment.'

Dansk prodded Rhees in the back with his gun. 'You don't have a moment. Keep moving.'

Amanda looked back and saw sparks float above the core of flame and up into the night. Sooner or later the cabin would be destroyed. Sooner or later she and Rhees would go the same way. No escape route came to mind. Dansk had the gun and the gun was the future.

'Over the bridge, cross the road,' Dansk said. 'Hurry. Move, move, move.'

The bridge was made out of wooden struts, decaying under a layer of moss. Amanda felt the structure sway when she and Rhees stepped onto it. Beyond the bridge, Dansk herded them to the right where his car was concealed under shrubbery. Behind, the fire roared with the noise of a small sun exploding.

'You're the designated driver, Amanda,' Dansk said. 'I'll just keep Rhees company in the back. I think that's the best arrangement.'

Amanda helped Rhees into the rear seat, then she sat behind the wheel. Dansk got inside, handed her the keys and said, 'Go back to the main highway, I'll give you directions along the way.'

She backed the car out from the shrubbery. When she reached the intersection of the highway, Dansk told her to turn left. She glanced at Rhees in the mirror.

Dansk leaned forwards. 'Keep your eyes on the road at all times, lady.'

'I was checking on John,' she said.

'John's fine. John's just hunky-dory back here. Right, John?'

Rhees said in a flat way, 'Sure, fine.'

'See? Don't worry about John.'

She stared ahead into the dark. Moths and bugs loomed up in the headlights and perished against the windshield. Mucus stains, broken wings trapped and flapping under wipers, a glass cemetery of dead insects. The road filled her vision, the white line bisected her head. Concentrate, figure a way out of this if you can; crash the car, swerve off the road, slam the brakes, anything you like. It didn't matter, because she had no doubt Dansk would shoot Rhees if she deviated by as much as a yard.

Dansk said to Rhees, 'This is nice, the three of us together like this. Cosy. I feel like I'm with old friends. We met before, John.'

'Did we?'

'In a French restaurant. We pissed side by side and talked about the merits of towels against forced-air hand-dryers. We discussed germs.'

'It escapes me,' Rhees said.

A French restaurant, Amanda thought. Was there any place Dansk hadn't followed her? His fingerprints were all over her life.

Dansk reached forward and touched her neck with the barrel of the handgun. She felt the metal against her skin and she remembered Dansk's distasteful kiss and moved her head just slightly. Dansk laughed and said, 'We're all happy. We're happy travellers. Right, John?'

Rhees said, 'I'm happy.'

'This is what I like. The only thing missing here is a picnic basket stuffed with goodies. A little roast chicken, a couple of cold brewskies to wash things down.' Dansk made another little move with the gun, some pretend fumbling, letting the weapon slip through his hands to his lap. 'Whoops. Gotta be careful. Don't want this to go off, do we?'

'Don't point that at Rhees,' she said. Dansk having fun with his gun, she thought. Dansk tightening the screws.

Dansk said, 'You hear that, John? Lady's worried in case I just happen to make a fatal slip. Zip. One bullet into the brainbox and goodbye Rhees. This concern's touching. I'm moved. I'm hearing the voice of love.'

She said, 'You don't know shit about love, Dansk.'

'Do I hear the expert's voice?'

'Death's what you know,' she said. 'All you know.'

Dansk made a mock sound of disapproval which sounded like choo-choo-choo. 'You're no slouch in that department yourself, sweetheart. Check the destruction in your own wake before you pass judgement on me. You're like some kind of fucking Typhoid Mary spreading a deadly plague. Instance, Bernadette Vialli. Instance, Willie Drumm.'

She said nothing, but kept her eyes on the road, as if all she wanted in the world was to get away from Dansk's voice. He was shifting blame. He was sprinkling fertilizer in the hope guilt would bloom in her.

'You want more, Amanda? Three dead guys in the woods, right? Who invited them in the first place? And the cop on the porch? Even poor Rhees here – he'd be in a damn sight better condition if it hadn't been for you. You drag death and pain behind you like luggage on a trolley, and the only thing I ever asked of you was to stay out of the way. Simple, but you didn't listen. Dumb, dumb, *dumb*.'

'I didn't kill those people, Dansk,' she said. Three men dead in the woods – people who'd come to protect her – and Thomas Gannon lying beneath the broken porch rail.

'You didn't pull any triggers, right. You just put certain people into lethal situations. I wasn't the one who did that.'

'You can't blame me for their deaths,' she said.

She was flooded with anger, but she couldn't tell if it was directed entirely at Dansk or whether some of it was channelled back in on herself. She recalled those moments when she'd thought of pulling out of the situation, when she might have chilled her mind and stilled all her impulses. But the tide had long ago gone out on those possibilities and the beach was a vast empty strand.

The road in front of her was empty.

'Where are we going anyway?' Rhees asked.

'A place. A couple of hours away.'

'What kind of place, Dansk?'

Dansk didn't answer.

A fire-engine, blue lights flashing and spinning, came out of nowhere and zoomed past the car in the opposite direction, and then there was a State police car, sirens going.

Amanda thought, Stop. We need your assistance. It's not only the forest that's burning. But the fire-engine and the State police car were already gone, and the road in the mirror was as black as the future.

74

Pasquale said, 'These digital numbers give you the location of Dansk's car and how far away it is and the speed. Right now it's three point two miles north of here and travelling at sixty-four m.p.h.'

McTell glanced down at the box. The numbers kept flickering. Pasquale said, 'You don't want to get too close to him.'

McTell nodded and said, 'That fire. Holy shit.'

'You figure he had something to do with it?'

McTell shrugged. He remembered being parked between trees just off the main highway and then whoom, all hell. 'All I know is what we saw. The whole place went up in flames and then the car's driving away and the woman's behind the wheel with the crippled boyfriend in the back.'

Pasquale said, 'I never figured he had the balls to go in and snatch the woman.'

'Balls,' McTell said, with some scorn.

Pasquale said, 'You think the woman and her boyfriend are a problem?'

'Nope,' said McTell.

Pasquale regarded the red numbers on the little black box. 'You know, Eddie, I think I'm over my doubts.'

'Sure you are. I told you they'd go away.'

'Dansk rescued me, OK. He gave me some purpose. But the way I'm beginning to see it, I paid that back with interest. I wonder what he thought when we didn't answer the phones.'

'Who gives a shit?' McTell glanced down at the black box. 'What's the numbers now?'

Pasquale examined the meter in his hand. The numbers went crazy suddenly. According to the digital register, Dansk's car was now ninety-seven miles away due west. Impossible. Pasquale tapped the box.

'You got a problem with that?' McTell asked.

'It's acting funny.'

'Funny?'

Pasquale gave the box a shake. The red numbers changed again. *5.8 m N 67 m.p.h.* 'No, it's OK now. Maybe there was some kinda interference.'

'A quirk,' McTell said.

'Yeah, a quirk.'

'Made in America, man. It's reliable.'

Pasquale said, 'Here's what I'm wondering. Why didn't he finish his business in the forest?'

McTell was silent, watching the dark highway. The trees had thinned, then vanished, and the landscape was desert again.

He snapped thumb and forefinger together in a click of realization. 'Forget that electronic box you got. I know where our boy Anthony's headed.'

75

The land stretched barren and flat all the way to the horizon where dawn was a few pale streaks. Dansk imagined this place in winter, a numbing wind howling over wasteland, the frozen bones of tumbleweed blowing across the narrow icy highway. Around here the season was basically always the same; dead.

He said, 'There's a turn coming up. Slow down.'

Amanda touched the brakes. The landscape was lunar and malignant in its indifference. She'd spent the last hundred miles or more ransacking her brain for ways she could shake off Dansk, but the ideas that came to her were fruitless. She was conscious of time seeping away. Only one thing was certain; Dansk hadn't brought her and Rhees out here for a barbecue.

Dansk had a map open under the rear light and one fingertip pressed to the paper. There were no colourful Native American attractions anywhere near here, Navaho rain ceremonies or Hopi dances, no trading post to attract tourists with trinkets and postcards. This was beyond nowhere, awesome in its desolation, perfect.

'Hang a right here,' Dansk said.

No track, landmark, sign. She felt the car rock as she turned off the highway. She wondered if she might find a ravine, hammer the car down it and hope for the best, but there were neither gulleys nor fissures deep enough for any action that desperate.

The dark was disintegrating. Dust blew from under the wheels, spreading a thin ashen film on the windows of the car. Dansk leaned towards her and said, 'You're looking pale, Amanda. She look pale to you, John?'

'A little,' Rhees remarked.

'She's wondering where we're going and how she can get out of it, except there's no way, not even for the lady prosecutor.'

Dansk tapped his gun a couple of times on Rhees's plastered arm and Rhees winced. 'Two professional types, and all I had was high school and two years in some sleazoid community college with metal detectors in the hallway.'

Dansk sat back again. Two educated characters, degrees and diplomas up the kazoo, and he had them helpless, playing a glissando on their nerves. They were afraid of him. This was a high. Watch me fly, Ma. *The respect I'm getting*.

He looked from the window. Out here was a hell of a place to die. Fifteen miles from the highway and you were in the heart of a zero state nobody claimed, nobody wanted.

The car swayed across ruts. Amanda's hands on the wheel were as white as her face. Dansk saw her eyes in the mirror. Our Lady of the Sorrows. She was no longer the smart-ass Amanda with the precious letter in her pocket. She was broken, afraid of where she was going and what awaited her when she got there. *Afraid of knowing.*

He remembered the way he'd kissed the back of her neck, prompted by mischief, but he'd liked the contact, the taste of salt and sweat on her skin. He'd imagined sliding down her jeans and fucking her from behind, right there on the porch with the gun in the back of her neck, and Rhees watching helplessly and the fire ripping through the pines. Little erotic signals from nowhere. The mind beamed out strange notions and impulses like a cock-eyed lighthouse in your head. He didn't want to fuck her, he wanted her dead. That was the square root of his desire.

'There,' he said, and pointed a finger. Strands of rotted wire hung between posts which rough winds had battered out of position. A sign, tilted backwards, bore a bleached message illuminated by the headlights of the car. All that was left to read were the meaningless fragments of words. *S DEP F AG RE.*

'What is this place?' Amanda asked.

Dansk said, 'Some kind of agricultural station once. I guess they were trying to develop a sturdy breed of soya bean or some such shit. They gave up twenty years ago. Nothing grows here. Drive between those posts.'

She drove where Dansk had indicated. Her heartbeat was violent and she couldn't slow it down. She turned and glanced back. 'John doesn't belong here,' she said.

'I've been waiting for that one. Oh, please, Anthony, let John go. Weep, weep.' Dansk gave his voice some falsetto, made a sobbing sound and pretended to wipe a tear away from his eye.

Rhees said, 'I'm here. I'm not going anywhere, Amanda.'

Dansk said, 'What a downright loyal guy.'

Amanda braked. 'Let him go,' she said.

'You heard what the professor said. Just drive.'

'This is just between you and me, Dansk.'

Rhees said, 'Don't, Amanda. Drop it.'

'See,' Dansk said, 'he's here for the duration. Now drive.'

Amanda clamped her hands on the wheel and stared ahead. 'Drive yourself.'

Dansk raised the gun to the side of Rhees's head. 'You don't drive, and guess what, Amanda.'

Her obstinacy against Dansk's gun, a serious mismatch. From the time Rhees had been beaten and hospitalized, Dansk had had the upper hand.

Dansk pressed his gun into Rhees's jaw. Rhees was maintaining a look of very quiet dignity. She wondered whether it was simply resignation or a façade he'd built against terror. She took her foot from the brake and the car slid forward. She stared through the dusty windshield. What had she expected from Dansk anyway? Compassion?

'Very sensible,' Dansk said. He lowered the gun. He'd wanted to blow Rhees's head away, but not in the car. He didn't need bloodstains in a rental car.

'Over there,' he said.

The structure was the colour of the land around it, camouflaged by years of exposure. It was a windowless wooden rectangle about fifty feet by thirty with a roof of rusted tin.

'Park,' Dansk said. 'Give me the keys, then step out the car.'

Amanda switched off the engine and handed the keys back to Dansk, who stuck them in a pocket.

She opened her door and got out, then helped Rhees from the back seat.

Dansk was already outside the car, gesturing towards the building. She didn't want to go inside. The absence of windows enhanced the general sense of doom, even with the rim of the dawn sun pale on the horizon. You could run, if Rhees was fit and healthy, if running could get you anywhere.

'Open the door,' Dansk said.

She didn't move. She looked at Rhees but she couldn't read his expression. Six years of living together had come down to this moment when he seemed remote. She walked a few feet, Rhees at her side. She wanted to say something but words wouldn't come. She took his hand. His skin was cool.

'Push it,' Dansk said.

She touched the door and it swung open. Beyond, she was aware of dark space, nothing else. Dansk came up behind and nudged her forward, then he edged Rhees inside. Dansk fumbled against the wall, pulled a handle, and after a moment there was a creaking sound that changed to a deep rumbling, a groaning, and the whole structure trembled. A strip of overhead light flickered a couple of times and then was steady but gloomy. The noise, Amanda realized, originated from an old generator reluctantly coming to life somewhere. It whined and rattled, complained and chugged.

Amanda looked round. One large room, three hundred square feet or more. Dust was everywhere; between rotted floorboards and on the shelves that lined the walls and clinging to the yellowy light-strip overhead.

Then she noticed the drums, dark-blue metal

cylinders stacked on the shelves, layered with the same dust as everything else. She saw stencilled letters on the sides of the drums: DANGEROUS. TOXIC WASTE MATERIAL. Drum after drum, each about two feet tall, perhaps thirty-five or forty of them, and they all had the same warning in silver letters.

Dansk said, 'Toxic waste.'

The sound of the generator roared in her head. She watched Dansk walk to the nearest drum, saw him reach out and tip it forward at an angle. The lid came off and went spinning away like a wheel beyond the reaches of the light, and landed, still spinning, in the shadows. Toxic waste, she thought. She realized she didn't want to see, didn't want to look at the drum Dansk was tilting downwards from the shelf.

The drum fell. The generator changed pitch a moment and the overhead light flickered a couple of times, and then the machine was rumbling again wholeheartedly, making the floor shake.

Dansk said, 'There's a profitable sideline in jewellery, money, whatever these people had. It's like a bonus system. This watch I'm wearing, for instance,' and he held up his wrist. He might have been talking to himself. 'A perk. Usually I don't touch any of the stuff, it goes to people of minimal sensitivity who aren't fussy about the previous owners, but this took my fancy. I'm just a little wary of the karma that might be attached to it. It's a nice watch though. I figured, take a chance, karma's a lottery anyhow.'

Perks. A bonus system. Karma. Dansk stared at the spilled contents of the drum, and Amanda turned her face aside. She felt her heart drop and go on dropping like a stone down a well whose depths were beyond measurement.

'Don't be queasy,' Dansk said. 'Professors and prosecutors, it doesn't matter. This is what we all come down to.' He was sifting through the stuff that had spilled from the drum. 'After we incinerate them, they're delivered here in these drums. We stash them and then dump them in the sea when air transport's available. Some of the work isn't up to scratch. Look at this.' He held something out in the palm of his hand.

She turned her face. She was aware of Rhees watching, his body hunched a little. Her eyes moved to Dansk and she stared at what he held in the centre of his palm.

'Now this is part of a fingerbone. See?' He plucked something else from the grey-white heap of human remains. The bone was charred and blackened and about two inches long. 'Looks like some spinal debris,' he said. 'Maybe even Benny Vialli's, huh?'

Benny Vialli's.

'Or maybe it's Isabel's,' Dansk said.

She'd known Isabel was dead, of course she'd known, but there must have been a level where she hadn't altogether accepted the fact, because she felt nausea. She folded her hands over her stomach. 'What else do you do? Wrench out the gold fillings, Dansk?' Her voice was dry. Her throat was parched. There was no oxygen getting to her lungs. Her heart seemed to have stopped pumping blood and she was outside of herself in a strange disconnected way.

'You make me laugh,' Dansk said. 'You've got this warped *thing* about justice. You go in a court of law and you think you're hot stuff, setting the world right. Bad guys go to jail, good guys don't. Except you have to make deals with some serious lowlife forms to get what you want—'

'It's the system,' she heard herself say. She was dizzy and there seemed to be ash in her mouth, a fine film of human ash.

'The system's fucked. But you were a serious player in the game. And there are people out there who ought to be behind bars or sucking on cyanide fumes, only they turned into songbirds singing tunes prosecutors need to hear, and you reward them by shipping them back out into society, which has rules and laws these lowlives have never paid attention to since the fucking day they were born. You think because they're in the Witness Protection Program they're all of a sudden saints? They go to PTA meetings and join the church choir? Make me laugh. They're shit on the sole of my shoe, and I wipe shit off.'

'They had guarantees,' Amanda said. She shut her eyes and swayed a little. Her stomach pitched, as if she was riding a boat on a very rough sea.

'Not from me they didn't,' he said.

'You're above the law.'

'There's more than one law in this great land, lady. You did your stuff on the surface where it shows and looks good. I'm the guy underground, I'm the miner working the dirty shafts all hours. You give your guarantees and I pop up and invalidate them. The scum you need to get your convictions, they don't deserve freedom. There are some evil fuckers wandering around out there, courtesy of people like you.'

'You select your . . . candidates and you bring

them here, you take them into permanent custody—'

'That's how it works, and it's beautiful. They go into the Program, they disappear and nobody ever comes looking for them, and even if somebody does get nervy – like Mrs Vialli say – there's too much security to get through. And if these people persist, hey, we solve that problem.'

'What in God's name did Benny ever do to deserve this?' She had her hands clenched so tightly she was stemming the flow of her circulation and her knuckles were white.

'Guilt by association. He was tainted.'

Tainted. It was lunacy. No, it was out there beyond lunacy in a place she couldn't describe.

'As for your pal Mrs Sanchez, she was also scheduled for disposal, except she happened to split, which caused some needless delay, as you know.'

'All Isabel ever did was testify against her husband, she wasn't a criminal—'

'She married one. She knew what Sanchez did for his money, but she went on living the life of luxury anyhow on the proceeds of his work. Then, when it suited her, she walked away and became one of your little songbirds, lady.' Dansk laughed. 'And all this time you figured Victor Sanchez was the one pulling the strings, didn't you?'

'You're cleaning up the country, Dansk.'

'I'm the Rotorooter man with a fucking vengeance,' Dansk said.

She stared at the drums and wondered how many had ended up in this place, sealed in cylinders, their names lost, their identities gone. Her brain was leaden. You couldn't take this in.

'I like my work,' Dansk said, and let ash sift through his fingers and looked thoughtful, maybe even a little serene. 'Some people came to me and told me I was the kind of guy they needed for this kinda operation. These are people who believe the Witness Program pumps megadoses of poison into the arteries of the nation. People who ask, What the fuck are we doing helping out the scum you lawyers pass down the line? People who say the whole thing is shaky on the morality issue – *aside* from the fact that it's costing millions and millions of dollars. And for what? To keep a criminal element safe and well? We've got thieves and killers receiving monthly federal pay cheques and job-training and relocation at the taxpayer's expense, and all this at a time when budget deficits are out of sight, and decent ordinary people can't find work and their fucking homes are being repossessed by banks?' Dansk, whose voice had been rising, stopped in an abrupt way. She heard the sound of his hand running across his wet lips.

She thought, Budget deficits, unemployment, the country stretched on a rack of cosmic debt, and certain people looked around for programs to slash. It didn't matter which ones, just cut the numbers. School lunches, kindergarten classes, welfare handouts, the Federal Witness Protection Program, wherever, it didn't matter.

Dansk said, 'These people felt a line had to be drawn somewhere, and this is the line right here, lady.'

'These people,' she said. 'Some of them work in Justice, some in the US Marshals Service. Places where ID cards can be made up in the blink of an eye, and messages intercepted, and official papers obtained without question.'

Dansk said, 'Where they work, what the fuck does that matter? The whole point is, what I do has moral merit. People like you leave a mess and I'm the guy who cleans it up.'

Moral merit. Morality was modelling clay. Shape it any way you like. Dansk had rationalized his role on the grounds that the Protection Program was wrong, but she guessed that whoever had dreamed up the unholy idea in the first place were more likely to be spreadsheet types on an economy drive than philosophers fretting over an ethical dilemma. She pictured memos going out in droves to assorted Federal agencies. She saw them landing on the desks of various department heads in these agencies. She imagined they all carried the same vaguely innocuous message, written by some bland bureaucrat in the Office of Management and Budget. 'At the present time, the condition of the general economy necessitates a reduction in Federal spending, consequently you are requested to analyse those areas of your operation where budgetary measures might be taken . . .'

And a devious functionary in Justice, Loeb say, had scanned his domain and seen the bloated form of the Protection Program, and he'd had a bright idea which he'd whispered to somebody else: here's a place where we can put the knife in, provided we go about it a certain way. So a sick scheme is born in furtive whispers and quiet consultations, and a few people like Dansk are recruited to implement it, people who lived on a dark rim of experience and who weren't particular, and they were issued cards that identified them as marshals or agents of the Justice Department. And money could be saved in accordance with the vague suggestions of the memorandum, and where there was money moral problems were nuisances that had a way of dissolving like a skeleton in acid.

She wondered about the mechanics. You didn't need hundreds of people to work it. You needed only some killers, a couple of supervisors in Arlington, two or three computer operators to falsify data, two or three insiders in Justice. Guys like Loeb.

Then, without any warning, Rhees moved, urgently and recklessly. As if he'd decided that his own pain was irrelevant, he grunted and threw himself against Dansk, who stepped effortlessly to the side. Rhees fell without making any contact and was lost for a moment in shadows, and when he tried to get up again Dansk kicked him in the ribs and Rhees clutched his side and groaned.

Dansk said, 'They always say it's the quiet ones you need to watch. It's the bookish types you need to keep an eye on.'

Amanda went to Rhees. His eyes were bloodshot and his face had shrunken in the bewilderment of pain. The generator faded, the rumbling was less intense, and the overhead light dimmed. She wished it would die completely so she'd be blind, immune to her surroundings. This place where all your curiosity ends.

She could smell death, death packed inside drums, and she wondered how many people had been brought here, three hundred, four hundred, and the process of flame they'd gone through, the furnace that had reduced them. She imagined rings and watches, lockets and ear-rings removed from limp bodies, ghouls sifting the possessions of the dead. She wondered about bank accounts and houses, and how monies must have been plundered and ownership documents transferred, and how many 'For Sale' signs throughout the country stood on posts outside homes where the lawful owners were never returning because they'd been shot and burned and brought here.

Dansk stepped towards her and placed a hand under her chin. 'Look at me,' he said. She kept her eyes shut.

'Look at me,' he said again.

But she didn't.

He thought, You don't want to see the face of your executioner, lady. You don't want me to be the last person you'll ever see. Carrying Anthony Dansk's image all the way into eternity with you.

She was thinking of dying. She'd hear the explosion of the gun. She wasn't sure. How could she know what she'd hear?

'Fucking look at me,' Dansk said.

'Dansk,' Rhees said hoarsely. 'Wait—'

'For what, John? The lady dies, then it's your turn. These are the facts. Face them.'

She felt the gun against the centre of her brow. She was linked to Dansk and the gun was a bridge. She heard the sound of the generator, the clunking and the asthmatic whirring noise which sometimes flared into a roar. Or maybe it was just the noise created by the broken dynamo of her brain. Outside, inside, there wasn't any difference, you knew you were going to die, you knew this was an ending.

She raised her face and looked at him finally.

He gazed into her eyes and saw what he wanted to see there, and it excited him. Defeat and despair, the pits of anxiety. It was how you looked when you turned the last page in your own history book.

'This is where curiosity gets you,' he said. He was the dispenser of darkness, the tourist guide to the other side.

'*Hey, Anthony! Check this out!*'

Surprised, Dansk turned. Amanda looked towards the doorway, dropped to the floor and shut her eyes.

The sound of automatic gunfire roared, shot after shot kicking up clouds of dust and splintering the wall behind Dansk. Amanda lost count, confused between the gunfire and the echoes it created. There was no spatial logic to the acoustics, just noise and more noise, until the place sounded like a shooting-gallery where all the clients had gone insane. Dansk was punctured everywhere, arms, legs, chest, skull. He took a series of staggered steps, and when he fell he rolled over and over, and was finally motionless a few feet from Amanda.

Two men in shadow. They walked to where Dansk lay and studied him, as if they half expected him to have survived the fusillade. One of the men kicked Dansk in the chest. The other said, 'Hey, enough.'

She couldn't see their faces. She didn't want to see them. The generator failed. The big room was suddenly quiet and dark, and the silence was strange and terrifying.

One of the men said, 'We ought to do surgery on this pair, you ask me.'

The other said, 'That ain't the way it was spelled out by Loeb.'

'No names, asshole.'

She heard them walk to the door where they stopped. She held her breath because she knew they were going to turn back and use their guns against her and Rhees. A bad moment, dust in your throat and the bitter taste of panic, but they stepped outside. Then a minute later she heard the sound of a car kick into life and then fade in the distance.

She moved to Rhees and held him for a long time, his face against her body, her arm round his shoulder. She sat until her body was numb and the sun had climbed high enough to send light through the open doorway into the room.

She wiped the gritty ash from her clothing and went to where Dansk lay. She searched his jacket for the car keys but didn't find them. Instead she found a notebook held shut by a thick red rubber band. She removed it, then rummaged in the pockets of his pants and found the keys, which were wet with blood.

The side of his skull was shattered. She could see bone and more blood than she would have thought possible. She had the impression he was turning to liquid. Hair sodden, mouth open and crooked. The eyes stared into nothing, but were curiously bright. A strange vigilance. She imagined some elementary form of life lingered in Dansk, that he was watching her, that when she turned and walked to the door with Rhees he was still following her movements and somehow in his ruined brain recording them.

She wondered how long it would take to liberate herself from this feeling, or if it was going to stalk her a long time. But she knew.

It wasn't going to go away.

76

Rhees sat in the passenger seat with Dansk's notebook in his lap, flicking pages in a listless way she found distressing, as if he'd used up too much of himself and had nothing left inside to give. The small arid towns they passed through had an air of despondency. In Holbrook they used the rest rooms of a gas station to clean themselves up. In Winslow she bought a pair of sunglasses and telephoned Kelloway from a pay phone outside a liquor store.

'I've been waiting,' he said.

'Let's meet in Flagstaff.'

'What's wrong with Phoenix?'

'Because I don't think I can make it without falling asleep at the wheel. I'm a road hazard, Kelloway.'

'Yeah, you're a hazard all right. Forest fires, serious loss of life. Name a location.'

'The airport.' It was the first place that popped into her head.

'I'll be there in a couple of hours,' Kelloway said.

She hung up and went back to the car. She sat

behind the wheel. Weariness was like woodworm tunnelling through her. But you're alive because Loeb had issued certain instructions. Maybe he'd come to the conclusion that enough was enough, no more killing after Dansk, because the whole sick clandestine business was coming apart.

Rhees hadn't even raised the subject. He seemed to accept the fact that he was alive without any curiosity. He was slowly turning the pages of the notebook as if he were reading text in a language he didn't know, one that held no interest for him.

Dansk's notes were centred on the pages, framed by sequences of tiny crosses and arrows and jagged lines that suggested thorns. One page contained a single word with a question mark: 'friends?' She couldn't imagine Dansk having friends.

Rhees continued to flick pages and sometimes read Dansk's notes in a disturbing monotone. In obscure ways, in phrases and fragments, Dansk had recorded his impressions. People were referred to by initials. L had to be Loeb. Dansk had written, 'I wish I could cut L's fucking throat like a pig.' She had no notion of the identities of Mc and P, initials that recurred. Willie Drumm's name was inscribed inside a rectangle, like a crude coffin.

Pages were crammed with letters, followed by abbreviated place names. BNDenv McKSeat FSaltLk RMDenv QDalbu RDalbu PROgd JROgd. In the back, the pages were covered with a series of digits, some of them phone numbers, others that looked like PIN codes for bank cards. You needed a key to unlock the significance of all these numbers. You needed another kind of key to reveal a different kind of accounting; the numbers of the dead.

A cryptic notebook, a cryptic life. She wondered

what could be deduced from these pages, from the abbreviations and the numerals, the mysteries in Dansk's world.

Something slipped out of the notebook into Rhees's hand. It was a folded newspaper clipping. He opened it.

'What's that?' she asked.

Rhees gave her the clipping and she read it.

LOCAL WOMAN SLAIN. Under this headline was a terse story:

> Mrs Frederica Danskowski, aged sixty-seven, of 2343 Drake, was killed yesterday by unknown assailants in broad daylight outside her apartment building. She was stabbed several times. She was taken to County Hospital, and pronounced dead on arrival. Police are asking for information from anyone in the vicinity of Drake Street between three and three-thirty yesterday afternoon to call the Patterson Police Department. Mrs Danskowski is survived by one son, Anthony, a surveyor for an oil company.

It was dated April 1994. A surveyor, she thought. She remembered the photographs Dansk kept. Mother and son. Anthony Danskowski, shortened to Dansk, a surveyor.

Somewhere between Winslow and Flagstaff she drove a hundred yards off the road. She got out, opened the trunk, found Dansk's case and set it down. She battered it open with a tyre-iron, sweating as she smashed the lid, the hinges, the lock again and again. She went down on her knees in the dust and rummaged through the contents, looking for papers, documents, files, any text of substance that might yield intelligible clues to Dansk's world. All she found were his clothes, folded neatly. His toiletries. But no papers. She kicked angrily at the stuff, scattered it around, then went back to the car. Sweat dripped into her eyes, blinding her.

She took the notebook from Rhees's slack hand, shut it and imagined this simple act might silence Dansk's voice, which had seemed to issue from the pages in whispers and incomprehensible asides. But it didn't quieten Dansk at all, because she could still hear him. *Check the destruction in your own wake before you pass judgement on me. You're like some kind of fucking Typhoid Mary spreading a deadly plague.*

Flagstaff marked a change, mountains and high green forests and a soft breeze. Amanda drove a mile or so beyond the town, where the airport was located. A small terminal, it served mainly short-hop commuter flights north to Las Vegas or south to Phoenix. A couple of picnic tables were situated at the edge of the parking lot.

She parked and bought two large sodas in the cafeteria and took them to one of the tables. Rhees sipped his in silence. Amanda smoked a cigarette and watched cars come in and out of the lot. A Cessna rose up from the runway. She imagined being inside the small plane, floating in a kind of light membranous sac through blue skies, where consciousness was suspended and amnesia a possibility.

She saw Kelloway step out of a car. He noticed Amanda and Rhees immediately and walked briskly to their table. He sat, waving smoke from Amanda's cigarette away from his face. She removed her sunglasses and looked at him, searching his expression for an indication of his mood. It was hard to tell.

'OK,' he said. 'Let's start with Tom Gannon.'

'Dansk shot him,' she said.

'And the other cops?'

She didn't say anything. She felt an unexpected reluctance to tell Kelloway anything else, but she wasn't sure why. Speech was an enormous effort suddenly. Words congealed and darkened like scars in her head.

'So he kills four cops in one swoop and burns down half a forest,' Kelloway said.

Amanda looked beyond Kelloway a moment. The breeze fluttered briefly, then faded. The windsock nearby deflated. This situation had the pitch of a dream, or of that moment when you experience the first slide towards sleep.

'And then where did he go?' Kelloway asked.

Rhees said in his flat way, 'Dansk's dead.'

'Dead?'

'There were two gunmen,' Rhees said.

'Where?'

Amanda said, 'A place we never want to go again.'

Kelloway looked into her eyes. 'What place?'

'I'll draw you a map,' she said. But all she could remember was wilderness and gunfire. The geography was missing.

Kelloway leaned forward, elbows on the table. 'These gunmen shot Dansk and left? You saw their faces?'

'It was dark,' she said. 'We couldn't see them.'

'So you can't identify them.'

Amanda said, 'Frankly, we weren't really looking. My best guess would be they were the same pair who attacked John.'

'Dansk's own people turned on him.' Kelloway swatted a fly from his arm. 'And left you two alive?'

'Maybe Loeb can explain that,' she said.

Kelloway made one hand into a tanned fist. 'Loeb was shot at close range outside a roadside tavern on I-Seventeen. We don't know who killed him. Nobody in the tavern heard any gunfire. You never find witnesses in these sawdust joints.'

She absorbed this information. No witnesses, she thought. No Loeb to answer questions. No Dansk to interrogate. Silenced voices. 'How much background have you looked into?'

'Ralph Loeb was with Justice for sixteen years. Terminal lung cancer, so he was going to retire one way or another pretty soon. I imagine he expected to croak in a hospital bed with tubes up his nose, but fate's a real joker. He told me he'd never heard of Dansk.'

'Surprise.'

'I have calls into various people. Top guys in Justice. The US Marshals Service. The Director of the Witness Protection Program. I'm also talking with the State Attorney-General's office. I have forensics examining the late Mrs Vialli for exact cause of death. The description of the guy you saw in the Hideaway Knolls has been circulated.'

'You've become a believer, have you?' she asked.

'Let's say I'm leaning,' Kelloway said, 'but I need anything you can give me by way of solid evidence.'

She thought of Dansk's notebook. She thought of the drums and the labels on them. She had the unsettling feeling that Kelloway was keeping something back from her and Rhees. She didn't know what.

Her attention was drawn to a car entering the parking lot and cruising close to the table. She saw the driver's face half in shadow, and she had a sense of recognition. The car moved past, then slid into a space about fifty yards away and the door opened.

The breeze came up again. The man who stepped out of the car put a hand to his scalp. His necktie, caught by a current of air, flapped up against his face and he smoothed it back into position. In his left hand he carried a briefcase.

Kelloway said, 'I'm looking at the possibility of a serious investigation here. One that's also very delicate.'

Amanda turned away from the man fidgeting with his necktie. 'Does the prospect scare you, Kelloway?'

'I don't scare, Scholes. I've got balls of steel. All I'm saying is, this isn't your run-of-the-mill affair. This is something you piece together, and if there's a case I'm gonna have to convince some pretty influential people I've got something worth pursuing. This one leads in all sorts of directions. Justice. The US Marshals Service. I can see FBI involvement. Beyond that . . .' He shrugged.

Amanda stared past Kelloway at the man who was struggling once more to keep his tie in place against the renewed mischief of the breeze. When he reached the table he smiled at Amanda.

She said, 'Lew Bascombe. Got a plane to catch?'

'No, no plane,' Bascombe said. He sat, opened his briefcase, took out an opaque plastic folder and laid it on the table. It was red and shiny, buttoned shut.

Kelloway nodded at Bascombe, then said to Amanda, 'I want everything you can tell me. A to Z.'

She wondered about Lew Bascombe's presence. She looked at the red folder. Lew was drilling his fingers on it. She leaned back, sluggish. When Kelloway spoke his voice came from a cloud of ectoplasm. 'I got some real thick doors to knock on and some heavyweight characters I'm gonna have to talk to. I need good stuff to show them, and where am I gonna find this stuff if I don't get it from you and Rhees? Not from Loeb, and not from Dansk, that's for sure.'

She said, 'Loeb and Dansk weren't working alone; they had support. People with access to information. People who knew what buttons to push on their keyboards. Others who specialized in violence. I don't know how many or how deep this whole sickness runs.'

'These are exactly the people I want to fucking nail.'

'Have you thought that Loeb had time to start covering his tracks before he died?' she asked. 'Maybe he made a few phone calls right after his talk with you. He realized things were beginning to fall apart, so he sent out messages. Eliminate certain files and records, et cetera.'

Kelloway said, 'You can't wipe out *everything*, Scholes. There are always traces left somewhere, and I'll find them. When I get my foot in the door I'm like some fucking Jehovah's Witness on Benzedrine.'

Kelloway looked at Bascombe, who unclipped the folder and opened it. He started to pull papers out.

Bascombe said, 'I've arranged a complete set, Amanda. Two birth certificates, two social security cards, two driver's licences issued by the State of Arizona. Two credit cards and a chequebook from a bank in Yuma. The key to a house in the same city, address attached. You'll see we've described you as married. I picked the names myself. Erika and Robert Bloom.'

'Wait,' she said.

Kelloway said, 'I can't begin to build a case without you two and I want to be one hundred per cent goddam sure any witnesses of mine are in protective custody—'

'*Wait*,' she said again.

'I want you both safe and sound while I work this business out. We have our own in-State witness protection program—'

'I'm aware of that—'

'It's small-scale compared to the Federal one, but at least it's secure, and I know where I can contact you when I need you. I can guarantee total safety, round-the-clock protection, a direct line to my office open all hours.'

Amanda looked at the birth certificates, the credit cards, the cheque-book. They appeared to vibrate in her vision. 'You're asking us to drop out of sight for God knows how long and assume new *identities*?'

'Nobody's gonna come looking for you. You don't have to live with an ongoing paranoia. You'll be safe in my care.'

Safe in my care. 'Is this mandatory?' she asked.

Kelloway shrugged and raised his eyebrows. 'Let me tell you what's gonna happen if you don't accept; you'll spend a whole lotta time looking over your shoulder. When the sun goes down, you'll wonder what lies out there in the darkness. When the doorbell rings, you'll jump. When somebody comes to fix your garbage disposal, you'll be reaching for a Valium or a gun, whichever's closer. And then there's Rhees to consider. He needs rest, time to mend.'

He'd fingered her weak point. She stared at the windsock and watched it fill with air. She listened to the breeze as if she expected to hear a message of guidance rustle out of the trees nearby, reliable counsel voiced by the shaken leaves.

'Maybe you don't trust me,' Kelloway said. 'But you have to trust somebody somewhere along the line. Begin with me. Who was it that gave you Tom Gannon for protection? Who was it offered you that? And those other cops? I walked that extra mile for you.'

She looked at Rhees, whose drawn face seemed to recede from her. Trust somebody somewhere.

Rhees said, 'Robert and Erika Bloom,' as if he were checking the flavour of the names in his mouth and didn't like how they tasted, but his voice was odd and lifeless.

She heard another small plane rise off the runway.

'Well?' Kelloway asked.

She raised her face and watched the craft, a dwindling gleam of quicksilver in the sun. The sound of the engine dropped a half-tone. She put on her sunglasses and the gloss of the day dimmed to an acceptable level. She looked at Kelloway, who was less harsh, less predatory, in reduced light. Then she stared at Bascombe for a long time. That bland face, that bad wig.

'What do you think, Lew?' she asked.

'I think you should go for it, Amanda,' he said.

'Just like that,' she said.

Bascombe said, 'I've already agreed to co-operate one hundred per cent with Dan to get this whole goddam business cleared up. I believe you should do the same.'

The same, she thought. Christ, she was weary, weary. She wanted a bed and clean sheets and a cool, dark room. Above all else she wanted Rhees to be safe. She looked at Bascombe and remembered Willie Drumm. 'Tell me, Lew. Did you ever get around to checking on Dansk?'

Bascombe said, 'Of course I did.'

'And?'

'Nothing,' he said. 'He wasn't employed by Justice. He wasn't employed by the Marshals Service. He came out of nowhere.'

Zero, she thought. A mystery. Now he was dead and she should begin the process of imposing amnesia on herself. She saw a State police car enter the parking lot.

'Is that our transportation, Kelloway?'

'Only if you accept,' he said.

She glanced at Rhees again. He made an indeterminate movement of his head. She knew what it meant: I'm in too much pain to think.

'What about my father?' she asked. 'He's going to wonder. I owe him a call.'

'Later, when you're relocated, we'll arrange for you to phone him. We're not talking for ever, Amanda. Three months, six, it depends on what I find. I might get lucky sooner, you never know.'

She closed her eyes against the light and finished the last of her soda. She thought of Morgan and his hacienda in the hills, Morgan waiting to hear from her. Later, like Kelloway had said.

Life was going to become a series of postponements and abdications. She removed the sunglasses and blinked.

'There's a notebook you're going to need,' she said.

77

Kelloway watched the state police car drive out of sight. Neither Amanda nor Rhees looked back at him. He turned to Bascombe and said, 'Where the hell did Loeb dig up a psycho like Dansk? What was the old clown dreaming of? He must've known the risk he was running trusting a guy like that. OK, so Dansk was a US Marshal with special undercover status, big deal, but Loeb should've checked on his mental stability, for Christ's sake.'

Kelloway picked up an empty soda container from the table and crumpled it in his hand. 'Then, lo and behold, Loeb changes tack and decides he wants Dansk dead because the guy's outta control and it's panic stations, and all the evidence has to get swept under the nearest rug immediately, and Scholes goes home happy and content because she imagines her personal nightmare's finished . . . A dying man finds some mercy in his heart. You think it was something like that with Loeb? Or did he just lose his nerve?'

'It doesn't matter much now,' Bascombe said.

Kelloway had a hard purposeful quality in his expression. 'No more fuck-ups. No more of Loeb's misbegotten judgements. No more Dansk.'

Bascombe smiled, a humourless effort. 'This wide-ranging investigation of yours. When does it begin?'

Kelloway said, 'What investigation?'

'I'm sorry for the woman, kind of,' Bascombe said.

'Save your sympathy, Lew. She got herself into this. She had her chances to back out. More than a few times.'

'Her father . . .'

'Tough one,' Kelloway said. 'But you can't have guys like Dansk doing this work. He fiddled around and he blew it, and along the way some unhappy sacrifices had to be made. Jesus, I hate losing men. It's a total waste.' He was silent for a time, staring towards the trees. 'OK, I figured Dansk was deranged enough and determined enough to get through to the cabin, but fuck, I really missed out on Loeb's misguided charity. Maybe the old fart saw Scholes's reprieve as an act of atonement or something, or maybe all the death just sickened him to the heart, which I could understand, believe me.'

'Who knows,' Bascombe said.

'Sometimes I get depressed and I think this operation's too much. The pressure-cooker syndrome. The whole act you have to go through; containment, keeping secrets, all the lies. Then I swing the other way and it looks good again, it feels right, it's running like a well-oiled clock and God's got a grin on his face. You think I need Prozac maintenance, Lew?'

'Drugs don't keep a man's head clear.'

'Whatever,' Kelloway said. 'She's all mine.'

'I don't have to ask what you intend to do with her, do I?'

A sparrow landed on the table.

Kelloway stretched a hand out and said, 'Boo,' and the frightened bird flew upward in a nervy flapping of wings and disappeared like a puff of woodsmoke or a dead soul in the direction of the freeway.

THE END

HEAT
by Campbell Armstrong

Frank Pagan, Special Branch's counter-terrorist agent, is being observed, his every movement tracked and recorded. His flat is broken into. The only object stolen is a photograph of his dead wife, which is later returned to him grotesquely disfigured.

But it is more than Pagan's home that has been invaded. His dreams, his every waking moment, are filled with hot, obsessive thoughts of a mortally alluring woman. For it is the most critical assignment of Pagan's career, as well as his fate, to bring to justice the enigmatic and ruthless terrorist Carlotta, who is wanted the world over for her hideous crimes.

Indifferent to the horror and destruction she leaves in her wake, yet curiously fixated on Pagan, Carlotta sends emotional depth-charges into his life to the point where his pursuit of her crosses the line that separates duty from sexual obsession. In a deadly cat-and-mouse chase, Pagan is destined always to stay just a step behind Carlotta, until the fatal day he catches up with his nemesis.

Riddled with intrigue, violence and sexual tension, *Heat* takes the reader on a thrilling journey into the darkest reaches of a man's soul.

0 552 14169 0